GUIAMO

GUIAMO

The Chronicles of Guiamo Durmius Stolo

Volume One

by

MARSHALL BEST

Chapter One - 60 B.C. Early Summer

"Be not afraid of greatness: some are born great, some achieve greatness, and some have greatness thrust upon them." Shakespeare, Twelfth Night, Act II Scene V

From the back of the two-wheeled, ox drawn cart, the boy listened intently to the bitter, barely concealed conversation between the ragged farmer and his sullen wife. He affectionately stroked the neck of the farmer's black and white dog. Disturbed by the discussion, he gave the dog a tender hug for reassurance.

"How can you do this?" said the woman in frustration, "I know we are in a difficult position, but Guiamo is my sister's son."

The man's face turned stony. "The world is a hard place, and right now he is a burden. I cannot feed that boy, and you know it. We lost the land, and that is that."

The woman's face pinched into a bitter scowl, "You lost the land. It was your drinking that caused it. It was all those wild nights with your worthless friends, gambling and drinking until dawn."

"Silence, woman," snapped the man.

"And now the boy will suffer for it," said the woman.

"I said be silent," he glared. "It is not my fault. The crops were bad this year. They have been bad for three straight years, and nobody can blame me for that."

He shifted in his seat and switched the whip at the ox. He turned to glance at the boy seated among their few belongings. It irritated the farmer that the dog had become so attached to the boy rather than himself.

Angrily he said, "There was a time when I could manage to raise your sister's boy, but now is not that time. I cannot find work, and both our bellies are empty." He fidgeted in his seat and muttered, "Maybe the butcher was right. We could sell the boy to him as a slave. You know we could use the money, and out here so far from Rome, no one would give it a second thought. It would give us a chance to start again. I still have a notion to sell him to Numerius Antoninus."

The woman's face became stony cold. She said bitterly, "My sister would never forgive me for that. Poverty is something we have had to deal with, and it is a life she would have expected for him. The life facing the boy will be unpleasant enough, but slavery is something else altogether. He will have a hard life, that is for sure, but at least he will be free."

The husband responded, "The butcher would make sure he is fed. That is better than starving to death."

The wife replied, "Slavery is not an option, and you know it."

The man paused gloomily. "I know, I know. But our options are few."

"True," she said. "It is a shame we cannot return to my homeland, but old grudges are never forgotten." She glanced at her husband to see what his decision would be.

He said, "He will not starve. He may be only ten years old, but you have to admit, he is a clever little guy. He will find a way, if anyone can."

The wife was doubtful. "Ten is too young. Anyone can see that. He will either starve or turn to thieving. He will get caught and they could put him to death."

The farmer replied, "Well, if he does, that is his problem, Namiotanca, not mine. Not anymore."

They both fell silent as the cart continued rolling across the dirt path.

Guiamo lay in the back of the wagon feeling very alone as it lumbered down the dusty road. The long-haired dog had cozied up to the boy's back for warmth, and it comforted Guiamo to know that at least his uncle's dog cared for him. He fiddled with the dog's long ears for which it had received the name Flaccus, which meant "floppy ears."

5

After hearing his uncle Valerius talking to Namiotanca, he knew he was in trouble. They had considered selling him into slavery! If things were that desperate, he knew terrible changes were coming for him. He tried to think of what his uncle's final decision would be for him, but the more he thought, the more frightened he became.

He had never trusted his uncle and aunt. Valerius was dangerous when he was drunk, and Guiamo had quickly learned to stay out of reach when wine was being poured. Namiotanca was selfish and begrudged every moment she had to spend taking care of the boy. Guiamo turned onto his side to put his arm over the dozing dog for comfort, and he drifted off to sleep.

Guiamo opened his eyes when the farmer's ox was reined in to a stop. He propped himself up on an elbow to find it was late morning, and saw they were under the shade of an ancient cork tree which stood alongside a small stream that fed into a large blue lake. Bare-chested fishermen were mending their nets on the shore a stone's throw from their oxcart. He could hear the songs of others laboring in their little boats as they cast their nets.

The boy realized that Valerius had been drinking the last of his wine while Guiamo had been sleeping. Facing his wife, Valerius spoke more to himself than to Namiotanca, "So it is decided then. It is time for it."

Namiotanca asked surprisedly as she looked around, "Here? In this desolate place?"

"Yes. Here." he said, angrily pointing to the ground next to the cart. "You do not like here? Fine. How about there?" he continued, angrily jabbing his finger toward a copse of oak trees on the right. Lifting his arm to point toward the horizon, he said "Not good enough? How about over by that hill? Anywhere will do, so I say it is here; and right now. I am done with him." He swayed slightly in his seat as he turned toward Guiamo.

"Boy!" Valerius barked drunkenly, "Get out of my wagon."

Confused at the gruff tone, Guiamo simply sat up.

6

Valerius stood and staggered as he stepped into the back toward the boy. "I said get out!" he shouted. His words were slurred from the wine. Guiamo looked at Namiotanca for help, but found only unsympathetic eyes glaring back at him.

"I do not care if you are the son of my wife's sister." his uncle shouted. "I have no means for feeding us, let alone you, too."

Guiamo realized that his drunken uncle had made the critical decision while he had been sleeping next to Flaccus, and Valerius was now abruptly taking action.

Valerius grabbed Guiamo by the left arm and shouted, "Get out!" He stumbled a bit and roughly shoved the boy out the back of the cart onto the hard dirt road. "It is time you learned to take care of yourself," he roared. Guiamo landed painfully on his right shoulder and crumpled into a heap.

Flaccus jumped out the back of the wagon and nuzzled Guiamo's face. The boy was so surprised with this appalling turn of events that he simply lay there with tears streaming down his face.

Valerius turned his back on the stunned boy, swayed back to the driver's seat, and whipped the ox to go. "Come on, Flacce! Let us go!" he called to the dog. Valerius was drunk enough that he did not glance back to see if his dog was following. He whipped the ox again, and the drunken farmer started down the path.

Flaccus stayed with Guiamo, protecting him while the boy slowly sat up. Guiamo wrapped his arms around his legs, and rested his chin upon his knees. He sat there in the middle of the road staring at the back of the ox cart as it slowly made its way around a grove of cedar trees and out of sight.

Guiamo sat dazed in the middle of the dirt road for over an hour, gazing off into the vagaries of the horizon, too stunned to react. A cloaked traveler with a walking staff passed Guiamo with no more than a casual glance. The abandoned ten-year-old sat uncomprehending, and took no notice. The breeze blew gently, the clouds drifted by, and the sun grew hot. A bothersome fly landed on his lip, and he brushed it away. With that, he took a deep breath, and began to shake off his stupor.

Guiamo gazed around and wondered what he should do next. Unfolding his arms to stretch, he realized he was thirsty, and slowly stood up. He walked over to the stream and dropped to his knees to take a drink.

The stream moved quickly, and the water was cool and clean. Guiamo took several sips of water and splashed some over his face. It felt refreshing in the heat, and reminded him of the stream by his mother's home. Flaccus lapped up some water and seemed to be having a good time sniffing around.

Guiamo's thoughts turned to his mother and father, now long dead. Guiamo's father had been a legionnaire in the army of Rome, and had been killed in battle with a barbarian tribe to the north, but Guiamo couldn't remember any other details. His mother had told him that his father had been a brave warrior, and that he, too, should be brave and strong like his father.

He'd been only five years old when his father, Appius Durmius Stolo, died, and Guiamo had few clear memories of him. While he had great respect for his father, Guiamo's love was held dear for his mother, Agesdaca. He later watched his mother and elder brother, Appius, suffer from a feverish wasting disease, and both had succumbed to it when he was eight. With no other family to turn to, *avunculus* Manius Valerius Ruga reluctantly took him in. Namiotanca Ruga never accepted his decision and acted accordingly, flaunting her contempt for his decision on a daily basis.

Guiamo walked downstream to see the fishermen mending the nets on the lakeshore with Flaccus following closely. He knew he needed help, and they were the only ones around. As he hiked barefoot across the pebbly shore, he decided that since he didn't know if these were good men or bad, he would be cautious. He also determined to be helpful to these men so that they would be willing to let him stay with them. Perhaps he could get some food to eat.

"*Adulescens, dic mihi nomen tuum, quaeo*" called the oldest fisherman as he watched the boy and dog draw near. "Young man, please tell me your name."

Guiamo replied with his full name, "Guiamo Durmius Stolo, *fortissimus senex*," referring politely to the fisherman as a strong old man. "May I help you mend your nets?" he asked in as cheerful a voice as he could muster.

The sinewy, aging fisherman laughed and said, "And what does a boy know of mending nets? But still, I see your manners are well taught. Come. If you will listen and learn, I will teach you." Guiamo studied the eyes of the men, and felt they were sincere and could be trusted.

The old fisherman introduced himself as Vibius Calidius Metellus. Calidius let Guiamo know that he'd seen the rough handling the boy had received from the drunk by the old cork tree.

"Who was the lout who so gently helped you down from the oxcart?" he asked sarcastically. Calidius listened patiently as Guiamo told his story of misfortune.

"By the gods, your *avunculus* deserves the life the Fates have given him." said Calidius grimly when Guiamo's story was ended. Then his voice softened, "Stay with me, boy. Work diligently on the nets, and your life will improve. The lot of a fisherman is a life of hard work, but it is honest work, and there is honor in that. We also eat well, and that is one of life's greatest joys."

Guiamo agreed with a nod, and said, "Then a fisherman, I shall be." Guiamo sat down and crossed his legs on the pebbly beach, readying himself to learn the ancient craft of net mending. "And Flaccus shall learn to eat fish." he added with a smile.

Calidius shared his simple lunch of bread and dried fish with Guiamo, who showed his appreciation with an unexpected belch and a nervous, giggling laugh. With that, Calidius saw the tension in Guiamo begin to melt away as they quietly finished their simple meal. Calidius fed some spare chunks of fish to Flaccus, who gulped them down with great enthusiasm.

As Guiamo watched Calidius and the others, he realized that, though poor, they were good honest men. He soon recognized that he had found the refuge he needed.

As the fishermen ate their meal, Calidius formally introduced Guiamo to them all as Durmius. In great detail, Calidius told them Guiamo's story with surprising accuracy. They said little, but listened well. Then Calidius introduced to Guiamo each of the seven fishers.

Publius Moravius Fullo was the tallest, and had worked for a time in Rome cleaning horse stalls for a nobleman. Spurius and Gnaeus Popillius Pulcher were brothers whose family had been fishermen on this lake for nine generations. Quintus Autronius Crispinus was a widower and had raised two marriageable daughters. Aulus Meridius Habitus, Guiamo noticed, walked with a limp. Calidius explained he had been severely wounded fighting in a Roman shield wall during his service with the *legio* and had nearly died from a stabbing thrust into his thigh. It was Meridius' melodic voice that led the singing Guiamo had heard coming from the boats. Gnaeus Equitius Nerva owned a team of oxen for hire and worked fields most of the time. He netted fish only when farming work slowed down. The short man with curly hair was Servius Caedicius Quadratus. He was new to the village and had taken a liking to the younger of Autronius' daughters, Autronia Crispinis Minor.

All the men agreed with Calidius that they'd help teach the boy, just so long as Calidius provided him with a place to sleep, food to eat, and a new garment about once a year. Then Calidius turned to Guiamo, "I shall feed you, Guiamo, but from tomorrow you must feed Flaccus."

Pleased with his new surroundings, and seeing the fishermen to be men worthy of trust, Guiamo then asked to speak. He told them, "I know it is proper that I should be called Durmius, but since you are all going to be my close friends, I would rather you call me Guiamo. It is the name my mother chose for me. Guiamo Laevinus was her father's name, I think. She told me he was a good man, even if he was not born a citizen of Rome."

Meridius laughed and said "As if being born a Roman is the sign of a good man." The others enjoyed his sarcasm and laughed heartily.

Autronius leaned forward and said "Your mother's father was a Gaul. It shows in your blue eyes. He also gave you your light brown hair. Did you ever meet him?"

Guiamo thought carefully and then said, "I remember seeing him working with horses. He was a big man with yellow hair and a long beard. His clothes were plain white. I think he had a big brown cloak that he would throw on top of me when I was little. I remember crawling out from beneath it. He was missing his front teeth. I remember that because he smiled a lot. I saw him kill a goose, and it flopped around for a while. That is about all I remember. He also sang songs to me when I went to bed. I liked his singing, but I did not understand any of the words."

Gnaeus Popillius asked, "Where did your parents meet?"

Guiamo gave him an impish smile and retorted, "I was not yet born, so how would I know?" Gnaeus Popillius grinned back at him. Guiamo continued, "I think they met when my father was serving in the *legio*. All I know is that he died in the north somewhere, and mother brought me back with my brother to his home to be raised a Roman. Then they both got sick and died."

The men murmured their sympathies for his plight. Moravius, Autronius and Equitius rose, and extended hands to Guiamo. "Welcome to our village, friend," said Autronius. "You have need of some things." Equitius then gave a length of rope to Guiamo. Moravius presented a well-worn iron knife, the blade a span in length, with a chipped handle of bone, and Equitius gave him a gourd water bottle. As the three returned to their places around the fire, Gnaeus Popillius then stood and presented Guiamo with a woolen hat. Caedicius then moved around their bonfire to greet Guiamo with a leather bag sewn with drawstrings and a shoulder strap. Spurius Popillius gave the boy a small clay oil lamp while Meridius limped closer. He gave Guiamo a clay jar of ointment for sore muscles. As everyone moved back to their seats by the fire, Calidius gave Guiamo an overlarge green blanket woven with a red fringe. "This should fit you better as you grow," he said. "All are good gifts, but as a fisherman, you will see that the ointment given you by Meridius is the greatest. He keeps its formula as a secret, and sells some in the village."

"Thank you," said Guiamo with tears in his eyes. "Such friends as this, I could never have hoped for. Perhaps the gods are smiling on me today."

"Indeed they are," Calidius said. "Indeed they are. You have shed an evil and have been delivered to good. That certainly is a blessing of the gods." He paused to reflect, and glanced at the sun. He spoke to the seven fishermen, "The day is passing. Let us now go back to our work. I shall teach the boy."

The seven gathered their nets and returned to their boats. Guiamo sat quietly with Calidius, and began to learn to mend nets. As they worked the ropes, Calidius varied the lessons from the practical skills of netting fish to the more important lessons of being a good man.

"What has two hands, the right giving joy and the left bringing despair?" he asked Guiamo as the day grew late.

Guiamo enjoyed riddles, but try as he might; he was just too tired to give a good answer.

"It is wine," said the elder. "A little wine makes a man merry, but much wine brings a man to ruin."

And so, an old, poor fisherman in a tiny village on the outskirts of Roman civilization began to teach the lessons of life to an abandoned orphan boy.

The summer lasted long, and Guiamo's skin tanned under the sun. His muscles grew stronger through the toil of a fisherman's life. Calidius taught Guiamo first how to mend the nets and weave baskets to carry fish to market. The boy's quick fingers soon outpaced his teacher, and he was pleased that his dexterity made the old man's work lighter. Calidius was surprised at the eagerness with which Guiamo embraced his teaching, and quickly found himself challenged to have fresh insightful lessons each day.

12

Guiamo was delighted when Calidius told him that it was time to learn to cast the net. The elder man showed how a twist at the wrist put the net into the beginnings of a spin which caused the net to spread wide. Guiamo rather quickly learned the need to spin the net, but found he didn't have the arm strength to cast it effectively. Undaunted, he spent many afternoons working to improve his skill.

Guiamo's catch went to Calidius who traded some with the villagers for their daily needs. Some they cooked fresh, and the rest was smoked or salted. They ate well, but Calidius never allowed Flaccus to have any of it. He insisted that Guiamo work extra to feed the dog.

Each day after supper, when the others had gone home, Guiamo tried his hand at netting fish so Flaccus would never go hungry. Even on the rainy days, he would go out to fish. Guiamo put on his wool hat and braved the weather for his dog's sake. He quickly grew tired of netting in bad weather and tried to think of clever ways to catch fish more easily.

One morning, when Calidius was feeling ill, Guiamo went alone to the lake. In his mind, he had devised a fish trap into which he intended to frighten the fish. He went to the east side of the lake where the water was only as deep as his waist for over fifteen *passuum*, or paces. He began pushing long, straight sticks into the muck on the lake's floor. They were placed closely enough together to form a nearly solid wall, quite sufficient to keep fish within.

All morning long, with his bone handled knife, he cut green branches in the wood nearby, trimmed off the stems, and then waded out with an armful to the fish trap. By the end of the day, he had created two long stick walls. They were only a hand's width apart where they began in the shallows near the shore and spread ever farther apart as they went out into the lake. He then sank a basket to the bottom, weighted with stones, near the shoreline at the place where the walls came together. Around the basket, he placed more sticks to form a complete wall around the basket.

Guiamo enjoyed the time he had to himself, but found that he had been so absorbed in his task that he had completely forgotten to eat his lunch. As the sun descended to the horizon, Guiamo ate his meal, and then headed back to the home he shared with Calidius.

Calidius was sick for the next two days, and Guiamo stayed with him, tending to his needs, keeping the fire, and doing other chores that needed to be done. Only on the second morning did Calidius feel well enough to let Guiamo go back out to the lake for a few hours as he slept.

Guiamo used the time improving his fish trap. Guiamo had determined that the trap was too weak to last long, so he interwove pieces of rope from worn out fishing nets among the sticks for strength and support. By noon, when he returned to his chores with tending Calidius, the trap was complete.

On the third day, when Calidius felt well enough to escort Guiamo out to the lake, he was delightfully surprised with the ingenuity the boy had shown. Calidius easily recognized their purpose of Guiamo's creation. Guiamo intended to drive the fish from open water in between the two stick walls. As the fish would swim away from Guiamo in open water, those that moved in between the two walls would be funneled into the narrow opening and on into the trap. Once the fish passed through the narrowest point, they would be blocked from returning by a gate Guiamo would then insert. The fish would be captured simply by lifting the basket out of the water.

Guiamo asked to demonstrate his trap to Calidius. He waded out beyond the two stick walls and tried to find some fish. At first, whenever he saw a fish or two, he'd smack the surface of the water with a stick trying to frighten the fish in between the stick walls. After a tiring hour of meeting no success whatsoever, he figured that all he really was doing was scaring the fish into flight in all directions.

Calidius patiently watched, and then, as he turned to go back to the village, advised, "You might have to guide the fish rather than frighten them."

Guiamo began to realize that by moving slowly through the water, he could nudge the fish in generally the correct direction. Experimenting by gently moving his arms out and forward under water to pressure the fish, he found he could sometimes steer the fish toward the trap entrance.

It took two evenings before he trapped his first fish. Guiamo excitedly called Flaccus, which came running. Guiamo picked up the basket and placed a cover over it. The flopping fish struggled in vain as the boy splashed through the water toward the shore. Once he was safely far enough from the water, Guiamo dropped the fish onto the ground. Flaccus lunged at the fish and in moments had it firmly in his teeth.

Guiamo was quite pleased with himself for having found a fun way to find fish for his dog. As he watched Flaccus consume the fish, he decided there must be an easier way to catch fish than swimming around all evening. Over the next week, he pondered ways to make his work easier.

Once, Guiamo found that a fish had swum into the trap by itself. He called Flaccus out into the shallow water. Once Flaccus saw the fish, he jumped over the stick wall to get it.

For the next fifteen minutes, Flaccus jumped, barked, splashed, chased and snapped at the frantic fish in the narrow confines of the stick wall. Eventually, Guiamo went into the tree line and returned with a large dead branch. He picked up Flaccus and put the soaking wet dog over the stick wall. Then, turning back to the trap with stick in hand, Guiamo waited patiently for the fish to stop swimming. It only took two tries. Guiamo swung the stick overhead to land flatly across the surface of the water directly above the fish. Stunned by the impact, the fish turned on its side and floated to the surface. In one fluid motion, Guiamo quickly grabbed the fish and heaved it onto the shore to Flaccus.

The boy soon grew tired of trying to guide the fish into the trap every evening, and decided that whatever found its way to the trap was good enough. He stopped spending his free time in the water and went back to his nets. Every day, Flaccus sniffed around in his trap and occasionally there was a fish or two in there.

While Guiamo spent some weeks casting nets with Calidius, the hard work motivated him to think of other ways to more easily catch fish. In the evenings when his daily work was completed, he tried spreading nets weighted with small stones on the bottom of the lake. With a pull on the attached ropes, he tried to raise the net as quickly as he could when a fish swam above. The resistance from the water always proved too great for his small arms and the fish inevitably escaped.

Then an idea formed into his mind. He could tie a net to one end of a rope, and a rock at the other. The rope would be draped over a tall forked pole which pointed straight up. He planned to have an adult pick up the rock as high as he could next to the forked pole, and Guiamo would then cast the net. When the adult dropped the rock, the rope would pull the net rapidly out of the water.

Calidius just smirked when Guiamo described his plan. "I am much too old to lift stones into the air. Perhaps someone else would be willing. However, before you build your engine, you should make a small one to test your idea."

The boy worked hard in his spare time to build a working model. He immediately found his idea needed improvement and made several versions. Several had extension arms to pull the net up from a distance. None worked as well as he would have liked, and some were dismal failures, but he took great joy in designing.

All this design work took up much of his free evening time. While the dog frequently had too little to eat, it was a rare day Guiamo caught nothing to feed Flaccus. On those days, Guiamo shared his own food with his dog, which seemed to understand his generosity.

Eventually, Guiamo abandoned his rock device. Lifting a net through the water proved to be too difficult. Then he realized he didn't need to lift the net out of the water to entrap the fish. All he needed to do was design a different kind of net. He decided to make a net which simply formed a wall to corral the fish.

Guiamo wove a net as high as his waist. It was large enough to form a circle two *passuum* in diameter. The bottom edge was secured to the lake floor with sticks pushed into the muck. On the top end, he tied bundles of buoyant

16

reeds. To the reeds, he tied heavy rocks which offset their natural buoyancy. The net would be carefully placed, laying flat on the lake bottom in a circle. Calidius showed him how to tie slip knots so that when a single cord was pulled, all the knots securing the heavy rocks to the reeds would release, and thereby allow the reeds to float to the surface, raising the net encirclement along with them.

Guiamo placed his special net on the lake floor, and watched from a small fishing boat for fish to swim by. Much to his own surprise, within the first hour, he saw a very large fish swim in. With a mighty pull on the cord, the knots holding the heavy rocks released, the reeds launched to the surface and the fish was encircled.

He had constructed a dipping net to secure his catch, which, to Calidius' surprise, proved to be a very useful tool in the hands of a motivated ten-year-old boy. Calidius gasped when he saw Guiamo quickly hauling his catch out of the water with his dipping net.

They marched home with their prize in the net, singing songs of conquest, and with Flaccus barking triumphantly all the way. Never had Guiamo tasted a more delicious baked fish than that evening, and the three had their fill.

Calidius saw that Guiamo was very intelligent, and unusually creative. The boy's efforts to find solutions were much more intense and detailed than mere child's play. He clearly was gifted and highly motivated to achieve success. As autumn breezes descended into the valley, Calidius decided Guiamo must be more than just a fisherman. "But for now," he whispered to himself, "he must learn the trade of a fisherman in full. Even a great man needs to know how to fill his own belly."

Throughout the fall, Calidius assigned Guiamo to the seven other fishermen to learn their particular insights and techniques. As the boy learned with eye and arm, he was quick to see what strengths each had.

Moravius had the advantage of height, and was able to cast his net further than the rest. His eyesight, however, was not as good as the others, so did not throw to the best advantage when boulders lay under the surface.

Meridius' injured leg gave him a disadvantage with endurance, but the patient, rhythmic style which accompanied his songs helped him through the long days. His fishing was steady, and his catch was good. Guiamo learned to sing Meridius' fishing songs, and the boy's high voice showed a natural talent. Each evening, he sang to Flaccus as the skies turned dark. The boisterous dog would grow quiescent to the lilting voice by the firepit, and gaze spellbound up at Guiamo as they quietly finished out each day.

Gnaeus and Spurius Popillius both had a wealth of knowledge about the lake, and knew where to fish during the different times and seasons. Of the two brothers, Spurious Popillius, Guiamo determined, was actually the more attuned to the lake. Gnaeus Popillius compensated with a continuous barrage of good humored bragging and brotherly insults, but the results of their daily catch regularly showed Spurious Popillius the better of the two.

Autronius was constantly bothered by his two daughters who seemed to argue incessantly, and regularly needed his intervention. Guiamo inwardly laughed as Caedicius' fishing rhythm was noticeably thrown off whenever Autronia Crispinis Minor ran to her father for aid. Guiamo recognized that she bickered purposefully with her older sister simply so she could justify being on the lake shore where she could be seen by the watchful eyes of handsome, young Caedicius.

Guiamo one day mentioned this to Calidius. "I suspect Caedicius will someday lose his balance altogether and fall into the lake when she comes to speak to Autronius," he said. "He is so miserably in love."

Calidius laughed quietly and replied, "This is true. Caedicius loves the girl, and she, him. Autronius also knows this, as does everyone in the village. It is plain to see. Autronius is waiting patiently for Caedicius to become brave enough, no, self confident enough, to speak with her. Caedicius is a brave man, but in love, he is not certain of his steps. For now, their love for each other is all at a distance. Give them time, Guiamo, give them time."

Equitius was the least skilled of the seven, but he had learned how to get the best exchanges for his catch. He was the best businessman of the lot, and worked hard to secure his profits. While not considered wealthy, he had managed to acquire the greatest estate in the village, and was well respected.

As his strength increased, Guiamo found that he was better able to feed Flaccus by simply staying out longer in the boat casting nets, than with his clever devices. The water also turned colder, and it wasn't nearly as much fun as it once had been. His fish trap slowly fell into disrepair, his dipping net broke apart and the models of his rock engines were discarded. He worked hard at fishing, but was never satisfied with it as a means to feed Flaccus.

One brisk early morning, Guiamo visited Moravius' home. As they chatted over breakfast about Flaccus' appetite and the hard work it took to feed him, Moravius stood up and strode into another room. He returned with an old bow and four arrows. "I should show you how to hunt." said Moravius. "This bow, I made some years ago after I returned from Rome. What a wretched place! It was both marvelous and disgusting. You should go someday, but be certain to return home soon, or its evil will cling to you. Meet me here tonight and I will show you how to shoot this bow. If you practice well, you will be able to hunt food for Flaccus throughout the winter. You will not enjoy being in the water when it becomes cold."

That evening Moravius taught Guiamo the basics of archery, and then set up a target at three *passuum*. Guiamo quickly and painfully learned to keep his left arm just out of the way of the bowstring as it snapped forward. "Those scrapes on your forearm will teach you to shoot properly." Moravius said when Guiamo's technique became sloppy. "Put some of Meridius' ointment on it when you return home tonight. It will help your arm heal quickly. Now, when you can hit this piece of bark every time, then I will let you shoot it at five *passuum*."

Guiamo practiced all evening until his fingers and arms were sore. He quickly caught on, and by the time the sun set, he could hit the piece of bark nearly every time.

"Come back tomorrow evening, and I will teach you more," said Moravius. "Now go home. I am certain Calidius has work for you to tend to. Will I see you tomorrow?"

"Of course!" said Guiamo with great enthusiasm as he headed home.

Guiamo showed up the next evening with supper in hand, and ate as Moravius gave instruction. They practiced that evening at five *passuum*. Again, Guiamo practiced diligently, but found this distance more difficult. By the end of the day, while still unable to hit the bark, could regularly place the arrows around it.

For the next two weeks, Guiamo worked diligently, and Moravius was pleased with his progress. As Moravius guided him on technique, Guiamo's aim improved. When he could hit the five *passuum* target about half the time, Moravius had him practice shooting alternatively between the three and five *passuum* targets. "This will help you shoot with accuracy more instinctively."

During periods of rest, Moravius taught Guiamo how to select good pieces of wood to be made into arrows. He showed Guiamo how to check for straightness by placing one end onto the fold of his left thumb when held at arms length, and, while holding the other end to his eye, spinning it with the fingers of his right hand. Guiamo clearly saw that any bowing of the wood immediately became visible.

Nocking the arrow shaft was the simplest task of all. He used his bone handled knife to cut out a groove across one end. He had to make sure it was centered properly, and was cut wide enough to accommodate the bowstring. It was then bound with sinew to avoid splitting the wood.

Fletching the arrows was more difficult for Guiamo, and he grandly fumbled his early attempts. He had a difficult time with the glue sticking to his fingers, and it tested his patience. After many attempts, a few angry bouts of an

20

erupting temper, and the destruction of many feathers, he finally was able to calm himself down enough to finish the fletching to Moravius' satisfaction.

Moravius purchased nine three-bladed iron arrowheads for Guiamo. He showed Guiamo how to mount them into the arrow shaft, and then bind them with sinew. Once Guiamo had finished constructing nine arrows, Moravius taught him the basics of hunting, and how to stalk his prey.

Guiamo soon spent most of his free time afield hunting hares and rabbits in the evening. He learned to walk slowly toward his prey without making direct eye contact. Moravius showed him how to draw close by walking slowly toward a spot to the left or right of the rabbit, and never directly toward it. As he moved toward this spot, his path was planned to always draw him closer. The animal usually thought it had not been detected by the boy and would sit still. Only when the distance was close enough, about three *passuum*, would he then turn at the waist and fire his arrow.

Guiamo practiced diligently, and his accuracy improved along with his stealthiness. The fields surrounding the village were quickly despoiled of rabbits, while Flaccus grew fat and his coat glossy.

As the rabbit and hare populations dwindled, Guiamo realized he'd have to find yet another source of food to feed his dog. He tried throwing nets, weighted on the ends with stones, to catch wild geese and ducks. Only with patience and crafty stealth was he able to get close enough for a cast of the nets good enough to catch a bird.

Caedicius taught Guiamo how to find a small animal's trail through the underbrush. He showed him that by placing sticks upright a few fingers apart along either sides of the tiny trail, the animal could be guided to a snare. The tiny fence would narrow to the snare, and when the animal tried to squeeze through the now narrow gap between the upright sticks, its head would enter the noose. As the animal tried to go forward, the snare would tighten around its neck. The animal's struggles would only further tighten the noose until it was strangled. By placing snares around, Guiamo would only need to make his rounds each evening to see what his catch would be.

Guiamo soon found that his catch was being eaten by a predator before he could retrieve the snared animal. In frustration, he decided to catch this animal. With some tools borrowed from Spurius Popillius, he dug a pit as deep as his waist and as twice as wide as his shoulders. He scraped the sides so they were straight and steep. He placed a few thin sticks across it in several directions, and then covered them with handfuls of grass and leaves. He then skewered a dead squirrel onto a stronger stick. He stuck one end deep into the grass to the side of the pit, leaving the squirrel dangling over the trap.

Guiamo came back the next morning to check his trap. As he was walking up, he saw that the squirrel was still on the stick, and the leaves were undisturbed. Disappointed, he came closer, only to find to his surprise that a section of leaves was missing. Quickening his pace, he fell to his knees, peered into the darkness and saw a fox standing at the bottom of the pit. Guiamo grabbed a fallen branch, whittled the tip into a sharp point, and spent the next few moments jabbing fiercely at the fox.

He soon was running jubilantly back to the village with a dead fox in hand, dangling from its furry tail. In a very short time, the fox pelt was drying alongside the dozens of rabbit hides Moravius had helped him prepare.

As winter passed, Guiamo began to think more about catching fish. One cold, rainy afternoon, Calidius and Guiamo stayed indoors, mending their clothes by the firepit and telling stories. Guiamo's thoughts wandered between his love for hunting these past cold months, and the tedium of fishing that would soon begin again in the spring. As his thoughts flitted between the two, an idea came to him. He looked up from his work to Calidius and asked, "Could a fish be hunted with a bow?"

Calidius paused his stitching and gazed into the fiery coals, contemplating the idea. "An arrow is a powerful weapon. If it can penetrate armor, surely it could penetrate water; at least a short distance." He turned his head to Guiamo, "I see you are being clever again."

Guiamo laughed and said, "I do like to consider myself cleverer than a fish." He put down the shirt he was mending. "When the winds turn warm, we shall see."

Chapter Two - 59 B.C.

"Amidst the simple-minded rabble of those scattered, brute tribes, when the earth was young and man had not yet learned to rise above their bestial ways, there arose from time to time, certain gifted individuals of surpassing brilliance whose exceeding wisdom shone as a gleaming light, and these, bringing discovery, eased the desperate plight of the others, and so by their guidance and accomplishments improved the lot of their kinsmen, and so the race of men began to thrive according to that degree accorded them. These men of wisdom were selected by the fathers to rule over them and made them into kings. Now some ruled benevolently, but others ruled as tyrants. These gifted ones, even today, are born into the world but on the rarest of occasions, for generations may pass before one arises, bringing prosperity and advancement through their creative endeavors or wise philosophy." The Remembrances of Sisythus 2:20

Spring came early, and Guiamo eagerly set out one windy, warm afternoon with his bow and five remaining arrows. He boarded his small fishing boat and headed toward the weedy shallows near the remains of his fish trap. Peering into the water, he searched for a worthy target. An hour went by before he spied a fish as long as his forearm near the surface. He carefully aimed and fired. The arrow disappeared into the murky darkness as quickly as the unharmed fish.

Guiamo dejectedly realized he had overlooked the most obvious thing; how would he ever retrieve his arrow? He sat down in his boat and thought this through. The answer came quickly enough. He needed to tie one end of a lightweight cord to the back of the arrow, and the other end to the boat.

He rowed to the shore, and ran all the way back to Calidius' hut to find a length of sinewy twine he knew was there. Totally winded by the sprint, he walked all the way back to the boat. He notched the arrow shaft near the nock, wound the cord around the notch, and tied it off. Then Guiamo tied the other end to the boat.

Searching again for a fish, he found another of similar size in front of a sunken log. Guiamo gave it his best aim and let the arrow loose. The arrow embedded itself into the wood above the fish. In frustration at the lost fish, and the firmly stuck arrow, he fired a second shot directly at the log.

To his surprise, it missed and passed on the far side of the log. He retrieved that arrow with the line and fired again at the log. It also missed, passing similarly beyond the log. Guiamo thought carefully about this for a while. He finally recognized that things below water appear higher than they really are. Testing his observation, he aimed deliberately a hand width below the log. The arrow sunk firmly into the log. "I must aim below my target when I shoot into the water!" he exclaimed his discovery aloud to himself. Then in disgust with himself, he said, "And I must remember to not waste my precious arrows by shooting them into sunken logs. Now I am down to only two arrows left."

He traded fifty of his rabbit skins for three more iron arrow heads. He couldn't afford the more expensive three-bladed arrowheads, but was content with the two-bladed ones. With his new purchase, he constructed three more arrows.

Guiamo spent his evenings alternately hunting rabbits and fish. His best success bow hunting fish came when the fish remained still hovering over their nests. He was a natural hunter, and though he enjoyed the retrieval of a flopping fish skewered by an arrow, he found that the stealth of hunting on land more fulfilling. He also relished the freedom he found in the field after a day at the nets confined to his small boat.

Guiamo spoke to Calidius during a quiet lunch on the shore of the beach. "I wonder if I could do something different from fishing for a while. I am getting bored, and my arms are always tired."

Calidius was surprised at this change in tone, "Bored? What has 'bored' to do with earning a living? Do you think we do not get bored with fishing? Certainly we do, but then, we are fishermen. That is what we do. Guiamo, fishermen do what to earn a living?"

Guiamo looked chided, and glumly said, "Fish."

Calidius looked him in the eye, "And what do weavers do to make a living?"

Guiamo looked even glummer, and replied, "Weave."

"And do weavers become bored?" asked Calidius.

"Yes." responded Guiamo.

"So what do bored weavers do?" asked Calidius.

"Weave." Guiamo replied with resignation.

"Yes. They weave while they are bored," said Calidius. "And for that, they make a living. Boredom means you have perfected a skill. Boredom is a price we pay to live well."

Calidius thought for a while as they finished their lunch in silence. As they rose to go back to their boats, he said, "A boy of eleven needs variety in his life. I will see what I can do to alleviate the pain of your boredom."

"It is a bargain then," Equitius said. "Guiamo will help me farm this summer."

Calidius reminded him of the terms, "He will help so long as you teach him the lessons we agreed to. He can start tomorrow."

"Tomorrow it is then," Equitius affirmed. "I need him to learn to milk the cows, so have him here at milking time. Better yet, have him stay with my family tonight, and I will wake him at milking time," Equitius said. He laughed and said, "The first lesson he will learn is the value of sleep. He will learn that quickly when I get him up well before the sun rises each day. I cannot have grumpy milk cows."

Equitius woke Guiamo in the middle of the night, led him to the barn and showed him the basics of milking. Though painfully tired, Guiamo did his best to learn milking. Equitius watched carefully, and gave clear instructions. He watched patiently while Guiamo struggled to do it correctly. It took twice as long as Equitius usually took, but he did finish the chore successfully. When the task was completed, he allowed Guiamo to go back to bed to sleep until sunrise.

When morning came, Guiamo was roused out of bed and told to feed hay to the oxen, horse and milk cows, scatter seed for the chickens and geese, and slop the pigs. "The animals provide you with food and drink. They must always eat before you do."

By the time Guiamo had finished these chores, he had worked up an enormous appetite. Equitius' wife fed him hot oat gruel mixed with milk and a little butter. Guiamo ate it all ravenously, wishing for a second helping, but knew better than to ask for more.

Throughout the rest of the day, Equitius introduced Guiamo to the daily chores required to care for the farm animals. By the end of the day, Guiamo was utterly exhausted.

Equitius sat with him by the firepit, relaxing after their supper, and said, "There are some things Calidius asked me to teach you."

Guiamo groaned, but nodded in agreement to listen. "Today, I will teach you numbers. You need to learn how to work with numbers." They worked together starting from the basics. Equitius taught Guiamo what the Roman symbols were for the numbers, and then the techniques to add and subtract with those symbols. Guiamo learned quickly, and practiced diligently. After a week, Equitius felt that, while Guiamo had not mastered it, he had become fairly proficient adding and subtracting.

After the first week with numbers, Equitius then turned to the letters. "I do not know how to read much, but I did learn the letter symbols some years ago. I will teach you what I know." Over the next several days, Equitius taught Guiamo the letter symbols, and some of what each meant. Guiamo became good enough at his letters that he could write the symbol correctly when Equitius called out the letter's name. "I wish I could teach you more about that, boy, but that is all I know. Come; let me now teach you more important things, like how to strike a good bargain."

"How do you get the most money for something you want to sell?" asked Equitius.

"Do not sell it to you," joked Guiamo.

"True," laughed Equitius. "I never pay top price. Well, not if I do not have a larger plan in mind. There is a time and place to pay full price, but when, do you think, is this wise?" he asked.

Guiamo thought carefully about this before venturing his answer, "Only pay full price if paying that price opens the door to something more important."

"Excellent answer," said Equitius. "It is also precisely true. There are times, when someone, usually rich, will open their rarities up for sale. You must use wisdom to discern these times. The seller must know you are a serious buyer set apart from the rest. You must not be one of the rabble clamoring for his goods. Paying full price for an item without barter can give you preference in their consideration of future sales. Always be respectful, for in these particular circumstances, you are being given a great privilege to merely see the items. Then, when he lets you see his treasures, he will tell you the price. You must decide, not what price to counter with, but rather, whether the price is acceptable or not. If it is acceptable, say 'Yes, I wish to purchase this item.' Pay your money and be content, for you alone will have the treasure.

"If it is not priced as you would prefer, or can afford, say, 'Not today, thank you, perhaps another day.' Any other response will be viewed as an insult. Do not haggle or you will never again be invited."

Equitius continued, "If it is not something you wish to purchase, take time to discuss its beauty, for it is beautiful and important to the seller. He will appreciate your interest, and genuine compliments will grow your relationship.

"Above all, when you have finished seeing these treasures, thank him sincerely. Only then will you be allowed in at another time. For your courtesy in this, you will be invited first when other treasures become available for sale.

"Further, never attempt to sell the item. If the original owner hears that his things are immediately being resold for mere profit, he will never invite you again. He sells them to you because he wants them to belong to someone who appreciates their beauty or importance. If you decide you must resell your purchase, be certain that you wait a year or more. If you wait to resell, no insult will be felt by the original owner if he hears of it."

Equitius stopped momentarily, and then continued with a firm tone, "There is another time to pay full price. Never barter with the gods."

28

With a twinkle in his eye, he added, "Haggle on everything else."

Guiamo learned to plow and sow, harness oxen, salve bee stings, slaughter geese, and a hundred other things of daily farm life during that summer. The work was hard, the nights short, and the lessons priceless.

As the hot days gave way to cooling winds, Equitius gave Guiamo a few days rest, and the boy returned home to Calidius for that time.

"All he wants to talk about is farming and haggling," said Guiamo as they strolled along a path through the woods behind their home. "I do not mind so much. I have learned a lot. He is a good man, but it is all farming and haggling, haggling and farming. Even when we fish in our spare time, all he talks about is farming and haggling."

Calidius was delighted. "Of course! Of course! Farming and haggling are what he does best. For that I have sent you to him. Farming I know a bit about. What did he teach you about haggling?"

Guiamo launched into a lengthy discussion about haggling. "He taught me where to sell my goods. The first question he asked me was 'Where should you go to sell your fish?' He laughed at the folly of my answer. I told him I would sell it in the village. He groaned at me and said 'You would sell fish in a fishing village? By the gods, that is a terrible plan. You need to sell the fish where people have no fish, but want it. A fishing village is where they already have fish and want no more. Did Calidius teach you that? No wonder he is still out in that broken-down, old boat casting the nets.' "

Calidius smiled broadly and slapped away a branch that had grown across the pathway.

Guiamo continued, "He took me to five different villages to see what prices for fish were. I was astonished that the further inland we went, how much higher the prices became. This was especially true for fresh fish. The prices were not so different for salted or dried fish, though. He told me to price the items so that you get the most money per piece and, just as importantly, you sell all your merchandise. 'There is no use carrying fresh fish back home because it will not be fresh when you get there,' he said."

"Trading is tougher because it is hard to know what the value is for the items you want. 'Know before you trade,' is his creed," said Guiamo.

"Equitius is a wise man," said Calidius. "He has taught you well. How successful have you been at putting his haggling lessons into practice?"

"I found out that fifty rabbits are worth more than the three arrowheads I traded last fall. But I was young then," said Guiamo.

"You were young…" thought Calidius as his voice trailed off in amusement.

Guiamo picked up his thoughts again, "I think my best trade was eleven boiled rabbits for an ingot of tin. A hungry family came through, and all they had left to trade was the tin. It came all the way from Albion. At least, that is what the father said. Equitius told me why he thought this was a very good trade. They needed something, in this case, food. I had something they wanted; boiled rabbits. They were willing to trade their most valuable possession for what they needed. The deal was struck, and everyone was pleased. Now I have the tin, and they had full bellies for a few days. I can get more rabbits. I do not particularly need tin, but I can trade it for some things I might need. Equitius told me he would take me this fall to a place I can get the best trade for the tin."

"Save some of your profits. You will need it later more than now," Calidius advised. "Save as much as you can. You have your entire life before you."

So another year passed with Guiamo toiling under the sun, learning the trade of fisherman, hunter and farmer, and listening to the lessons a boy needs to mature into manhood. Calidius watched him become consistent and reliable. He was by nature generous and forgiving. Sometimes his temper flared up, though his natural stubbornness was slowly transformed, shaped by Calidius into more of a controlled

30

desire for self-determination. At twelve years old, Guiamo was clearly becoming his own man.

Chapter Three - 58 B.C.

"And the priests were so incensed at her words that they seized hands upon the oracle and bound her and slew her upon the tripod, for they deemed that she had done some impure thing to have been rejected and punished so by the gods. Her memory was despised by many, but the high priest, Manius Aemilius Scaurus, knew she had done no wrong, having only asked the god, as was their custom, concerning a certain young man of Gallia from the town of Gobedbiacum, but he held his tongue for fear of the crowd and so she died." Lives of Nicaea, Timophilus 17:81

On the second day of *Martius*, Calidius sighed as he passed the platter of baked fish to Guiamo for a last helping at the evening meal. "I may seem an old fool to you today."

Guiamo was taken aback. "Why should you say that? I have never thought you so. Have I become so arrogant under your teaching?"

Calidius smiled at his pupil's humble demeanor. "No, my boy, arrogance never found a foothold with you. No, but with what I have to say, you may disagree. For that, you may see me a fool."

Suspicious of this unfolding riddle, Guiamo sat back from the low beech wood table to lean against the wall of their mud and wattle home, and guardedly folded his arms.

Calidius continued, "Guiamo, I have known you for two years, and each day since we met, every day, I have known you are special. Within a few weeks, it became clear to me that you have a gift given by the gods which not every man receives."

Guiamo looked confused. "I have received a gift from the gods?"

"Observe my words carefully," Calidius explained, "I said 'you have a gift given by the gods which not every man receives.' When I say 'receives,' I do not mean in a way that a gift is thrust upon a man by the gods. Rain is a gift of the gods which is received whether or not a man would have it. There is another way to 'receive.' By this, I mean that the gift which is presented by the gods is accepted by a man who chooses to receive it fully into himself. Truly, you have been given such a gift by the gods. Will you receive it?"

"And what should the gods demand of me for such a gift? Why should the gods bless me with a gift I know not?" asked Guiamo cautiously. "I have friends, a home, I eat well. I am content. Let them keep their gift."

"Now it is your turn to play the fool, Guiamo," chastised Calidius. "Your home, friends and food certainly are gifts of the gods, but of these, I am not speaking."

Guiamo grew impatient and his temper showed itself. "My gift is where? Hiding under the table? No. Perhaps it is behind the door. Ah, there it is, let me go fetch it," he said sarcastically and half rose as if to retrieve it.

"Silence child!" commanded Calidius. "Order your thoughts and be still." He sat unmoving, but held a fierce glare to control the young man. "Your gift is before you. I have but to name it, but I shall not. Not yet."

Calidius' tone softened, but his will remained firm, "To receive your gift, you must give up your friends and your home. And you may not eat well. For that, you may see me a fool, for your life is at rest and goodness surrounds you. What ordinary man would give this up? I see, though, that you, my son, are not an ordinary man. I tell you, truly, that the gift lies before you. Pass it over, and you shall stay and be with friends and home, perhaps be wed someday, and be content with your daily bread. But your rejected gift will haunt you throughout your life, though you cannot name it."

Guiamo was bothered by this riddle and did not know how to respond.

Calidius broke the silence. "Your gift has a price to be sure. It is a gift, however, that is worthy of this price." He paused and let his words soak into Guiamo.

The young man grew more thoughtful and deliberate with his tact. He reviewed Calidius' statements in his mind and pieced the clues together. "You say I have a gift, but have not yet received it. To receive this gift, I must give up my friends and home. My life will be difficult. I must go away." He paused in thought and then his mind expanded as he continued, "So I must go away. Where must I go?"

" 'Where' is not so important," said Calidius. " 'Why' is the key."

"So, why must I go?" Guiamo asked. "Why must I go to receive the gift?"

"Because your gift cannot be found here," replied Calidius. "I have known since the day your *avunculus* dumped you off the cart. I knew from the moment you picked yourself up, walked across the beach with the feeblest, most pain-ridden smile I have ever seen, and asked to help me mend those nets.

"You have strength in you, boy, strength and wisdom. I have seen how you chose to work hard to be useful to complete strangers. You did not say to me 'I need this, give it to me,' like a beggar on the street. Instead, you decided to make yourself useful to me without reserve in the hopes that you would eventually obtain what you need. Your idea worked. If you had asked me for food, I would have sent you on your way.

"You are an unusually contemplative young man. You use your wits. I have seen you create unusual answers to solve many problems. How many engines did you create to catch fish for that mongrel Flaccus? Do you think everybody would do this? No! Only you. I see in you intense curiosity, and an even greater desire to conquer problems. You are creative. You have a great mind. To stay here would be a waste. You must not stay here."

Guiamo paused before answering, "So you think my mind is this gift of the gods?"

"No," Calidius replied. "Your mind is not the gift of which I speak. A gift it is, but merely as the rain that is a gift of the gods. You have no choice in that matter. Your intellect, your creativity, and your desire to succeed are the tools that allow the gods to give you a better gift, a gift greater than mere intelligence. That is the gift you must receive within yourself."

"So what is the gift, Calidi?" Guiamo asked in frustration, "I cannot see it."

Calidius looked at Guiamo squarely in the eyes. He spread his hands towards the boy's face, placing his palms

34

gently on each cheek. With a tear flowing down his face, Calidius choked with emotion as he smiled, and whispered, "An extraordinary life, my boy. An extraordinary life."

As the sun rose the next morning, Guiamo found Calidius already busying himself with their breakfast. Calidius turned at the noises Guiamo made stretching and said "Today is the beginning of your journey. I have packed your things while you slept. After you have eaten, you must say goodbye to your friends."

Guiamo found the rapidity of his departure a bit unsettling. "So, 'good morning' and out I go. I do not even know where I am going." He rose and walked to the firepit to take a piece of bread. "So, where am I going?"

"North. Take the first left when the path branches. In three days, you will come to the village of Gobedbiacum. Ask for Lucius Gabinius Malleolus. He will teach you metalworking. You are to stay with him for three years. Trust him as you trust me. Serve him well. His lessons will prove far more valuable than my feeble attempts." Calidius' eyes twinkled as he thought, and he smiled insightfully. "And his riddles more difficult to answer."

"He knows my mind and will direct you to your next destination all in good time. Gabinius is a learned man. He has promised to teach you to read. That will give you advantage above the rabble."

"I have saved for you as much silver as I could from your haul of fish these past two years." Calidius opened a rag filled with silver and bronze coins. "Place these in the purse Caedicius gave you, and guard it carefully."

Guiamo was surprised at this unexpected gift. He took the coins and inserted them into the leather bag he kept slung around his neck and shoulder. He sat down next to the firepit to eat. As they ate together in silence, Guiamo became tearful. Calidius ignored his emotions and rose to finish packing.

"Will you come with me?" he asked.

"You know the way," Calidius replied as he tied the top flap to the leather bag securely.

The boy's face fell as Calidius handed it to him to sling over his head and shoulder.

"It is a long way," Guiamo implored.

"Life is a long journey. It is one that you must take alone. I have cared for you for two years. I have walked alongside you during this portion of your life's journey. I have prepared the way for your next steps. Gabinius will guide you well from here, but I will not take you. You must take yourself. By taking this trip alone, you will more fully receive the gift of the gods set before you. If I should go alongside you, the ties you have to me will never be truly severed."

Placing his hands about Guiamo's shoulders, Calidius said, "Go. Take my love with you, but leave me behind. May the memories of my voice guide you. May my lessons be remembered. As your life's journey takes you to fascinating places, and you meet people good and bad, remember that though they may walk beside you, it is your journey alone, not theirs. Decide things with your own mind and conscience, for you must bear the consequences, not they."

Calidius continued, "Trust Gabinius as you trust me. We served together in a *legio* of Rome, and I know his heart. He is wise and will tolerate no evil around him. His servants also are honorable, for he would have no other."

"Are you certain you will not go with me?" pleaded Guiamo once again, already knowing the answer.

Calidius smiled compassionately, and long embraced him in his strong arms. "My boy, I will certainly not go with you; only in my heart." Then, with a twinkle in his eyes, he said "You see, my nets and I have an appointment with a fish that craves to be my supper.

"Now greet your friends goodbye. It is time for your journey." As Guiamo stooped to pick up his possessions, Calidius added with a smirk, "Be sure to tell old Gabinius that at the raid we made near the *oppidum* of Bibracte, it was his fart that startled the Gaul's horses, not the voice of their thunder-god as he told that fool of a scribe who wrote the conquests of our *legio*."

Guiamo turned toward the northern path and found his fisher friends gathering for their final parting. Each embraced him as a son, and presented him with a parting gift. Gnaeus Popillius tied a harp onto his blanket roll. Moravius gave him the bow Guiamo had used for hunting along with a bundle of fifteen newly fletched arrows tied with a cord. Guiamo untied the bundle and placed his three remaining arrows with the others, and then tied them up again. Meridius presented him another bottle of ointment for sore muscles. Spurious Popillius handed him two large rolls of freshly baked bread for the journey.

Only Caedicius had his thoughts elsewhere as he chatted awkwardly with a glowing Autronia Crispinus Minor, pausing only briefly to embrace Guiamo, and say a blessing of safety for the journey.

Autronius had made a walking staff sized for the young man, and whacked Guiamo on his rear in a parting jest. Guiamo rubbed his bottom to ease the pain, but gratefully accepted the staff with a smile. Equitius waited to the last to embrace him, and then handed Guiamo a single small bronze *as* coin, "To remind you of my haggling lessons," he said.

As some turned back to home and work, Calidius approached Guiamo. "I have not fed your dog for two years. It is not that I do not like Flaccus, but rather you have had to learn to be responsible for someone other than yourself. He has proven to be a good dog and loyal companion, so today I will at last feed him." Calidius handed Guiamo a heavy sack. "Here is a supply of meat for him that should last the journey. You will not have time to hunt."

Guiamo thanked Calidius for all he had done, and for his immense generosity. He then called Flaccus, which came bounding out of the wood line behind the hut.

As his final piece of advice, Calidius embraced Guiamo and said in parting, "You have much to carry and the trip is long. Do not neglect to eat and drink to keep your strength. Rest frequently. A tired traveler is a target. Walk with confident steps and evil will remain in the shadows. Sleep unseen a distance from the path."

With a final wave to his friends, Guiamo turned and headed north with Flaccus trotting alongside. The sun quickly grew hot, and he drank water from his gourd bottle. His sadness at parting with his friends soon passed. With the excitement of new adventure, he began to enjoy his trip through new regions never before seen. He soon felt reinvigorated.

He was tempted to hunt the rabbits that ran across the road from time to time, but realized his priority had to remain with placing one foot in front of the other. Hunting would mean delay, and he had food enough to sustain him the distance.

With a wistful look, he bypassed the rabbits and continued on at a determined pace. Flaccus stayed close to Guiamo, largely ignoring the animals except for an occasional bark.

He rarely passed travelers, but the few he met passed by with little more than a disinterested word of greeting.

The day passed quickly as Guiamo found the left fork and walked north. Despite the advice of Calidius, Guiamo rarely stopped to rest. He paused only long enough to get some food for Flaccus and himself. He fed the dog small pieces of rabbit meat which were quickly gulped whole. Guiamo then walked on, eating his own bread and meat as he went.

As the sun drew down to the horizon, Guiamo decided to settle in for the night. He checked the road north and south, and saw that no one was in sight. He turned left off the road, and headed into a rocky wood twenty *passuum* off the road.

Carefully setting down his possessions, he opened his leather bag to check everything over. After clearing the ground of underbrush and stones, he spread out the overlarge green blanket.

The sun went down with Guiamo resting on the blanket with one-half folded over across him. Flaccus settled next to Guiamo, pressing against the boy's side for warmth. As Guiamo quietly sang the fisherman's songs, the dog drifted off to sleep. Guiamo felt pleased with this first day on his own and looked forward to the next day, another day of adventure.

38

In the morning, it rained.

Soon after he set off down the road, the rain came with a cool gust of wind. It poured rather abruptly and heavily at the outset, and then quickly tapered off to a slow steady rain for the rest of the day.

Guiamo soon became chilled, wishing he was sitting with Calidius by the firepit inside the hut. The road turned slippery and, as the rain water soaked into the soil, became a muddy morass. The mud clung to his feet and he struggled with his walking staff to avoid falling. He walked along the side of the path on the weedy edge, preferring the occasional scrape of a thorn or stick to the struggle in the mud.

His progress slowed, and his remaining loaf of bread got wet. Flaccus seemed unhappy, and stayed close to Guiamo. The twelve-year-old trudged quietly on throughout the day, and when the rain stopped, evening came. Resignedly, he slept uncomfortably in a muddy thicket with a damp blanket.

Morning of the third day came with a warming wind and soggy bread. Guiamo set out with Flaccus along the weedy edge of the muddy path. By midmorning, the sun had dried his wet clothing to the point of mere discomfort, but by noon was fully dried. Flaccus seemed much happier and his appetite had grown.

As Guiamo trudged north, he saw more farmsteads and lanes branching off. The number of travelers increased, coming from crossroads of the surrounding villages. He kept to himself and was polite to those he met, but marched resolutely on. Flaccus seemed to be tiring more easily as the hours went by.

As the path turned around a large formation of broken, tumbled rocks, Guiamo came upon a Roman army encampment. Each log of the wooden palisade was sharpened to a point. Two sentries with long spears guarded the gates. Towers were built of timbers at each corner, and along each side at regular intervals. He watched, spellbound, at the troops marching out of the fort armed as if for battle. The *cornicen* sounded the commands of the *centurio*. The large circular horn curved downward from the mouthpiece, under his right arm, on around his back, and up over his right shoulder. His excitement built quickly as he thought of his father's service with a Roman *legio.*

Guiamo wandered over to the gate to peer inside the fort.

"What business do you have here?" challenged the stocky, bearded guard. "Move along, boy."

Guiamo kept his composure and glanced curiously at the guard. "I am just looking," he said calmly.

"Looking for something to steal, more likely," grumbled the taller guard. "Look, boy, move on."

"I am doing no harm," said Guiamo. "I have never seen an army encampment before."

The stocky guard motioned toward Guiamo with his spear and snarled in his most threatening tone, "If I catch you sneaking inside, we will eat you for supper. Now move along, you thieving rascal, before I skewer you through and roast you on the spit."

Guiamo blinked in surprise at first, but then quickly realized the bearded guard's vicious threats were meant to simply intimidate him into moving along, but not to be taken literally. Their rough jests were obviously used to keep troublemakers out and to secure the camp.

The twelve-year-old realized that with his light brown hair, blue eyes, and bedraggled, road-weary appearance, they mistook him for a Gaul, no doubt up to no good.

He tried to not look intimidated, so he respectfully, but firmly, continued to speak with the guards. "I am Guiamo Durmius Stolo, and I am a Roman citizen. My father served and died in Gallia with a *legio* in service to Rome. May I pass into the camp?"

"A citizen of Rome, you say? Truly? You do not have the look of a Roman. Mistook you for a Gaul, I did. My apologies, Durmi," the stocky guard said. His demeanor changed radically from disdain to respect. He paused to reflect on the boy standing before him, and leaned forward as he spoke a quiet blessing to Guiamo. "May your father be forever honored by the gods, and the memory of his devotion to Rome be a light to guide you." Straightening to attention as he resumed his role as guard, he instructed Guiamo, "You

40

may enter the camp of the Seventh *Legio*, but your dog must remain outside."

Turning to point out directions, the stocky guard told Guiamo, "Stay on the main road, the *via praetoria*, through the camp and report to the officer in the building you see there at the end of the road. He will instruct you with the camp rules for visitors. Stay on the *via praetoria* until then or someone really might skewer you on the spot. "

Guiamo turned back to Flaccus. He tied a cord around the dog's neck and staked it to the ground. "I will be back to get you in an hour or two," he said. Guiamo then went back to the gate and, thanking the guards politely, entered the camp.

"He has an odd name for a Roman, that one does," said the taller guard as they watched Guiamo walk down the *via praetoria*.

"Perhaps, but he bears the dignity of a Roman," replied the other.

After receiving the required instruction for visitors, Guiamo was given freedom to wander the camp. He knew he could not enter the soldier's quarters or take food prepared for them, but these were no bother. He was fascinated with the camp and the life of a soldier, and enjoyed observing all aspects of a soldier's life. He was amazed at the orderly layout of the soldiers' tents, the straight streets, and the methodical way their lives were conducted.

He stood for a long time watching a *centuria* of eighty *tirones*, the new recruits, on the drilling field receiving their first instruction on swordplay. The *centurio* demonstrated how to thrust horizontally with the blades of their swords, the *gladius Hispaniensis*, a design which was developed from the weapons encountered during the campaign in Spain. Guiamo laughed aloud at the awkwardness of some of the young men as they handled their weapons for the first time. The second in command, the *optio*, barked his commands in a frustrated rage at the inept recruits.

A second *centuria* of soldiers with obviously more experience was practicing in a shield wall formation. He watched as they practiced not only the basic thrust to the abdomen, but also the disabling stabs to the knee and foot. With a strong, commanding voice, the *centurio* reminded them how this attack was particularly useful when facing an opponent also fighting from a shield wall.

Watching the soldiers drill dredged up memories of his father. Guiamo faintly recalled seeing his father's uniform. The horse-hair plume which splayed from ear to ear over the helmet of each of the shouting *centurionis* matched the distant memories he had of his father. Guiamo realized his father must have been a *centurio*, and not a common *milites gregarius* foot soldier as in the second *centuria* as he had imagined.

As he stood at a distance from the drilling formations, Guiamo noticed the fierce barking of a dog from out of sight behind a row of large white tents. Curious, he wandered around them to see the animals. His first glimpse showed a powerfully built black dog of an impressive stature. Its massive jaws and short, square muzzle on the large head sported long projecting fangs. The dog's short hair emphasized the muscular outlines on the neck and shoulders. As it ran aggressively across a fifty *passuum* fenced-in field, it barked in a deep, intimidating way that made Guiamo shudder.

"Attack, Laeleps, Attack!" shouted the young handler. The animal leaped over four obstacles laid across its path. Guiamo's view of the dog became obstructed by a wooden hut on his right, but he could hear ferocious snarling as Laeleps lunged into the target and sank its teeth. Guiamo could hear the dog thrashing the target from side to side in quick, vicious motions.

"Release, Laeleps, release!" commanded the handler, and the sounds of the dog's attack immediately dissipated. "Come, Laeleps, come!" he shouted.

Guiamo watched the powerful dog return to its master, carrying an aura of confident satisfaction in its long, leaping strides. As the young man reached a hand out to greet the dog, he glanced to the right and noticed Guiamo coming closer to watch. Guiamo stood by the fence and watched with great interest.

Showing off his training achievements to Guiamo, the handler commanded Laeleps to leap over a high wooden bar on the obstacle course. From a standing position, Laeleps jumped immediately, and easily cleared the crossbar. The young man shouted out more commands, and Laeleps raced downfield, muscles bulging. The logs across his pathway were easily crossed in fluid motions. As Laeleps passed the final obstacle, he slowed only minutely to circle it, and then raced back over the logs to the handler. Panting excitedly, Laeleps nuzzled the young man's left hand.

The handler commanded Laeleps to lie down. He then motioned for Guiamo to come closer.

"Hey, boy!" he yelled to Guiamo. "Come here. Do not be afraid. Laeleps will not hurt you."

Guiamo was surprised and pleased at this invitation, but entered the training field through the gateway with some hesitation. As Guiamo approached Laeleps, he paused to search his pack. He pulled a piece of Flaccus' rabbit meat and asked the young man if he could give some to Laeleps.

"Let me introduce Laeleps to you properly. He can be quite dangerous, and only those I let close to him are truly safe," said the handler.

The young man told Guiamo to extend his hand palm down. He spoke firmly to the dog, "Greet, Laeleps, greet." The massive dog stood and walked calmly forward. He sniffed Guiamo's hand and licked it.

The handler said, "You may now give him that piece of meat."

Guiamo presented the large piece of rabbit meat to Laeleps who accepted it with enthusiasm. The dog lay down and began to work at the dried meat, holding it with his front paws while chewing on one end.

"When he is finished, I will let you stroke his fur," said the young man. "He is the best dog I have ever trained. He obeys very well. Just do not touch him when he is eating."

Guiamo introduced himself. "I am Guiamo Durmius Stolo. I am on my way to Gobedbiacum. I have a dog named Flaccus. The sentry made me tie him up outside the camp gate. He is the only dog I have known. Laeleps is so much larger than he. "

The young handler said, "Oh, yes. He is a very large dog; one of the biggest I have ever seen. He is intelligent, too. I have really enjoyed training him. The Gauls will soon learn to stay away from our camp at night."

He changed the subject, "So you are Durmius. I am Decimus Ursius Praeconinus. I have been assigned to train a few dogs to be sentries for the camp. Right now, I have five dogs. Laeleps is the strongest. The others are named Heracles, Antaeus, Argos and Cerberus."

Guiamo was intrigued by the names, "Heracles I know from the old legends. Was Antaeus the strong man Heracles wrestled but could not defeat?"

"Yes," Ursius responded. "Antaeus was the son of Poseidon and Gaia. She is the goddess of earth and Antaeus gained his strength by being in contact with her. Antaeus would kill all challengers in wrestling matches, and hoped to build a temple to his father, Poseidon, from their skulls. At first, Heracles could not defeat Antaeus, but Heracles eventually realized that Antaeus' strength came from the ground. Heracles picked him up. Once Antaeus was no longer in touch with the earth, he became as weak as water. In that way, Heracles was able to defeat him, and crushed him to death with a great bear hug."

Ursius continued, "Laeleps is named after the father of all dogs. He was forged of Demonesian bronze by the god Vulcan. Vulcan then put a soul into him and gave him as a gift to Jupiter. He was eventually turned into stone, but before he died, he sired a litter of pups from which all dogs descended."

Guiamo said, "I like these names. You have chosen strong names for your dogs."

Ursius agreed, "I like to have good names for my dogs that command respect. Have you heard of Cerberus? Now that is a name that is to be feared. Cerberus is the demon hound with three heads which guards the gates of Hades. He

44

has a snake for a tail, and snake heads that grow out of his back like a mane."

Guiamo said, "I have heard of him, but I do not know Argos. Who was he?"

Ursius answered, "Argos was the dog of King Ulysses. Ulysses left his dog Argos behind at his home in Ithaca when he went away to war against Troy. Twenty years went by, and though everyone thought Ulysses dead, Argos alone waited faithfully for his return. Eventually, Ulysses returned in disguise as a beggar, and Argos was the first one to recognize him. When he saw Ulysses, he whimpered and wagged his tail, and then died. He is known as the most faithful of all dogs."

"These are all good names, and fitting," said Guiamo earnestly.

"Would you like to see them?" asked Ursius.

"Absolutely. Where do you keep them?" asked Guiamo.

"Their pens are over on the west side right over there by that tent with the eagle banner," Ursius said as he pointed to the left.

The two jogged to keep up with the trotting Laeleps as they returned him to his pen. The four other dogs, though not quite so massive as Laeleps, were clearly formidable animals, and all had black hair. Ursius explained to Guiamo that the color black made for better sentry dogs, enabling the animals to surprise the enemy at night. It also was a very intimidating color when encountered during daylight.

Ursius brought each dog out one at a time, and went through the formal greeting process with Guiamo. As each dog was returned to its pen, Guiamo was allowed to give them a piece of dried rabbit meat. They all lay down and chewed on the dried meat as Laeleps had done.

Ursius asked, "So you are going to Gobedbiacum? You do not have far to go. It is only five hundred *passuum* north from here. Have you traveled far, Durmi?"

"I have traveled for three days," Guiamo explained. "I have been sent to work for Lucius Gabinius Malleolus for three years. He is to be my teacher. He is a worker of metal."

Ursius gave a look of recognition at the name. "I know the man. Well, more truthfully, I have heard of him more than know him."

Guiamo said, "My friend, Calidius, served in a *legio* with him."

"Then your friend is old indeed. It has been many years since Gabinius left the *legio*," Ursius observed. "Today he sells swords, helmets, various pieces of armor, metal fittings, tools, nails… things like that. I have never met him. I know he is skilled enough to make the really good armor used by the wealthy *equites*."

Guiamo stared blankly at Ursius' comments.

Ursius looked surprised, "Have you never heard of an *eques*? Where have you been all your life? Stuck in a stupid little boat in some wasteland fishing for your supper?"

"Well, actually yes," said an embarrassed Guiamo. "My friends and I are fishermen."

"Truly? By the gods, I am sorry. I was simply joking," Ursius said apologetically. "I meant no insult to you."

Guiamo brushed it off, "Let us let it pass. I do not know what the *equites* are, but it sounds like they are horses."

Ursius laughed at Guiamo's ignorance and said, "The *equites* are among the best of soldiers, and they frequently have horses."

Guiamo took this in and continued, "I do not know much about the *legio*, but I do know my father was killed fighting for the *legio* up north somewhere when I was a young boy. I think he was a leader of some kind. He had a horsehair mane that went like this." Guiamo gestured with his hands over his head to illustrate the ear to ear splay of the horsehair ornament atop the helmet.

Ursius recognized his demonstration immediately. "He was a *centurio*, Durmi. What was his name?"

"Appius Durmius Stolo." Guiamo replied.

"Do you know the *legio* to which he was assigned?" Ursius asked.

"No, I do not," said Guiamo.

Ursius thought a moment and then said, "How long ago did he die?"

46

"About seven years ago," replied Guiamo.

Ursius frowned and then said, "I will ask around. Perhaps someone will remember him, or would know which *legio* he served with. The *legiones* are formed up for a while, and then are disbanded. I do not know much about those old *legiones*."

Ursius thought a moment, and an idea came, "Let us go speak to the *praefectus castrorum*. He has been in service a very long time, and he should know if anyone does."

Ursius took Guiamo to the same building the gate sentry had sent him to when he had first walked down the main camp road. Ursius politely asked to see the camp prefect.

The prefect's assistant admitted Ursius and Guiamo after a short wait.

"What do you want?" asked the bored prefect as he sat behind a wooden table covered in documents.

Ursius politely asked, "My friend, Durmius, is the son of a *centurio* who died in battle seven years ago. I am wondering if you might know of his father."

"What was his father's name?" asked the prefect blandly.

Guiamo gave his father's name, "Appius Durmius Stolo, sir."

The prefect sat back in his wooden chair with a very clear look of surprise on his face. "You are the son of Stolo?" He sat forward peering intently at Guiamo. "I knew him well. You have his look, though your eyes and hair are that of a Gaul. I served with him in another *legio* some years ago. He was *primus pilus* in command of the first *centuria* of the first *cohors*, a position of high honor. I was *tertius pilus prior* commanding the first *centuria* of the third *cohors*. Your father was slain by an arrow fired at random by the Sequani. It struck him in the neck and he bled to death before our second assault overran their positions. His death was a great loss to the *legio* and the Sequani paid dearly in blood for his life."

He continued, "I met his wife on several occasions. I remember her as a very gracious lady. Is your mother well?"

"She died a few years ago," Guiamo replied.

"Then you stay with family?" asked the prefect.

"I was abandoned by my *avunculus*, but for two years now have been well cared for by Vibius Calidius Metellus, an old fisherman who was once a legionnaire. He is an honorable man whom I hold dear. He has sent me to learn from Lucius Gabinius Malleolus," said Guiamo.

"I know him. Malleolus is a good man. He is one of the best." The prefect looked pleased. "He will teach you well. Listen to him, and you may trust him fully."

Sitting back in his chair, the prefect puzzled over the boy's situation and then asked, "What service may I render to the son of Stolo?"

"I only wished to know of my father," said Guiamo.

"He served Rome with honor. If life should lead you to return, I would welcome you to join this *legio*," the prefect solemnly said.

Ursius and Guiamo thanked him for the information and his time, and left. As they walked together toward the front gate, Ursius said, "I must return to my duties. I have enjoyed meeting you, and am pleased that I could help you learn more about your father. He was a great man to have become the *primus pilus*."

Guiamo nodded silently as they neared the gate. As they reached the gate, Ursius stopped and would go no further. "I must remain inside the gate. Where is your dog? Is he where I can see him?"

Guiamo said, "He is just over there on the left. I shall untie him and show him to you. He is not at all like Laeleps, but he is still a very good dog."

Guiamo quickly returned with Flaccus and, separated by the gate rules, spoke to Ursius from a space of two *passuum*. "I think Laeleps and the others shall make excellent sentry dogs. If you had one hundred such dogs, I should think you could defeat an entire army of Gauls. I can just see them running away!" he laughed, and Ursius laughed with him, but the creative idea intrigued him.

Guiamo continued, "Flaccus and I are going now on to Gobedbiacum. Perhaps we could visit from time to time."

Ursius, mulling this new idea over in his head, saw that Guiamo could prove to be a good friend. "Please do. Please do. I have enjoyed your visit immensely. I would enjoy more time with you. Now travel safely."

With that, Guiamo and Flaccus headed north for Gobedbiacum and a new life with old Gabinius, the metal smith.

As Ursius turned back into the camp, he pondered on Guiamo's idea. "A hundred dogs!" he said to himself. "A hundred dogs! That would indeed be a formidable weapon. Perhaps that boy has an insight the *legio* had not yet considered. A hundred dogs attacking together would be terrifying on the battlefield to men on foot as well as horse. I must think further on this."

Gobedbiacum was an unpretentious village, with most families living in mud and wattle hovels similar to that of the fishermen. Guiamo walked quietly into the village square amongst a scattering of chickens and a half dozen poorly clothed children playing in the dusty street. Flaccus was tired, and ignored them all, preferring to stay close to the boy.

Guiamo stopped to drink and cool his face with water from the village well in the center of the square, and poured some onto the ground, forming a puddle for Flaccus to lap from.

The mother of two of the children came out of her hut and called the children inside to eat their evening meal. She then called out curtly to Guiamo, "What do you want?"

Guiamo replied, "I am looking for the home of Lucius Gabinius Malleolus."

"He lives down the trail that leads out of the village to the east. He is very busy. I am sure he has no time for you," she said rudely as she turned back into her hut and shut the door.

Half-heartedly thanking her through the closed door, Guiamo led Flaccus to the east side of the village and easily found the trail. It led up into the hills, through groves of olive trees, orchards of apples and plums, vineyards, and vast fields of wheat. Neatly groomed, orderly and meticulously clean, the estate of Lucius Gabinius Malleolus spoke of uncommon wealth and a disciplined life. Guiamo had never seen such beauty and felt awkward and alone walking the pathway to the home, worried about his insignificance and poverty.

Servants in the fields tended to their work, giving Guiamo nothing beyond a single glance. Guiamo was surprised at the large number of servants working the estate. If Gabinius was merely a metal smith, how did he obtain so much wealth? Guiamo plodded along, apprehensive of meeting this important, prosperous man. But continue he did, setting one foot ahead of the other until he came to the courtyard in front of the villa.

A thin, elderly servant greeted Guiamo warmly at the door. "May the gods be praised, you have arrived safely," he said. "We have been anxiously awaiting your arrival. Brigands are about these days, and my master, *Dominus* Malleolus, has feared for you. Please do come in."

Guiamo stepped inside, but paused to push his dog back out the door into the yard when Flaccus tried to sneak past him into the house.

The old man nodded appreciatively at Guiamo's thoughtful action and continued, "I have prepared your *cubiculum* sleeping room, but for now, let us set your things here."

Turning to a young woman cleaning the next room, he commanded "Ulleria, fetch *Dominus* Malleolus. Young Durmius has arrived."

Guiamo was brought past the entry *vestibulum*, passed through the *fauces* corridor and shown into the open aired *atrium*. The wait was long. Guiamo became entranced by the beautiful mosaic tiles on the floor and the frescoes painted on the walls depicting scenes of the gods in heroic struggles. Ulleria eventually returned breathlessly and said, "Sertori, *Dominus* Malleolus wishes the boy to join him in his workshop."

Guiamo followed Ulleria and the old steward, Sertorius, back out the front entrance and turned to the left toward a cluster of some twenty wooden buildings laid out with military precision astride a well constructed stone pathway.

The first building they passed was a storage shed. Glancing into the opened doorway, he saw stacks of iron ingots, brass and copper. Inside, a servant was picking up a heavy iron ingot to set alongside another on a handcart placed just outside.

Just beyond stood a second building, open-aired, the largest in the cluster where two dozen craftsmen worked busily with hammers falling with noisy clangs on the glowing hot pieces of iron. Young men stoked three raging furnaces to keep their fires glowing intensely.

Guiamo's eyes showed his amazement at the sheer volume of production in Gabinius' estate. He had expected to see old Gabinius working alone in a shack, struggling to produce a few swords each month. Instead he found an industry prepared to outfit entire *legiones*.

He saw two burly men carrying a pot of molten iron with two wooden poles. They carefully tipped it and the glowing orange metal flowed out into molds placed on a long wooden table. They moved from one mold to the next, and Guiamo guessed there were at least twenty molds on the table.

As Guiamo followed the two servants as they led him between the worker's shops, they passed a building where six young men worked at cutting and shaping pieces of leather. He passed several more buildings, each with a group of craftsmen cutting and carving wood, sewing, weaving or stitching fabric, polishing, grinding and sharpening, or riveting and assembling. Guiamo estimated there were well over one hundred and fifty people laboring in these workshops. Stacks upon stacks of baskets filled with semi-finished goods were placed at the back of each building, and young men were making their rounds, loading them onto horse drawn wagons for delivery to their next destination.

As the three passed the final building, Guiamo saw two more buildings set apart a distance from the rest. The path led them directly to the structures. The closer building on the right was an older building of mud and wattle, though in good repair. The farther building on the left was built open to the air and was clearly a blacksmith's workshop.

As they neared, Guiamo saw an extraordinarily tall, profoundly muscular man striking a glowing orange sword blank with a large hammer in one hand and tongs in the other. Guiamo gaped when he realized the enormous size of the blacksmith's biceps.

The smith struck the blazing hot metal with powerful strokes born of decades of hard work. Clearly an aging man, he still had not lost any of his strength.

He spoke without turning his head or missing a strike, "Pardon me, young Durmi, I must strike while the iron glows red. The metal cannot wait."

He continued for a long time, patiently working the metal with steady, powerful blows, each placed precisely. He spoke not a word beyond his initial greeting, concentrating fully on his work. Guiamo and the two servants stood patiently and watched silently.

When the sword blade has been worked to his satisfaction, he hung it carefully on a hook to allow for the cooling time necessary to relieve the stresses in the metal. Gabinius then set down his tools, and turned to greet Guiamo.

"So, Calidius thinks you are something quite special. I have learned to trust his judgment. Hasty his words are not. Welcome to my household, young Durmi. I have sons and daughters of my own, and now they bring me grandchildren. But much too infrequently do they visit. I miss the freshness of life young voices bring. So you are welcome indeed."

Gabinius moved a few paces to reach for a pottery mug full of water. He drank it down without pausing to take a breath. "Ah, water is much better than wine when I am working." His expression changed to embarrassment as he looked down at young Guiamo, "Oh, my apologies. I should mind my manners. You have traveled far and I have been a poor host. Have you need of water or food?"

Guiamo replied, "I am fine, thank you. I was well supplied for my journey."

Gabinius continued, "Yes, Calidius would be certain of that. He would have well planned your traveling needs.

Well, now that you have arrived, do you have any initial questions?"

Yes, sir, by what name should you be addressed?" asked Guiamo. "The servants refer to you as Malleolus, but Calidius spoke of you as Gabinius."

Gabinius replied, "Calidius refers to me as Gabinius in remembrance of our friendship from years gone by during our days of soldiering in the *legio*. Others will refer to me as Malleolus out of respect for my position as a wealthy *eques*. My estate has grown vast since the days of my youth when I was just a simple *pleb* like you. Still, your life lies before you, and being a freeborn Roman citizen will give you advantage to prosperity and acquiring wealth. My slaves will call me *Dominus* Malleolus. By what names did you speak of each other?"

Guiamo replied, "I spoke to him as Calidius, and he named me Guiamo."

"Truly? Not as Durmius?" asked Gabinius. "Then you were dear to him indeed." He paused to reflect and then said, "If he is such a close friend that he allows you to call him Calidius, then I, too, shall be your close friend as well as teacher. You may call me Gabinius rather than Malleolus. The servants shall name you Durmius, but Guiamo you are to me."

He continued, "Calidius has sent you to me conditionally. I have agreed to teach you all I can, but for your part, you must learn with a teachable spirit. If this attitude changes, I am to turn you out. He has assured me that you are an eager student who strives for excellence. He has told me of the potential of your great mind, and your abundant creativity. As is his way, Calidius has not asked for any favor in return, he simply asked for your sake. A request from him is something I take seriously. Not only were we very close friends in the *legio*, I owe him my life from two occasions in battle. For the sake of our long friendship, I have promised to receive you. So, this I require of you in return for my shelter, support and training; that half the money you acquire while under my tutelage be put under my care. Twice each year, I will have that money delivered to Calidius for support in his old age. He is becoming too old to cast nets in the sun. What have you to say of this?"

Guiamo looked up at the tall old craftsman and said, "These things I shall do willingly."

Gabinius laid his hand on Guiamo's shoulder, looked him squarely in the eyes and said, "I will teach you, but you must obey me in all things, speak the truth in all things, and you must never be condescending to my servants or punish them. Some are slaves, most are hirelings, but all are virtuous and worthy of dignity. This you will observe faithfully."

"You shall be a guest in my home, to share in my bounty as a son while you remain under my roof, but you shall have no authority as a son over my servants. In all things you are to ask of them, never to command. Sertorius will instruct you of the order of our lives and be your counselor when I am busy."

Gabinius turned to the older man, "Sertori, Guiamo needs to bathe, and his clothing must be replaced. Have Naevia provide him with new garments fitting for work and leisure. He is to be given a golden *bulla praetexta* necklace. The pouch attached to it is also to be of worked with gold. We will later select the protective amulets to be placed inside the *bulla* pouch. For work, he will also need a full leather apron and gauntlets. For formal occasions, she is to prepare him a *toga praetexta* over a striped tunic as is appropriate for the son of an *eques*. He will need both sandals and boots. Have Sallustius cut his hair in the style of Rome, but do not curl his hair, and give him no perfume. He is a boy, not a prissy girl, and vanity is a vice I will not introduce to him. When I return tonight for supper, I wish to examine his possessions with him."

"He has a dog, *Domine*," said Sertorius.

"Do you, now?" Gabinius asked Guiamo in surprise.

"Yes," Guiamo replied. "His name is Flaccus. He is a good natured dog and well mannered. He will not be trouble."

Gabinius contemplated on this for a moment, and then said, "You must be certain of that always. I suspect my huntsman, Salonius, can teach him some skills so he can be useful rather than merely a burdensome form of entertainment continually despoiling my grounds with his droppings. Flaccus is not allowed indoors in my house or any building. If he can be taught by Salonius, then he will earn his meals. If not, the dog must go."

"Thank you," said Guiamo earnestly. "I do love that dog, and I know he can learn his lessons as well as I."

"You may go now," said Gabinius. "I have much work to do on *Tribunus* Dolabella's *gladius*. And you," he said, pointing to Guiamo, "need a bath."

With that, Gabinius turned back to his work.

Supper in the *triclinium* room consisted of roast duck, boiled apples in a honey sauce, and a variety of fancy dishes with delectable sauces and exotic flavors he had never before experienced. It was exciting, strange, and delicious, but Guiamo quietly missed his simple meals of fish, rabbit and bread.

While he enjoyed his new woolen tunic, he felt awkward wearing a *toga*. He also found the three *lecti* around the table in the *triclinium* dining room to be strangely designed. Lying on his left side on a *lectus* couch seemed to Guiamo to be a most peculiar way to eat. He was used to sitting on the dirt floor beside the firepit with Calidius, not reclining on stuffed cushions.

Gabinius recognized Guiamo's unfamiliarity with his surroundings, as well as his discomfort at being served. He informed the boy, "Your first lessons will be to act, dress, and eat like the son of a Roman *eques*. The lessons of Calidius at being a *vulgus* peasant are now concluded."

Gabinius rose from his *lectus* and motioned for Guiamo to follow him to an adjacent room. The *tablinum* served as Gabinius' study, and Guiamo found that Sertorius had moved his belongings there for Gabinius to inspect.

Gabinius silently picked up the bow and inspected its construction. After setting it back down without comment, he untied the cord binding the arrows together. He selected each of the eighteen arrows one at a time, and checked them for straightness in the same manner Moravius had taught

Guiamo. He inspected the arrowhead mounting and checked the nock.

He then picked out the three built by Guiamo and looked them over carefully again. "These are all well made arrows, and while they are of the same style, these three are from a different craftsman. They are assembled better, well fletched, and the arrowheads are sharper, though they are not new like the others. I am looking for more arrow makers. Would you help me contact him?"

Guiamo smiled as he responded, "I made those three. The others were a gift from a friend in parting. He also made the bow."

"Well, now I know how you can earn some money in your spare time," said Gabinius. "So, do you hunt?"

"Yes, I have hunted mostly rabbits and hares to feed Flaccus. Calidius would not feed him," said Guiamo.

"That sounds like Calidius," smiled Gabinius, "and it sounds like me. It teaches responsibility and also skill. We are very much alike, you know. That is why we have been such close friends."

Gabinius set the arrows down and looked over Guiamo's belongings. He picked up the ingot. "You have some tin. I use tin, so if you care to sell it, I am interested in purchasing it."

Guiamo realized quickly that whatever price Gabinius set would be fair, and decided it would be rude to haggle with so generous a host.

"It is for sale or available for trade," he replied courteously.

Gabinius was pleased and said, "Let us weigh it tomorrow morning and set a price."

Gabinius then emptied the bag of silver *denarii* and bronze *as* coins, fingers flicking them to the side as he quickly counted their value.

"These coins are yours, but remember, half of what you earn beyond today shall go into my keeping for Calidius' sake. However, the sale of the tin ingot will not be shared with Calidius."

Gabinius began separating Guiamo's possessions into two groups. On the right side, he placed the bow, arrows and the walking staff. He placed with them the clay oil lamp and the green blanket with red fringe. He said, "My servants shall wash this cloth tomorrow and return it to you."

He emptied the bag of rabbit meat toward the left, beginning the second pile. The bag was then placed on the right side.

"What is in this jar?" he asked Guiamo.

"It is a balm for sore muscles. It is very effective and soothing," he replied.

Gabinius placed it beside the green blanket on the right side. He then inspected the gourd bottle and placed it next to the rabbit meat on the left. With a look of disdain, he picked up the woolen hat and with ceremonious flourish, dropped it on the left.

He then picked up the knife with the chipped handle. "I will have someone repair this for you," he said, placing it on the right.

He picked up the coil of rope which was frayed from much use. "This I cannot repair," Gabinius said as he placed it on the left.

Lastly, he picked up the harp. "Do you play well?" he asked curiously.

"Actually, not at all," Guiamo replied. "It was a parting gift from a friend who I suspect had nothing else to give. I do not know why he ever had it. I never heard him playing it."

"Well, music lessons will be given to you to make use of your friend's generosity," Gabinius responded.

Pointing to the pile of possessions on the left, Gabinius said, "Guiamo, these things are no longer fitting or useful to you in my house. I will have these things traded in the market for whatever they will bring. Whatever is obtained will be given to my huntsman Salonius to compensate him for the extra work he will bear to provide food for Flaccus. You will be far too busy to find meat for the dog, so Salonius will carry this burden. The rabbit meat resting here will also be used to feed Flaccus. The rest of the items in the other pile on my right, you may keep."

Gabinius then gave Guiamo a tour of the house, and recognizing that Guiamo had never been inside a home like this before, spent time to explain the particular uses of each room. Gabinius struggled to maintain a straight face as he laughed inwardly at Guiamo's incredulous reaction to seeing an indoor bathroom. It was located adjacent to the open air *peristylium* garden room.

When the tour was completed, they returned to the *tablinum*. Gabinius picked up Guiamo's coins and said, "I shall keep your money in safe keeping for you. As you need it, 'need it,' mind you, not 'want it,' I shall give it to you for your purchases." Gabinius helped Guiamo gather his things from the right pile into his arms, and directed him to his *cubiculum* where he bid the boy goodnight.

After two years of simply fishing and farming, Guiamo was amazed at the variety of activities and lessons Gabinius had set up for him. After an early morning breakfast of *puls* porridge and his favorite, an apple, Guiamo spent two hours with Sertorius reviewing what he had learned from Calidius of numbers and letters. Sertorius was pleased with what he had been taught, but quickly ascertained that Guiamo had much to learn in writing words and sentences.

To assist Guiamo's lessons, Sertorius gave Guiamo a writing tablet and *stilus*. Constructed as a shallow wooden box with raised edges, the tablet was filled with reddish brown wax. The *stilus* was bronze, pointed on one side for making marks in the wax, and flattened at the other end for scraping the wax smooth for reuse. Guiamo proved proficient with his letters, and quickly learned to use the *stilus* and writing tablet. Sertorius found him to be a gifted boy, and eager to learn. The morning passed quickly, and as the day's lesson concluded, Sertorius promised to bring some rolled manuscripts called *volumen* for Guiamo to read from.

Sertorius took Guiamo to his next assignment. They walked outside through a drizzling rain to the open walled blacksmith shop. "Durmi, today's assignment is to clean up this workshop. Show me what you can do, but stay out of the craftsmen's way. Your job is to help them, not disrupt their work. Someone will fetch you when it is time to eat our midday meal." Sertorius bent to pick up a broom lying on the stone floor, held it out to Guiamo, and said, "Here is your broom. Now, get to work."

Guiamo looked around at the workshop, took a deep breath, and began sweeping around the closest furnace. He worked his way through the building, sweeping thoroughly, and whisking the dusty piles into a wooden bucket. As he moved into each craftsman's work station, he politely introduced himself and asked permission to do his duties. His humble demeanor surprised some of the workmen who had heard the story of this talented boy, and they quickly accepted him as one of their own.

Toward noon, the rain lightened and then stopped altogether. Ulleria walked up to the edge of the workshop, glanced around, and then walked around the building to speak with Guiamo.

"Durmi, Sertorius has your lunch prepared. Wash up quickly and meet him in the *triclinium*," she said.

"Finally! I am so hungry, I thought I would fall over," he said with enthusiasm, and started toward the house. He stopped in midstride, and turned back to the workshop. Self-consciously, he set the broom down and shook his head at himself. Guiamo picked up the bucket and carried it over to one of the young men tending a furnace.

"There are many tiny pieces of iron in this bucket mixed in with the dirt. I think we could put it through the fire and draw iron from the slag," Guiamo said.

The young fire stoker looked at the dirt in the bucket and saw many tiny flecks of iron shavings and nuggets of iron splattered from the pour of molten metal into the molds. "I will try what you suggest, and I will send word of how much iron there was in this bucket."

With a grin, Guiamo thanked him, and set off at a run down the pathway to lunch. Ulleria served Guiamo his meal alone in the *triclinium*, while Sertorius ate with the servants in the kitchen. Guiamo was given bread, figs, and strips of lamb prepared in olive oil. He had grown to like Sertorius, and felt awkward that the custom of class separation included his teacher. With his humble background, he thought he should join them, but realized this was all part of Gabinius' plans.

Sertorius took Guiamo after lunch to the stables and introduced the boy to a large chestnut mare. "This horse is named 'Honestia' which accurately describes her true character as a beautiful, proper horse. She is very gentle, gives us no problems, and you shall learn to ride her."

Having worked the stables and farm for Equitius, Guiamo felt quite comfortable around Honestia. His lessons with Honestia amounted to cleaning her stall and learning proper grooming techniques. Once these tasks were completed to Sertorius' satisfaction, the elderly man placed a rope around her neck.

"You have been around animals, I see," said Sertorius. "Once you have learned to care for Honestia, and are comfortable with her, then I will let you ride her. But that is not today. Today you work with her."

He gave the rope to Guiamo and had the boy lead Honestia across the riding arena to a grassy area used for grazing. Sertorius said, "I will come back later after she is fed. She will not wander far. Just keep her away from the crops."

As Sertorius walked back to the house, Guiamo dropped the rope to let Honestia graze in peace, and he then sat down to rest under a cluster of shady trees. The cool water in a trickling stream babbled quietly as Guiamo patiently watched Honestia eat and drink for the rest of the afternoon.

Guiamo was grateful for a time of rest, but wished the ground was not so damp. He felt at ease in his new surroundings, and appreciative of all Calidius was doing for him by sending him to learn from Gabinius.

He thought about his stonehearted *avunculus* Valerius, and thanked the gods that his drunken uncle had abandoned him unwittingly in such a blessed place. Building on the lessons of Calidius, Gabinius stood ready to give to him such training as to prepare him for an exceptional life, gifted as few others ever had experienced. He vowed to himself and the memory of his mother to never struggle against Sertorius or Gabinius, to be a willing vessel for them to pour their teachings into.

The lazy afternoon closed gently when Guiamo noticed Sertorius walking across the riding field. "Durmi, it is time to bring Honestia back into the horse barn," said Sertorius as he drew near. "Have you had a pleasant afternoon?"

"Yes indeed, Sertori," Guiamo replied. "I was thinking how completely generous Gabinius has been to me. I am just a poor orphan boy, yet he treats me like his son."

Sertorius looked Guiamo in the eyes and clearly saw the boy's sincerity. "*Dominus* Malleolus is a good man, a man of principle, integrity, and wisdom. He knows of your great potential, and agrees with Calidius that you are someone who must not be wasted in squalor and ignorance.

"In his old age, with sons and daughters gone from his household, he is lonely. Eight years ago, his wife died. He is like a drifting boat. Though he has much wealth, he is not content. He works hard to mask his emptiness. He needs a purpose greater than mere profits. Calidius has given him that purpose. *Dominus* Malleolus will have you taught, trained, disciplined and strengthened. All his focus is bent on you. He will demand honesty, wisdom, virtue and temperance. When he releases the bowstring of your life, he plans to launch you into the world as an arrow fired into the sun. You could change the world, Durmi, you could change the world. Did *Dominus* Malleolus tell you of the oracle?"

Guiamo answered, "He spoke of no oracles to me. What did he want the gods to tell him?"

Sertorius realized he had spoken of a subject Gabinius had withheld from Guiamo, and deflected the boy's question, "I suppose he will tell you when you are ready, and he is bored."

After a brief pause, Sertorius changed topics, "Did you know his reputation is known across Gallia?" He let his statement sink in. "He is a master craftsman of the highest order, and a tireless businessman. I have heard that some of his best work is prized by the *legati* in Rome. They are the highest officers who are given command of the *legiones*. Well, enough of my chatter. Come, Honestia needs to be returned to her stall."

Guiamo quietly walked over to the mare, took the rope, and with Sertorius, led her back to the stable.

Supper with Gabinius was as delicious as the previous night, and afterwards, they again retired to the *tablinum* for after-supper discussions. Gabinius picked up a weight measuring scale and the tin ingot, and quickly determined the weight and value of the tin. "I would pay four *denarii* and seven *asses* for this amount in the market. Are you agreeable to this?"

"Certainly," said Guiamo as they both sat down on a cushioned bench.

Gabinius replied, "Then it is settled. I will have this amount placed with your other money for safekeeping."

Gabinius produced Guiamo's repaired knife and placed it in the boy's lap. The chipped handle had been replaced with elegant stag horn. The blade had also been reworked, polished, sharpened and oiled. Guiamo ran his thumb sideways across the blade, feeling its sharpness. It looked newly made, as for a wealthy *patricius*, not a fisherman.

Guiamo was nearly speechless, and stammered out his thanks. With great satisfaction, Gabinius saw the delight and awe in the boy's eyes. "Soon I will have lessons prepared for you so that you, too, can craft such a beauty as this." They both sat quietly, enjoying a slight breeze flowing from the *atrium* into the *tablinum*.

Gabinius then said, "Sertorius informs me that today you gathered the floor sweepings from the blacksmiths' workshop. He said you suggested to the young man who stoked the fire refining the iron bits for reuse. We never gave much thought to it. We knew the dust contained iron, but assuming it was not worth dealing with, swept it out of the building onto the ground. They did put it into the fire as you recommended. Do you know that nearly half the dust must have been iron? They recovered enough iron that, well, I figure the value at one *denarius*, two *asses*. I have given orders to have every building swept each week, and the dust sent through the fire when the bucket becomes full. You had a good idea. Now, I will not pay you for iron I already own, but I thank you for your helpfulness. A skilled craftsman's daily wage is eight *asses*, so the savings is meaningful.

"I also am told that the men like you," Gabinius said. "This is good. Courtesy always wins over a haughty spirit."

Gabinius changed subjects again. "Your dog, Flaccus, is being taught to hunt game. He is not large enough to be a proper household guard, but he will do fine as a hunting dog. Unfortunately, you will not be seeing him very much. His attention must be on my hunt master, Salonius."

Gabinius looked at the boy and asked, "Guiamo, I would like to prepare you for your life ahead, but I am an old man. Is there anything I have missed that would make your task here more enjoyable?"

Guiamo knew immediately what would please him most. "If it meets with your approval, I should like to visit my friend, Ursius, at the Seventh *Legio* encampment from time to time."

Gabinius looked surprised at himself, "Of course! All boys need companions. I should have thought of this. What a fool of an old man I have become." Gabinius thoughtfully mulled this over for a few quiet moments, and then decided. "You may visit him one day out of sixteen. Each week of eight days begins with market day. You may go every other market day, but always return before dark. Also," Gabinius said, tapping on the knife in Guiamo's lap, "you must always take this."

The eleven days until market day passed quickly, but Guiamo was so busy with his lessons, that he nearly forgot to prepare the night before market day.

Gabinius found Guiamo packing his food the evening before market day. "I am glad you remembered. I was not going to remind you. In my house, you are responsible for your own calendar. If you do ever forget, you will have to wait another sixteen days."

The trip was easy, the sun was warm. With great enthusiasm, Guiamo arrived at the camp late that evening on the seventeenth day of *Martius*. He greeted the same two gate guards he met before, and was courteously granted access. After checking in with the office of the *praefectus castrorum* at the end of the *via praetoria*, he headed directly to the dog training area.

As before, Ursius was out training the dogs, but Guiamo was surprised to see that Ursius now had eleven dogs, all staked apart on short tethers. He waved at Ursius and walked over to the perimeter fence. Ursius waved him in, and Guiamo sauntered over.

Ursius greeted Guiamo with a triumphant grin. "I spoke to my *centurio* about your idea of one hundred war dogs. It so intrigued him, that he has allotted enough money to buy thirty dogs, and hire three helpers. I have been able to purchase six more dogs already, and I think I will be able to buy seven more in the next few days. I am still looking for three good helpers. Is there any chance that you would be interested?"

"Well, certainly, I am interested, but I cannot. Still, I can visit every other market day," said Guiamo, "and help you then."

"Then visit as often as you can." Ursius replied thankfully. He noticed Guiamo's newly remade knife tucked into his belt. "Where did you get such a beautiful knife?" he asked.

Guiamo took it out and let Ursius hold it. "Gabinius had my old fisherman's knife rebuilt. His craftsmen's' skills are amazing."

Ursius said, "I wonder how much it would cost to buy one like this? Probably more than I could ever afford." Ursius looked disappointed, but not depressed or jealous, and carefully returned the knife to his friend.

Guiamo and Ursius talked about dogs the rest of the day, trying to think of clever names, teaching the dogs basic commands, and simply enjoying each other's company.

Not unexpectedly, Guiamo had to run the entire distance back to Gobedbiacum to beat the setting sun, and gasping for breath from his exhausting run, stumbled into the house where Gabinius sat writing a letter.

Without a word, Gabinius looked up through the open-air *atrium* at the darkening sky, turned his face slightly at the breathless Guiamo. He caught the boy's eye with an authoritative stare and, with a smirk on his face, returned to his writing without comment.

Fifteen days passed with Guiamo improving his writing and reading, and testing his arithmetic skills each the morning. Lat in the day, he had rotated through several of the different buildings, sweeping the floors and picking up scraps. The craftsmen liked Guiamo's demeanor, and included him in their discussions. He wanted to do more than just clean, but Sertorius had told him it was a good way to meet everyone and learn how the craftsmen's work progressed from start to finish.

The horse grooming work was always interesting, for it appealed to the caretaker instinct in him. Of all his lessons, he enjoyed riding Honestia most. He seemed to have a natural ability to fall off on turns, but bruised arms and legs taught him to hold on more tightly to her mane, and grip her body with his knees.

Still, he felt uncomfortable, so one day he tied a rope tightly around Honestia's chest to give him something secure to hold onto. Sertorius looked dubiously at it, and almost told him to remove the rope, but then thought it best to give the boy some room for his creativity. He smiled as Guiamo trotted Honestia in great circles, triumphantly holding tightly to the rope.

The next day was the second day of *Aprilis*. It was also market day. Guiamo hurried to the camp and found Ursius again working with the dogs. This time, Ursius had twenty-two dogs, and had hired the three helpers his *centurio* had authorized. Ursius introduced Guiamo to the hirelings and they spent the morning together with the animals. At noon, they staked out the dogs on tethers, and went to get their lunch. As the five young men walked along, Ursius motioned for Guiamo to slow down so they could talk privately.

Ursius glanced over his shoulder as if someone might disapprove of what he was about to say. "There are rumors about that the Seventh *Legio* is going to war soon. The men are working at gathering supplies as if for a march. There also is talk of a shortage of foodstuffs. I spoke to my *centurio* about this yesterday. He was most particular to not confirm or deny the rumor, but did say that if the *legio* ever went to war, I would stay behind with the camp guard to train my dogs. They are not ready for war."

Guiamo promised to not say anything about it to anyone in the camp, and they went on to eat their lunch. The afternoon went by quickly as they worked to train and exercise the dogs. Guiamo remembered the painfully long run he had to endure to be back home before dark, and so left with plenty of time to spare.

Gabinius was quiet during their evening meal, and allowed Guiamo to chatter endlessly. As they finished eating, Gabinius set down his goblet and silently motioned for Guiamo to follow him into the *tablinum*.

Gabinius stretched his arms and back muscles, stiff from his labors and old age. "Guiamo, we have other matters to discuss. Change is coming in Gallia that may lead to war. Stories have reached the ears of my friends at the encampment of the Seventh *Legio*. It appears that a tribe to the east, the Helvetii, desire to move through Gallia to better lands. We have a new provincial governor who believes they must be kept in their ancestral lands. For my part, I agree with him, though I cannot say I like the man. He is a scoundrel who is fleeing from Rome even today, for his consulship has just ended. He has friends in power who have protected him, giving him immunity from prosecution for corruption by granting him this governorship for five years. Five years! Five years is outrageous! Governors are to be appointed for one year, just as are consuls. He is a power hungry, corrupt man surrounded by other corrupt men. Well, I have learned that, while not all people in power are corrupt, power attracts corruptible people. As you grow into manhood, Guiamo, above all, keep your integrity intact, for your reputation follows you as closely as a shadow.

"I have also heard that this governor, whose name is Gaius Julius Caesar, is in debt to the point of drowning in it. Guiamo, debtors can be desperate people, and people without the fortitude to maintain their integrity, in time of trouble may stoop to unimaginable depths. Be wary of debtors, not for their poverty, for poverty is not a vice, but for their moral vulnerability."

Guiamo nodded, knowing the pricelessness of these lessons of life.

Gabinius continued, "The Helvetii are a large and powerful people, proud and wild. If this Julius Caesar wants to stop them, he will have a difficult and bloody fight.

"Our craftsmen will be working hard for the next few months, as Julius Caesar will be raising two new *legiones*, the Eleventh and Twelfth. That means arrows, belts, shoes, swords, *pila*, shields, breastplates, all the supplies needed to equip twelve thousand soldiers. We will be busy, indeed. I just hope my iron merchants deliver the ingots I need by the scheduled dates," Gabinius winked at Guiamo, "or Julius Caesar will be going to war with twelve thousand naked soldiers.

"Guiamo, I need your help. I am short on arrows. I need you to spend your afternoons, while Honestia grazes, making arrows. I will supply you with materials and pay you for your labor. Be diligent in your work, and hold to the quality shown in the three I saw earlier.

Guiamo felt like trying his hand at haggling. "Well, I am certainly willing to help you, and you have been most generous to me. Perhaps we can work a deal favorable to us both. I am interested in acquiring a knife, a duplicate to my own that was so beautifully remade. I would be interested in working, making your arrows in exchange for the knife. Would this be possible?"

"Certainly," replied Gabinius, and he mulled the idea over for a few moments. "I need all my craftsmen right now to work diligently on the needs of the *legiones*. After the *legiones* have marched, I will be able to assign a craftsman to build your knife. On another point, let us remember to not cheat dear old Calidius. Half your profits must go to him. So, I shall apply half your labor toward the knife and half shall be set aside in coin for Calidius. Agreed?"

Guiamo smiled and said, "Agreed."

As the days passed, Sertorius brought more *volumen* for Guiamo to read. Gabinius had little in the way of a library, but knew several other wealthy *patricii* who did. In the mornings, Guiamo found himself assigned to reading the grand, epic poem *Annales* by Ennius. He enjoyed the warfare recorded of the fall of Troy, but bored with poetic style, preferred to read the writing of Polybius about military tactics. He was fascinated by the battle strategies and techniques used by both the Greeks of old and more recently, his own countrymen. He tried his hand at drawing sketches of what their formations looked like, and imagined the warriors in desperate battles fighting bravely against overwhelming foes.

Gabinius had his craftsmen introduce the boy to tending the furnaces rather than sweeping floors. Guiamo learned to use charcoal to generate the hottest flame, and was taught when to add more to the furnace. They showed him how to use air to increase the temperature as needed by blowing air with a bellows through a tube into the furnace. They taught him that each type of metal softened or melted at different temperatures. Depending upon the stage at which a blade was in production, the iron would be worked when it glowed red, other times orange or white. He also learned that he needed to wear his leather apron and gauntlets to protect his body and arms from the continuous barrage of raging heat.

The days passed with more reading lessons, furnace tending, stall cleaning, horse grooming and late afternoons of arrow building. The iron arrowheads were well made and very sharp. The feathers for fletching were plentiful, but the arrow shafts were of variable quality. Guiamo rejected nearly half of his arrow shaft supply for being warped. One afternoon, Gabinius inspected Guiamo's work. Guiamo felt like hiding the growing pile of warped arrow shafts, but decided it best to let Gabinius see everything. Rather than being disappointed with the high rate of rejection, Gabinius was pleased that Guiamo was keeping his reputation for quality in mind. "It is not your responsibility to provide good components, only to build good arrows. If others are slack in their assignments, it is they who must be corrected. I shall see to it that the quality of arrow shafts you receive improves."

Guiamo loved to ride Honestia, but still felt uncomfortable on the turns. While he no longer fell off the horse, he wanted something to secure him on the horse besides the rope tied around the horse's chest. He let his thoughts wander creatively as he worked on the arrows throughout the afternoon. An idea came to him that he thought might work, and he focused on how best to construct it.

When his duties for the day were completed, he ran to the workshop of the leatherworkers, and selected some pieces of discarded leather, and cut a long piece off a tanned cowhide. He searched through some other buildings, picking up bits of material he thought might be useful for his design. He also borrowed an awl and hammer from the stores of spare tools. After supper, he quickly excused himself, and retired to his *cubiculum* to work on his idea.

The next afternoon, he retrieved his creation and carried it out to the stalls. He picked up the rope which he daily tied around Honestia and, no longer needing it, returned it to where he originally found it. He threw his leather device over Honestia's back, and secured it around her chest by tying it up with leather laces. Attached to each side of the encircling leather band, he had stitched strips of leather, each a handbreadth in width, which hung down the horse's sides. At the bottom of these hanging strips of leather, he had looped the leather upwards and stitched it again.

He led Honestia out into the riding arena and placed his left foot into the loop. Honestia stood quietly while Guiamo grasped her mane and stepped up to sit upon her back. He slipped his right foot into the opposite loop and surveyed his invention.

Sertorius came out to check on the boy, and was surprised to see Guiamo sitting on Honestia's back, grinning like a fool. "Durmi, have you cleaned her stall and fed her so soon? Or, have you decided to ignore your responsibilities and play all afternoon?"

"Oh, Sertori, please be patient with me today. I have worked a long time last night on a new idea, and I just had to try it out as soon as I could. I will clean her stall, and brush and feed her soon enough. Look what I have made."

Sertorius walked up and examined the leather device. He muttered something under his breath. Guiamo could not hear Sertorius clearly, but thought he could make out the words, "foolishness" and something about "ride like a Roman."

Sertorius looked up at Guiamo and said, "I see you are being clever again. What, pray, do you call your device?"

Guiamo recognized Sertorius' sarcasm, and was disappointed that his idea was being rejected out of hand. Maintaining his dignity, Guiamo calmly announced, "I shall name them 'riding steps.' I think they will make me much more stable as I ride. And look," Guiamo said as he rose up by standing on the loops, "I think I could throw a spear better than when riding bareback. I have support for my feet. Do you not think this is a great idea?"

Sertorius looked dubiously at Guiamo and sarcastically said, "I look forward to announcing your invention to *Dominus* Malleolus this evening. Now do not forget your chores, and do not neglect to make the arrows. The *legiones* are in great need of arrows, and you must not dawdle on silly things."

Gabinius inspected the riding steps after supper, but to the boy's dismay, his opinion had already been influenced by the skeptical Sertorius. Gabinius encouraged Guiamo to continue being creative, but thinking that the riding steps looked unmanly, decided to not show it much attention.

Rather, he switched Guiamo's lessons from horse care and riding to exercise and weaponry training. Beginning the next day, Sertorius was to have Guiamo run long distances to build up his endurance. Following his daily run, Guiamo would now practice throwing the javelin.

Market day of the eighteenth day of *Aprilis* arrived, and Guiamo gleefully set off toward the encampment of the Seventh *Legio* riding on Honestia. He could hardly wait to show Ursius his riding steps. The trip went quickly, but his enthusiasm was dampened when the gate guards denied entry of his horse. He tied Honestia to a post and walked in to visit with Ursius. He knew he could not leave Honestia out at the post for long, so planned on a short day at the encampment.

He was astounded to see that Ursius had purchased another group of large dogs, and the count now came to thirty. Ursius showed them all off to Guiamo. Ursius excitedly told Guiamo, "I have received an increase in pay by one *as* per month, and I report directly to the *optio* now. My helpers work directly for me, as well."

Guiamo was quite disappointed that, with Ursius being so excited about his good news, Guiamo had no time to tell him about his riding steps. The rain squall that burst over them sent Guiamo scurrying out the gate to retrieve Honestia, and with a short visit cut shorter, he quickly set off for home again.

As they walked into the *triclinium* for supper on the twenty-seventh day of *Aprilis*, Guiamo realized that Gabinius regularly spent much time stretching his back muscles and massaging his massive arms as they prepared for their evening meal. The next evening, Guiamo brought his jar of ointment made by Meridius. Setting it on the *mensa* serving table, he said, "Meridius has made this balm which is useful for easing the pain of sore muscles. I would like for you to try it. It works very well," said Guiamo. "All the fishermen use it."

Gabinius said, "So you have noticed my sore muscles. It is all part of growing old, and lately, I have been growing old all too well. On my next birthday, I shall be seventy-three years old. I was young like you once, but so long ago it seems now." His voice trailed off as he thought about his many years. He then grew more cheery, and said, "Still, I do not mind birthdays. They are good for your health. You see, the more birthdays you gather, the longer you live. I have even heard that the person who has the largest collection of birthdays lives the longest of all!"

Guiamo smiled at Gabinius' joke.

Gabinius continued, "Do not grow up too fast, Guiamo. Enjoy your youth while you have it. These aches have become quite tiresome and take the joy out of living."

He switched topics back to the ointment. "So, what is this balm made of?" Gabinius asked.

Guiamo shrugged his shoulders. "No one knows, only Meridius. He keeps it a secret."

Gabinius picked at a piece of food stuck in his bottom teeth. "Well, he knows its value, and keeping it a secret maintains his reputation of being a bit of a healer then. Let me try your ointment, and I will tell you what I think of it. I am a serious expert on sore muscles, you know."

The next morning, an energetic Gabinius woke Guiamo. "Guiamo, that balm of yours is very soothing. I noticed my pains fading late last night as I got into my bed. This morning, the pains are gone and I feel more limber. As effective as this balm is, I must have some, not only for myself, but for my craftsmen as well."

Guiamo recognized a business opportunity as Equitius had taught him, and formulated a plan. "Gabini, if you would permit me to return to Meridius for a short time, I believe I can arrange to have a steady supply of this balm available to you."

Gabinius was very pleased. "That would be wonderful, my boy. I shall make arrangements for you to leave tomorrow. You will need someone to escort you, what with the brigands that have been about. Sertorius is too old. Perhaps I could send my huntsman, Salonius along. He also rides a horse."

Guiamo was surprised at Gabinius' quick assent, and asked, "Do you mean I will ride rather than walk?"

Gabinius replied, "Certainly, you will ride Honestia. Riding will save two days of travel time. You cannot afford to miss your schooling."

Guiamo thought about this chance to see his friends, and was extremely pleased. He realized he had a unique opportunity to work several business deals with his friends in the fishermen's village.

"Gabini, you liked my arrows," Guiamo stated. "Were the others acceptable?"

Gabinius thought back to the evening in the *tablinum* when he sorted through Guiamo's possessions. "The others were not so well built as yours, but they were acceptable. What do you have in mind?"

Guiamo said, "I am thinking of hiring my friend, Moravius, to make arrows which I could sell to you. He would provide his own materials. What would your price be?"

Gabinius knew his market well, and quickly replied, "I would pay two *denarii* for ten acceptable arrows. You will be responsible for assuring their quality. You must inspect each one, and deliver them to me tied in bundles of ten."

Guiamo then asked, "What of his bow? Is it acceptable?"

"No," said Gabinius. "It is a hunter's simple wooden bow, but Rome wants bows made of wood as the central shaft, but with rams' horns on either end. These bows will fire much farther than a hunter's bow. I am not interested in his bows."

Guiamo changed topics to another business idea he had, "Does the *legio* need fish? I have heard that food is in short supply. The village catches much fish, and I could provide it to the Seventh *Legio*."

Gabinius was surprised and pleased with Guiamo's ability to recognize and seize an opportunity. "The *legio* needs everything, including fish. It must be salted or smoked, of course," said Gabinius.

Gabinius smiled at Guiamo's motivation, and said, "Go make your business arrangements with your friends. I have suppliers who regularly pass along the south road which you travelled. I will see to it that your purchases are picked up whenever they pass that way. They will also deliver payment on their return trip.

"You certainly have an eye for business opportunities. This is good. Be careful to do what you say in everything. Promise less than you can do, and fulfill more than they expect. In this way your reputation will grow, and that will draw even more business to you. Your reputation is worth more than the mere profits of a business venture."

He continued, "I will have your travel needs prepared by morning. Now, after supper, I want you to go to bed early so you are rested when you awaken in the early morning."

On the twenty-ninth day of *Aprilis*, Guiamo ate a quick and informal breakfast of simple *puls* porridge in the kitchen, known as the *culina*, with Gabinius, Sertorius, Ulleria and Salonius. Afterward, Guiamo mounted his horse, Honestia, while Salonius checked their packs one last time. Guiamo motioned to Gabinius that he had remembered to bring his knife along, and Gabinius nodded approvingly. Salonius carried a sword, and it was obvious that he knew how to use it. Waving goodbye, the two headed south.

The weather was fair and hot, but windy, with few clouds scattered across the blue sky. Salonius spoke little, but listened patiently to the talkative Guiamo.

Guiamo enjoyed the company of his confident companion, and reveled in the joy of riding Honestia, though he remained unsure of his riding skills. The trip was uneventful, which suited Salonius just fine. Gabinius had firmly instructed his huntsman to guard Guiamo with his life, and Salonius took this charge seriously. There had been reports of brigands wandering the region, and Salonius kept a wary eye as he listened to Guiamo's chatter.

Only one time, in the early afternoon, did Salonius hush Guiamo and lead the two off the trail. Unaware of the two young men hiding quietly in a stand of woods, a disheveled, ragged group of twenty mounted riders passed by across the roadway, carrying a battered collection of spears, swords, damaged shields and helms.

When the brigands had passed far off the trail out into the wild, Salonius led Guiamo out of hiding back onto the trail.

As evening came, the two adventurers settled off the trail for the night by a stream on the edge of a wood. Salonius let the horses graze in a nearby meadow while Guiamo set up camp.

The wind died down, and the welcome cool of evening settled in. As the sun descended, Salonius gathered the horses. To keep the horses from betraying the location of their camp, he tied them to a tree a distance deeper into the forest. Salonius and Guiamo made their beds of blankets and soon fell asleep.

With the brigands well behind them, and headed in a different direction, Salonius became more confident in their safety, and began to talk. "I came into the employ of Malleolus three years ago. I had won an archery tournament, but was challenged by a weasel of a competitor who came in second place. He tried to have me disqualified by saying I had stolen his arrows. I was shocked by this accusation, and had to think quickly, for my accuser had already won the support of other competitors.

"I told the competition judge, an *optio* from the Seventh *Legio*, to ask my accuser how many turns of twine were used around the arrowheads. I told him I always used eleven turns. I never use more or less because everyone knows even numbers are unlucky. He counted the turns on three of my arrows picked at random, and knew the truth.

"The *optio* then asked the weasel how many turns of the twine were on the arrowhead, and you should have seen the scoundrel squirm. He sputtered out his answer, 'I do not know. It depends on how many the arrowhead needs to be secure.'

"I thought the *optio* was going to kill him on the spot. He drew a dagger, and the man ran. You should have heard the crowd laugh at the fool. He tried to dodge their fists, but they gave him a good beating.

"Malleolus was in a generous mood and hired me after I had received the prize. He told me he liked the way I defended myself in a clever and dignified manner.

"I have served him ever since and enjoyed every day of it. I get to do what I like to do most of all. I hunt. In return, Malleolus gets what he wants. He loves to have fresh, wild game on his table."

Guiamo said, "I am a hunter also. Moravius taught me how to shoot a bow and make snares. He shared all his hunting tricks with me."

Salonius said, "We must hunt together one day. There is a dangerous old boar that comes around from time to time. It killed my last dog, and I am eager to claim my revenge. During *November*, he comes into the sacred oak grove on the greater hill above Gobedbiacum to eat the acorns. We shall lie in wait for him there, just outside the sanctity of the sacred grove."

Guiamo was excited about the hunt for this dangerous quarry, not only for the thrill of the hunt, but also out of his concern for Flaccus' safety. Guiamo was pleased that Salonius was happy to train his dog, and asked about him, "How is Flaccus? Is he learning to help you hunt?"

Salonius replied, "Flaccus is a good dog, mild tempered, and well built, but not fast. He is a little old to help me hunt live game, but do not worry, he is learning enough to earn his keep. I do not think you have any worries that Malleolus will make you be rid of him.

"I think I can best use Flaccus to retrieve the animals I shoot, such as birds and hares. He has a good nose to find the game that has fallen, and has patience to stay still behind me as I stalk. However, I do not think he could be a good hunter that chases down running quarry like deer and wild goats. He would need more speed and be of a larger build. Still, he is a good dog. I am glad to have him."

Guiamo was quietly pleased at the news, knowing Gabinius would let Flaccus stay. As he thought further on this, he realized that his close attachment to his dog was fading. Flaccus would become Salonius' dog as time passed.

The day passed quickly, and toward evening, the travelers entered the quiet village. They rode unnoticed down the deserted street directly to the mud and wattle hut of Calidius.

Hearing the unusual sound of horse hooves clomping on the ground just outside his hovel, Calidius cracked the door to peer outside, and his eyes widened in surprise.

Guiamo sat confidently on Honestia's back calmly awaiting the old man's response, but burst into a broad smile which quickly changed into a laugh of delight at seeing his friend.

Calidius was equally as happy. "My boy, my boy," shouted Calidius with hands raised with delight, "You are back so soon! You look so fit up on that horse, and your clothing is so fine! I see Gabinius is treating you well. My boy, what brings you back?"

Guiamo dismounted and walked up to greet Calidius. "It seems Equitius has turned me into a merchant after all. I have some business proposals, but first we need to visit. Later tonight, it would be good to gather the fishermen so we can talk. I must return in the morning."

Guiamo, Salonius and Calidius shared a simple supper around the firepit. Guiamo savored the simplicity of not-quite fresh bread and fish stew. When they had finished, Calidius went next door to the home of Autronius to ask him to spread word to all to gather at Calidius' home, but would not divulge why. Autronius was surprised at this request, and though it interrupted his supper, quickly went out to the fishermen's homes.

Each man was curious who the two riders might be, and why they had come to visit old Calidius. When they had all gathered outside, a smiling Calidius stepped out of the doorway, followed by Guiamo and Salonius. All the men were surprised and delighted to see Guiamo, particularly Equitius, and they all gathered around to greet him. Guiamo asked them all for news, and Autronius spoke first. He cheerfully announced, "Caedicius had finally found his courage, and is now engaged to be married to my youngest daughter."

Everyone cheered loudly, and Caedicius beamed with joy at first, but then began to wince with pain from the hard back slaps and shoulder punches given by his delighted friends.

When the boisterous fishermen quieted down, Spurius Popillius spoke next. "You have such fine clothing," he said, and then looking more closely at Guiamo's waistband, asked, "And how did you come by such a beautiful knife?"

Guiamo answered, "Moravius gave it to me."

Moravius blinked at Guiamo's statement, "The knife I gave you was useful enough, but it never gleamed like that one you carry now."

Guiamo said, "Gabinius has had it remade, but this is the same blade you gave me."

Moravius stood obviously impressed, "Clearly, he has gifted craftsmen in his employ." Moravius was curious about the happenings in Guiamo's life. "What else has happened to our dear Guiamo in the past weeks?" he asked.

Guiamo looked at Gnaeus Popillius and said, "Gabinius has promised to have me learn to play your harp, though other things are more pressing right now. When I return, I must hurry back to those vital tasks to which I am assigned, such as sweeping out the workshops and removing horse dung from the stalls."

Everyone chuckled at Guiamo's good natured sarcasm, knowing full well that Guiamo had to do his work as everyone else.

The men were pleased with the lessons in reading and writing, and were curious about Gabinius' home. The life of a wealthy man was totally foreign to them, and Guiamo elaborated long on the layout of the house as well as the customs of the home.

Eventually, Guiamo spoke to the fishermen of the needs of the Roman army. "The Seventh *Legio* needs food. If you can provide me fish in quantity, smoked or salted, I will buy it all, and provide transportation to a ready market."

Equitius, ever the haggler, spoke for them all. "The harvest this year has been good. We have more than enough fish to meet our needs. How much will you pay?"

Guiamo had rehearsed his pricing with Gabinius and knew just what to first offer. "I will pay one *as* for each *libra*," he said, referring to the Roman pound.

The men murmured their surprise at so high a number, and with the sound of their obvious approval, Equitius saw his room to haggle even more profits quickly diminishing. He turned unhappily to brusquely hush them. He ventured a counteroffer, "Give us three *asses* for two *libra* and we will work from dawn to dusk so long as you need our fish."

Guiamo, recognizing Equitius was positioning himself for negotiation, laughed and said, "You already work from dawn to dusk, and, yes, we have an agreement." Guiamo was pleased, for he knew he could sell the fish at three *asses* for one *libra* to the *legio* and double his money.

Guiamo turned to Meridius. "Meridi, I need your balm for sore muscles."

Meridius said, "I have a jar in my house you may have. Are your muscles sore from riding that beautiful mare?" He grinned mischievously at the boy and asked, "Shall I go fetch it so you can rub some on your sore bottom?"

Guiamo blushed with embarrassment and everyone laughed along with the joke. "Meridi, I need your ointment to sell to hundreds of people, possibly thousands. I need as much as you can make. Can you make it in large volumes?"

"Well, yes, but it will take me a few days to gather all the ingredients," Meridius replied.

"Good, then let us set a price," Guiamo said.

With a look of helplessness, Meridius glanced at Equitius to intervene on his behalf.

Equitius understood and immediately spoke up for him, "Meridi, do you have to purchase the ingredients, or do you gather them at no cost to you?"

Meridius said, "I gather them myself in the fields."

Equitius continued, "Are they in plentiful supply?"

"Yes, though I prefer to not tell what they are," Meridius said.

"That is wise," said Equitius approvingly.

Equitius thought for a moment and then asked Meridius, "How long would it take you to gather enough ingredients to fill a *congius* of your ointment, and how long does it take to make it?"

Meridius thought about it and said, "It would take two days to gather the ingredients, and an evening to make it."

Equitius thought carefully about the time lost from fishing, and then said, "If it were me, I would charge forty *denarii* for a one *congius* sized jar filled with balm. You will lose your profits from fishing during this time, so that needs to be made up somehow. The ointment, we all know, works very well, and no one else makes anything nearly as good. That makes this balm unique and desirable; therefore it can bring a good price. We all know how expensive amulets and potions are. Forty *denarii* is a good price, Meridi."

Meridius turned to Guiamo and, with false confidence, said, "I will make as much balm as I can if you pay forty *denarii* for each *congius* of my ointment."

Guiamo said, "Then we also have an agreement."

Equitius turned to speak to Guiamo, "Guiamo, I would recommend you charge five *denarii* for each jar the size Meridius gave you. Those are *quartarius* in size. Five *denarii* for a *quartarius* of balm would be in keeping with other things I have seen at the market and more than double your money."

Guiamo nodded his appreciation for Equitius' insightful advice. He knew his profits would be lessened by the cost of the small jars he would need to sell in small quantities. He quickly calculated that each *congius* would make twenty-four *quartarii* portions, and since the jars cost one *as* each, his profits would come to fifty-six *denarii* on every *congius* of ointment he purchased.

Guiamo turned next to Moravius. "Moravi, you taught me to make arrows. I need arrows. Lots of arrows. If you could make arrows for me, I would pay one *denarii* for ten arrows, but only for good ones, straight and true. They must have two-edged iron blades suitable for the *legio*, and sharpened, ready for battle. You would have to provide your own materials at this price. Are you interested?"

Moravius was pleased, "Three day's wages for ten arrows? Yes, of course. The arrowheads will be the most expensive part, but that still leaves me over a day's wage profit for a few hours work. I can do this in the evenings after the fishing is completed for the day."

Guiamo said, "Then we have an agreement. I need as many as you can possibly make, and arrows are far more important than fish. I would prefer that you work all day on arrows rather than fishing."

Turning to speak to the group, Guiamo said, "Gabinius told me his supplier will arrive here in two weeks to pick up whatever you have available. Your payment will be brought back a few days later on his return trip home. It has been good to see you all again. Now go home and get to work!" he said with a laugh. "We have much money to earn."

After the enthusiastic fishermen left, Guiamo and Calidius talked long into the night while Salonius sat quietly and listened. Calidius was surprised to learn of Gabinius' accumulation of such great wealth, having only known of his work in the *legio* as a simple blacksmith. He was also pleased to hear of Gabinius' plan to provide income to Calidius from Guiamo's earnings.

"From what I have heard tonight, I expect to become far wealthier than at any other time in my life, though that is not saying much. Perhaps I will splurge a little and buy some new nets," said Calidius.

Guiamo half-expected this response and chided the old man, "Calidi, I was hoping to keep you from having to fish at all anymore."

"We shall see, Guiamo. We shall see," he replied.

Salonius and Guiamo left early the next morning on the second day of *Maius* in high spirits. Their return trip was as uneventful as it was pleasant, and they arrived back in Gobedbiacum the evening of the second day's travel.

Guiamo looked refreshed rather than road-weary, and sitting on cushioned benches in the *tablinum*, Gabinius listened intently to the boy. When Salonius interjected their sighting of the twenty mounted brigands, Gabinius asked numerous questions before allowing Guiamo to continue. He was particularly interested in hearing a description of the pack's leader. Salonius described him as either dirty or with a dark complexion, bearing a spear, and riding a dusty white horse that looked ill-kept. He wore a heavy silver collar around his neck, and his arms and body were covered in tattooed symbols. He rode at the front alongside another man, larger and bearing a spear. They rode together as friends, but the leader clearly commanded the group. They all wore the clothing of Gallia rather than Rome, and their hair was pulled back and as coarse as horse manes. The leader wore a long moustache which grew long enough to completely cover his mouth. A few wore short beards. The rest preferred to be clean shaven, though all were in need of grooming. From the growth of their unshaven beards, he guessed they had been traveling for five days.

Gabinius looked at Guiamo and said, "Clearly they are Gauls. Did you know they wash their hair with lime? That is what makes their hair look so rough. No self-respecting Roman would consider such a barbarous practice."

Turning back to Salonius, he said, "You have done well, my friend. Without your sharp eyes, this young lad might now be lying in his grave." He reached into his purse and pulled out two gold *aureus* coins. "These are for you, Saloni. You have done well."

He turned rather quickly back to Guiamo who sat with jaw gaping at the first gold coins he had ever seen. "Tell me of your negotiations," Gabinius said.

Guiamo went into great detail explaining his business dealings while Gabinius sat listening intently. Only occasionally did he probe with a question, and then fell silent while Guiamo answered.

Gabinius was well pleased with the success of the trip and the business deals that were made. "We shall have to wait two weeks to see the results of your friends' productivity. I just hope I do not run out of this fine balm in the meantime."

Gabinius then spoke of the latest news of war. "Word has it that Julius Caesar has built a rampart sixteen *pes* tall with a deep trench that runs for eighteen thousand *passuum* in an attempt to stop the Helvetii. There has been some skirmishing, but the Helvetii have been pushed back every time. The wall is as tall as three men, and the Helvetii have not yet figured how to cross it. Julius Caesar left *Legati* Titus Labienus there in charge of the Tenth *Legio*, and is coming here to Gallia Cisalpina to take command of the three *legiones*, the Seventh, Eighth, and Ninth stationed in this region. He may arrive by tomorrow.

"The Seventh *Legio* is demanding delivery of all my weaponry stores immediately, while the Eleventh and Twelfth *Legiones* are still ill-equipped. I have nearly run out of iron, though my copper remains well stocked. Tomorrow, three wagonloads of badly needed tanned leather are to arrive, though the wet roads may delay them. With that, I will be fairly well supplied. It all depends now on the iron from Noricum. Well, the Seventh *Legio* can demand all they want. Provincial Governor Julius Caesar has final say, and the instruction I have received is that outfitting the Eleventh *Legio* commands the highest priority, followed by the Seventh.

"It is decided, then," Gabinius said gravely. "Rome is going to war against the Helvetii. Though the *milites gregarii* have not been informed, the camp activities reveal to everyone Julius Caesar's intent to march soon, probably by the *idus* of the month of *Maius* when the moon is full."

Guiamo was eating his lunch the next day with Gabinius, eagerly describing how he had been allowed to pour molten metal into molds set on a work table. Gabinius asked what he was doing to keep from being hurt. Guiamo was surprised at the question but smiled and said, "I know better than to work with fiery iron without wearing my gauntlets, apron, and boots, if that is what you mean."

Gabinius relaxed a bit and said, "That is exactly what I mean. You must be always careful when working with hot metal."

Just then, a fat and sweating textile merchant came to the door to bring news to Gobedbiacum. Gabinius graciously brought him into the *triclinium* to join them for the midday meal. The overdressed fat man could hardly contain himself, and the anxious words fairly spilled from his mouth, "Our Provincial Governor has arrived this morning at the encampment of the Seventh *Legio.* This Julius Caesar is creating quite a mess of things. Everything is in utter chaos, with everyone bustling about and acting as if the world was coming to an end. 'Line up here!' someone shouts. 'Stand at attention and look smart,' says another. It is all quite upsetting, you know. I am glad to be outside the camp this morning, I should say."

Gabinius smiled pleasantly at the man and said, "Is there any word of Julius Caesar's plans?"

The man spoke with a mouth full of bread, bits spraying onto his clothing, "Oh yes, though I must say, I am not certain of the surety of the report."

He spoke more closely to Gabinius as if he held a great secret. "They say that Caesar intends to take command of the Seventh, Eighth and Ninth *Legiones* immediately and march with all haste to defeat the Helvetii. I have even heard," he paused to look around as if someone might have been listening in, "that he is going to enroll two new *legiones*, the Eleventh and Twelfth. The Helvetii are also said to be negotiating with the Sequani to the west to allow them peaceful passage through their lands."

He dramatically moved his arm in a curving gesture, "They intend to sneak around *Legati* Titus Labienus' Tenth *Legio* stationed at that very long barrier wall he built. Some say that the Helvetii are coming here, and that they will be here in days."

Gabinius was doubtful and asked, "Days?"

The merchant nodded almost frantically, with his fat jowls flapping as he did so. He was clearly frightened, "Days, just a few days," he said. "I am leaving tomorrow morning. I just hope," he said, dramatically placing his hand over his heart, "our brave men can hold them off that long." He breathed deeply, and let out a long sigh of despair.

Gabinius knew the gossip was filled with inaccuracies, and tried to calm the man down. "Has anyone asked why the Helvetii would even want to come here? The lands to the north of Gallia are fertile and more easily taken. I would think, rather, that they intend to simply go where the land can be seized with little effort. They will fight, but only where we try to stop them. No. I do not agree that they would come here. It would take eight days to travel here, anyway. You are quite safe, my good friend. You are quite safe."

Gabinius spent the rest of the afternoon looking at the merchant's bolts of cloth and fabric. Guiamo was relieved to finally be excused to pursue his regimen of long distance running. He found this tiresome, but realizing its importance, he did his best. He preferred weaponry training, and looked forward to his lessons of fighting with a spear.

After supper, Gabinius told Guiamo, "Tomorrow is the day for your market day visit to the encampment. Watch everything, listen carefully, and let me know what you find out."

Guiamo agreed cheerfully, and then made ready for the next day's outing.

The encampment was indeed busy, with soldiers readying their equipment, lining up to receive necessary supplies, loading wagons and practicing for war. Ursius was assigned to other duties, so Guiamo was not able to see him. As he wandered the camp, looking at the soldiers preparing for war, a *centurio* spotted him and shouted, "You! Boy! Go directly to the office of the *praefectus castrorum*. All visitors are being removed from the camp."

Guiamo glumly walked to the building at the end of the *via praetoria* and quietly entered. A legionnaire there instructed him, "You are to leave the camp immediately. No visitors will be allowed in camp until after the *legio* marches."

Guiamo walked out the door, and as he glanced to the left where men were noisily unloading a wagon filled with wheat, he noticed a number of officers huddled around a table. He recognized the *legio's* commander, the *legatus legionis*, speaking to an angry stranger of obvious high rank. The furious visitor was barking out commands to the *legatus legionis* who saluted respectfully, and in turn, began issuing orders to the senior officers surrounding them. Guiamo realized that the visitor was the new Provincial Governor, Julius Caesar. As the governor allowed the *legatus legionis* time to issue the orders, Caesar glanced at the young boy walking alone on the *via praetoria* toward the camp gate. The two caught eyes for a moment, and Julius Caesar then turned back to his work.

"I saw him today; the governor, I mean," said Guiamo at supper. "He was speaking to the *legatus legionis* outside the office of the *praefectus castrorum*. There is a war coming. That much is certain. I was told there would be no more visitors until the *legio* marches."

"Then much of what the textile merchant said was true." Gabinius said. "Guiamo, if ever there was a man I would not want you to become, it is that fat coward."

On the fifteenth day of *Maius*, merchants from the south arrived at Gabinius' home with wagons piled high with merchandise. Among the stocks were large quantities of smoked fish, bundles of arrows, and eight *congius* jars filled with ointment. Guiamo was delighted. Gabinius had the merchants take Guiamo's purchases aside.

"How much do I owe the merchants for delivering my merchandise?" Guiamo asked Gabinius.

Gabinius shrugged it off and said, "Nothing. I told them that if they wanted to continue selling me their stock, they would pick up your items at no cost. Obviously, they do want to sell me their wares, so they agreed. It would be good of you, though, to feed and water their animals to show them your appreciation. It was the animals that did the work carrying your shipment, after all."

Gabinius then said, "Guiamo, you need to give these men far more silver than you own to purchase these items from your fishermen friends. I will loan you the amount lacking, and you can repay me when your sales are made to the *legio*. In return for my help, you will provide me a supply of your balm to ease my aches and pains. Is that fair enough?"

"It is quite fair and most generous, Gabini," said Guiamo.

Gabinius had his servants empty the wagons, and everything was counted, measured and verified. As the merchandise was being unloaded, Guiamo took the eight bundles of arrows, untied the cords and inspected each arrow. All were satisfactory, and Guiamo retied them into bundles of ten. Gabinius counted out his payment for his own purchases. "This," he then told the merchant leader as he handed out more gold *aurei* and silver *denarii*, "is for the smoked fish, the jars, and the arrows. Deliver this money to the fishermen as we agreed."

As the merchants left with empty wagons and purses full of gold and silver, Gabinius said, "I will go with you tomorrow back to the encampment, and help you sell your things."

Gabinius continued, "You were ejected today from the camp as were all visitors, but tomorrow, I will be welcomed with open arms. Tonight, Ulleria will help you scrape the ointment into *quartarius* jars. I have purchased one hundred *quartarii* for your balm. First fill these for sale to individuals. The rest is to be sold in bulk to the *legiones*. Sell me first, though, the first twenty *quartarii* for my craftsmen."

The morning trip to the encampment started late. Gabinius had his servants load every cart, wagon, ox and horse with supplies of all kinds. As things were loaded up, Gabinius carefully wrote an itemized list of the entire inventory with prices and final tally.

When his supply train arrived at the encampment, Gabinius and Guiamo dismounted and walked together to the office of the *praefectus castrorum* while the wagons, guarded by his servants, waited outside the gate.

Gabinius greeted the prefect who sat busily working at his desk, "I understand that our new governor is raising two more *legiones*. From what I saw walking in this morning, one is being marshaled here alongside the Seventh."

The prefect answered, "You have observed correctly. I also see you have the son of Stolo here with you." He turned to greet Guiamo, "Health and strength to you, Durmi." Guiamo was surprised that the prefect had remembered his name, and courteously replied, "And to you as well."

The prefect turned quickly back to Gabinius, "Gabini, the Eleventh *Legio* is forming quickly. Their assignment, along with the Twelfth, which is forming alongside the Ninth *Legio*, will be to guard the supply line and the reserve stores."

Gabinius spoke authoritatively, "My instructions from Governor Julius Caesar are to outfit the Eleventh first. Only afterwards is the Seventh to be supplied."

"Yes," said the *praefectus*, "my orders agree with you. I am acting in support of the Eleventh, so your sales to them will be through me. It is my responsibility to sort out the needs. Let me see your inventory."

"They will need much of everything, I suppose. Here is my supply list," Gabinius told the prefect as he handed the parchment to him. "As usual, it is all waiting outside the camp gate. What are you interested in purchasing?"

The prefect scanned the list, checking quantities and prices. "I will take all of it except the balm." With that, Guiamo's heart fell as his profits plummeted. The prefect continued, "Most will go to the Eleventh *Legio*, of course. Your prices are acceptable overall. Bring me three more shipments like this and Caesar can have his war."

Gabinius asked, "What timeframe have I for the quantities you need? Since time is probably short, an updated listing of your needs delivered to me tonight would be most helpful."

The prefect replied, "Caesar plans to march on the twenty-fourth day of *Maius*, but tell no one. Provide me as much as you can from my list before that day. I am counting on you."

Gabinius nodded and said, "I understand." Gabinius turned to go, paused momentarily, and then said, "I am curious why you are not interested in the balm. I recently discovered its value. I will stake my reputation on its effectiveness in treating the pain of sore muscles. Your legionnaires will certainly need it after a week of hard marching."

The prefect reconsidered and said, "Well, based on your recommendation, I will try it. If I hear back on its usefulness, I will consider purchasing more in future."

Gabinius and the prefect completed the transaction and the supplies were turned over to the *legiones*. Guiamo smiled all the way home.

After supper, Gabinius and Guiamo sat again in the *tablinum* to review the day's negotiations. "Guiamo, I have been calculating your sales from today. As I figure it, your profits came to 580 *denarii*, 8 *asses*. From that, you can return my loan of 354 *denarii*, 3 *asses*." Gabinius raised a finger to show he hadn't forgotten anything. "You also had some money coming to you from your construction of arrows during the afternoons. Let us call that amount 16 *denarii*. That brings your total profits to 242 *denarii*, 5 *asses*." Gabinius smiled as Guiamo turned speechless and blinked at the magnitude of his fortune. "We also need to consider the 17 *denarii*, 9 *asses* you brought with you originally. That must be deducted from the total to figure what Calidius' half comes to. As I see it, Calidius should receive 224 *denarii*, 12 *asses*. Your total funds after today are 242 *denarii*, 5 *asses*. You have made a vast profit today. Your friends will be delighted with their proceeds, and the Roman *legiones* are becoming ready for war. All in all, it has been a very good day indeed. Wealth can come quickly, if you are willing to seize the opportunity. Remember, though, days like today are rare."

Gabinius thought for a moment and then said, "I forgot you were working on the arrows as payment for the knife you wanted. Your account should be changed to read 226 *denarii*, 5 *asses*, and I'll have my craftsmen begin building your knife when the *legiones* march."

Gabinius made daily excursions to the camp with wagons loaded with merchandise, but since Guiamo had nothing to sell, Gabinius required that he remain at home to continue his lessons. Guiamo knew he was not allowed to wander in the camp on market day to see Ursius, so was agreeable with Gabinius' instructions to stay behind. He spent the afternoon riding Honestia, and grew to enjoy the confidence his riding steps gave. Sertorius clearly disapproved of the boy's novel idea, but said nothing.

The craftsmen worked as fast as they could, producing weaponry of all kinds in abundance. By the twenty-third day of *Maius*, the final shipment was delivered. The men were exhausted, but happy to know the Eleventh *Legio* had enough basic weaponry to function properly. Gabinius had also made plans for additional supplies to be sent along in the baggage train as the *legiones* marched.

On the twenty-fourth day of *Maius*, Provincial Governor Gaius Julius Caesar led his Seventh *Legio* out of camp with the sound of blowing trumpets and rousing cheers of enthusiasm. The supply train followed, with the Eleventh *Legio* acting as rearguard. As they passed through the town of Gobedbiacum, the villagers gathered to watch, with Gabinius' slaves and craftsmen joining them with shouts of encouragement and praise.

As the last of the Eleventh *Legio* passed over the hills and on out of sight, the crowd dispersed back to their homes and to work. Only then did the worrying truly begin. While all had great confidence in their men, everyone knew the enemy was potent, and that disaster could befall the *legiones*. Even in victory, death could still take their father, son or brother. So with fear gripping at their hearts, gnawing every waking moment, they did the only thing they could. They returned to work, hoping that the days would pass quickly before the one they loved returned safely.

The herald from the Seventh *Legio* came into camp riding at a gallop on the sixth day of *Iunius*. He dismounted at the office of the *praefectus castrorum* to deliver his message, and entered to meet the prefect privately. Word of his arrival spread quickly and the soldiers who remained in the camp drew near knowing that word of the battle had finally arrived.

Among the crowd was Guiamo, having returned to the camp that market day to visit with his friend Ursius. As the boy sat with Ursius eating his lunch, he watched the herald dashing in, and the two quickly drew close with lunch in hand to see what the news would be.

The prefect strode confidently out of his office into the center of the milling crowd. "*Roma victrix!*" he shouted. "The Helvetii are defeated! Victory to Rome!" As the cheers erupted, he motioned to the herald to announce the details of the battle.

The herald stepped forward and raised his arms for all to be still. "The Helvetii passed through the land of the Sequani, bypassing the rampart wall built by the Tenth *Legio.* Our triumphant governor, Julius Caesar, met the Helvetii as they crossed the river Arar. As he drew near to battle, his scouts discovered that a large formation of the Helvetii had not yet passed over to the west side of the river and were extremely vulnerable. It is estimated that this group was one quarter of the entire Helvetii army. Seeing them cut off from support of the main enemy formation, Caesar attacked this group on the east bank with three *legiones* and massacred them on the spot. They were destroyed almost to the last man. The surviving Helvetii on the west bank have withdrawn in great confusion. As I left to deliver this message, the *legiones* are pursuing them."

The soldiers again erupted in boisterous cheers which the prefect indulged. As the cheering began to subside, the prefect announced, "Men of the Seventh *Legio*, our wounded brothers will be arriving in a few days. We must prepare to receive them." The men grew quiet at this news, and as the grim reality of brutal casualties among their absent friends gripped each man, the prefect invigorated them anew with a commanding shout of "*Roma victrix*! Hail Caesar!" Their pride returned again, and they returned his call with an echoing shout of "*Roma victrix*! Hail Caesar!"

After supper, Gabinius took Guiamo outside for a walk in the cool of the evening. Curiously, he carried a leather satchel in his hand. They walked a distance past a copse of trees talking of Guiamo's work in the blacksmith shop. Guiamo told him that he enjoyed learning to sharpen arrowheads, though it made his hands tired and his fingers sore.

"All in good time, you will become used to the work and the pain will subside. You need to keep your hands strong, so work diligently," advised Gabinius. "Sertorius will have you expand your exercise to include short sprints. Endurance is important, but nimbleness is as well. He will also begin teaching you to fight with your spear while holding a shield. The tactics are quite different."

When they were clearly out of hearing of others in the courtyard, Gabinius began to speak in quiet tones.

"Guiamo, we must speak of more serious things," he said. "Our world is turning to a time of war. Julius Caesar must secure the regions in his new governorship, and the tribes are restless. Do not believe the war will end quickly. Our enemies have vast armies, though undisciplined. One battle seldom ends a war if the loser is still motivated.

"I also believe our new governor has aspirations to expand his territory and increase his power. Some believe he has eyes on Rome itself. With such a mindset, I believe we will see much warfare within the boundaries of Roman rule and without which could span decades. This thought of enduring war has brought me to speak to you this evening of something I have revealed to none save Sertorius."

Gabinius paused and took a deep breath as he prepared to launch into a weighty topic.

"Before I agreed to Calidius' desire to have me train you, I sent a request to the oracle at Nicaea to receive advice from the gods. I do this from time to time when I am faced with important issues. Would you like to know what reply the gods gave to my query?" asked Gabinius.

Guiamo was unsure of himself, and knew little of oracles. He said, "I suppose I would, though I cannot imagine why the gods would be particularly interested in me."

"Oh, they are, to be sure, though the meaning behind their words is hidden. The gods always speak in riddles, and the answer I received this time is beyond my understanding," said Gabinius. "It would seem that Calidius has found a jewel in you after all, though I remain confused."

Gabinius opened the leather satchel and pulled out a scrolled parchment, a small *volumen*, and unrolled it for Guiamo to see. Awkwardly, the boy read aloud the script, while, with eyes closed, Gabinius mouthed the words silently from memory.

O, Land beyond the *fasces*,
  The son of Mars comes!
With wit and cunning,
  He slays the dark oppressors.
Wail, ye destroyers!
  Despair, ye tyrant!
The son of Mars comes!

O, Land prepared, Romulus follows.
  The son of Mars comes!
Clad in woad,
  He prepares the way.
Trioculis dimmed.
  Horned sages cleaved.
Behold! The son of Mars comes!

Guiamo looked up at Gabinius with confusion on his face. "What does this mean? I am totally confused at what the gods are saying. Is this gibberish really trustworthy?"

Gabinius cautioned the boy, "Be mindful of the gods, for they do not lie. These words are intended to answer the question I asked of the oracle. My question was simply this, 'Tell me of the boy being sent to me.' "

The surprise was clearly seen on Guiamo's face. "So this is truly about me?" he asked.

"It is," replied Gabinius.

"Gabini, tell me about Mars. Who was he?" asked Guiamo.

Gabinius closed his eyes as his thoughts turned to the legends told of the ancients. "In the earliest time, when the heroes, gods and demigods walked the earth, in the days of

Neptunus, Juno and Pluto, when Jupiter was the ancient king of what is now the land of Rome, long before Heracles lived, a man-child was born to the king, and the child was given the name Mars. When this child had grown to manhood, he created a new thing never before seen upon the earth; a thing of such power as to change the course of history. With this new device, he could take what he would and bend men's lives to serve his will."

Gabinius turned to Guiamo and said, "Do you know what this great thing was that Mars brought into the world?"

Guiamo shrugged his shoulders and said, "I do not."

Gabinius said, "His invention was the first spear. Never before was there a weapon crafted with such power over other men. With the coming of the spear came conquest and dominion over others. For this, many generations later he was honored with godhood for his ingenuity, and declared the god of war.

"Now, this Mars had two sons, one named Remus and the other, Romulus. The time came when Romulus killed Remus. Your oracle states that Romulus will follow the son of Mars. How is it possible for Romulus to follow himself or dead Remus?" Gabinius said pointing to the text. "I do not understand what it means."

Guiamo was equally confused, and chose to ask of another mystery, "What is woad?"

Gabinius replied uncertainly, "It is a flower. Why would anyone be dressed in flowers? I do not understand the oracle's meaning."

Gabinius scanned the text and pointed at several different lines. "The one thing that seems to stand out is 'the son of Mars' is coming. I have been pondering this for some months now. This oracle is clearly about you, and with this understanding we must look at the message. It is possible that the lines speaking of 'the son of Mars' are not directed at Romulus, but rather at you, Guiamo. Mars was the great inventor of the most important weapon of all time, the spear. Guiamo, you are gifted, particularly with inventiveness, and with creativity. I believe the oracle refers to you as 'the son of Mars' for the weapons of war you will someday invent."

Guiamo was taken aback, and looked up hesitantly at Gabinius. "I am the son of Mars? That is not possible. I am just a boy."

Gabinius looked calmly back, and with a quiet voice, firmly said, "Do not doubt the gods. Today you are a boy. Tomorrow you could be Great Alexander the Macedonian. An auspicious destiny lies before you. The oracle declares it."

Guiamo turned his eyes away, and then read again from the *volumen*. "What is this word?" he asked, pointing to the first line.

Gabinius peered at the text and then said, "*Fasces*. *Fasces* are special bundles of rods carried by the *lictoriae* who acted as bodyguards for magistrates in Rome. *Fasces* themselves are simply bundles of white birch rods tied together with red leather ribbons. Sometimes a bronze ax blade protrudes out the side. They are mostly symbolic of the power to punish errant people, though they are occasionally used to beat someone if he should threatens the magistrate. The red ribbons which tie them all together are symbolic of the judicious restraint the *lictor* needs when wielding that power.

"Now the real question is 'What is the land beyond the *fasces*?' as spoken by the oracle. My interpretation would be rather straightforward. The land beyond the *fasces* would be some region of the world beyond the reach of Roman law. If this is accurate, then it would seem, Guiamo, that your life's work will lie in a far off distant land."

Guiamo stood silently absorbing Gabinius' comments. He looked to the bottom of the text and stated, "What do you think this part about '*Trioculis* dimmed' and the 'horned sages cleaved' mean?"

Gabinius looked as puzzled as Guiamo had ever seen. "I think it means 'three eyes dimmed,' but it makes no sense to me whatsoever. I am just as confused by the 'horned sages' part as well. Only time will tell. Anyway, I wanted you to see the oracle. You may keep it, for it speaks to you alone, it would seem."

Gabinius handed the *volumen* to Guiamo, and they walked silently back to the house pondering the mysteries of the oracle, and the life lying before the boy.

Late in the afternoon of the tenth day of *Iunius*, the wagons came, rumbling quietly through Gobedbiacum as they hauled their grisly cargoes toward the encampment of the Seventh *Legio*. The moans of the wounded and dying were filtered by the trees, and only an occasionally shrieking scream reached the ears of the servants working in Gabinius' fields.

Gabinius was quickly summoned and he immediately mounted a horse, racing down the pathway to Gobedbiacum. He counted the wounded at eighty-four. He found eleven had died en-route and knew another dozen would not survive the night.

What surprised him greatly was that every wound had been generously covered with Meridius' balm. He carefully examined several wounds and found that healing had begun.

Gabinius spoke quietly to the *centurio* assigned to lead the caravan. "This balm on the legionnaires... how did it come to be used on these wounds? It was intended for use on sore muscles, not flesh slashed by iron."

The *centurio* replied uncertainly, "When this healing balm was delivered to us, we received no instruction as to its use. It seemed natural to use it on these wounds, and as I see it, seems to work well. I wish I had known it was meant for sore muscles, for I have been marching for days, and these old legs ache badly."

Gabinius asked, "How goes the war?"

The *centurio* said, "Very well, indeed. The Helvetii are withdrawing, trusting their safety in the river Arar which flows between us. Governor Julius Caesar has since built a bridge to span the river to allow his *legiones* to pursue the Helvetii.

"Even with the river between us, the Helvetii were clearly terrified at our victory as we slaughtered their clansmen in great heaps. The victory was complete. Anguished lamentations at their own impotence were heard from across

96

the Arar as we butchered their wounded as they lay on the field of battle.

"When we left the *legiones*, the bridge had just been completed. We set out to return home the same hour our Seventh *Legio* led the other *legiones* out across the Arar.

"This war is not over. We certainly have hurt them badly and demoralized the survivors, but they are still powerful and eager for revenge. Caesar intends to either pursue the Helvetii back to their homeland or destroy them in a decisive battle.

"I understand his desires and agree with his plans, but I fear for our food supply. We may overreach and be forced into battle with empty bellies. As I see it, the food supply will win or lose Caesar's war. As soon as the wounded are delivered and their blood is washed out of the wagons, we are to return with as much grain as we can haul."

Gabinius looked at the wagons full of writhing misery and said, "I shall send some of my servants to the camp to help tend these men. We must not cheer at our victories while ignoring our wounded."

The *centurio* nodded in agreement, thanked Gabinius for the promised help, and then continued down the road toward the camp.

Calidius' second shipment arrived the next day and was quickly taken to the camp. Again, the *praefectus castrorum* purchased everything, but he also told Guiamo that he was so impressed with the healing properties of the balm on the wounds of his returning soldiers that he wanted Guiamo to have even greater quantities delivered.

Guiamo was quite pleased with his growing fortune, and asked Gabinius that evening, "Rather than earning the duplicate knife by making arrows each afternoon, may I simply pay the balance in coin?"

Gabinius frowned at this question, and said, "No, you may not. I need those arrows, and we have an agreement," and walked abruptly out of the room.

Guiamo was shocked at this response and did not know what to do. Gabinius returned a few moments later with the same stern expression, and motioned for Guiamo to sit. He glared at Guiamo as the boy sat paralyzed on the cushioned bench. He held the stare for several heartbeats, then his eyes transformed into a twinkle as he broke out into a great toothy smile. "No, you may not, for you have earned it already."

He reached behind his back and pulled out a beautiful, gleaming blade affixed with a stag horn hilt. He held it out to Guiamo.

"It is finished!" exclaimed Guiamo enthusiastically as he took it from Gabinius. He turned it carefully in his hand to examine both sides. He walked into the *atrium* where the direct sunlight was better. The reflected light flashed across the boy's face.

Gabinius asked, "I have been curious about this. Why do you want two identical blades?"

Guiamo glanced up from the mesmerizing knife and replied, "I am going to give it to my friend Ursius. He really liked mine, and we have become such close friends. I know he will truly appreciate it."

Gabinius said, "That is a generous act, indeed. Know this, Guiamo, a gift given in such a spirit may return a blessing to you someday when you most need it, and least expect it. Your heart is good, Guiamo. Give your gift and be content."

The wounded struggled in over the next five days, some in wagons and some on foot, all with bloody bandages, wounds smeared with balm.

With them came news of the pursuit of the Helvetii. The words of the *centurio* who led the first group of wagons filled with casualties proved prophetic. Food supplies were growing short, and Julius Caesar had been consulting *Legatus* Titus Labienus about their options. Labienus favored a move toward their stores at Bibracte to consolidate and reequip, while Caesar preferred a bold, forced march to engage the Helvetii decisively. News dried up after the last group of wagons filled with wounded arrived.

Market day on the twenty-second day of *Iunius* came none to soon for Guiamo, and he hurried at first light to the encampment to see Ursius.

He found Ursius eating *puls* porridge for breakfast with his three assistants in a large tent near the dog cages. Guiamo sat on the ground beside Ursius and pulled out a small loaf of bread from a bag he carried. He wanted to find occasion to give Ursius the knife. As they ate together, Guiamo tried to act nonchalantly as he pulled out his knife to fiddle with it as if he were bored.

The three assistants noticed it immediately and Guiamo handed it around for them all to see.

"What does this new carving on the hilt say?" asked Ursius as he held the knife. "I cannot read."

Guiamo replied, "I carved it into the stag horn last night. It says 'Guiamo, friend of Ursius."

Then, reaching into the bag, he pulled out the second knife and passed it to Ursius. "This is for you, Ursi," he said as Ursius took it into his hands. "Yours says 'Ursius, friend of Guiamo."

Ursius stared as he held the identical blades side by side, comparing their similarity. He carefully handed the first blade back to Guiamo, and said, "This is for me? I am overwhelmed, Durmi, my friend. That you should give so fine a blade as this to me… With all my heart, I thank you. I shall treasure it always."

Guiamo said, "Ursi, you have been my good friend. Please name me Guiamo from this day forward. The gods have smiled on me, and I wish to share my joy with you."

Ursius smiled, Guiamo grinned back, and the three assistants sat quietly in awe at this tremendous show of generosity and brotherly love.

The next day, a herald arrived to the camp of the Seventh *Legio*. As before, he made his way to the office of the *praefectus castrorum* to declare his message.

The two walked out to speak to the gathering crowd. "*Roma victrix!*" the prefect shouted, and the soldiers' shouts of cheer resounded throughout the camp.

The herald raised his hands for quiet, and began, "Our brave Provincial Governor, Gaius Julius Caesar, has again defeated the Helvetii in battle. Our six *legiones* pursued the Helvetii after our first victory at the crossing of the river Arar. We harried them for many days, forcing them to move at our will, but they dared not engage us in full battle. Our supply train became stretched and vulnerable. Rather than fighting on without sufficient foodstuffs, Caesar wisely chose to move back to Bibracte where our supplies were guarded.

"As we marched the eighteen miles to Bibracte, the Helvetii turned to harass our rearguard. Caesar realized the battle he wanted was at hand. Near Bibracte there are two large hills. Caesar deployed all six *legiones* upon the slope of the larger hill in our standard three line formation so Dumnorix and Divicus could see our full strength.

"Our Seventh *Legio* was placed near the foot of the hill alongside the Eighth, Ninth and Tenth *Legiones* while the newly raised Eleventh and Twelfth *Legiones* were stationed farther up the hill to guard the supplies. Caesar wanted the Helvetii to fear our strength, and I doubt very much whether Dumnorix can tell an experienced *legio* from a newly raised one at that distance."

The crowd of veteran soldiers laughed at his criticism of the enemy chieftain.

"When the Helvetii saw our *legiones* ready for war, they moved their supplies behind their own ragged masses for protection. Then they attacked in a tight phalanx formation.

"They did not anticipate the power of our first volley of *pila* javelins. We threw our *pila* when they were eight *passuum* from our lines. Their front ranks stumbled upon our volley and nearly broke. Our ranks charged and fought with *gladius* and shield like warrior-gods against those howling demons. At last their tribes retreated to the opposite hill, leaving their dead in piles, and abandoning their wounded to our thirsty blades.

"As the Helvetii fled across the plain, turning toward our right, the Boii and Tulingi tribes arrived on our left flank to assist them. Our brave and wise governor turned our third rank to oppose them on this new front to our rear. Battle continued on, but eventually the Eighth *Legio* pushed on to capture their supply stores in the rear. At that, the Helvetii fled in confusion.

"The *Legati* were chafing to pursue the fleeing Helvetii, but Caesar held our men in formation, not willing to risk the chaos of pursuit when so low on food. At the time I was commanded to return to deliver this message, the six *legiones* were being reorganized for the final march to Bibracte."

The herald ceased speaking and with a roar, everyone shouted, "*Roma victrix*! Hail Caesar!"

As the wounded began to arrive from the battle of Bibracte, word of subsequent events spread. Caesar saw the Helvetii fleeing northeast toward the territory of the Lingones tribe. Cleverly, Caesar sent messages to the leaders of that tribe insisting that they offer no assistance to the Helvetii. He then marched out in pursuit. Soon after he marched, the Helvetii, seeing their dire situation, sued for peace.

One tribe of the Helvetii, the Verbigeni, refused to accept the surrender by Divicus and fled. Caesar ordered them arrested. They were quickly captured by neighboring Gallic tribes, and Caesar had all six thousand executed. The surviving Helvetii, only one in three that originally went to war, sheepishly complied when ordered to return to their homeland.

The region settled into an uneasy peace as the governor exerted his will powerfully over the rival tribal groups. The number of wounded in battle was greater than Guiamo had anticipated, and it bothered him greatly to see them suffer. The balm was a surprising blessing as it helped stop infection and encouraged more rapid healing. In this, Guiamo took comfort, knowing he had helped save many lives.

He also enjoyed his work in the smithy. His tasks in the late morning recently had been to place strips of iron over a wooden mold, and hammer the heated pieces into shape. His arm muscles ached, and he was pleased he had set aside a portion of ointment for his own use.

One night while readying himself for bed, his thoughts turned to Ursius' thirty war-dogs. He realized that they, too, would be hacked and hewed in battle by desperate warriors. He decided he should create an armor shielding to protect the dogs as they savaged the enemy. He knew it must be both flexible and lightweight so as not to slow them down when in pursuit.

As he lay in bed, his mind raced with creative ideas and he worked on various designs. He thought how a dog's torso moved as it ran, trying to determine how best to put flexibility into it. He had to visualize the dimensions of Laeleps, stitching leather to leather, designing in freedom of movement. He also had to deal with adding leather laces to allow the leather armor to be adjusted for each dog. Sleep did not come until he had finalized his design.

The next afternoon, he gathered pieces of leather and the tools he would need, and placed them in his *cubiculum*. After supper that night, he worked late, cutting, shaping, and piercing the leather.

Market day came on the ninth day of *Quintilis*, and again, Guiamo hurried to the encampment to speak with Ursius. "I have built something I would like for you to see," Guiamo said as he pulled his invention out of a gray cloth sack.

Ursius had learned to listen well as Guiamo explored new ideas. Guiamo continued, "The dogs will certainly be ferocious on the battlefield, but like a bare-chested barbarian warrior, they are vulnerable to a blade or spear."

Guiamo knelt and set three leather pieces on the ground so Ursius could examine them.

"This may sound silly, but I think this leather harness could serve as light armor to protect the dog. It is rather simple, but could save them. The way I see it, the most vulnerable parts of a dog will be his belly as he leaps onto his target. This would be particularly so if the enemy is armed with a sword. As the dog leaps, the swordsman would thrust his sword upwards into the dog's vitals. Now, if the enemy has a spear, I should think the dogs most vulnerable parts would be his shoulders, chest and back for a spearman will attack as the dog approaches."

Ursius looked carefully at the dog armor. "Guiamo, we need to put this on one of the dogs to see how well it fits. Laeleps is the biggest, and I trust him to obey more than any of the new dogs."

The boys walked over to Laeleps' cage where the powerful dog eagerly greeted Ursius. With Ursius handling the dog, Guiamo carefully fitted a broad leather collar around Laeleps' neck. He stitched it carefully with long leather laces along the dog's throat. Laeleps stood quietly panting as Ursius spoke with a calming voice.

The second piece covered the belly and wrapped up around the dog's back. The leather stitching was tied up along the dog's spine. Guiamo pointed out to Ursius that the armor was sewn double thick along the belly. See here," Guiamo said as he pointed to the belly section, "This is for extra protection from sword thrusts."

The third piece fit around the dog's shoulders. Loosely fitting, it was designed to fit over both neck and chest pieces to avoid pinches and abrasion. Like the belly piece, the shoulder and chest section were sewn double thick. Guiamo fit this piece onto Laeleps and laced up the leather ties along the dog's back. When the armor was all in place and stitched up properly, he said, "I think we should watch how well he runs."

Ursius agreed and took Laeleps out onto the training field. With a shout of command, he ordered the dog to run downfield, over obstacles, around the final barrier and back again.

As Laeleps returned, Ursius said, "He seems a little stiff."

Guiamo replied, "I think the leather around his chest and stomach is too stiff. I think I can work the leather there to increase its suppleness."

Ursius tried to keep an open mind. He knew Guiamo was on to something and mustn't let trivial issues curb his creativity. "Let us try this on a smaller dog and see how adaptable this armor is."

Guiamo agreed, and the two worked to fit it onto Argos. It fit well, proving the armor was well designed to adapt to all the dogs.

Ursius saw the value of this invention and encouraged Guiamo, "Can you build more of these? I would like one for each dog."

"Yes," Guiamo said, "though it will take some time. I will bring all I can on my next market day visit. I think this design is a good one, but I would like to see how well the dogs bear it in the heat. I will work to make more, but I must take this one back to Gobedbiacum to use as a pattern for the others. Let us run Laeleps hard today and see if he overheats quickly."

Laeleps wore the leather armor through the early afternoon and became exhausted early from the heat. The dog was given water to drink and placed in the shade to cool down. "We shall have to make sure they do not overheat on the day of battle," said Ursius, and Guiamo agreed.

On the tenth day of *Quintilis*, merchants from the south arrived with Calidius' third shipment. As the wares were being unloaded, Guiamo hurried over to find the bundles of arrows. He inspected them individually and retied them into bundles of ten.

Gabinius listed every item and calculated his purchases, and Guiamo's. He paid the merchants and invited them for the midday meal.

They feasted on fresh eel fillets with a spiced plum sauce. Guiamo did not care for the plum sauce, but relished the eel. Even the fattest merchant raised an eyebrow when Guiamo took a third full helping.

Gabinius and the merchants spoke of the war in great detail. All agreed that the battles had to be fought, but to a man, they were truly appalled to see so many casualties among the young men. Guiamo was surprised to find that Gabinius alone was the only one who would have been willing to forfeit all his profits from the campaigns if it meant avoiding the many deaths and injuries of the legionnaires.

Guiamo, usually quiet, asked his guests if they had any worries on their trip. The oldest merchant replied, "Word has come to us of a band of robbers that have been wandering the region as of late."

"I have seen them," Guiamo said enthusiastically. "Some weeks ago while traveling south, the brigands nearly rode up across our path. They were a miserable lot of about twenty armed men."

The elderly merchant said, "I have heard they are Belgae. Their chieftain had over two hundred men when he ventured south into Aquitania two years ago. Some returned home, a few married and settled, not a few were caught and killed. Today, they are but a remnant."

The shortest merchant said, "One story that has been told is that their chieftain was driven out of his homeland across the waters with curses written into his flesh."

Another merchant said, "Some say that they are not so much wicked as desperate. They take what they will, but kill none unless necessarily."

"Well, desperate or wicked, we bring enough spearmen that they dare not attack our caravan," said the leader of the merchants.

When their meal was completed, Gabinius retired to the back of the house. When he returned, he handed a heavy leather bag to the merchant leader, "This money is to be delivered to Calidius the fisherman."

The merchant opened it to peer inside, "So much silver! Would it not be better to send him gold instead?"

Gabinius shook his head and said, "The way Calidius lives, he would have nothing to spend so great an amount on. He would buy a tunic, not a chariot. His purchases will be small. He needs silver *denarii* and bronze *asses*, not gold *aurei*."

"I have seen how he lives. No one would ever suspect that he has so large a fortune as this. It will be done as you wish, Gabini," the leader said.

On the twenty-fifth day of *Quintilis*, Guiamo delivered to Ursius thirty sets of leather dog armor in a large sack dragged behind Honestia. The horse balked at the rope brushing her left hind leg, but Guiamo had no other way to take them to the encampment.

He spent much of the morning lacing the armor onto the thirty dogs and demonstrating to Ursius and the assistants how to fit them properly. The three assistants spent hours running the dogs to familiarize them with the restrictive leather. By day's end, Ursius was completely pleased with the design and with the dogs' progress.

Guiamo returned again on market day on the tenth day of *Sextilis*, and Ursius was as excited as Guiamo had ever seen. "Guiamo!" he exclaimed. "My *optio* has returned to the encampment on behalf of our *legati* and stopped by to inspect my work.

He was astounded at your idea for armoring the dogs. He carefully examined the armor and was surprised with how much thought had gone into designing it, as well as how well it was stitched together.

"We demonstrated the dogs running over the obstacles, and they performed remarkably well. He was so pleased that I received a bonus of eight *denarii*, and he has given me approval to purchase another seventy dogs if I can provide armor for them all. I can also hire seven more assistants!

"The *optio* is bringing the *legati* to inspect them when the *legiones* return from the wars. When the thirty dogs are trained sufficiently to obey commands and fight effectively, he wants me to begin training them to work in packs, as on the battlefield."

Ursius looked wistfully at Guiamo and asked, "Will you help me? I do not know any tactics for using the dogs in battle."

Guiamo said, "I have been thinking of this problem as I made the armor these past days. The dogs will tend to run in a pack on the field of battle. Whoever they attack is sure to be killed, but I do not think this is the best way to utilize them to turn the tide of battle.

106

"I think we should consider sending them out in groups of ten some moments apart. Now one pack of dogs will tend to follow another, so I had to think of a way to send each pack in different directions. I think we could train the dogs to run after an arrow, flaming brightly, and fight only when they get close to the fallen arrow. It would take much training and effort, but I think it might just work.

"Imagine having an archer fire the first flaming arrow on one part of the battlefield, and then loosing a pack. Once these dogs are on their way, a second arrow could be fired elsewhere. Another pack is sent on its way. Dogs could be sent to various parts of the battle as needed. If fifty dogs were needed to break up an enemy formation, we would just fire one arrow and release five packs of dogs."

Ursius was pleased with this idea, and the five young men began to formulate training methods for working the dogs in packs.

On the eighteenth day of *Sextilis*, Gabinius watched Guiamo running the trail leading from the village of Gobedbiacum up the hill to his home. His strides were long and smooth.

Sertorius said, "His endurance is remarkable. His fishing days have made him strong for such a young boy."

Gabinius nodded in agreement. "He is lean but becoming ever more muscular. Have you noticed how his appetite has grown?"

Sertorius said, "Yes, he eats everything and wants more."

"Well, he is growing and you work him hard," said Gabinius.

Sertorius laughed, "No, you work him hard. I just do what I am told."

Sweating profusely and breathing loudly, Guiamo finally ran past Gabinius and Sertorius, and on to the creek. He dropped to his knees, knelt forward, and put his entire head underwater. He sat back with a great splash and tossed his head to shake off the water. Then, he bent again to the creek to take a long drink.

Sertorius called him, "Durmi, come here when you catch your breath."

Guiamo said nothing, but waved his hand as he panted heavily.

Presently, he sauntered over as Gabinius and Sertorius were busily speaking in serious tones. As he drew closer, Sertorius abruptly stopped speaking and the two turned to face him.

Gabinius said, "That was a good run today. I would like to see your skill with a spear in a little while, but first, we have something of import to discuss.

"A herald from the Eleventh *Legio* arrived today. It looks as if our governor has brought Rome another victory. He is quite clever, that one, though the *praefectus alae* of the cavalry reserve seems to have saved him from an embarrassing defeat."

Guiamo gave Gabinius an exasperated look. "Well, at least tell me who Caesar fought!" he said impatiently. "Was it the Helvetii again? I thought they went back to their homeland."

"No, not the Helvetii. They have been disgraced and subdued. This time it was the Suebi," Gabinius replied.

"Who?" asked Guiamo.

"The Suebi. They are a tribe from Germania. Their leader is Ariovistus. He is a brute of a man. I have heard he stands taller than I do and wears a great bear cape. It is said he has six wives and over twenty sons."

Sertorius chuckled and said, "All as ugly as he."

Gabinius laughed and said, "His sons, too."

Guiamo and Sertorius burst out laughing.

"So how did the battle unfold?" Guiamo asked when his sides began to hurt.

Gabinius wiped his tears of laughter and struggled to speak seriously, "First you need to understand what led Caesar to fight the battle. After the battle of Bibracte, Julius Caesar clearly proved himself a strongman that none could contend with. All the tribal leaders of Gallia met with him with praise; all maneuvering for favor with bribes and empty

108

promises. Out of all this grand show of support for our governor rose the true issue of note.

"The Arverni have been squabbling with the Aedui for some time now. I have heard it had something to do with some stolen cows and a barn burned down a few years back. They have been feuding ever since. The Aedui were angry that the Arverni had hired an immense force of mercenaries out of Germania from the Suebi tribe. The Arverni hoped to tip the dispute in their favor. It clearly put the Aedui at a marked disadvantage. The Aedui are laughing now for Ariovistus turned on his benefactor, took some children of the Arverni nobles hostage and has upset the whole struggle.

"Caesar waded into the mess with all six *legiones* to settle the matter. He bullied Ariovistus' forces in minor skirmishes, and boldly forced them into battle even though Caesar's army was less than half that of Ariovistus."

"So how did Caesar fight his battle?" Guiamo asked again.

Gabinius squatted to the ground and drew three parallel lines. "With great difficulty. Caesar wanted to force the battle. Ariovistus had maneuvered to threaten Caesar's supply line, and we needed to relieve it. Caesar marched his *legiones* right up to their encampment and deployed for battle.

"Caesar fought with the standard tactics of Rome. They were positioned in three lines. Caesar saw their weak spot was on their left, so like any good *legati*, that is where he focused his attack. Caesar favors the Tenth *Legio*, so he placed *Legati* Labienus on his right where he could press their weak left.

"As we advanced, the Suebi charged across a broad front. We were prepared for this, but to Caesar's surprise, as our *legiones* pressed forward, the Suebi brought a new tactic to the field. They moved into columns here," he said pointing to his map in the dust, "here, here, and here.

"Their advance in column was quick. It was done so rapidly that we lost our advantage. The Seventh and Ninth *Legiones* had no time to hurl their *pila* at their front ranks. We were forced to meet them with *gladius* and shield. The fight was brutal. This is where the Seventh *Legio* took most of its casualties. The Ninth was also savaged, but not so dearly. Most importantly, though, our front held. The Suebi eventually fell back to regroup and we pursued them.

"Now the *praefectus alae* of the reserve cavalry is Publius Crassus. He had his men maneuvering around the battlefield searching for vulnerable spots among the Suebi which he could exploit at a pivotal time in the battle.

"I have told you how a cavalry charge at the right time and place can penetrate the enemy defenses, and so shock their morale that the entire enemy army becomes paralyzed with fear, and they flee in panic.

"As he approached our left, he saw that the Seventh and Eleventh *Legiones* were locked in a vicious struggle, and looked as if they were about to break. If they fled, Caesar would not be able to keep the other *legiones* from joining them in flight, for panic spreads as fast as lightning.

"Crassus saw what Caesar could not, for he was with the Tenth *Legio* on the far right, so took action on his own initiative. He ordered the third line held in reserve to reinforce the Eleventh and our Seventh *Legiones*. They rushed forward, rallying the faltering Eleventh which was ready to collapse. Many of them quickly fell back a few paces to recover from exhaustion. The Seventh *Legio* held until Crassus' men arrived moments later. The Suebi still pressed the battle, but had no reserves. They were locked in battle for longer than expected, but tripping on their own dead and dying, could not press forward in strength. As the Suebi came to realize they could not force the Seventh and Eleventh into flight, their momentum waned.

"At this point, Crassus saw his time to clinch victory had arrived. He launched a renewed push that swept past their front ranks, and the Suebi right broke. The Tenth *Legio* also pushed and forced back the Suebi left. Fearing envelopment and annihilation, the Suebi pulled back.

"Their withdrawal quickly turned into a rout. They fled in utter panic, many dropping their weapons as they ran. Crassus led his cavalry in pursuit and the slaughter was beautiful and terrible to behold. All the *legiones* followed

110

and cut down thousands, for the Suebi were exhausted from battle.

"Unfortunately, our men did not kill Ariovistus, but he has crossed the river Rhenus to lick his wounds. I doubt if he shall return any time soon. There is little worry that he will fight for the return of his wife and daughters that were captured. They are all ugly as bulls.

"Crassus saved the battle, and Caesar has his victory. It would seem he has taken complete control of Gallia. This will mean some level of peace for the rest of this year, but the tribes are still restless. To protect his governorship, I would expect Caesar to move aggressively to crush any rebellions. A subdued region is a profitable region, and Caesar desperately needs funds. His debts must be paid or he could still be removed from office. However, I do not think he is overly concerned about his debt.

"One principle of debt Caesar seems to understand is this; if I owe you ten *denarii*, you have a measure of control over me. If I owe you ten thousand *denarii*, I have a measure of control over you. Do you understand this, Guiamo?"

Guiamo thought about this and replied, "Yes, I think so. Caesar owes so much money; the lenders have become financially vulnerable, and are now dependent upon Caesar's ability,"

Gabinius interjected, "and desire."

"and desire to repay," said Guiamo.

"Correct," said Gabinius. "Only if he remains in power as governor do they have any hope of repayment. They will press him as hard as they dare, but in the end will be forced into being his strongest supporters to keep him in power."

Gabinius continued, "So these are the events in the world. Sertorius tells me you have learned much of spear fighting. Now, fetch a spear and show me your drill."

Salonius and Guiamo spent their evening together on the sixth day of *September* outside sitting around a small bonfire. Guiamo practiced playing his harp in the quiet of the cool evening as Salonius poked at the coals with a long stick. Guiamo was pleased that Ulleria had been assigned to teach him to play the harp some weeks past. His music was not flawless, but he did show some skill. When he had finished playing the seven songs he knew, he began to improvise.

The music soothed his own spirit, for though he had been glad to see his dog, he was mildly discouraged that Flaccus lay at the feet of Salonius.

As the evening turned to darkness, and orange sparks flickered up into the night sky, Salonius' thoughts turned from the music to his first love, the hunt.

"Durmi, the acorns are soon to fall," said Salonius. "Are you ready to slay the boar with me? He will return to the sacred grove in just a few weeks."

With a chilling breeze and rising sun, Salonius and Guiamo set out on foot on the fourth day of *November* for the sacred grove atop the hill east of Gobedbiacum. They each carried a spear, while Guiamo also carried his bow. An hour of silent marching brought them to the rocky crest where they planned to lie in wait for the legendary old boar.

The acorns had fallen in abundance under the ancient oaks in the sacred grove. Salonius hushed Guiamo as a sow with seven piglets crossed their path as she led her young to her morning feast.

Guiamo was surprised to see wild pigs so quickly, and his hunting instincts switched on. Salonius pointed to the path the sow had taken and then showed Guiamo where to conceal himself. He was placed to the left of the trail partly obscured behind a boulder on his right, and a thick shrub on his left which had not yet lost its dried leaves. Guiamo surveyed the hunting ground and quickly saw that if the boar should come up the trail toward the acorns in the sacred grove, it would not see him. Guiamo would have a clear shot at its left side from the rear.

Salonius continued on to place himself near the opposite side of the crest, hoping to kill the boar if it came from the other direction.

Guiamo cleared the ground around his feet of sticks and leafy debris to avoid revealing himself to his prey if he should need to move into position for a clear shot. He could clearly hear the grunts of the sow as she devoured the acorns spread thickly under the oaks.

Guiamo patiently stood with bow in hand, leaning against the rock. He had learned to be patient, remaining quietly attuned to the sounds around him, while his eyes scanned the undergrowth. He allowed himself only the slowest turns of his head, for he knew quick motion would give himself away.

He listened as Salonius' muffled steps grew ever fainter, and then abruptly stopped. He heard Salonius scraping the ground free of sticks and leaves as he had, and then all went silent again.

Guiamo enjoyed the early morning chirping of the birds as they flit from tree to tree. The wind slackened and the air grew comfortably warm. He could still hear the sow foraging, and it encouraged his hope to see the boar that had killed Salonius' dog. Aside from the birdsongs, the occasional scurrying of a squirrel and the faint noises from the pigs at a distance, the world was silent. It was one aspect of hunting that appealed to him most. He loved the world at peace. For nearly two hours, he listened and his heart was joyful.

Before he saw it, he felt its motion through his feet. The hunter came alive as the silent steps reverberated through the soil. It was near. He could feel it walking toward him, its heavy feet compacting the ground. As it neared, he heard its rough exhale and the rustle of vegetation being brushed aside. Guiamo knew the boar was on the trail, just on the other side of the boulder. Salonius had chosen this spot well, generously giving Guiamo the favored location.

It breathed heavily again and moved forward. Guiamo carefully raised his bow, ready to draw the bowstring as the boar passed him. The boar noisily exhaled again and ambled forward at a cautious pace. It grunted as it appeared from beyond the boulder.

Guiamo's heart leaped as he saw first the enormous snout, and then the entire head come into view. This was no ordinary pig raised in the farms around Gobedbiacum. It seemed nearly the size of an ox, larger than any he had ever seen. The tusks were each over a span in length.

Guiamo realized for the first time that his own life was truly at stake and Salonius was too far away to help. Guiamo had to decide right then whether he should let the boar pass safely, or shoot and hope for a quick kill.

As the boar shuffled forward, Guiamo steeled his resolve, drew the bowstring and let loose the arrow. The shrieking squeal that erupted from the boar shook Guiamo to the core. The boar spun left toward the injury, and Guiamo saw to his dismay that while the arrow had pierced the left shoulder, it had been stopped by the bone of the shoulder blade.

The wounded boar spied the hunter as he nocked his second arrow, and charged. Guiamo realized he had no time for a second shot, so he dropped his bow, turned and ran, leaving everything behind. As the gap between the two narrowed quickly, Guiamo sprinted to a small elm tree with low branches, and scrambled to safety just before the boar reached him. Hauling himself as high as he dared, Guiamo gasped for breath, and broke out in a sweat as he watched the boar circle the tree again and again.

The arrow was hanging loosely now, and Guiamo clung to the tree in sheer terror. As it became apparent the boar could not push the tree over and he was safe for now, Guiamo's panic subsided. He began to call out to Salonius.

"Saloni! Saloni! The boar is here and wounded!" he cried.

Salonius called back, "Durmi, are you safe?"

Guiamo yelled, "Yes, but I am caught in a tree and have no weapons."

Salonius replied, "Some great hunter you are today, Durmi. If that old boar is wounded… how badly wounded is the boar?"

"Only hurt enough to make him angry," said Guiamo.

"Then you stay in your tree until he leaves. I have no desire to fight that old boar face to face when he is in such a foul mood."

So Guiamo clung to the thin branches of the elm for an hour as the boar moved around grunting angrily. Eventually, the old boar moved away, and soon after, Salonius came in to rescue the frightened and embarrassed Guiamo.

114

Gabinius listened quietly to the tale of the two mighty hunters that evening. Rather than discouraging any further attempts as Guiamo had expected him to, Gabinius chose a different tact. "Boys, you have faced a monster and survived. It would be easy to quit, but sometimes," and he raised a finger to emphasize his thoughts, "sometimes, you must act the man and not the boy. Saloni, Guiamo, that boar is as dangerous as a wolf or bear. It must be killed, and if you two want to be men and not just half-grown boys, you must do this. Guiamo, you are not strong enough to fight this animal on equal terms. You must use your wits to defeat him. Think on how best to kill this beast, and let me know your thoughts."

Guiamo's mind began churning the moment Gabinius finished his words. He thought of nets and snares, rocks thrown, hidden pits, and traps of flame. As his mind explored wild possibilities, by next afternoon, he finally settled on an idea, though some details had yet to be defined.

"I need an arrow, Saloni. A big arrow," he said. "It must be as long as a spear and I need a bow designed to launch it. I want to skewer that boar with an arrow so large and powerful that the boar will drop in its tracks with a single shot. It must pierce flesh and shatter bone."

"Why not just throw a spear?" asked Salonius.

"I cannot throw it hard enough for a certain, quick kill. I would just make him angry again," said Guiamo. "I need this arrow, and I need a bow large enough to shoot it powerfully."

Salonius thought about this for a moment, and skeptically asked, "Durmi, you are but twelve years old. How would you draw back such a bow?"

Guiamo understood the difficulty and said, "That I have not figured out yet, but I shall, Saloni, I shall."

Guiamo began sketching ideas in the dirt. Frustrated with his primitive drawings, he ran to the workshop, and grabbed a dozen pieces of scrap leather. He cut them roughly to the same size and returned to his *cubiculum*. He spent the afternoon alone, refusing to construct arrows or tend Honestia. "I have something important I need to work on, and I will come out when I am finished!" he shouted to a worried Sertorius, who scurried off to alert Gabinius.

After hearing Sertorius' report, Gabinius chided him, "Have you not considered he just possibly might really have something important he needs to work on? Do not worry about him or pester him. He will come out to eat or use the bathroom. A dozen arrows fewer will not bring Caesar's armies down in ruin, and Honestia is better groomed than my own horse. No, dear Sertori, we should leave him be."

Sertori found him slumped over, breathing noisily as he slept among his drawings. "Durmi, Durmi," he called quietly, "it is time for breakfast."

Guiamo awoke from a heavy sleep and stretched to work out kinks and stiffness in his muscles. "Sertori, would you please have Ulleria fetch me some bread and water? I am almost finished with my design, and I must continue here in my *cubiculum* without distraction."

"Certainly, Durmi. It will be just a short time for her to gather it," said Sertorius politely.

Guiamo reorganized his sketches and hardly noticed eating his breakfast, much less Ulleria bringing it.

When supper was prepared and set for Gabinius, Guiamo walked in confidently with a dozen pieces of leather stacked neatly, trimmed to equal sizes, and bound together on one edge with a length of leather cord spiraling through a series of holes pierced along the edge.

"What is this you have created, Guiamo?" asked Gabinius as he bit into a serving of cow's udder stuffed with boiled goose eggs and garlic cloves.

"What? This?" he replied, pointing to the leather pages. "I bound these leather skins together to keep my sketches orderly. I think it is easier to find what I am looking for than the *volumen* you have had me reading from. See? I can flip

116

through them quite easily." Guiamo demonstrated by turning some leather pages.

"Clever," said Gabinius, "but what are your sketches about?"

Guiamo explained how he had designed a device that would be able to shoot a large arrow whose design is based upon a spear. Gabinius was clearly intrigued as Guiamo turned the leather pages to show various aspects of its design.

Guiamo showed how he had devised a way to draw the bowstring back mechanically. He would affix one end of a beam of wood to the bow where a man's hand normally would grasp it. At the opposite end of the beam he would anchor a loop of iron. Between the bow and the loop, he would set a hand crank that would be attached to the loop and the bowstring. By turning the hand crank, he could pull the bowstring back in increments to a full draw. The bowstring could then be secured in place with a metal hook. The hand crank would then be removed. The entire bow would be positioned horizontally and the huge arrow would be dropped into a shallow trough. The entire engine would be mounted to a post so that it could be turned in any direction and pointed up or down. When ready to fire, Guiamo planned to move the metal hook away, releasing the bowstring and firing the arrow.

"How will you mount this to the ground?" asked Gabinius. "It is much too large for me to carry, let alone a twelve-year-old boy."

"I am not going to put this on the ground. I shall put it in a tree where the boar cannot gore me. I have faced him once, and have learned my lesson," said Guiamo.

"Up in a tree?" Gabinius asked.

"Yes," replied Guiamo, "on a platform where I will not have to cling to the branches like a squirrel. It must be mounted to the post which will be affixed in the center of the platform. Positioned there, I can turn it in any direction for a shot without fear of falling out of the tree."

When Guiamo had finished, Gabinius commented, "The bow must be made of iron, tempered for flexibility. Even the bowstring might best be made of wire strong enough to hold the tension. Let us show your design to my craftsmen and they can make this arrow engine far more quickly than you could. This could prove a magnificent weapon. Do you doubt the oracle now, Guiamo? Son of Mars, indeed!"

The craftsmen worked diligently for nine days, with Guiamo guiding the overall design, while Gabinius gave instructions in the details of construction. As they labored on the arrow engine, Salonius worked rapidly to design and build the wooden platform in a tree near the sacred grove. Guiamo graciously agreed that Salonius should be allowed to select the post location and build it as he would.

When the arrow engine was nearing completion, Salonius was brought into the smithy to see Guiamo's invention. As he studied the mechanism in wonder, he asked, "How will you aim this? I shoot bow by experience, and know how to hit the target near and far, but this... this is something new altogether. We must test fire it to learn its aim."

They brought out the four arrows. Their iron tips were long and each had four blades for cutting. The fletching was not of feather but thin, hammered iron, shaped to spin the arrow in flight for stability. The shaft was made from oak spears. The nocks were cut deeply and reinforced with a covering of hammered iron to keep the shaft from splitting.

They spent the afternoon firing the arrows at various distances while the craftsmen looked on. It proved consistent in its firing pattern and Guiamo became quickly adept at using the hand crank to draw the bowstring. Locking it back was a little awkward, but achievable.

When the day drew to a close, Guiamo and Gabinius disassembled it for the ease of the next day's transport to the platform near the sacred grove.

By late morning of the fifteenth day of *November*, the arrow engine had been hauled in pieces on horseback to the platform. With ropes, Salonius and Guiamo hauled the pieces up onto the wooden platform. Final assembly took more time than Guiamo thought it should, but at last the work was completed and the horses returned to Gabinius.

They both slept on the platform that night and awoke as the birdsong filled the air. They waited all day in the tree hoping to spot the boar. Nothing showed.

They had planned for a long hunt, so brought provisions for several days. The morning of the second day, Salonius awoke first, and climbed down the tree to find a quiet place to relieve himself.

As Guiamo stirred, he heard a panic-stricken shout of alarm. He peered over the platform edge in time to catch a glimpse of Salonius sprinting for the safety of their tree. Right on his heels was the old boar, charging with fury. As Salonius jumped at a branch, the boar caught the hunter's right foot and knocked him off balance.

Guiamo sprang to his feet, and began to draw the bowstring back as quickly as he could with the hand crank.

Salonius fell to the right of the tree trunk and the boar veered to the left. As Salonius scrambled back to his feet, the old boar spun around and charged again. Salonius did his best to keep the trunk between them as he went for another branch. He pulled himself up tightly against the underside of the thick limb just out of the boar's reach, and called out for help.

Guiamo latched the bowstring back, unhitched the hand crank and loaded a massive arrow. The boar was beneath the platform and Guiamo moaned in frustration.

"Hold on Saloni!" he shouted. "I cannot shoot him until he moves off a ways."

Salonius struggled mightily to climb to safety without dropping his legs within the boars reach. After a few tries, he finally pulled himself up and onto the platform.

The old boar began circling the tree, and Guiamo could see the scabby, infected wound on its left shoulder. At long last, the boar wandered off to stand at a distance behind another oak, and facing to the right. Guiamo waited patiently with the arrow engine pointed to the right side of the far tree hoping to get a shot when the boar moved forward. After a few minutes, it snorted and stepped out, giving Guiamo a perfect shot.

Guiamo aimed as well as he could. With a gentle motion, he released the bowstring and let the arrow fly.

The arrow was so large, it seemed to fly slowly, but it flew straight and with tremendous power right into the boar's right flank behind the shoulder blade. It punched through a rib into the right lung, slicing through the heart, passing through the left lung. It continued out the other side and burrowed into a tree. The boar fell dead on its belly without so much as a twitch, and then rolled slowly onto its left side.

Salonius and Guiamo let out shouts of cheer and fairly tumbled out of the tree in their eagerness to claim their prize.

"Now what do we do with it?" Guiamo asked as he stood over the dead boar.

Salonius said, "Cut it up and haul it back, of course. I should think Malleolus and his craftsmen would like a taste. This monster is the largest I have ever heard of. Look at the immense tusks! They are well over a span long! You should cut them out as trophies from today's hunt."

Salonius looked slyly at his friend and said, "Your fame will grow, you know." Guiamo was not so certain he liked that idea. "You will be known across all of Gallia as Fearless Durmius Stolo, the mighty pig slayer of Gobedbiacum," Salonius teased. Guiamo rolled his eyes in dismay, and Salonius continued his joking. "Yes, old men will cheer as you pass, and beautiful girls will swoon at the sound of your name." Guiamo covered his face with his hands and groaned.

As the autumn months turned to winter, Guiamo spent more of his free time playing legionnaire. He loved to roam the orchards with his practice spear and wooden *gladius* to fight the imaginary Helvetii as they charged his positions.

Using fighting techniques Sertorius had taught him, and embellishing them with dramatic jabs, turns and kicks, he fought with all the valor of a Hector fighting in the defense of Troy.

The leafless trees became charging horsemen, their branches, swords and spears; and the battles raged. Sometimes he brought his wooden shield and imagined fighting in a Greek phalanx or a Roman shield wall. With cries of '*Testudo!*' he would raise his shield in the tortoise defense as the *legiones* were taught to block a volley of arrows in flight. By bringing their shields together, they formed a solid wall in front and overhead which arrows and spears could not penetrate.

One cold evening, he charged after his panic-stricken Helvetii into a thicket of saplings. Unable to effectively fight with his spear among so many foes, he valiantly drew his *gladius* and stabbed and hacked to his heart's content.

As the exhausting battle drew long, he realized that the Gallic warriors were so close together, it was difficult to change direction of his *gladius'* thrust. He kept his foes at bay, but swung clumsily as the tip of the *gladius* frequently clattered unexpectedly against the weapons of the Helvetii.

He grew frustrated and on impulse drew his fisherman's knife. With great effort, he whittled and cut the tip of the wooden *gladius* down by a full span. As he reshaped the blade, he gave it a sharp pointed tip.

The Helvetii charged again, and this time, the blade flicked effortlessly from warrior to warrior, dealing death at every blow.

Sertorius was not pleased. "Why did you ruin your practice *gladius*?" he asked in exasperation. "It was so well made. Now someone will have to make you another."

"I do not want another. I like this one. It is much better this way than before," replied Guiamo.

Gabinius stood silently in the *tablinum* listening to the boy's explanation.

"The other is too long. I can stab one target and switch to another more quickly. The extra reach might be necessary when fighting from a horse, but up close in battle, I will not need to reach so far anyway," Guiamo said.

Gabinius was mildly intrigued and called out, "Guiamo! Sertori! Come here. I wish to join your discussion."

As the two came into the *tablinum*, Gabinius saw the modified wooden *gladius* for the first time. "Bring it here,

Guiamo. I am not upset at the change you made. I want to know your reasoning."

Guiamo told the story of his play battle and his frustrations when fighting close in with such a long blade.

When he was finished, Gabinius said, "I do not know if this has to do with your stature and reach, or the close proximity to a number of enemy warriors. Let me think on this."

Gabinius kept Guiamo's shortened sword and excused the two. As Guiamo left, he glanced behind and saw Gabinius with the *gladius* in hand feeling its balance while slowly moving it around in front of him.

Midmorning, Gabinius called Guiamo outside to watch him drill. Guiamo found him holding a shield and iron *gladius* shortened to the length of his wooden pattern. He stood in front of eight wooden posts placed closely together. Guiamo recognized Gabinius was simulating a close-quarters fight similar to his own imagined fight among the saplings.

Gabinius changed to his fighting stance; shield tightly positioned, feet spaced with the left forward and prepared for action, *gladius* prepared for attack. Without warning, he launched himself into a vicious assault with a flurry of blows.

Alternating his rapid horizontal thrusts with overhead chops to the head and ankle stabs, he moved with fluid movements which belied his age. His speed was as quick as snake bites as he switched between target posts. The pace quickened as he forcefully stabbed each of the posts in random fashion. Then he charged bodily into each post with forceful shield rushes while making powerful stabbing body thrusts as if locked shield to shield.

Abruptly, he stopped. He turned, breathing heavily, clearly weary, to speak to Guiamo. "I believe you have a good idea," he said. "The extra reach of a normal *gladius* is actually a disadvantage when in extreme close-quarters. When we fight, we are used to the extra reach of a longer blade, but I think the advantage of extra length is outweighed by an increased ability to maneuver in close-quarters. My

122

thrusting hand does not have to reach nearly so far backwards to make a body stab when our shields are touching.

"The Eleventh *Legio* is stationed near Durocortorum, a trading village settled recently. Our *praefectus castrorum* is still managing their affairs. I am told they have placed an order for three hundred *gladii*. I shall make these in Guiamo's shortened style. I know I can persuade him to test them as a possible improvement."

The *praefectus castrorum* carefully examined Gabinius' shortened sword. He practiced thrusting it, going through the motions of close in combat as had Gabinius, but in slow motions. He thought of the critical distances of combat and the subtle motions of hand and arm. He eventually handed the *gladius* back to Gabinius and smiled slightly as he realized the tremendous advantage his customers would have in battle.

"Your proposal is approved. The length is much more precisely fixed to maximize its effectiveness of a reaching stab or slash to the head, and shield-to-shield body thrust. All further purchases will be in this style. I shall send word to all the other *legiones* of this design and recommend all new purchases be specified so. It will be up to each *legio* to make their own decisions, of course, but the Seventh and Eleventh will be so equipped as demand arises.

"Additionally, I would like to purchase one myself, but ornately crafted. I cannot afford your finest work, as you well know, but I would like it made more elaborately than the *milites gregarii* would have."

"I would be delighted to craft your new *gladius*," Gabinius replied. "It should be ready by springtime."

Rumors came with the bitter cold winds of winter. The Belgae to the north were spoiling for battle, eager to push the Romans out of their ancestral lands. Boduognatus, the tribal chieftain of the Nervii, was known to be sending spies and raiding parties southward into Roman territory contrary to the wishes of Galba, king of the Suessiones. Galba preferred to appear docile while he quietly gathered his strength for an unexpected attack on the traitorous Remi tribe at their *oppidum* at Bibrax.

To counter this growing menace, Caesar gave orders to organize two additional *legiones*, the Thirteenth and Fourteenth and that they should be sent from Rome to Gallia in the springtime.

As the *legiones* trained replacements, the need for equipment continued though at a more leisurely pace for Gabinius' craftsmen. Gabinius was pleased that they had time to make better quality weapons. He also found time to build the very ornate pieces for which he was famous, and for which his wealthier clients clamored.

Winter passed and his fortune grew. Guiamo also had come into great riches, having a sum in his account with Gabinius of over fifty gold *aurei*. Calidius received his final payment for the year, an equivalent amount but in silver of over fourteen hundred *denarii*.

Guiamo was too busy to worry much about his growing fortune. Mornings were spent reading and working with Gabinius in his private smithy. Sertorius kept him busy in the afternoons exercising and practicing for war even on the coldest days. He grew strong and showed a natural aptitude for fighting.

Chapter Four - 57 B.C.

"The gods do not see all ends." Androteus, circa 230 B.C.

Guiamo visited the encampment as usual on market day on the seventh day of *Ianuarius* only to find that Ursius had been ordered to take his ten assistants and one hundred dogs to Agedincum to join the Seventh *Legio* at their temporary encampment in preparation for combat operations in the spring.

He missed his friend dearly, and it was small consolation for Guiamo to be informed that Ursius had been promoted to *optio* of fighting dogs and assigned directly to the *primus pilus*.

On the third day of *Maius*, Sertorius sent Guiamo to Gabinius' private workshop late one morning. As he approached, Gabinius set his engraving tools aside and motioned for Guiamo to come closer. The boy was curious about what might have occurred that was worthy of interrupting his lessons.

Guiamo took a seat on a wooden stool, and Gabinius said, "Guiamo, the first battle of the season has been fought near the river Axona against King Galba of the Suessiones.

"There was nothing particularly notable in this fight. We met for battle, but they refused it. That is typical of them. How they must cheer as they set out for a fight, but more often than not, they do all they can to avoid it. That is, when they are not in a drunken stupor. The glint of sunlight sparkling off our *pila* seems to take the fight right out of them. Rather than face our iron man to man, Galba sent a fair sized force around our flank and attacked over the river. It was actually a clever move, which is the surprising part about this battle. Galba is not particularly known for his skill in warfare. To counter his assault, Caesar sent in our cavalry along with Numidians, archers and slingers. We caught many of their men in the water and the slaughter was great.

"Seeing their ambush turn to disaster, their main body of warriors fled. Caesar was surprised at so easy a victory. It was too easy. He decided it might be a trick to bring us into a trap, so did not pursue them.

"Only when morning light rose did he realize they truly had withdrawn. Caesar sent three *legiones* and the cavalry in pursuit. While the Suessiones' rearguard fought well, everyone else fled for their lives which, thanks to our brave men, proved very short indeed. We slaughtered far more as they ran than in the river where they at least fought bravely.

"Such is war. Guiamo, it is always better to stay together to fight to the end as did their rearguard than to scatter and be stricken down like a flock of chickens."

Gabinius saw that Guiamo was worried about his friend and gave Guiamo what news he had. "I have heard that Ursius' dogs fought well, but he had trouble gathering them back afterward. He is still missing twenty or so. Still, he is making quite a name for himself. The leather armor you designed has also been very successful in keeping the dogs from harm. Some dogs were killed with blows to the head, but many more were spared by your armor.

"The flaming arrow idea seemed to work fairly well to direct the dogs to the chosen target area, though in the excitement of battle, some dogs still chased after the closest target. Fortunately there were no reports of any of our men being mauled. Ursius was hard pressed to keep up with the dogs as the Suessiones fled, and the dogs ran freely about the battlefield. The dogs did seem to know our men from theirs, which is fortunate. Word has it that the *primus pilus* is pleased overall with Ursius' plans and will continue using them."

Guiamo was pleased that Ursius' dogs had performed so admirably in battle. He missed his friend and asked, "Gabini, is there any news when the Seventh *Legio* will return?"

Gabinius said, "My hope is that they should arrive before winter sets in, but no one knows for certain. Not all the tribes are yet subdued. Perhaps, if they delay, I shall send you to visit him."

On the second day of *Quintilis*, in the dusty courtyard in front of Gabinius' house, Salonius approached Guiamo with shield and wooden *gladius*. Holding his shield to cover his body, he advanced carefully toward Guiamo's spear. Guiamo thrust the spear forward with a quick jab. Salonius met the blunt wooden tip with a sideways swipe, knocking the spear tip to Guiamo's right. As Salonius moved forward, Guiamo stepped back and recovered his fighting stance.

Salonius placed his feet carefully in preparation for an attack, positioning himself to move quickly past Guiamo's spear point.

Recognizing Salonius' plan, Guiamo steeled himself for the impending onslaught. He knew this was where he had met repeated failure in combat practice with the skilled huntsman. Only the night before had he finally decided how to try to meet this challenge. Today, he would see how well his strategy would work.

With a fluid motion, Salonius stepped forward, slightly extending his shield ahead. Sweeping his shield to the left to knock the spear tip aside, he lunged forward with his *gladius* to deal a decisive blow. To his surprise, his shield made no contact with Guiamo's spear.

Anticipating this move, Guiamo hopped backwards one step, tossed the spear in his hands back an arm's length to shorten its forward length. Once secured in its new position, he thrust the padded spear forward to impact squarely against Salonius' unprotected chest.

Salonius dropped his *gladius* and fell to his knees clutching his chest. "Oh, that hurts, Durmi," gasped Salonius. "How did you do that?"

"It is my secret," laughed Guiamo. "Would you like to try again?"

"No. Not today, anyway. That was a good move," groaned Salonius. He looked up and saw Gabinius driving a wagon up the pathway more hastily than usual.

The old man climbed down from the wagon and strode over to the two weary fighters. "Guiamo, walk with me," he called out.

Salonius took Guiamo's spear and returned it to storage.

"When they were beyond earshot, Gabinius turned to Guiamo and said, "What I have to say is not yet for the ears of the common folk. I want you to know, but you are to say nothing at this time. Caesar wants to tell the story to the public as he wants it told. There has been a fierce battle and the casualties are great."

Guiamo stood silently, taking in the sobering news. "What happened?" he whispered.

Gabinius breathed deeply as he sorted his thoughts. He let out a long breath and began. "Our friend, Julius Caesar, has been caught like a fly in honey, it would seem. You know how I told you the Nervii have been causing us some problems of late. Caesar first marched on to the Suessiones town of Noviodunum which surrendered quietly.

"Our *legiones* then moved on to the Bellovaci *oppidum* of Bratuspantium. The Bellovaci also surrendered without any terms demanded which is fortunate for they are the greatest nation in this region. Caesar secured the city, demanded six hundred hostages and confidently moved on to face the Ambiani who followed in like manner some days later.

"With three nations easily subdued, his six *legiones* boldly marched out to face the main Belgae encampment at the river Sabis. The baggage train had not yet arrived, and the Thirteenth and Fourteenth *Legiones* were trailing behind as rearguard. There had been some skirmishing, but nothing serious. As the day was late, Caesar ordered the construction of our encampment. What Caesar did not know was that the Nervii and their allies were hiding in the forest just across the Sabis.

"While our men were busy building the fort, the Belgae came charging out of hiding. Our men were completely surprised. They charged across the river, being only waist deep, and were nearly upon us when we were first able to react. Everyone scrambled to secure their weapons, and though there was no time to gather the men into groups by *cohors* for a proper defense, the *milites gregarii* knew from experience what needed to be done without having to be given orders. Everyone rushed about preparing for the onslaught, and we were just able to form up in time, though many had to fight without helmets or shields.

"The Nervii, commanded by Boduognatus, came out to face our *legiones* on our right, while the Atrebates were on our left. The Viromandui controlled the center. Caesar prefers the Tenth *Legio*, so he moved to place himself with them on our left with the Ninth *Legio*."

Guiamo asked, "Where did our Seventh *Legio* fight?"

Gabinius replied, "They were on the extreme right next to the Twelfth *Legio*. The battle quickly split into three distinct struggles. Caesar, with the Ninth and Tenth *Legiones*, met the Atrebates and fought them back across the Sabis, putting the Atrebates to flight.

"In the center, our Eighth and Eleventh *Legiones* met the Viromandui. With steady advances, we pushed them back as well, but not across the Sabis. It was here that Caesar nearly lost the battle.

"As our center advanced, a gap appeared between the center and our right, which is where our Seventh *Legio* was fighting. The Seventh and Twelfth *Legiones* were attacked by the largest force, the Nervii, who poured through the gap like water. We were nearly overrun. The Seventh and Twelfth *Legiones* were cut off and became surrounded. The Nervii captured our camp as well.

"The Twelfth *Legio* was so pressed that our men were squeezed shoulder to shoulder. They no longer could fight effectively and the battle became desperate. This is the point when Caesar saved the battle.

"The Twelfth had lost nearly every *centurio* including the *primus pilus*, Publius Sextius Baculus. Caesar seized a shield from a legionnaire toward the rear and joined the front ranks. He gave orders to have them spread out to give themselves room to swing their *gladii*. He brought courage with him, and the panic subsided.

"As he held the line against the Nervii, he ordered that the remnants of the Twelfth should join together with the Seventh *Legio* to form square. They were able to do this with some difficulty, and afterwards the Nervii broke on our formation like water upon the rocks.

"It was at this point that two wonderful things happened that secured our victory. *Legati* Titus Labienus saw our distress from across the field of battle. He immediately commanded his Tenth *Legio* to turn back from sacking the Belgae camp across the river, and came to the rescue of our right wing. Soon after, the Thirteenth and Fourteenth *Legiones* that had been trailing the baggage train arrived to support him.

"With these new reinforcements, Caesar was able to encircle the surviving Nervii and killed them almost to the last man. I have heard that out of sixty thousand Nervii, only half a thousand survived.

"The battle was successful, but our losses were immense. Over half the Seventh *Legio* has fallen."

Guiamo was clearly worried about his friend, "Have you news of Ursius?"

Gabinius replied confidently, "Ursius travels with the baggage train and did not arrive until this battle had turned in our favor. There never really was much opportunity for his dogs to fight, for the Nervii were encircled already, and the other tribes had crossed the river beyond the dogs' reach. Ursius is safe, though I suspect he is quite disappointed in having missed the battle altogether."

Gabinius led Guiamo back to the house for a drink of water. As they entered the doorway, Gabinius cautioned, "Again, I tell you, speak no words of this to anyone. Our governor, though victorious, will have great difficulty persuading everyone so through the laments which will be heard from so many homes. Twelve sons of *senatoris* were killed and their deaths will not go unanswered. Caesar will find he has few supporters in Rome. Victories like this can prove a sure path to a recall from Rome and a career in ignominy."

On the morning of the eighth day of *Quintilis*, Gabinius came into the *tablinum* to fetch Guiamo as his reading practice with Sertorius was ending. "Guiamo, there has been another battle." Sertorius and Guiamo both turned to listen. "Do not worry. Caesar won this battle, too.

"There is a tribe called the Aduatuci who had intended to aid Boduognatus in the battle at the river Sabis we heard about six days ago, but their arrival was delayed. About the time we heard of our victory over the Nervii, the Aduatuci also heard of their defeat. To avoid our *legiones*, they moved upstream seeking sanctuary in a fortified city situated where the Sabis joins the river Mosa.

"We engaged them in skirmishes and were repelled, but without relent continued our advance until we pressed at their gates. Our men threw up a wall encircling their *oppidum*. They saw our *legiones* in strength, and were not afraid. They saw us constructing a tower at a safe distance, but thought it too far away to be effective. How they laughed from within the safety of their walls. But when our tower was moved forward on a ramp, they realized we could have the city if we forced it.

"Their legs became weak and their courage fled. Within hours, they sent men to negotiate a settlement of peace. Caesar agreed to generous terms provided they turn over their weapons. The Aduatuci had a chance for an honorable settlement, but they tried to concoct a clever way out. They claimed to be afraid of the neighboring tribes, so said they were reluctant to turn over their weapons to Caesar. Our governor saw this was a ruse, for the neighboring tribes were subdued, so he forestalled their objections in the guise of graciously offering to protect the Aduatuci from harm once they were disarmed. The Aduatuci knew they had been outfoxed, and reluctantly conceded. Under the guise of avoiding strife and looting of the Aduatuci, Caesar also promised to remove any Romans sent into their *oppidum* after the surrender. In actuality, he wanted his men safely away when the Aduatuci moved to escape.

"They turned over many weapons, but secretly withheld a large store. In the middle of the night, they swarmed out of the *oppidum* and attacked. Caesar's men were lying in wait and fought viciously, killing four thousand as they struggled unsuccessfully to break through our wall. When escape was no longer possible, they fled back into the *oppidum*. When morning came, there was no fight left in them. We simply smashed their gates and entered.

"In normal situations, Caesar has proven himself generous to his enemies, but he was furious at their deceit. When he had finished taking the *oppidum*, he had all the Aduatuci sold into slavery. The single buyer, it is said, purchased over fifty thousand men.

"Now this slave merchant has moved many of these men to Lugdunum for resale. I have need to purchase a slave, so we shall be traveling to Lugdunum to search him out."

Guiamo was confused. "Why travel all the way to Lugdunum? Surely there are others available locally."

Gabinius replied, "Guiamo, I have need of a certain type of slave, the type that cannot be found here, so we go to Lugdunum tomorrow. I have hopes to find what I need there among that rabble."

Six days they traveled to Lugdunum, arriving on the fourteenth day of *Quintilis* to the sweltering markets teeming with jostling crowds, rolling carts, vendor stalls manned by shouting merchants and hucksters. The streets were filled with poor farmers, arrogant priests, destitute beggars in rags, proud nobles, thieves, squawking chickens and busy servants going about their daily work. Amateur oracles conned the unwary with ecstatic visions mixed with the exotic aromas of smoldering incense.

Guided by Gabinius, Guiamo and the two servants threaded their way to the center of the crowded market where statues of the gods had been placed around a circular pool of water. In the center of the pool stood a marble statue of Jupiter Olympus. All the sculptures were painted in vibrant colors, giving them a most realistic appearance, though the pigeons had left them in need of a cleansing wash.

Gabinius led them to the east to the entrance of a great temple where they paused to look at the impressive painted carvings on the pedimental triangle above the six-columned portico.

"We must see this temple to Mars. Surely you remember the words of the oracle," stated Gabinius.

"Of course, I remember," replied Guiamo. "You think I am the 'son of Mars.' "

"Perhaps Mars may speak to you here today," cautioned Gabinius.

Gabinius led Guiamo, Sertorius and Ulleria through the bustling crowd and up the twelve steps which spread across the entire front of the temple. Guiamo guessed the temple to be ten *passuum* wide. He walked to the left side of the porch to see more fully the building's design. It looked to be a building of marble walls, outside of which was an encirclement of crafted stone colonnades identical to those of the portico at the front, and about fifteen *passuum* long.

Gabinius turned to look around the portico and was nearly knocked off balance by a number of priests who ran out shouting excitedly and calling for the *augur*. Sertorius saw first what they were agitated about as they pointed toward the sky. An eagle was soaring serenely overhead. Guiamo walked back to Gabinius, Ulleria and Sertorius and together they gazed for a while as the great bird floated effortlessly across the city.

"They get so excited about the calls of birds, which way they are going and if they are accompanied by other birds," said Sertorius. "I do not know what to make of it all."

"Who are you speaking of?" asked Guiamo, not understanding.

"The *Flamines Martialis*, those priests of Mars you saw running past as geese when the fox is about," Sertorius replied.

Ulleria became upset with Sertorius' flippant comments. "Be respectful, Sertori. They are men chosen of the gods."

"Men chosen by men to serve the gods, you should say. By the looks of their fat bellies, I should think they wanted this honor simply as a sure means to fill their gullet. It is a much easier path to riches and good food than honest work," Sertorius snorted.

"Sertori!" Ulleria hissed in dismay. "For such disrespect, the god will surely strike you down with a bolt of lightning!"

Sertorius said, "Among so many fat men, I should hope he has good aim," and he roared in laughter.

Gabinius laughed quietly behind a hand raised to hide his enjoyment of their spat, but finally choked down his mirth enough to say soothingly, "That's enough, you two."

Guiamo watched the priests pointing out the direction of the eagle's flight and their frustrated efforts to determine its meaning. They were clearly disputing among themselves.

Gabinius said, "The gods speak in many ways. Our priests seem to know how to interpret them, though I have seen that some of them may disagree to the point of blows."

An older priest, senior to the others, came out to see the bird aloft. Gabinius pointed him out to Guiamo and said, "This one is the *augur*. He will 'take the *auspiciis*' and decide the meaning of this event. This could take some time and I have not the patience to wait. In the meantime, we should visit the temple."

Gabinius led the three into the building through two massive doors. The silence within the walls was profound, but Guiamo found it wonderfully serene rather than stifling or oppressive. Guiamo saw a solitary structure in the center, a small building, and before it stood a stone table. On the table he saw a sword, quite a few coins, and two small statues.

Gabinius said, "The room you see before you is called the *cella*. This is where you will find the image of Mars, the god of war. The plinth table in front of the *cella* is where the people are to place their offerings. People will give money, votive statues, and weapons."

Gabinius strode forward to the plinth table and placed a dozen silver *denarii* upon it, and then motioned for Guiamo to do likewise. "Place a few coins here," he said.

Fumbling for his purse, Guiamo grasped the first three coins he found and placed them upon the table. To his dismay, he saw they were gold *aurei*. He was too self-conscious to exchange them for silver, so left them as they lay.

A priest had been watching the four to be sure that none of the gifts given by others earlier in the day were being stolen. As Guiamo's hand revealed the three gold coins, the priest walked briskly over. He smiled greedily and said,

134

"You are most generous to the great god. Mars shall surely smile on you today."

Gabinius took Guiamo alone with him into the *cella* where the image of Mars was placed. It was carved of wood and painted in vibrant colors. He stood naked with one foot upon a fallen enemy, holding a spear triumphantly in his outstretched arm. He carried a shield and wore a bronze helmet in the style of Corinth.

Gabinius stood respectfully and bowed with his right hand on his heart and the left lifted up in supplication. He quietly offered up a prayer of protection for them all during their trip. Guiamo felt out of place and hesitated from offering up his own prayer. Gabinius saw his embarrassment, and without comment, led him back out of the *cella*.

Gabinius took the three around the perimeter wall of the temple, showing them the beautiful stone carvings of the heroes of old battling the classical enemies of Rome. He explained each of the battles to Guiamo who was completely captivated, and listened with rapt attention. Sertorius knew the stories well, so lingered behind with Ulleria who clearly had no interest in history whatsoever.

When they came to the back of the temple, a very old man with a wooden staff exited the *adytum*, a small chamber behind the *cella*. Gabinius recognized his garments and hat. "That old man is the *pontifices*. He is the chief priest in this temple to Mars," he said to Guiamo.

The *pontifices* glanced at the four visitors and then paused as he looked intently at Guiamo. Gabinius found it a little unsettling and kept them walking to the far wall where he continued his history lessons. He noticed that as they slowly made their way to the entrance, the *pontifices* kept staring curiously at the boy.

As they exited the building, Guiamo lingered behind to look again at the *cella*. Gabinius, Sertorius and Ulleria had nearly crossed the portico to the steps when Guiamo finally stepped out of the temple into the sunlight.

Just at that moment, the eagle swooped down out of the southeastern sky and lighted upon the uppermost branch of an ancient tree just to the side of the forum. The brilliant sunlight shining on the eagle cast a shadow directly onto the temple doorway just as Guiamo stepped forward through it. As Guiamo emerged, the eagle spread its wings and screamed into the morning air.

While the *flamines* yelled eagerly about the eagle landing so closely, the *augur* alone knew what to look for. He turned quickly to see where the shadow was cast, and saw Guiamo in the doorway. The *augur* shouted loudly to the *flamines* and pointed at Guiamo. The priests ran to surround the boy.

Gabinius saw the rush and hurried back to the temple doorway to secure Guiamo from the crowding rush of the younger priests who were overly eager to please the *augur*.

The boy was confused by the sudden crush of shouting priestly bodies, but Guiamo calmly stood his ground. He realized that he was not being attacked, and was being treated more as a great prize.

Gabinius elbowed his way into the tight circle of triumphant *flamines* and boldly pushed them back into a larger circle. "Hold, I say!" he roared, and the *flamines* fell silent. "Why detain you this boy unjustly?"

The *augur* gently pressed his way through the excited young priests and motioned for all to remain silent. Ignoring Gabinius' commanding stance, he looked first at Guiamo. Then he spoke gently to all. "Today I have seen a most auspicious sight, of such import that few have been so urgently counseled by the gods. We must take this boy inside to see the *pontifices*."

Once Gabinius saw that Guiamo was not in danger, he conceded to the wishes of the *augur*.

The boisterous crowd moved into the temple hall where the *pontifices* was already hurrying to the disturbance at the doorway.

The *augur* hurried forward to greet the *pontifices*. Breathless with excitement, he said, "A great sign has been given this day about this boy!"

"Tell me what you saw and divine its meaning," commanded the *pontifices*.

"I saw a great eagle circling the city. It descended and landed in a tree. At that moment, it cast its shadow upon the temple doorway just as this boy emerged. The eagle screamed and spread its wings," said the *augur* excitedly.

"A great sign it is, indeed," said the *pontifices*. "What is its full meaning?"

The *augur* took a breath to calm himself and said, "The meaning is manyfold. The sign being an eagle shows the boy to become a great warrior. Its flight from the southeast tells that the boy will travel to the northwest. The eagle settling into a tree tells me that the boy will settle in that land. The shadow cast on the doorway to the temple shows me that he has the guidance of Mars. With spreading wings, the war god will enlarge his lands, and the screaming voice tells me of triumphant victory. This is the meaning of the portent."

The *pontifices* looked down at Guiamo and said, "He does not look like much, does he?"

Several of the *flamines* laughed a little too loudly.

"But then, Mars himself was once just a boy," said the *pontifices*, annoyed with the fawning priests.

The laughing abruptly stopped.

He looked back to the *augur* and said, "During my meditation and prayers early this morning in the *cella*, the image of Mars seemed to come to life, and the face of Mars turned to speak to me as man to man. He told me that a great one was coming to carry his strength to a new land.

"He said to me, 'Place my sacred spear into the hands of the great one.'

"I asked of him, 'Surely it must be kept here safely for all ages!'

" 'Nay,' said he. 'Only for a season have I placed it into thy keeping.'

The *flamines* murmured unhappily at the words of the elderly *pontifices*, and it was clear that they believed his mind had fallen into dotage. The *augur* became frustrated that the *flamines* were so clearly motivated by greed, and most did not have not a truly devout mind. Without the sacred spear to draw gifts to the temple, the *flamines* knew the supply of money would dwindle precipitously.

" 'How shall I know the great one?' I asked.

" 'The *augur* shall name him even yet today,' he replied, 'but say nothing to anyone until he is revealed. By this sign you will know him. He shall be the least to come into my holy temple, yet his offering shall be the greatest.'

"I see now that this boy is the one spoken of by Mars."

Turning to Guiamo, he spoke with command, "Come with me."

The *pontifices* put his arm upon Guiamo's shoulder to direct him, and they walked directly to the *cella*. After signaling that the other priests were to remain outside the *cella*, the two walked up to the image of Mars. Without fanfare, the *pontifices* reached up and grasped the spear. It came easily out of the painted wooden hands, and the *pontifices* said to Guiamo, "I do not understand the reasoning of my god Mars, but I certainly obey him." He put the sacred spear into Guiamo's hands and released it with only the faintest hesitation, but still with trembling fingers.

"This sacred spear is the very spear that Mars invented when living among us as a mortal in ages long past. This is the spear for which he was honored with godhood. What most people do not know is that Mars crafted his powers into the bronze spear point. If he shouted *"ibur"* it would hit whatever he threw it at, and if he cried *"athibar"* it would always return to his grasp.

"I know not your destiny, but Mars sees much. I see you shall have need of his spear to survive your ordeals to come. The spear's name is Lúin. He has a twin named Assal with the same powers, but he is lost in the mist of time."

Guiamo asked, "How did this temple in so remote a location come to have such a great treasure?"

The *pontifices* replied, "Some generations ago, it was stolen from a greater temple in Rome by the command of a corrupt *pontifices*. Even today, they do not know they have a replacement. The *flamines* and *augur* here know its worth, but not its powers. Only the *pontifices* is allowed to know its full story. Since you are taking the spear of Mars with you, I shall have to quickly put a replacement in the image's hands so that the masses will not know."

Concerned he was hearing only bits of a critically important discussion, Gabinius stepped forward silently into the *cella* to stand beside Guiamo. "Your gift confirms, and yet deepens, the mystery of the oracle sent to me from Nicaea."

"Speak to me of the oracle," asked the *pontifices*.

Gabinius quoted the oracle to the elderly *pontifices* who listened intently.

The *pontifices* replied, "Great destiny awaits this boy. He is covered by the guiding hand of Mars. Remember this," he advised, "someone will surely try to steal Lúin. If they should succeed, remember to call '*athibar*' and he will return to you."

The three walked quietly out of the *cella* to the anxious *flamines*. The *pontifices* commanded all the priests to stay within the temple hall so Guiamo could leave without attracting too much attention. The *pontifices* announced, "The will of Mars is that this spear be given to the boy. We are all bound by a vow of eternal silence on this matter. Whosoever objects must say so now."

His challenge was met with silence, for all knew an objection would result in expulsion from the order of priests.

Turning to Guiamo he asked, "Before you go, tell me, then, your name."

Guiamo answered, "Guiamo Durmius Stolo."

"Then go with peace, Durmi, for surely the strife of battle awaits you in years to come," the *pontifices* said in parting.

Gabinius put his arm around Guiamo and led him out of the temple hall. Guiamo felt very self-conscious and small carrying such a valued treasure, but walked with confident steps knowing it truly was meant for him.

As they exited the temple, Sertorius and Ulleria quickly found them.

"What happened in there?" Sertorius asked curiously.

Gabinius replied, "Nothing of consequence. It seems Guiamo gave such a large offering that they generously gave him this old spear in return." Gabinius winked at Guiamo, while Sertorius looked at Guiamo suspiciously.

Ulleria was simply relieved that her time to shop was no longer being delayed, and she quickly turned her attention to the exciting throngs milling through the streets. For her, the attraction of the market was the wares of the merchants, and all the noise, confusion, and odors foul or savory simply added to the flavor of excitement for the day's outing.

Ulleria was delighted with the opportunity to buy fabrics and foods unavailable in the markets around Gobedbiacum, but Gabinius clearly saw the fear she felt for her safety. "Sertori, I am taking Guiamo to the docks. Stay with Ulleria today, and protect her. We shall meet you at the inn for supper," he said.

They parted and Gabinius led Guiamo through the alleys toward the river knowing that he docks were where the slave sales were conducted. "I am looking to buy a slave today, but not a strong-back," Gabinius said to the boy. "I need a slave who is very special.

The docks were filled with cargo ships busy disembarking lines of dirty, downcast slaves, chained, their blond, brown and red hair matted and filthy. Their eyes betrayed their fears, flitting back and forth at any perceived threat. The first belligerent few who defied their handlers were dragged before the slave lines and unceremoniously executed with a *gladius* thrust into their bowels. The excruciating pain lasted long, and they were left to thrash about in agony as they slowly bled out. The bodies were displayed openly for all to see. None resisted after that. With heads bowed and shoulders slumped in resignation, they shuffled in lines to be sold in groups to the waiting wealthy *patricii*

Most would end up working to death deep in the iron mines of southern Gallia, or as galley slaves chained to their oars in the *Mare Nostrum*, the great sea around which the nations of the known world dwelt. The lucky ones would work as laborers on expansive farming estates or in cramped, smoke-filled workshops toiling alongside a skilled tradesman.

Gabinius searched out the chief agent of the slave sales. He was found in a shabbily made shanty arguing with a shipmaster over the disposal of the dead and dying.

Gabinius and Guiamo waited patiently for the two to finish. At long last, the shipmaster stormed off angrily, muttering under his breath and looking back in disgust.

Gabinius took on a pleasant tone and asked, "Pardon me, but I have a particular need."

"Yes?" replied the still agitated slave merchant. "Please be quick. I have more shiploads arriving this minute."

Gabinius spoke directly to the heart of the matter. "I need to purchase a slave who knows many languages."

"An interpreter, you say? Go out to the quay near that ship with the broken mast, and ask for Mandudagus. He can help you," said the slave merchant.

Gabinius thanked him and led Guiamo out to the wharf as directed. Mandudagus was easily spotted as he was obviously in charge, shouting commands at the slaves in their dialect. Gabinius strode directly up to him, his height and massive build commanding attention from all around.

Mandudagus stopped abruptly, looked up at the aging man and asked, "How may I assist you, my lord?"

Gabinius said evenly, "I seek to purchase a slave who can be an interpreter of many languages."

"Yes, my lord," Mandudagus replied. "Let me see what we have currently in inventory. Most all of our stock are illiterate and brutish. Few have value save for the virtue of their strength."

Mandudagus called over three Gallic assistants and quickly issued orders to them. Gabinius and Guiamo watched as the three men walked along the lines of slaves calling out in various languages and dialects. Occasionally a slave would raise a hand. These slaves were pulled out of line and led into a fenced corral apart from the masses.

A galley laden with more slaves rowed up against a pier and one of Mandudagus' assistants hurried over. He shouted loudly to the slaves in a variety of languages. One old man toward the back raised his hand. The assistant called him to come onto the pier. Once unchained, he crawled with great difficulty through the men and had to be lifted over the side by others. His right leg was totally limp, his left was crippled, and both bore scars from battles fought years before.

The assistant ordered two slaves to carry him to the corral.

Gabinius and Guiamo were led by Mandudagus to the corral and Gabinius began inspecting the men who now stood in an uneven line. Though defeated in battle and distraught with their helpless plight, they all eyed Gabinius curiously as he began the sorting process.

Guiamo stood quietly, carefully holding his spear, and counted thirty-seven men including the cripple who was carried in last.

Gabinius called out loudly in Latin for all who spoke the language of Rome to step forward. Sixteen men stepped forward, and the lame man pulled himself in line with them as well.

Gabinius dismissed the others who were then removed from the corral to be sent back to the chained lines. Gabinius then went down the row and asked each man what other languages they spoke. Most could speak only Latin and their mother tongue of the Aduatuci.

Gabinius found one muscular man who could speak several languages. He was pulled out of line apart from the rest. Gabinius continued down the line and finally arrived at the lame man. When Gabinius asked him what languages he could speak, he replied, "I speak many languages and dialects of Germania, Gallia as well as the tongue of Rome."

With a dismissive hand, Gabinius told Mandudagus that he might consider the lame one as well. Gabinius motioned that the rest of the slaves should be led back to the slave lines. Gabinius spoke to the two remaining slaves, asking about their accomplishments.

The first man was heavily muscled, with ragged brown hair that came halfway down his back. He was about twenty-five years old and bragged of his great daring in battle, that he had taken five heads which still hung outside the doorway of his home. He owned seven horses, and had two slaves of his own. Throughout, he bared his teeth as he spoke with jaw jutting, nostrils flaring, and head held high.

The cripple sat quietly as the younger man boasted. When he had finished, Gabinius turned to Mandudagus and asked, "How much do you ask for this great warrior?"

"Three hundred *denarii*," he replied.

Without comment, Gabinius turned to the old cripple and quietly asked him of his accomplishments. The old man spoke softly, so no one else could hear. "I am the neck that turned the head of my lord, King Lucotorgetorix."

Gabinius asked, "You were councilor to Lucotorgetorix?"

"Yes, my lord," replied the lame man. "For seventeen years I have guided him and represented him as ambassador and judge."

Gabinius raised his eyebrows in surprise. He glanced at Mandudagus who did not reveal any signs of interest in following the conversation. Gabinius asked, "Tell me of your legs."

The old man motioned at them with a wave of his hand. "No matter. They are just my legs. I lost the use of my legs serving my king some thirty years ago, but not my wits. There was once a time when my legs would carry me where I would go. Since that day of battle, it has been my mind and voice which have carried me to the council hall of my lord, King Lucotorgetorix."

"Did you advise him to fight with the Nervii against Rome?" asked Gabinius.

"Yes, my lord, for we wished to be free of the yoke of any man," he replied.

Gabinius probed further, "Did you counsel him to surrender the *oppidum*?"

"Yes, my lord, though I could not sway him against his plan to fight again in the night," the old man said.

Gabinius stood and returned to the young warrior who stood with pride and strength. "A fine specimen he is, indeed." He let the words of praise sink into Mandudagus' thoughts. "The only one to compete against this strong one is that old man, lame and dirty. That is not much of a choice."

With a mocking laugh, Gabinius said, "What price would a fool have to pay to rid you of him?"

"One hundred *denarii*" Mandudagus answered.

Gabinius acted visibly surprised, "So much? He is crippled, old and lazy." Gabinius ventured, "I will give you one hundred thirty *denarii* for the warrior."

Convinced that Gabinius desired to buy the young warrior, Mandudagus held close to his original price. "Two hundred eighty *denarii* and not one *as* less."

Gabinius sputtered out, "I cannot pay this amount, though he surely is worth it."

Mandudagus said derisively, "Then if you cannot afford him, perhaps you should buy the cripple and let me go back to my work."

Gabinius looked outraged, "Look at his hands. I see no calluses. None! He has done no work for years. This lout is a mouth to feed. Nothing more. Even a fool would not pay more than forty *denarii* for his miserable life." Dismissing the lame man with a wave of his hand, he said, "Sell me the warrior for one hundred fifty *denarii*. I implore you!"

Mandudagus laughed at Gabinius' plight and, pointing to the young warrior, sparred back. "If you cannot afford this choice, juicy grape, then you must settle for the raisin. In my market, raisins sell for fifty *denarii*."

Gabinius huffed angrily, pulled the fifty silver coins out of his purse, and with a frown, begrudgingly placed the coins in Mandudagus' outstretched hand.

Mandudagus spoke quickly to one of his helpers who set off at a run to obtain a means of transporting the crippled slave. He returned in short order with a wagon pulled by a dusty, aging donkey.

"I am sorry you had to settle for the lame man," said Guiamo as the slave was picked up by two of Mandudagus' helpers. Without any sign of gentleness, they placed him in the back of the hired wagon. "The younger slave would have been better."

Gabinius did not reply until the slave handlers had returned to their work on the quay. When they were safely beyond hearing, Gabinius said, " 'Settle for?' 'Settle for?'

Do you think I could not afford the warrior? Surely you know I could have purchased ten slaves at his price, but I never even wanted him."

Guiamo looked up in surprise. "But you argued so forcefully to bring his price down!"

"No, Guiamo, I argued to keep his price high. It was the lame one I wanted all along. Did you notice how his value to Mandudagus kept dropping lower and lower? I was arguing to reduce the cost of the lame man. The young man would be nothing but trouble for me. All my praise and argument was mere posturing to get a better price for the old man. The lame man has wisdom beyond mere knowledge of many tongues. Being counselor to a king means he was considered trustworthy. With him, I will not have to worry about having my throat slit in the night. I would not have taken the warrior if the slaver had paid me the three hundred *denarii*. Guiamo, do you not see? I have bought a premium slave at the lowest imaginable price."

The streets were busy with shouting merchants and animals burdened with tall packs tied precariously on their swaying backs. The delays were long as they threaded their way through the narrow streets back to the inn. Gabinius turned from the front of the hired wagon to speak to the old man. "I am Lucius Gabinius Malleolus. You shall call me *Dominus* Malleolus. What is your name?"

"Catocarogus is how I was called in the hall of my king. I was his 'fortune teller of battle,' as the name implies. It is a good name, though Suadusegus is the name given to me by my father," he replied.

"Then by which name do you prefer me to call you," asked Gabinius.

"I am no longer advisor to my king. I prefer to be named Suadusegus, *Dominus*."

Gabinius put his arm around Guiamo's shoulders and said, "This boy is my pupil. His name is Guiamo Durmius Stolo. You will call him Durmius.

"Your *praenomina* is Guiamo?" asked Suadusegus inquisitively. "That is a name from among the Bellovaci. Did you know this?"

Guiamo was intrigued. "No, though I know my mother's parents were from Gallia," replied Guiamo. "Guiamo was my grandfather's name."

"It is a good name," replied Suadusegus, deep in thought. "A good name."

Suadusegus turned to Gabinius and asked, "If it pleases my lord, *Dominus* Malleole, to what end have you bargained so effectively to purchase me?"

Guiamo listened intently, for he, too, was curious about this unusual slave.

Gabinius said, "I wish to have you teach young Guiamo here to speak the many tongues you know."

Suadusegus replied, "That I can do, my lord. I have acted as interpreter to King Lucotorgetorix in dealings with many tribes, and have even travelled to Rome on his behalf some years ago." With sarcasm drawn from the unpleasant memory of this ordeal, he said, "Forty blissful days sweating in a wagon pulled by an ox with diarrhea, and the merchant I was to meet proved too ill to see me." The memory almost made him blanche. Bringing himself back to the present, he said, "From what I heard of your haggling, I think my lord is very shrewd, though I must admit it was a most humbling experience when being referred to in such distasteful terms."

Gabinius said, "Shrewd? I suppose I am. I prefer to be described as wise, but in negotiation, shrewd will do. As a master of iron working, I prefer to be described as highly skilled. As an employer, generous; as a slave master, gentle.

"Let me tell you of your future. I am a man of great wealth and have earned it as a skilled blacksmith, a *negotiator gladiarius*. My estate is vast and I have nearly two hundred craftsmen and farmers in my employ. I have thirty-eight slaves, mostly tending the fields, orchards and vineyards. All are treated well.

"If you are dishonest, steal, cause me trouble, or are slothful, my response shall be the worst possible punishment

146

I can imagine. I shall not beat your or mistreat you in any way. I shall simply sell you. Think on this well.

"If, however, you are diligent in your work, are cooperative, and are honest in all things, your life will be blessed. I feed my people well, respecting them as the men and women they are. You will have a home of your own. You will be free to marry if you so choose.

"I am an old man and have seen much in my life, good and bad. I know what it is to work under the yoke of another man's whims. These lessons have taught me how to be the master I have desired to become. One lesson I learned is that a slave without hope makes for a poor servant. Therefore, your enslavement to me is not to be forever. I have stipulated in my will that all my slaves are to be freed upon my death. As old as I am, I should not expect it to be too many years."

Gabinius looked sideways at his new slave, "Do you already have a wife?"

"Yes, *Dominus* Malleole," the slave replied.

Gabinius was not surprised. "If you wish it, she may live as a free woman with you. I can send word to her if you desire it."

Suadusegus brightened considerably and said, "I desire it greatly, my lord. My four daughters are grown with children of their own. She will come."

Gabinius said, "Your typical duties will be to teach languages to Guiamo each morning after breakfast under the supervision of Sertorius, a slave in my house. Late morning the boy will be working in the smithy and you will be free from work until after the midday meal. Your afternoon work will be food preparation.

"You will need assistance moving around, so I will task Guiamo" he continued, patting the boy on the knee, "who you will find is quite inventive, with finding something useful to aid you."

Gabinius arrived back at the inn with Suadusegus and Guiamo before the others. They stayed the rest of the afternoon resting in their room. Gabinius and Suadusegus napped, and after putting his spear under his bed, Guiamo soon fell asleep as well.

After Sertorius returned to the inn with Ulleria, the four travelers and their one crippled slave sat down to eat a supper of bread, knuckles of pig, and a brothy fish and vegetable soup.

Ulleria opened the evening by showing off her purchases of fabric and hair decorations. With forced patience, the men agonized as she gave moment-by-moment, detailed descriptions of every hard-found purchase. Sertorius squirmed in his seat as Ulleria elaborated on each of the many items she had decided not to purchase. It was almost more than Sertorius could bear to listen when she elaborated on the intricacies of the latest in hair fashion. None of the men had any interest whatsoever in what she enthusiastically described, but Gabinius smiled graciously, listened and asked questions about her purchases and her day's outing. She was delighted.

When she had finished her long and detailed story, Sertorius audibly sighed in relief. Gabinius kicked him under the table and shot him a hard glance as a word to mind his manners with a lady. Fortunately, Ulleria had not noticed, and she smiled contentedly as she put away the many bolts of fabric and her other sundry purchases.

Conversation turned to Gabinius' single purchase who sat on the roughly made wooden bench at their table next to Sertorius. Gabinius introduced Suadusegus to his slaves, Sertorius and Ulleria who greeted him politely.

Much to Gabinius' embarrassment, Guiamo broke the rules of etiquette by speaking of Suadusegus' most prominent feature. Guiamo bluntly asked, "When you were counselor to King Lucotorgetorix how did you move from place to place without good legs?"

Suadusegus answered, "I had two slaves given me to carry my worthless carcass around. The best way was a board with great loops of rope on either end. Each slave would put a loop over his shoulder and I would sit on the board with my arms around them. It was a bit awkward going through doorways, but more dignified than being carried like a babe."

Gabinius interrupted Guiamo's further overly-blunt questions and said, "Suadusegus is here to help young Guiamo learn languages of the people who surround Gallia and Rome."

Sertorius was puzzled, "Why do you want him to learn languages?"

Gabinius bit into a chunk of pork and said, "I travel to the western coast of Gallia to negotiate with tin merchants and copper mongers about every third spring. I have always been at a disadvantage for I do not know their tongue. They speak the language of Rome, and can understand all that is said among my troupe, but I understand nothing of their private conversations. This they know, and use against me.

"However, if I brought Guiamo along with me, they would not know he could understand them. They speak their tongue openly, knowing I cannot understand them. If he could tell me their words, I could negotiate from a stronger position. Guiamo, you are to be my little spy."

Guiamo's eyes widened in surprise. Then he nodded in understanding and approval. "I am to go with you to the coast?"

Gabinius replied, "Of course, my boy. I also know how much fun a trip can be to a young boy. My grandfather took me to Athens when I was a lad. Such wonders to see! You will enjoy our trip which I anticipate will be next spring."

"So which language do you wish me to teach young Durmius?" asked Suadusegus.

"Eventually all you know, but the most pressing need is the three languages of Gallia. How well do you speak the tongue of the Aquitani?" asked Gabinius.

"Well enough, *Dominus*," he replied "to negotiate the release of the king's cousin who was captured with a raiding party on the near edge of the territory of the Tarbelli at the river Garumna."

"Excellent, but we shall begin with the languages of the Belgae," replied Gabinius.

The return trip proved uneventful, with Ulleria remaining happy throughout, sated with the delight of her many purchases. Sertorius barely endured her endless prattle which irritated him greatly. Gabinius drove the wagon in good humor with Guiamo by his side holding his spear. Suadusegus grew ever more content with his lot in life, looking forward to reestablishing his life in a home alongside his wife, though of humbler station.

The morning after they returned to Gobedbiacum, Gabinius came to Guiamo's *cubiculum* and told him, "Today, you will begin to learn the ways of Lúin. Dress and eat quickly and join me outside with your spear. Bring food enough for our midday meal."

In a quieter voice, he cautioned Guiamo, "Be careful always around others to treat him as just an ordinary spear obtained on the trip. You may show, however, that he is special to you, so that others leave him alone."

Gabinius stepped outside the *cubiculum* and left Guiamo to dress.

When Guiamo was finished with eating and preparing for the day out, he retrieved Lúin from his *cubiculum* and walked out into the sunshine to find Gabinius.

Gabinius took Guiamo far afield where the land was unplowed and open meadow. Setting their supplies on the ground, Gabinius took Lúin from Guiamo. He carried the spear ten *passuum* across the field and set him down in the tall grass. He returned to Guiamo and said, "Say the word to retrieve Lúin."

"*Athibar*," said Guiamo.

The spear lay on the ground unaffected. Guiamo looked profoundly disappointed.

"Say it with command as the *pontifices* instructed you," said Gabinius.

"*Athibar!*" shouted Guiamo.

Lúin rose vertically from the grass and turned to point at Guiamo. With a smooth motion, it glided directly at the boy. Guiamo flinched in fear and raised his arms to deflect the spear. But rather than knocking the spear away, Guiamo felt Lúin moving to nestle into his hands.

150

With a shocked look on his face, Gabinius stepped forward to congratulate Guiamo. "The *pontifices* was correct!" he said in amazement. "This is truly the spear of Mars. Though I knew he spoke with the truth as he knew it, I harbored doubt in my heart that he was simply mistaken. Now we know the truth. This is Lúin of a certainty!"

Guiamo shuddered with excitement and said, "Let us practice again!"

Gabinius took Lúin out farther and farther with each successive try, and he returned through the air with each cry of "*athibar.*" Even a commanding whisper traveled through the air to reach Lúin.

Guiamo could feel Lúin enjoying the practice. Lúin seemed eager to return at Guiamo's call, and the two bonded more with each passing hour.

Gabinius stuck the bronze spear tip into the ground, and still Lúin returned. He tried hiding the spear behind a tree or under stacks of wood. Lúin spun around the tree and out from under the heavy weight effortlessly.

Once as Gabinius carried Lúin into a nearby stand of woods, Guiamo teased him by calling "*athibar*" early. A frowning Gabinius walked back out of the woods empty-handed to see Guiamo clutching the spear, laughing and running to return it to his teacher.

Guiamo soon lost his fear of his spear, and boldly held out his hands. He learned he did not have to catch the spear, but that Lúin would come to him.

When Guiamo's confidence had grown, Gabinius told him, "It is time to learn to throw Lúin."

Guiamo asked, "What should be my target."

Gabinius replied, "You have learned that Lúin can be called from great distances. Let us try his skill at a target at a far distance. Throw him at the dead tree on the edge of yonder wood."

Guiamo saw that the broken, lifeless tree was well beyond bowshot, but chose it in his mind. As he threw the spear, he cried, "*Ibur!*"

Lúin gained speed beyond that given by Guiamo and raced in a great arc of his own choosing. With a mighty thud, he pierced fully through the trunk and rested there.

Gabinius said, "My aging eyes have lost sight of Lúin. How well did he fly?"

Guiamo said, "He hit it straight and true! I saw him strike and the tree shook mightily from the blow!"

Gabinius said, "Then call him back."

With a shout of joy, Guiamo cried, "*Athibar!*"

Lúin moved immediately out of the trunk and flew back to rest in Guiamo's palms.

For the next two hours, Guiamo selected targets for Lúin. Guiamo could feel Lúin's love for him grow, and they both exercised joyfully in the sun while Gabinius sat in amazement, eating his meal of bread, cheese and water.

In the late afternoon, Gabinius guided Guiamo back to his home.

"Lúin is a mighty weapon, Guiamo, but you must never forget to practice diligently with regular weapons," cautioned Gabinius, "or on the day of battle, you may find your skills insufficient to meet the foe."

It only took eleven days and little convincing for Suadusegus' wife to return. On the twentieth day of *Quintilis*, Gabinius sent Salonius on a wagon to find Suadusegus' village near Aduatuca.

On Gabinius' advice to send a token of good faith, Suadusegus had pulled a necklace from around his neck. It bore a protective amulet carved from a red stone. "Give this to my wife, Susama, and say 'Suadusegus asks you to join him. All is well.' Demand nothing of her, but await her answer. Tell her nothing more. If I know her well, and I do, she will agree. Show her courtesy, for she is well respected and none will allow her to suffer maltreatment."

Guiamo had asked, "Why do you trouble yourself to fetch a slave's wife?"

Gabinius replied, "He will be more amenable to settling in to his new life if his wife is here with him. It is a great hardship to be parted from family, and I would not require that of any man."

Mid-afternoon of the first day of *Sextilis*, Ulleria sighted the caravan kicking up dust on the pathway leading up from Gobedbiacum. She walked over to Gabinius' private smithy to give him the news that merchants were coming.

He stood at his front door to watch the four wagons roll toward the house. To his surprise, he saw that the lead wagon was driven by Salonius. Seated next to him rode a young woman in her mid-twenties. On each of the other three wagons rode two women of similar age, though the rider on the second wagon was in her late fifties. Each of the wagons was piled high with wooden crates, barrels, two-handled clay *amphorae* jars filled with wine, rolls of tapestries, and large and small pieces of furniture.

As Salonius drove his wagon up to stop in front of Gabinius, he shrugged his shoulders wistfully and jumped to the ground. "I have brought the wife of Suadusegus as you instructed me. One wagon was not enough."

"So it would seem," replied Gabinius as he shook his head incredulously at the tremendous amount of goods she had brought with her. He let his thoughts drift away with a sigh, "Women..."

Gabinius strode over to the second wagon to greet the stately lady who sat calmly with head held high. The fabric of her clothing was of elaborate pattern of red, white and the rare purple of the spiny sea snail. The edges were trimmed with gold thread to match the golden slippers upon her feet. Her sleeves were full, nearly covering the back of her hands. In her reddish hair were golden combs and around her neck was a golden collar inset with red rubies. On the index finger on her right hand, she wore a golden ring.

Sertorius and Ulleria came out of the house to stand beside Salonius. Gabinius turned to Sertorius and said, "Sertori, fetch Guiamo and Suadusegus." Gabinius held out his hand to the lady to assist her off the wagon. She stepped carefully to the ground and waited for Gabinius to introduce himself.

"My lady," he said, "I am Lucius Gabinius Malleolus. I am he who sent for you on behalf of your husband, Suadusegus. I hope your journey was pleasant. Your safe arrival is a delight, to be sure."

She nodded courteously and replied, "My lord, Malleole, I thank you for your gracious invitation to join my husband in exile. I pray that my presence will not inconvenience you."

"Your prayers have been answered in full, I assure you," Gabinius replied. "I have sent for Suadusegus."

She glanced to her left in the direction Gabinius pointed, and saw the astonishing sight of her husband sitting stiffly in a chair which glided unnaturally through the grass. As they moved closer, her confusion at this mystery dissipated when she saw that the chair had been cleverly fitted with four wheels, each two spans across, and her husband was being pushed from behind by a young boy. Though the clumps of grass and rocks caused it to bump along unevenly, it moved quickly and without too much effort.

"Susama! Susama! You have come to me! May the gods be praised!" cried Suadusegus when he recognized his wife among the crowd by the wagons.

"And may the gods be praised that you survived to call for me," she replied as he drew near. She knelt before Suadusegus who leaned forward to embrace and kiss her. "My dear Susama, how I have missed you," he whispered, and their tears fell as they wept with joy together.

"And I, you," she replied, stroking the hair on the back of his head. "Now we shall be together again, my love."

He released her gently and she stepped to his side. Her hands touched the chair and she looked inquisitively at it.

"What is this chair with wheels you ride upon? How came you by it?" she asked.

"This brilliant boy, Guiamo Durmius Stolo, has built this for me. Is it not a marvelous thing? Would that I had owned it these past thirty years. See here where my feet rest upon this board to keep them from dragging in the dirt," replied Suadusegus as he pointed to his feet. "Is it not a wonder?"

154

She turned to Gabinius and said, "A blessing of the gods be upon you, lord, for the generosity you have shown to us this day."

Gabinius nodded graciously and said, "Your quarters with Suadusegus, while of humble station, will prove dry, warm and secure. You will be free, of course, to have additional rooms constructed as your finances allow."

Gabinius instructed Sertorius to show her maidservants where to take the four wagons. He also told Salonius to organize a team of men to begin construction of servants' quarters to house the young women. "And put a lock on their door with a strong crossbar." With a wink at his hunt master, he added, "We cannot have our craftsmen bringing kisses to these lovely ladies unannounced in the night, now, can we?"

When the evening meal was completed, Suadusegus was excused from work duties for the remainder of the day. As Guiamo returned him to his small home, he saw that Susama's maidservants were being housed temporarily in a hastily converted workshop. They worked busily unloading the many supplies that filled the wagons, and Guiamo realized that not everything would fit inside.

Suadusegus found his wife waiting silently for him sitting in his house on an elegantly carved chair. The abundance of possessions befitting a noblewoman were out of place in the humble mud and wattle structure built by Gabinius' craftsmen, but Guiamo said nothing. He quietly helped Suadusegus onto an equally ornate reclining bench placed closely to her chair so that husband and wife could speak intimately together.

"What remains of the Aduatuci?" asked Suadusegus after Guiamo left.

"Tears and hardship," replied Susama. "The children have no fathers, the women, no husbands, and the fields, too few workers. Many fear the coming winter, for food will be in short supply.

"It is in some ways very difficult to leave our people during this time of sorrow, but in truth, it is good to be away from such overwhelming misery. I rejoice to be with you, my husband, knowing our daughters and their children are well. Valena's husband, Lugucumbus was sold into slavery, but I have sent many of the older men to search him out. If he can be found, he will be redeemed from his master regardless the cost."

"That is good," said Suadusegus. "He is a good man. I suspect that his tall height and balding red hair will make him easier to find. If he is sold as an oarsman on a merchant vessel, though, we shall never see him again."

Susama looked into her husband's eyes and asked, "And what price did Malleolus pay for your life?"

Suadusegus did not know whether to laugh or hang his head from embarrassment. He said quietly, "Fifty *denarii*. It was only fifty."

Susama was surprised, and turned her face away in sadness. "Such a paltry sum for so dear a part of my life." With a sorrowful look, she said, "Tomorrow I shall pay Malleolus five hundred *denarii* for your freedom."

Suadusegus replied, "I have thought long of this during the nights, and I have decided that, while you could buy my freedom, you must not." He touched her chin gently and turned her face to him. "You have already said that the land of our people is now a desolate place. There can be no joy of life there for a generation. I could be freed, but even then, the hand of Rome will be upon our throats. Freedom, true freedom as our grandsires knew, is forever gone. Rome dominates all.

"Purchasing my freedom shall grant no joy to me. Here, though a slave, I am held in honor as a teacher to Durmius. To be a slave in this place bears no shame. In the ancient days of Greece, honored Aesop the story maker was also a slave. Malleolus treats me far better than did King Lucotorgetorix, and I have no desire to serve the brat he calls cousin who surely will succeed him. I am at peace. I eat well, my work is easy, and you are here with me. The day will come when Malleolus dies and I shall be free again. Until then, save your money, dear one. Use it to live well with me here."

Six days later, as Suadusegus completed Guiamo's daily language lesson in the pasture, Guiamo asked, "What does a counselor to a king say and do that is different and more valuable than the other courtiers?"

Suadusegus looked sideways at him in surprise. "What an astute question! It is far better than a simple 'what did you do as a king's counselor?' I see you seek wisdom rather than mere information.

"Let me spend part of each day's lessons on how to be a wise counselor to a king. Much of what I will teach you will be less what to say to your king than when to speak and how to phrase it. Every bit as important is when to be present.

"I once saved our king an embarrassing defeat by simply not being present at his council of war. I know my voice would be shouted down by his generals, but I also knew Lucotorgetorix would not decide without hearing my blessing. When the war council broke up undecided, as I knew it must, Lucotorgetorix came to my chambers privately. There in the quiet of my study, my reasoning was heard in full and uninterrupted. I prevailed.

"Remember this, Durmi. A king's summons must sometimes be disregarded for the greater good, but he must always, in the end, see your actions as in his best interest. He will thereby indulge the unpredictable behavior your duties will require.

"Your opinion must be a prize the king does not control. He must come asking of you for your wisdom to be useful to him. Your erratic behavior sets you apart from the rest, and above them.

"If you are common in behavior, your advice will be given only common consideration. You must be eccentric, occasionally defiant, always unpredictable. A king may use a fart as his answer when ambassadors from a rival king present charges against him, but a king's counselor must never demean himself.

"Under most circumstances, the king's counselor must not speak to those in the king's court, but to the kings ears alone. Above all, the courtiers must learn to respect, even fear the counselor.

"Never say the obvious unless everyone refuses to speak it. And if you do name it, you must also tell the solution to its riddle. Otherwise, be silent.

"Tomorrow we shall practice these lessons."

The next morning, Guiamo enjoyed his time of reading with Sertorius after an early breakfast of *puls* porridge, for several *voluminis* of philosophers and historians had recently been borrowed from Aulus Geminius Barbatus, a priest of the war god Mars, who had moved to the encampment to serve alongside the Seventh *Legio* which was still afield near the land of the Aduatuci. Guiamo opened each one carefully to discover what he could, and found much to his liking. The priest collected writings mostly of the methods of warfare and the philosophy of conflict between nations.

After his time of reading had passed, he worked with Suadusegus with language instruction. It came easily, for he had an excellent memory, but Guiamo enjoyed most the short daily lessons of the art of counseling a king. Suadusegus also relished this time, for it spoke of the joy of his life's work. With Guiamo posing as king, Suadusegus demonstrated how best for the counselor to enter and stand before his king. He showed the boy where to stand and how to place his feet and position his hands in a dignified manner. Suadusegus also taught him to nod in recognition to the king but never bow as others.

Guiamo was beginning to tire of his metal working sessions with Gabinius' craftsmen which followed, but put in his best effort to learn diligently. His assignment for the day was to affix the individual pieces together to make *pila*, which he found a tedious task. He much preferred working with glowing hot metal.

Lunch came later than he liked, and he ate ravenously, though he still did not like the spiced plum sauce on his fish. As usual, he had several helpings and took a roll of bread with him when he hurried out to his next assignment.

For the rest of the afternoon, Guiamo spent much time working through a regimen of strenuous exercises followed by weapons training. By late afternoon, his arms were thoroughly worn out from repeated and rapid volleys throwing *pila* at long distance targets.

He was pleased when Gabinius came by to give him instruction on battle strategies, and taught how commanders of Roman *legiones* used couriers, drums and horns to relay their commands during the tumult of combat.

Gabinius drew battle formations in the dirt along with terrain details, and drilled Guiamo in what each opposing general knew of the other's strengths and positions. He then played out the battles with Guiamo serving as rival general. Gabinius always had a surprise in store for Guiamo, such as cavalry hidden in the woods or spies in his camp, which threw him off balance, but Guiamo fared better than Gabinius expected. Guiamo quickly learned to look for the unexpected, and used his scouts to good advantage, frequently discovering Gabinius' surprises.

Supper was supplied by Salonius, who had killed a young wild sow in the forest down by the river. Gabinius ate enthusiastically and was in a good mood, telling funny stories of days gone by. When supper was finished, Guiamo excused himself and searched out Suadusegus.

He found the lame slave sitting with Susama and watching the sun setting behind the wooded hills. He realized he was intruding on their solitude and turned to leave.

Suadusegus saw Guiamo change directions awkwardly and called him over. "Durmi! Come here. Is this not a beautiful evening? Come join us."

Guiamo stopped and then turned back to join the relaxing couple. "Yes, it is a wonderfully quiet evening. I did not mean to intrude," he answered.

"No trouble, my boy. Did you have anything in particular you wished to discuss?" Suadusegus asked.

"I so enjoyed our discussion today about the king's counselor, that I wanted to speak more of this with you tonight," said Guiamo.

"And so we shall," Suadusegus replied. Susama listened with great interest as her husband began to teach. "I have been thinking of something I taught you this morning which needs correction. I said earlier that the king must know that all your actions are in his best interest. This is only partly true. The wisest counselor, the most respected advisor must prove to his king that he holds one thing in greater regard than the king himself; truth. You alone will be his moral guiding light, to correct him when he strays.

"Your devotion to truth goes in several directions. First, you will guide him through webs of lies spun by others. Secondly, you will call him to account when he deals out falsehood to you. Also, the king cannot force you to join with his deceitful ploys. You are above that as the representative of truth. And lastly, you will impress on him the truth of his responsibilities to rule justly as king.

"The role the king plays in this world is a paradox. As a man, he must speak the truth always. As king, he must use deceit and lies to secure his country and confound his enemies. The best way for a king to rule is to always speak the truth plainly and without guile to both foe and neighbor, but skillfully wielding others to deceive when necessary. With truthful speaking, the king will be renown in far distant lands as a good king, but his discreet use of others for deceit will gather him fame as a wise and resourceful king.

"To all, the counselor must be enshrouded in a cloudy aura of mystery. You are not a general or friend. You are a sage. You will walk in the shadows, but not stalking like a fiend. No! You will tread quietly with head held high. You will have your own majesty, appearing in the light at the king's side as his rescuer in his time of trouble.

"I will teach you where to sit, how to stand. You will carry a staff which gives you the image of authority. You will always speak with command; with certainty. You will give your answers as precisely as a *gladius* thrust, not as merely one of the clamoring rabble begging for the king's attention. Keep your words few, and spend them solely on the king's ear, though all will hear, and this is to your gain. Answer only the important questions, and never bandy words with your lessers. Boldly rebuke your king's enemies on his behalf. Proclaim the solution, and hold the king's hall in silence with staff and arms boldly raised, if need be. Let this silence linger to dominate your rivals.

"Be absent from the king's presence when your critical advice is not needed, but always be available at a few paces in the shadows when it is. Enter into the king's presence at the pivotal point of the debates. Speak just before the time of decision is at hand.

"Since you will be absent frequently, you must develop reliable informants to provide you with critical information in order to know what is going on within your king's realm and without. Never reveal these sources and never give full explanation for your counsel for you must never reveal the chain links of your reasoning. Your knowledge of events in the world must astound those around the king. The mystery of your reasoning shall give you power."

Susama watched with delight as Guiamo absorbed her husband's teaching. She saw that he understood and took it deeply to heart. When Guiamo stood to go back to Gabinius' house, she laid her hand tenderly upon his and said, "Durmi, I see there is much wisdom in you, and you are worthy of my husband's teaching. I foresee your life will be challenging beyond measure. Your survival and rise in power depend upon the lessons my husband shall give you, and truly, the days are soon coming. Listen well."

Guiamo looked at her for a long time, and then nodded his thanks for her words. He turned quietly and walked back to Gabinius' house but found sleep would not come.

The next day, Gabinius and Guiamo walked quietly together between the rows of workshops in the cool of the evening. Guiamo's legs were sore, particularly his calves, from an extra long run that lasted most of the afternoon.

"Gabini, Suadusegus has told me of the people to the north where my name is known," Guiamo asked.

"Yes, I know the Bellovaci. They are a most populous nation. Babies everywhere! Some say the goddess Venus visits every home there in the springtime to bless each mother with a child," Gabinius replied.

"Do you think she really does this?" asked Guiamo.

"I suspect it has more to do with all the fathers not being killed off in battle on a regular basis," said Gabinius. "There is more to a nation's success than the spoils of war. For a people to become great, the population must increase, and to accomplish this, the fathers need to be at home with their wives. The leaders of the Bellovaci understand this, I suspect, and are farsighted in their thinking. More so than most peoples anyway. They did not grow to be such a great tribe by happenstance. They have learned to choose their battles very, very carefully, always weighing gold against blood."

Guiamo looked into Gabinius' eyes and said, "Gabini, I would like to visit the Bellovaci. It is possible I still have family there. My mother's father may still be alive. He was old, but not exceedingly so. Perhaps I have other kin as well. I should like to know them. Suadusegus has told me the region where they live, and Bratuspantium is not too far away from where the Seventh *Legio* is stationed. If you would be in agreement, I could visit with Ursius as well."

Gabinius had been expecting this question, and replied, "Well, I would counsel patience for the world is still in turmoil, but you certainly are not my servant. With some restrictions, you are free to come and go as you will. Has Suadusegus taught you well the tongue of the Bellovaci?" asked Gabinius. "You must be able to converse with them."

"He assures me that their dialect is similar to what he has taught me thus far. Some words will be strange to my ears, but I think I shall be able to understand them," said Guiamo.

"The Bellovaci have been allied with Rome since their submission at their capitol of Bratuspantium. The trade between Rome and the Bellovaci is beginning to grow and the roads are guarded. I think it would be safe enough for you to travel there, though I think Suadusegus should go with you. I do not want trouble for you in a strange land, and his skill with language and wise counsel could prove invaluable. Take his chair with wheels and I shall send Salonius as escort. When do you want to go?" asked Gabinius.

"Is tomorrow too soon? I am anxious to find my family," said Guiamo.

162

"Then spend the rest of today gathering your supplies. Tomorrow morning you three will go. Visit with Ursius also. A friend such as he is a friend for life," replied Gabinius.

Guiamo asked, "Should I take my spear, Lúin?"

Gabinius replied, "No, I think not. Your life's challenges will come later. Leave him here. Besides, the *legio* would not permit you to carry him within its walls. I shall miss you. I know you look to find your family, but I allow this trip conditionally. You must return to me, and before winter sets in."

The trip to see Ursius took longer than they anticipated, for the roads were poor and the frequent rains left mud everywhere. Throughout, Salonius proved an excellent guide. The abundance of rabbits along the trail supplemented their meals, and the time spent hunting rejuvenated their morale.

After fifteen days, the bedraggled travelers wordlessly drove their wagon to the gate of the temporary encampment. Guiamo jumped off the wagon and made steps toward the camp guards, but Salonius called, "Not yet, Durmi. We must first find a place to pitch the tent and a source of unspoiled water. Both horses need a field to graze, so let us first search it out."

Guiamo was clearly disappointed, but followed Salonius' lead. The horses of the Roman cavalry had overgrazed nearby, and the three had to search far down the road to find a suitable grazing field with clean water flowing nearby.

As the sun began to set, Guiamo realized he would have to wait until morning to meet with Ursius. The two young men worked together to set up the tent as Suadusegus prepared their supper.

The evening winds were faint, and the coolness that set in was welcome after the hot, dusty travel of the day. Salonius tied up the horses for the night, and then returned to the fire where Suadusegus began telling stories of heroes long ago before the Aduatuci came into the land they now called home.

Guiamo was surprised to see that he was not the first to rise that morning. Suadusegus was stirring under his blanket, but Salonius was already stoking the fire outside. He could see that Guiamo was impatient to go to the encampment. "We have the whole day, Durmi, and your friend Ursius must have time to rise and eat as well. Come. Sit beside me and eat your bread."

Guiamo sat as he was instructed and the two ate and talked of the day's plans. Suadusegus soon joined them, dragging himself along the ground, and they relaxed by the fire as the sun came fully up. All three wanted to meet Ursius, but Suadusegus preferred to tour the Roman camp and visit the market to the west of the camp. Salonius agreed to push his chair of wheels and look after the horses, so they agreed to meet back at the main gate in time for supper.

They set out in the wagon back to the Roman camp and, leaving the horses and wagon tied outside the gate, passed through the guard onto the *via praetoria*. It had been a long time since Guiamo had been to the *legio's* encampment near Gobedbiacum, and he was surprised to see that the *praefectus castrorum* had been transferred to this temporary camp at Agedincum.

The camp prefect recognized Guiamo as he walked toward the *praefectus castrorum*'s wooden building, and gave him a pleasant greeting. He looked at Salonius and then Suadusegus, who sat upon his unusual chair, with a curious eye. "Are these two your slaves?"

"Salonius is a free man, and Suadusegus is the slave of Gabinius," answered Guiamo.

The *praefectus castrorum* instructed Guiamo, "Suadusegus shall always be attended by you or Salonius while in the camp. You are responsible for him always."

Guiamo noticed that the encampment was laid out in the same pattern as the permanent camp near Gobedbiacum. He walked briskly toward where he expected to find the training field Ursius used for exercising his dogs.

As he drew closer, Guiamo saw eighteen young men, each controlling packs of five dogs held on leashes, running

164

inside the perimeter fence. Three men stood in the center of the field observing the exercise. The tallest was a *centurio*, another an *optio*, while the third had no apparent rank. The *optio* was pointing out one particular group of dogs to the *centurio*. The *centurio* said something and the *optio* responded by giving commands to the third man, who immediately sprinted over to the handler.

Guiamo came closer and saw that the *optio* was Ursius. As he passed through the gate, he had to dodge a pack of five large black war dogs. As they ran past, the young handler shouted, "You are not allowed in here!"

Guiamo stopped abruptly in surprise, but knowing his friend would want to see him, continued on. The *centurio* noticed Guiamo entering the field, and pointed him out to Ursius.

Ursius saw a young boy walking nonchalantly across his practice field, so he stormed off to chase the boy away.

As Ursius approached, he saw the boy raise his hand to wave. Instantly, Ursius recognized his friend. His angry marching changed to a sprint with delight and the two met, clasping forearms in friendship.

"Guiamo, you have traveled so far! I am so pleased to see you. Come, let me introduce you to my *centurio*, Gaius Cordius Libo. He is the *primus pilus*, and a very brave man. He saved our *cohors* in battle recently, and you know what they say, 'He who saves the *cohors*, saves the *legio*.'"

The two returned to the commanding officer who stood waiting for his *optio* to deal with the young intruder. As they drew near to the *centurio*, Ursius called out, "*Centurio* Libo, this is the dear friend of mine who used to visit every other market day. He is the one who gave me the knife."

Libo replied, "Ah, yes, you must be Durmi, the son of Stolo. I do remember seeing you working the dogs with Ursius. You are welcome indeed. In a few hours, we shall eat our noonday meal. Would you care to join us?"

"Most certainly, *Centurio* Libo," Guiamo replied gratefully.

"Good! Spend the rest of the morning with Ursius and I shall see you then," Libo said. Turning to Ursius he said,

"Continue your exercises with the new dogs as I instructed you earlier. They must learn to not fight each other so."

Excusing himself politely, the *centurio* left the two to return to his duties elsewhere.

Ursius was delighted to see his good friend and spoke eagerly in his enthusiasm, "You have grown taller, I see. Soon you shall be as tall as I. You look healthy, Guiamo. Malleolus feeds you well."

Patting Guiamo on his sinewy arms, he said, "And it looks as if Sertorius is having you exercise regularly. Your muscles are more developed. You are starting to have the look of a man rather than a boy. Your voice is deepening too!" Looking at Guiamo's face, he squinted his eyes and chided, "Is that a whisker I see on your chin?"

Guiamo blushed at Ursius' teasing for he knew his face had no beard hair, but his voice had been changing recently. He tried to control the pitch of his voice, but it was to no avail, for the embarrassing skips from high to low pitch were powerfully in play. Manhood was approaching and he was beginning to feel the awkwardness that came with this time of transition.

Guiamo was not about to let Ursius pummel him with his jokes. "No, no whiskers yet, though I am still far more handsome than you," he teased back. "I think you are beginning to look more like Laeleps, though your dog might be insulted if he knew I said so. It is a good thing you wear the helmet crest of an *optio* so *Centurio* Libo does not confuse the two of you."

Ursius laughed with Guiamo, and they walked together into the center of the practice field where Ursius called all his dog handlers in for instructions.

The morning went by quickly, with the boy and the *optio* thoroughly engrossed in training the dogs. Ursius was becoming comfortable with command, which had come as much of a surprise to himself as to Guiamo. Ursius was now charged with the responsibility of twenty-eight young men. He had twenty dog handlers, three hunters to gather meat, and five workers tasked with any job needing to be done, from cleaning after the dogs to running errands.

Soon enough, Ursius sent his men off for their noonday meal, and he led Guiamo to the officer's mess to dine with *Centurio* Libo.

They sat at a long wooden table in a tent of sewn leather skins. They sat upon cleverly designed wooden chairs that could be folded to be stored away when not needed. There was seating enough for sixty men, though only twelve were present for the noon meal.

Centurio Libo rose to greet Guiamo and Ursius. Calling attention from the other officers present, Libo introduced Guiamo as the son of *Primus Pilus* Stolo. The men all stepped forward to greet him. Guiamo was surprised at the heartfelt respect they had for him and for the memory of his dead father.

Servants brought hot loaves of bread with a roasted goose on a silver platter and wine was poured generously. From their reaction at seeing the bird, Guiamo perceived that meat on the table was a rare treat and that their regular fare was only marginally better than what the *milites gregarii* received.

As they ate heartily, *Centurio* Libo asked to see the matching knives Guiamo and Ursius carried. They set their knives on the table in front of him. Libo was clearly surprise at the striking similarity and approved how precisely the inscriptions had been carved. As he handed the knives back, he asked, "Durmi, what plans have you on your journey?"

Guiamo said, "After visiting with Ursius, I intend to travel north to the land of the Bellovaci. My mother was from this people. My hope is to find my grandfather, should he still be alive. I go first to the *oppidum* of Bratuspantium."

"You travel alone to that dark part of the world?" asked Libo in surprise.

"No, I have two companions. We should be safe enough if Rome guards the way as I have been told it does," Guiamo replied.

Centurio Libo frowned and said, "Rome has patrols out to secure the way, but danger still lurks in the shadows.

Some might say you are braver than you are smart. It is a dangerous path. I would warn the uninformed traveler to return home, but I must admit, if I were in your stead, as one looking for family, I would still chance the danger and continue on. My advice to you is to search out a Roman patrol, and travel near to them."

The *centurio* clapped Ursius on the back and said, "Ursius has proven to be quite an exceptional thinker, for did you know it was he who first brought to the *legio* this new way to employ dogs beyond mere watchers over the camp, but as dogs of war fighting in disciplined groups? Further, he also designed a very clever protective armor for them as well. It is most ingenious. Has he shown you his design? He is another Mars, it would seem. His insightful ideas have brought him respect within the *legio*, and outside, his fame grows. Already, several other *legiones* are copying Ursius' ideas, and detachments of 'Ursius dogs' are being trained for war. I particularly like his idea of using a flaming arrow to guide each pack of dogs to a particular area of the battlefield."

Ursius looked away awkwardly from Guiamo as the *centurio* praised him.

Guiamo smiled contentedly, knowing Ursius had benefitted from his ideas, but it gnawed a little at his heart in disappointment that Ursius had claimed these ideas as his own.

As the noon meal concluded, and the men all rose to return to duty, one veteran *centurio* paused long enough to caution Guiamo, "Be cautious of the Bellovaci. Kin they may be, but they are wary of outsiders. They will not hesitate to kill you if they believe you have come to spy out the land or are perceived as a threat."

Centurio Libo said, "When do you leave us?"

Guiamo answered, "I was hoping to stay a few days."

The *centurio* looked at Ursius and then replied to Guiamo, "I am afraid Ursius has been tasked to go afield tomorrow with his dogs for a seven day trip with three *cohortes*. You can wait for him here, but this assignment has been ordered already. I am sorry, Durmi, for you may not go with him."

Guiamo clearly looked disappointed, but decided to make the best of it. He said, "Then I shall enjoy each moment of our short time together all the more."

Centurio Libo left them, and Ursius led Guiamo back to his practice field.

Guiamo enjoyed seeing Ursius succeeding in a command position, and the young men under him clearly respected their *optio*. Ursius' orders were precisely stated, timely, and thought through.

As the day wore on, Guiamo told Ursius he must leave to meet with his friends for supper. As they prepared to part once again, Guiamo said, "You might consider teaching all one hundred dogs to attack at one particular spot in the enemy line rather than across a broad front. If they could break the line, your spearmen could pour in behind the dogs and make permanent the breach, thus splitting the enemy."

Ursius looked pleased at this suggestion and said, "I shall work on this, Guiamo. It could help us win on the day of battle. Travel safely my friend."

As he turned to go, Guiamo paused and said, "There is another thing you might consider. If you wish to advance beyond the rank of *optio*, you cannot do so while commanding the dogs. Spend your spare time learning infantry tactics, and the command calls and strategies of a *centurio*. Make yourself skilled and available for promotion. To do this, you must train someone to replace you as *optio* of war dogs, or you will always be needed where you are now."

As an afterthought, Guiamo said, "If I were to make your choice, I should prefer being *praefectus alae* of cavalry."

Guiamo met Salonius and Suadusegus back at the entrance of the encampment, and they made their way back on the wagon toward their tent. Guiamo said, "We leave tomorrow, for in the morning, Ursius must take his men and dogs afield for seven days."

Suadusegus replied, "I am sorry your visit has been cut so short, but we still shall have further adventures to look forward to. For myself, I have enjoyed the day immensely. The organization of the Roman army has always been a mystery to me, but I see now that, far more than our tribal leaders, your *legatus legionis* truly commands and all others obey.

"My people, like the Belgae, do much as they like without regard to the desires of the tribal leaders. Our chieftains must cajole, entice, bribe or shame our men to action. In contrast your *legatus legionis* simply speaks and it is done.

"I suspect your visit to the Bellovaci will be as eye opening to you as today's visit with the *legio* of Rome was to me."

They saw many on the road, traveled occasionally with Roman patrols and merchant caravans, and found no troubles. The trip was long, dusty and hot, and Guiamo enjoyed every moment. Guiamo became quite excited when they passed the first village of the Bellovaci, but was taken aback by the suspicious looks given by the old women. Suadusegus spoke courteously to many Belgae as they traveled, and they consistently pointed the correct way to the main village.

His enthusiasm grew with each passing day, and on the evening of the fourteenth day of *September*, they arrived at the outskirts of Bratuspantium, the main village of the Bellovaci.

Bratuspantium was not half the size of Lugdunum, and much simpler in construction. Many homes were simple huts made of wooden poles covered with hide, and the people looked impoverished.

The meeting hall of the Bellovaci king was located in the *oppidum* itself, and that was where Suadusegus told Guiamo they should first go. Salonius drove the wagon through the squalor of the village up the hill to the *oppidum*.

As they neared the wooden fortress's iron bound gates, Suadusegus told Guiamo, "Before we go inside, give to me two *denarii* and one gold *aureus*."

170

Though confused by this request, Guiamo searched his purse quickly, pulled out the three coins, and put them into Suadusegus' outstretched hand.

The gate guards waited patiently for the wagon to roll close before the oldest spoke. "What business have you here?" he asked.

Suadusegus quickly spoke so Guiamo did not have to speak with a foreigner's accent, "To meet with the king's advisors. They have sent for us," he lied.

"Go up the hill and park your wagon on the left," the guard replied with total boredom.

Suadusegus winked at Guiamo as he motioned for Salonius to move along. The path curved along the hillside past horse stables, living quarters, kitchens and the armory, all nearly deserted. A single column of spearmen on horseback rode past down toward the gate.

As they came to the top of the hill, Salonius drove the wagon to the left of the king's meeting hall which was constructed of wood and had a thatched roof. The massive wooden doors had iron hinges, and were decorated with deeply cut carvings of entwined serpents. Traces of inlaid gold reflected from the doorposts.

Up a wide stone staircase, two heavily muscled men stood guard in front of the hall's doors with spears and sheathed swords, men who clearly were veteran soldiers of many battles. Two shields leaned against the walls. Off to the right stood another fierce looking veteran who watched the three visitors with wary eyes. Guiamo recognized that he could call out a large force of warriors to defend the king at a moment's notice.

One of the door guards stepped forward to the edge of the steps and shouted, "Leave all your weapons in your wagon."

The three removed their weapons and with exaggerated movements so all could see, placed them clearly in the back of the wagon. Salonius brought down the chair with wheels and helped Suadusegus into it. The three went to the broad stairway where Salonius picked up Suadusegus, and Guiamo awkwardly moved the chair to the top. Setting Suadusegus into the chair again, Salonius moved him forward a few steps to speak directly to the two guards.

When the two guards moved closer, Suadusegus quietly slipped each of them a silver *denarius*, and said, "I wish to speak to the king's counselors on this boy's behalf. The boy should come with me." Pointing to Salonius, he said, "The young man can stay here outside."

Seeing no threat, the guard let Guiamo push Suadusegus through the doorway. Salonius sat down on the steps.

The lighting was poor, and it took a while for their eyes to adjust. As they came into the first hallway, they were greeted by an older man who was missing four fingers of his right hand. Accompanying him were two guards even more fierce looking than the two door guardians.

"State your business," the older man said brusquely.

Suadusegus spoke gently, "My lord, I wish to speak with the king's counselors, but do not need to disturb the king himself." With subtle motions, he slipped the man the gold *aureus*. "I seek information on behalf of this boy."

The man glanced at the gold coin and mumbled, "Let me see what I can do."

He turned back into the deeper chambers and soon returned. He led Guiamo and Suadusegus into an adjoining antechamber and motioned for them to wait.

"Why did you bribe them?" asked Guiamo. "That is not the act of a moral man."

"I have served my king, Lucotorgetorix, for many years and know the ways of the court. You do not. You are correct in saying it is not a moral act, but I am prepared to do what is necessary. I bribed them so you did not have to," replied Suadusegus. "We have been received, and your moral standing remains intact."

Guiamo was not pleased and scolded Suadusegus. "Do no such thing in my name again. What you do is an extension of my reputation," Guiamo said in exasperation.

Suadusegus' reply was firm but without belligerence, "I shall do what I must in the role I am required to play. Remember, I serve *Dominus* Malleolus, not you. To him you must take your case."

Guiamo glared at him with displeasure, but knew he could not change his teacher's mind.

After a short time, three men of commanding presence and ornate clothing with lightweight capes entered the room and motioned for Guiamo to sit on one of the wooden benches.

"My lords," said Suadusegus as he bowed in courtesy as well as he could in his chair, recognizing their authority.

"I am Cumbdubno. I am King Nertorecturix's high counselor. Speak your names and your request," said the tallest counselor.

"My lord, I am Suadusegus, and this boy is why I have come seeking your wisdom. His name is Guiamo Durmius Stolo, son of Appius Durmius Stolo, a *centurio* who died in the service of Rome some years ago," said Suadusegus.

The three counselors all looked startled with surprise. Before Suadusegus could continue, the three counselors stopped him to speak quietly among themselves. They looked at Guiamo carefully, as if in wonder, and then motioned for Suadusegus to continue.

"This boy's mother was born of the Bellovaci and died in Gallia some time ago. We seek his family. He has some memory of a grandfather of the same name and we hope you could guide us to him," Suadusegus said.

"Wait here," replied Cumbdubno. "This may take some time. I shall have someone bring you water and bread."

The wait was long, and the sun descended over the hills. As the chill of night descended upon the great hall, Guiamo wished he, too, had brought a cape with which to warm himself. Suadusegus and Guiamo had little to say, and both sat quietly waiting for the counselors to return. An attendant brought more water, bread and some strips of roasted veal. Guiamo wondered if Salonius was being fed as well, but rather doubted it. He was not too worried for him, though, for the wagon held plenty of foodstuffs he could eat as he needed.

The three counselors so abruptly entered the antechamber that Guiamo nearly fell off the bench. Suadusegus had been dozing, and was startled awake.

"You will see King Nertorecturix now," said Cumbdubno when he had their attention.

Guiamo rose to push Suadusegus out of the antechamber, and they followed Cumbdubno out the door into the first hall. They proceeded through another immense set of doors into the grand hall. The hall was filled with many soldiers, and the king sat upon his throne raised upon a dais, and was surrounded by many grandees and attendants.

Guiamo had expected a king's hall to be filled with marble columns, colorful banners, sculptures of valiant battles of years gone by, and mosaics in the flooring depicting scenes of the gods at play, as he had seen in the temple of Mars in Lugdunum.

Instead, he found the hall to be drab, poorly lit, smoke-filled, and needing to be swept. The roof timbers were beginning to sag, and the remains of shattered cobwebs dangled from the crossbeams. It was utterly devoid of decoration save for silver candle holders which had long needed polishing. Guiamo looked up and saw that the thatching was old and needing to be replaced. The wooden throne itself was ancient, and the horse and wolf figures carved upon the base were chipped and worn.

Cumbdubno led them directly before the king. "My lord, King Nertorecturix, the boy, Guiamo Durmius Stolo and his slave Suadusegus," he announced loudly.

Suadusegus was surprised he was known by the Bellovaci to be a slave, but he was positively shocked that such intense attention was being shown to Guiamo. He recognized that important things were happening of which he knew nothing, but felt that they were not being threatened in any way. Rather, he felt all around had a profound sense of curiosity about Guiamo. He bowed again in his chair, but remained silent. Guiamo moved to the right side of the chair to follow his example and bowed politely.

Cumbdubno moved forward to stand beside the king. The king spoke briefly to him in whispered tones and

174

Cumbdubno stepped quickly down the dais steps to Guiamo. He said, "This is yours, I believe." Cumbdubno held out his hand and placed two silver *denarii* and one gold *aureus* in Guiamo's hands. The high counselor glanced sideways at Suadusegus, and then spoke to the boy. "You are most welcome in this hall. The normal, um, courtesies to the king's staff are not needed. You have access to the king's ear."

Cumbdubno returned to his station beside King Nertorecturix and the murmuring voices in the hall fell silent.

The king spoke to Guiamo, but loud enough so all could hear. "You are wondering why mere travelers should merit so much attention. Yestereve, a holy man came to my chamber to speak of a vision sent to him by one of the gods. Would you like to know the god's message?"

Guiamo nodded silently.

"I will have him tell you himself," said the king. "Camulvellaunus, come forward and speak to us all of your vision."

An aging, bearded man, quite tall and dressed in a long white robe, stepped forward from behind the throne. He wore a garland of mistletoe upon his head and a thick golden collar about his neck. His long white hair had only remnants of the golden tones of his youth, and a bald spot could be seen above the garland. His vision was poor, and he was led by a young boy by the hand. Guiamo could see that he bore a circular mark upon his right forearm and a gold ring on the index finger of his right hand.

Camulvellaunus found his place and raised both hands high into the air. With a strong voice, the man spoke. And as he spoke, Guiamo saw that his front teeth were missing.

"That is my grandfather!" Guiamo whispered excitedly to Suadusegus.

"He is one of the *Druidae!*" exclaimed Suadusegus to Guiamo with a voice half hushed. "Apparently an important one. Now, be silent!"

Camulvellaunus' voice carried strongly across the hall, "The great god Lugus came to me as I worshipped and prayed among the sacred oaks atop the hill of Duthmorno.

As I stood in supplication, a great mist arose and filled the grove. The birds fell silent, and the sun became dim. From out of the foggy mist came the voice of Lugus, strong and commanding. Thus he proclaimed:

"I, Lugus, Fierce in War, am come to thee, oh Camulvellaunus, for the time of strife comes. Thy kin need deliverance, for the foul servants of the abyss rage again. From across the sea, the terror of their might pours forth unchecked.

"I, Lugus, the Eye of Wisdom, say unto thee, 'Camulvellaunus, thy strength wanes with age, so another must rise on the day of great deeds. Wisdom and might as yours I have given to another. The deliverer from Gallia comes!

"I, Lugus Path Maker, named thee well, Camulvellaunus, for a powerful seer you are indeed. Now another sage comes bearing the name given by your father. My path lies before him, his steps are directed to you, oh Camulvellaunus. Behold, he comes to your doorstep, to your door he comes tender and pure of heart. He who shall surpass you draws nigh.

"I, Lugus, Protector of Children, command you, 'Embrace him, Camulvellaunus! Teach him your secret ways! Fill him with your wisdom! Love him as a son, for a son to you, he shall be!'

"I Lugus, Embodiment of the Seven Truths, say, 'Test him with the golden serpent which does not deceive. The golden serpent shall reveal his face to you.' "

Camulvellaunus closed his eyes and lowered his hands. "Thus said Lugus to me," he said in closing.

He took his gold ring off and threw it at random into the air. It sparkled faintly in the dim light and with a light ringing sound bounced across the wooden floor of the dais off to his right.

The ring rolled two *passuum* toward the right edge of the dais and bumped against the wooden base of a candle holder. As the ring wobbled backwards, it fell off the first step and picked up a little speed. It bounced down each step and rolled at a leisurely speed toward the crowd. As the ring slowed down, it curved toward the left and rolled under Suadusegus' chair of wheels. As it passed beyond the chair, it rolled slowly on and, with a final spinning whirl, came to rest in front of Guiamo directly between his feet.

The hall was filled with a loud collective gasp from all the people present, and King Nertorecturix stood suddenly to see more clearly.

"Where did it stop?" asked Camulvellaunus.

King Nertorecturix replied, "It came to rest between the feet of the boy."

Satisfied, Camulvellaunus prodded his young guide to take him down the steps to meet the great one. Camulvellaunus walked forward to Guiamo. He placed his face extremely close to Guiamo's and moved around so that with his poor eyesight he could examine Guiamo's face. When he was satisfied, he said, "Pick up the ring and look at it."

Guiamo stooped to retrieve the gold ring. As he looked at it, he saw that it was carved in the image of a snake circling around to devour its own tail. He recognized that it was similar to the tattoo on the old *Druides'* right forearm.

Camulvellaunus instructed Guiamo quietly, "This serpent does not lie." Taking the ring gently from Guiamo and holding it aloft, he shouted. "This serpent does not lie! The servant of Lugus has arrived!"

The hall reverberated with shouts of joy as the people cheered triumphantly. The king, accompanied by the grandees, descended the stair to greet Guiamo who stood stunned at the spontaneous celebration.

"What is your name?" asked Camulvellaunus.

"Grandfather, I am Guiamo Durmius Stolo come back to you," said Guiamo.

Camulvellaunus drew in a gasp of air and stepped back in surprise.

As the king drew close, Camulvellaunus turned stiffly in shock to face him. With an expression of disbelief, he exclaimed "My lord, this boy is my grandson!"

"Truly?" said King Nertorecturix. "Then he is welcome indeed. Bring him to a private room. We have much to discover about him and more yet to discuss."

The audience was dismissed and they filed slowly out, looking in awe after Guiamo as he was led deeper into the private rooms behind the great hall. Suadusegus was pushed by an attendant who looked curiously at the wheeled chair as they went.

Camulvellaunus had Guiamo act as guide and the king led them to a private office where they sat quietly around a rectangular wooden table. Large, ornately carved cabinets sat at opposite ends of the room, and candles burned low on an iron-reinforced wooden chandelier which hung on chains from the ceiling.

Camulvellaunus looked visibly relieved at seeing his grandson. He said, "If the gods had not brought you back to me, son of my eldest daughter, I should have thought you were lost forever. Word came to me that she had died along with your brother Appius. I sent for you, but your uncle had already taken you away beyond my reach."

"I would have been lost had not the Fates been kind to me," said Guiamo. "My *avunculus* Valerius abandoned me when his fortune was lost."

"I do not trust the Roman Fates or their gods," said Camulvellaunus. "They are weak and fickle. I listen to the voices of the gods of our ancestors and it is they who brought you back to me. I see you have much to learn."

"Then learn, I shall," said Guiamo. "I am confused. I was told your name was Guiamo Laevinus, not Camulvellaunus."

"So your Roman uncle taught you," said his grandfather derisively, but his tone softened quickly. "As a boy, I was named Guiamoluvino by my father, a name well known by your uncle. When I entered the priesthood of the *Druidae*, and my talents became known, my name was changed to Camulvellaunus which means 'powerful seer.'

King Nertorecturix interrupted impatiently. "Yes, yes, this is all very nice. You shall have time for tears and rejoicing later. I need to know now what threat there is to me

178

and my lands. Camulvellaunus, you spoke of some enemies rising up to fight me. It is my time to speak to this boy."

"No," said Camulvellaunus, "it is time for me to meet with him for the concerns of the *Druidae*." Dismissing the king with a wave of his hand, he said, "I will later inform you of what might concern you." Deliberately snubbing the king, Camulvellaunus commanded, "Shut the door as you leave."

King Nertorecturix stormed off shouting "Impudent *Druides*! Next time I will remove your head and take it with me!" He slammed the door as he stomped out, leaving a cloud of profanities as he went.

Suadusegus smirked at the intrigue of the court which was so familiar to him, while Guiamo glanced anxiously at Camulvellaunus, fearing for his grandfather's life.

Camulvellaunus saw Guiamo's distress, and dramatically mocked the king, "Impudent *Druides*! Next time I will remove your head and take it with me!" Camulvellaunus laughed easily, "Think nothing of it. That is what he always says when we part."

Camulvellaunus leaned forward with confidence. "He will go to sulk over his cups, and by morning will be more concerned of the pain inside his head than the frustration he has with me. Our king is much too fond of his wine."

Guiamo was clearly confused, so his grandfather explained, "Nertorecturix knows I spoke against choosing him king, but he needs me to rule the people. Guiamo, we are actually closer friends than most realize, though with our conflicting roles, I must challenge him always. I constantly tease and belittle him as friends sometimes do, but only in private. I goad him to emphasize that he has named me his High *Druides* and he is still only the king. It torments him to no end, for he has an unquenchable thirst for power."

"It is a strange arrangement," said Guiamo.

"True," said Suadusegus, "but it works."

They spoke long into the night. Guiamo spoke of his life's journey, of Calidius and Gabinius, of oracles and fish traps. He spoke of lessons and responsibility, of Ursius and his promise to return home before winter. Uncertain of the trustworthiness of the Bellovaci, and knowing the urgency with which he had to keep Lúin a secret, he chose to say nothing of the spear. Throughout, Camulvellaunus said little, and Suadusegus, less. When weariness finally overcame curiosity, they walked to another part of the *oppidum* where Camulvellaunus had a private sleeping chamber, and they settled in for the night.

Morning came too quickly for Guiamo, but he did not complain. Picking up a fabric bag, Camulvellaunus took Guiamo outside, leaving Suadusegus behind. He left word to have attendants assist him until their return. With Guiamo leading his grandfather according to his instructions, they walked out the *oppidum* and descended the hill upon which it was built. Guiamo was hungry and was surprised he was not offered bread. They talked of Guiamo's mother, Agesdaca, and it comforted him to hear words of her life and interests.

Camulvellaunus was not pleased that his two daughters had both married men of Rome, but knew that Agesdaca had married well to a good man. Manius Valerius Ruga was very different from *Centurio* Appius Durmius Stolo. Camulvellaunus could see into Valerius' corrupt heart, while Namiotanca had been blinded by his wealth and charm. In the end, Camulvellaunus had lost both his daughters. Guiamo also learned his grandmother had died within the year, and Guiamo could clearly see the pain of it in his grandfather's eyes. To Guiamo's comfort, it was also plainly obvious that he had instantly become the joy of his grandfather's life.

They came to a stream in the valley, and Camulvellaunus stopped. "For the *Druidae*, it is time to bathe. The ritual cleansing of the body is done each morning of every day." Without hesitation, he removed his white robe and stepped into the cool water at his feet. Beckoning Guiamo, he said, "You shall wash as well."

Guiamo removed his *toga* and *subligar* loincloth, and walked into the water. Though cool, the water was not icy, and Guiamo enjoyed splashing water onto himself while standing in the knee-deep water. When Camulvellaunus had finished washing, he stepped back onto the grass and shook much of the water off. He then patted himself down with his robe, and Guiamo did the same.

When they had put their clothing back on, Camulvellaunus directed him to take a familiar pathway which led to the nearby hill of Duthmorno. Guiamo saw that it was covered with oak trees and looked forward to seeing the sacred site. The pathway was smooth, straight and old, for it was pressed deep into the soil. From its narrowness, Guiamo guessed that his grandfather was one of very few who regularly visited the grove. Even with his poor eyesight, the aging *Druides* knew the way from years of holy devotion.

When they passed into the shade of the ancient trees near the crest of the hill, Camulvellaunus heard Guiamo's stomach growling. He said, "Each day, we must honor the gods before we honor our bellies. We shall eat after we return from our prayers."

Camulvellaunus led Guiamo through familiar territory, and they soon came to a clearing at the high point of the hill. Standing just at the edge of the grassy hilltop, Camulvellaunus instructed Guiamo to remove his sandals, explaining, "This is holy ground."

Guiamo removed his sandals as did his grandfather, and leaving them behind, walked toward the center of the grassy clearing. The open area had been kept well groomed, with fallen branches and protruding stones removed.

Camulvellaunus showed Guiamo a scorched patch of ground in the very center, and said, "Our sacrifices are burned here. We have no stone altar as others may carve with their hands. To the *Druidae*, they are an abomination. The ground itself, pure and untouched, is most holy and part of the realm indwelt by the gods."

Guiamo was interested, for while the religion of Rome seemed impressive in its wealth, artistry and construction, it seemed but empty in its heart. Here in a grassy field among the oaks, it was simple in form, but the connection to the gods ran deep. Guiamo could feel the power of the gods in this place, and out of the corner of his eye, just beyond his vision, he caught faint glimpses of motion silently encircling them.

"This place is truly holy, grandfather. I sense it." Guiamo asked, "Tell me of the *Druidae*."

"The *Druidae* are the order of holy followers of the gods of our ancestors, the gods of earth and sky, future and past, mountain, stream and tree. We serve by learning, teaching, remembering, serving, judging, guiding. Beyond this I will not say. If you wish to know more, you must enter into the order of the *Druidae*. Know this, I am forbidden from asking you to become a *Druides*. You must request it," said Camulvellaunus.

Guiamo became even more intrigued, "If I wished to become a *Druides*, what commitment must I give?"

"Nineteen years of learning. Until this is completed, you may not marry. You must commit to learning all presented to you. It will be difficult. Not all initiates are capable of completing the learning, and as the years pass, not all remain committed to attain it. They remain within the *Druidae*, but their roles are diminished. Only a fully trained *Druides* can wear the garland of mistletoe, and all with garlands are considered equal. King Nertorecturix calls me his High *Druides*, but in truth, that is a name only he recognizes. All *Druides* are equal.

"You would be free to abandon the time of instruction, but you would forever be bound by the vows of silence on pain of death. When called, you would be required to submit; when disciplined, you would bear the pain willingly."

Guiamo said, "I am desirous of becoming a *Druides*, grandfather, but I am committed to returning to Gabinius before winter sets in."

"You are still young. What is your age?" asked Camulvellaunus.

Guiamo said, "I am thirteen years old."

"Yes, you are big for your age," Camulvellaunus replied, "and I feel in your arms that you are strong." He paused before continuing, "And you have much wisdom in your heart. It would be possible for you to enter into the order of

182

the *Druidae* while you are here and begin your instruction. When winter nears, you could return to Gabinius for a season. When you are ready to continue to your lessons, return to me."

Camulvellaunus stood silently and Guiamo looked at him, awaiting further information. Camulvellaunus continued standing silently. In the awkward moment, Guiamo realized his grandfather was waiting for Guiamo to ask to join the *Druidae*. Guiamo said, "Grandfather, I wish to join with you in the holy order of the *Druidae*. I would be honored if I could stand among them."

Camulvellaunus took an oak twig and a sprig of mistletoe from his sack. Placing these into Guiamo's hands, he smiled and said, "Swear this oath before the gods in this holy place: 'To the gods above, I pledge my life and my will to serve as one of the holy *Druidae*. I will learn what I am able, do what I must, serve when am called. I vow to keep its secrets safe and venerate the sanctity of the hallowed places. I, Guiamo Durmius Stolo, swear this today in this holy place.' "

Guiamo repeated the words precisely and when he was finished, looked proudly into his grandfather's eyes.

His grandfather smiled back the said, "Today, you have become *Druides*. Now sit in the grass. There is one more thing to do here today."

Camulvellaunus sat beside him and opened his sack. He removed a sharply pointed bronze tool, a vial of dark blue liquid, and a clean rag. "Hold out your right arm palm down."

It took two painful hours, but Guiamo bore the stinging pain well. He was surprised to see how precisely Camulvellaunus put the tattoo onto his arm. His grandfather's vision was poor, but by placing his face extremely close to Guiamo's arm, he could still put the bronze tool precisely where the design required. When it was finished, Guiamo inspected the raw flesh gingerly, and was satisfied that the image of the serpent swallowing its own tail was beautifully drawn.

Camulvellaunus put his tools back into his sack, and they strolled back to the *oppidum* to eat a late breakfast.

Suadusegus was surprised to see the serpent tattoo on Guiamo's tender arm. He beckoned Camulvellaunus to speak privately with him. When they were alone, Suadusegus said, "I see that you have enticed the boy to join you with the *Druidae*. I have something to speak to you of this. While I am not a *Druides*, I know some of their ways. In the house of Malleolus, there is a *Druides* who could continue his teaching there when he returns before winter."

Camulvellaunus was intrigued with this development. He asked, "Tell me, do you know this *Druides* well?"

"Yes," replied Suadusegus. "She is my wife, Susama of the Aduatuci."

"Is she also a slave to Malleolus?" asked the *Druides*.

"No, she is a freewoman. Malleolus sent for her to join with me after my capture and enslavement," Suadusegus replied.

"Then I will spend some weeks with Guiamo, to evaluate him, and I shall send with him instructions to Susama on how best I recommend she train him," said Camulvellaunus.

His tattooed arm hurt for many days until the skin had healed. Camulvellaunus had him demonstrate his strength and skill at war through several days of exercises and drills, and his sore skin kept him from his best performances. Overall, Camulvellaunus was pleased with his grandson's progress toward manhood.

The next few weeks were spent in reviewing and improving his abilities in writing, speaking, ciphering with numerals, and they had many lengthy discussions of philosophy. Camulvellaunus understood Guiamo's bias toward Roman teaching, so spent much time teaching him the ways of the Belgae.

Suadusegus understood the direction Camulvellaunus led in Guiamo's teaching, and agreed to support the *Druides* in grooming the boy for life among the Belgae.

Guiamo thoroughly enjoyed his time in the north with his grandfather, and devoured his lessons. Mornings were spent in exercise, and he poured himself into his studies, staying up late working by candlelight.

Idle since they arrived, Salonius chose to make himself useful by spending his time hunting game, and as the winds turned cooler, he began to plan for the return trip.

And then the day came for the three to return home. Camulvellaunus embraced Guiamo and gave his final goodbyes. The wagon lumbered slowly away down a narrow trail and Camulvellaunus wept, unable to see his beloved grandson pass into the distance.

The trip lasted many days, but their supplies were plentiful and the weather pleasantly cool. Guiamo was eager to return to Gabinius, and Suadusegus, his wife. Salonius was weary of travel and eager to collect his reward. All were in good spirits and anxious to reach Gobedbiacum, and the days passed quickly.

Noon came as Guiamo, Salonius and Suadusegus lumbered along on the cart, with Guiamo practicing his words. The sun was unusually hot and the wind was building.

Guiamo was glad to pass through a wood where the overhanging branches blocked the rays of the sun. Their horse plodded down the windy path. The recent rain had left puddles in the wheel ruts, and the shadows slowed the evaporation, leaving muddy spots. The weary horse struggled to pull their wagon through a particularly long muddy hole and Salonius jumped off the cart to lighten the load.

As he pushed on the back of the cart, a group of horsemen burst out of the woods on the right. With spears leveled at Guiamo and Suadusegus seated in the wagon, and Salonius standing behind, they fanned out to encircle the three startled travelers.

The tattooed leader of the group said, "Your purse, good sirs."

185

Guiamo groaned and Suadusegus slumped dejectedly. Salonius stood apprehensively in the mud motioning that he was unarmed.

One of the brigands noticed Guiamo's knife. He spoke in a dialect Guiamo recognized from his lessons.

"The boy has a knife. I claim it," said the red-haired brigand to the leader in their native tongue. Guiamo was pleased he understood some of their statements but tried to not betray his insight by reacting in disappointment to the pending loss of his favorite possession.

"I say who gets what," said the leader who rode closer to inspect the knife.

"The knife, please," said the leader with mock politeness as he stretched out his hand. Guiamo reluctantly pulled the knife out and slowly placed it in the man's hand. He also pulled out his purse filled with silver *denarii* and handed it over as well.

The leader opened the bag with a grim smile of satisfaction and said, "Enough for us all," in his native tongue. All the brigands broke out in smiles. The knife was passed to the red-haired man who looked it over carefully and then contentedly slipped it into his waistband.

The large man who rode beside the tattooed brigand leader said, "We should take their food as well."

"See it done," said the leader, and the strong man motioned to another to take the foodstuffs out of the wagon. He did so quickly and returned with two large leather bags filled with the remains of the food supply.

One of the brigands armed with a bow spoke in low tones to the leader, "The old man there, I have seen him somewhere."

"Yes, I, too, recognize him," the leader replied as he examined the scars on the old man's legs.

"He might be the one who was once counselor to the Aduatuci king. Do you remember the lame advisor who spoke to Borumatus about the stolen horses? That might be him."

"I am he," said Suadusegus in their dialect, surprising them all. "And the horses were returned to you, if I recall correctly."

"Yes, they were," said the brigand leader.

Suadusegus continued, "King Lucotorgetorix wanted to keep them, for they were taken within our land, but I cautioned him that our friendship with the Eburones was more important than fifty horses."

"So, are you a freeman or slave?" asked the brigand leader.

"I am a slave," replied Suadusegus.

"Come, let us kill these two and you can be free with us," offered the leader.

Suadusegus thought about the offer to join them, and judiciously replied, "Your offer is appealing, but hear me. My master is a good man and well respected by those in his employ as well as his slaves. He has given me a home and brought my wife to me to live as a free woman. My work is light, chiefly to teach languages to this boy. I also have been promised freedom, and I believe his word is true.

"Your offer is generous and freedom is appealing, but my lameness, my age, the loss of my wife, and quite honestly, your own dire condition bring me to say no. I also could not bear to see this boy killed to hide my escape."

"What value is he to you?" asked the leader.

"He is a good boy," pointing into the back of the wagon he continued, "He has built for me that chair of wheels that gives me the ability to go where I will. To kill him, he who does so much good, would be wrong."

The brigands sat for a minute before Suadusegus ventured an idea, "May I discuss something privately with the boy for a moment?

The brigand nodded and said, "Yes, but no trickery."

Suadusegus huddled together with Guiamo, quietly talking. The boy gestured frequently with his hands, and nodded his head.

Suadusegus said, "Perhaps my young friend and I could make an offer which might appeal to you. My master is wise and influential. We both believe that if you come to him for sanctuary and turn from your banditry, he can provide you a safe haven where you may prosper and receive a pardon from our governor."

"Why would he do such a thing for thieving refugees such as we?" asked the leader.

Suadusegus replied, "I have heard of your story. Some say you were driven from your homeland, and while you are desperately in want, you are not by nature wicked. Would it not be better to remove robbers from Gallia by restoring them to good?"

Pointing to Guiamo, Suadusegus said, "This boy was taken in by my master. He is an orphan who had nothing of his own, yet my master was merciful to him; merciful and generous. He did this simply because a friend asked it of him. He is this sort of man, rare and pure. It could be the same for you and your men. We have but to ask.

"A similar story is my own experience. He treats me as a man, a philosopher and teacher, yet I am a slave. He even brought my wife to me from my homeland. He loves this boy, and will listen truly. It is within his ability to grant."

Guiamo spoke up, "He always has need of workers and is willing to forgive transgressions, provided from this day forward all is done honestly."

The brigand leader suddenly appeared weary. "Your words astound me. I am intrigued, for our life is difficult. Let me speak of this with my men," he replied.

Guiamo watched their discussion without understanding so many words as Suadusegus could, but their reactions were obvious. They were at first profoundly surprised, and some laughed loudly as if it were a jest. As the leader explained the seriousness of the offer, their eyes revealed their astonishment. They began to talk excitedly about the proposal. Some were immediately opposed to it and spoke loudly against it, but others argued and pleaded in its favor. The soundness of the proposal proved irresistible, and even the most belligerent eventually softened and acquiesced.

"We are agreed then," the leader said to Suadusegus. "Your proposal is generous, though a betrayal would mean instant death to both of you."

188

Guiamo heard his words, but realized the voice betrayed a lack of commitment.

"How do you propose we meet with your master?" asked the leader.

"He is only half a day's travel from here. Let us return together," said Suadusegus. "Salonius and I will go ahead to prepare *Dominus* Malleolus. He will want to be certain you have not come to rob him. Understand that he will be guarded when we speak. You may carry your weapons, but do not brandish them aggressively. Carry an olive branch and dismount courteously when you arrive. The boy, Durmius, will approach freely ahead of the twenty of you. Once he is with *Dominus* Malleolus, you alone shall approach to reach settlement."

On command of their leader, several men dismounted to help coax the horse and push the cart out of the mud.

Toward evening, Salonius drove the cart with Suadusegus up the path to Gabinius' home while Guiamo remained at a distance with the brigands. Ulleria saw the two drawing near as she fed the chickens, and confused that only two were returning, ran frightened into the house.

Sertorius came outdoors as quickly as his aging legs could carry him, followed by Ulleria, and shouted, "Where is Durmius?"

Suadusegus motioned for Sertorius to calm down and replied, "He is quite safe, but I must speak at once with *Dominus* Malleolus."

Sertorius was visibly shaken and Suadusegus saw him trying to control his nerves. "Ulleria, fetch *Dominus* Malleolus at once."

Ulleria turned and dashed off toward the private smithy.

When Gabinius came, he looked very concerned. "Where is Guiamo?" he asked.

Suadusegus explained, "My lord *Dominus* Malleole, Durmius is safe and down the pathway. Let me explain. We were waylaid by the troupe of brigands that have been seen about these past five years. As we spoke with them, an idea came to me which I believe you will find agreeable. They recognized my face and the scars on my legs. Remembering my favorable dealings with them in years past, they offered to give me freedom and would kill Guiamo and Salonius to hide the act.

"Rather than seek a life with them at the cost of their lives, I offered the brigands a new opportunity totally unexpected. Guiamo is in agreement with my plan and is down the lane playing his role.

"Our plan is that they give up their wretched lives in the wild, for wretched it truly is. We proposed that they become workers for hire in your shops and with your influence could obtain a pardon for them from Governor Caesar. They seem most eager to comply. Will you agree to such terms?"

Gabinius turned to Sertorius and with a serious and even tone said, "Fetch all my men who can bear arms. Gather them out of sight behind the house fully equipped, and on my word, bring them out as a group. Do not surround the brigands, but form up in two lines behind me. I do not want to appear as if threatening an assault, but I must appear the stronger. Bring a horse to Salonius here."

When Gabinius' armed men had formed up behind the house, he sent Salonius down the road to find Guiamo. He returned a short while later to inform Gabinius that they were coming and Guiamo was on foot leading them.

Salonius told Gabinius, "Their demeanor, though guarded, is still as I left them. They are weary men looking to be rescued from themselves."

Soon after, Guiamo came into sight, and he waved a hand in greeting. Sertorius and Salonius waved back, but Gabinius stood unmoving.

Behind him came twenty-three men on horseback, all in armor but with weapons sheathed or held at ease. The leader carried an olive branch, signifying peace, freshly plucked from Gabinius' orchards.

Guiamo walked forward confidently and greeted Gabinius politely. He then turned and stood beside the old man.

The leader of the brigands drew near, and commanded all to dismount. As they came closer, Gabinius spoke quietly to

Sertorius who signaled for the seventy armed men to come out from hiding and line up behind Gabinius, but with *gladii* sheathed.

The brigands froze in their tracks at the sight of so many armed men, but their leader, seeing Gabinius' men stood without drawing their *gladii*, told his men to stand easy. Alone, he walked up to greet Gabinius.

"Lord Malleole, I greet you in good faith," said the leader.

"My good faith is extended to you this day, sir. By what name are you called?" replied Gabinius cautiously.

"In the land of my fathers across the sea, I am Valmatus, son of Nertotarvus, but to these men, I am Actus, 'the Driven One.' It is the name I prefer. Your servant Suadusegus has offered us sanctuary with terms which are acceptable to us. If you would but agree to their proposal, we would be most pleased."

Gabinius spoke firmly in his most authoritative voice, "I understand you desire sanctuary and a pardon from Governor Caesar. You also desire to be hirelings in my workshops. Your reputations here are, shall we say, tarnished. Why do you not simply return home? Or is it that you would not be welcomed home if you should return?"

The tattooed man replied, "My lord, these men, the few who remain, are loyal to me, and have chosen to remain as my company. For my part, I cannot return to my homeland on pain of death, though not for evil deeds. Rather, the dark forces of evil that abide there, those who stole me away, who wrote their cursed words on my body, would kill me on sight. Nay, I cannot return. I sought refuge in the lands to the north, but the Belgae flinch in fear of these words and will not abide me."

Gabinius took this in and then responded, "Not without reason do I surround myself only with virtuous people. Though a pardon from Caesar is achievable, I can find no place in my heart to hire you."

The leader grew tense, and chafed at Gabinius' surprising denial. "To what end could we accept his pardon if we have no means to put bread into our stomachs?"

Guiamo realized the plan was falling apart and quickly spoke up. "Gabini, I have a thought." He whispered into Gabinius' ear.

Gabinius looked surprised, and then silently agreed with a nod. He spoke quietly to Guiamo and pointed to the east.

Guiamo turned to speak to Actus, "I am not without wealth of my own. Since Gabinius has chosen to not hire you, I have asked him permission that I should hire you myself. There is a plot of land over across the river which is for sale, and suitable for farming. I will purchase this land upon which you may settle. I will have much work that needs to be done, and you may earn your living there.

"Like Gabinius Malleolus, I will be fair and just. If, in time, you prove your worth, he is agreeable to offer additional work suitable to your talents. Additionally, he will negotiate to have Caesar extend to you a pardon of amnesty. What say you?"

In reply, Actus turned back to his men waiting at a distance, sought out the red-haired man and removed Guiamo's knife from his waistband. Quietly returning to Gabinius, he placed it gently in Guiamo's hand. As he returned the purse filled with silver *denarii*, he said, "My lord, Stolo, we agree."

Gabinius sent Sertorius to negotiate the purchase of land across the river. The purchase was approved by both parties and Gabinius deducted the price from his account. The twenty-three men were shown the way and given a wagon full of supplies and food to enable them to begin their work.

Gabinius spoke to Guiamo at supper. "You are certainly clever and clear thinking in a time of stress. I just hope you are not overgenerous."

"Overgenerosity is preferable to tightfistedness," Guiamo replied.

"True," answered Gabinius, "though, be careful always with your money."

"For my part, I shall send word of your proposal for your men to the governor and ask for a pardon. Amnesty will not be easy, for they have committed many crimes, but I have

192

friends who can bend Caesar's ear in our favor. We must be patient, for this will take some time."

The next evening, Guiamo strolled with the letter toward the home of Suadusegus and knocked on the doorpost. Suadusegus was pleased Guiamo had responded so quickly to his request. "Come in, come in, Durmi," shouted Suadusegus from inside the home. As Guiamo entered, Suadusegus motioned for his wife to join him, and the three sat together on ornately carved chairs.

"Susama, I have a surprise for you," said Suadusegus mysteriously.

"What mischief have you been up to on this trip?" she asked inquisitively.

"Roll up your sleeve, Durmi," said Suadusegus, and Guiamo obliged.

"You have become *Druides*!" exclaimed Susama when she saw the serpent tattoo. "What kin of yours is one of the *Druidae*?"

"My mother's father is a *Druides* of the Bellovaci. He has asked me to give you this letter," Guiamo replied, and he handed her the rolled parchment. "Are you of the *Druidae*?"

"I am. Does this surprise you?" Setting the letter aside, she rolled up her green embroidered sleeve and revealed to Guiamo a serpent tattoo similar to his own. She then held her right hand up and showed him the gold serpent ring she wore on her index finger.

Guiamo asked, "Does not a *Druides* always wear the garments of white as my grandfather told me?"

Susama replied, "In a foreign land, where the *Druidae* are feared, I dare not wear my *Druides* garb. Here, I dress the part of a noblewoman of the Belgae." With a lilting laugh, she added, "Besides, I enjoy indulging myself in these beautiful clothes, and to be beautiful for my husband is not a sin."

She picked the letter back up, glanced over it and quickly realized it was an assignment of teaching responsibility from Camulvellaunus to her. She looked up at Guiamo and said, "Durmi, your grandfather is instructing me to teach you. So I shall. Each evening after your meal with Malleolus, you are to come here. We begin tomorrow. Is this understood?"

"Yes, my lady," Guiamo said.

" 'Yes, Priestess Susama,' " she corrected.

The first lessons were simply discussions of how the nineteen years of education would unfold. It was not until their fourth lesson that Guiamo asked about the legendary magic powers of the *Druidae*.

She put her hands in her lap and said, "There are two kinds of magical powers. The first power only is allowed to the *Druidae*. It is the power to use those gifts offered to us by the gods. My serpent ring is of this kind. It has the enchantment of Discernment. Words of the ancient tongue are used to call the enchantment into action. You can say the word without calling upon the power of the word. The word must be said as a command to empower the word."

Guiamo asked, "How is the enchantment put upon the ring?"

Susama replied, "A lump of purified gold is presented to the god by the *Druides* initiate in a sacred ceremony. If the initiate is approved by the god, the god transforms the lump of gold into a circle, shapes it, and imbues it with the power requested. It is the god who shapes the lump of gold into the ring. Usually he chooses the shape of the serpent.

"I have seen a *Druides* die while wearing the serpent ring. As his breath left him, the ring fell off his finger and returned to an unformed lump of gold again. It cannot be given, taken away, or left as an inheritance.

"There is another kind of magical power which the *Druidae* detest. This is the magic of witches, conjurers and warlocks. With their abuse of the words of power and with shameful potions, elixirs, curses and spells, they attempt to wrest from the gods the powers they desire. Cursed they are for their acts of blasphemy."

"Do you know the word '*ibur*?' " asked Guiamo.

Susama raised her eyebrows in surprise. "Where did you hear this? It is a mighty word of power."

Guiamo evaded her question by asking, "What is its meaning?"

Susama replied, "It is a word of Striking, meaning 'to pierce.' Where did you hear such a word?"

Again Guiamo ignored her question by asking, "What is the meaning of '*athibar*?' Do you know it as well?"

Susama said, "You are full of surprises! This is another strong word. It is a word of Summons. I would use this word to call someone I loved dearly to come back to me. A little child, upon hearing '*athibar*' would take it to mean I wanted her to come to sit upon my lap and receive tender caresses."

Susama looked with a stare of authority at Guiamo and said, "Tell me how you know these words of power."

Guiamo replied, "I must go speak to Gabinius. Only with his blessing can I reveal this to you." He rose and left hastily.

Guiamo returned with Gabinius and Lúin. When Susama saw Lúin, her expression became a confusing mix, transitioning between recognition, disbelief and astonishment. Bereft of words, she raised a wavering hand to point at the spear Guiamo carried.

She finally said in a hushed tone of utter disbelief, "Treasure of treasures! You have Lúin, the fabled spear of Lugus!" She put her hand to her mouth, looking back and forth between Lúin, Guiamo, Gabinius and Suadusegus in shock. "He has been lost for over a thousand years! I suspected a connection to a gift of the gods from your use of the two words of command '*ibur*' and '*athibar*,' but I did not think it possible Lúin had been found! How came Lúin into your possession?"

As Suadusegus and Susama sat in amazement, Gabinius told the whole story of what happened at the temple of Mars the day he purchased Suadusegus at the slave market.

When he had finished, Susama said, "Durmi, I will teach you the words you will need to draw upon the power of Lugus in Lúin." Shaking her head in amazement she said,

"To think that the spear of Lugus should visit me in this poor home in exile!"

Over the next month, Susama taught Guiamo the secret words of power most suited to apply to Lúin. Beginning with the simple words of the elder tongue, she showed Guiamo how to teach Lúin. Guiamo could sense that Lúin was eager to learn. Through Susama's instruction, Guiamo taught Lúin to cause his spearhead to become warm. With practice, Lúin could become extremely hot, and though occasionally the spear tip turned molten red, remained as strong and sharp as ever.

Lúin was also taught to point to the east, and Guiamo began to teach him to point at hidden things. Susama revealed to Guiamo several words that Lúin could understand to mean 'butt against' and 'knock down.' The spear would reverse course, and with the blunt end of the spear, attack objects Guiamo set up for him as targets. Guiamo worked diligently and eagerly with Lúin, and they bonded together. Over the weeks, Guiamo became fluent with the words and Lúin seemed to rejoice at his commands.

As the month passed by, Gabinius called Guiamo into the house one day to speak quietly together. "Your generosity to Actus and his fellows has proven quite expensive. Caesar demanded twenty-three *aurei* for a pardon of amnesty, one for each man. This is an expensive plan you have embarked upon. The plot of land alone cost sixteen *aurei*. I shall deduct the price of the pardon from your account."

Guiamo smiled up at him and said, "Expensive, yes, but worthwhile. They do work hard and enthusiastically. Their homes seem well built, they ask for little, and the well is nearly completed already. Once they have lined the well with stone, they will begin clearing the fields. I hope to buy some oxen for plowing in the spring. The men will need four iron plow blades, so I shall ask you now to schedule their construction. I shall also need scythes for each at harvest."

Gabinius said, "It will be a fine estate in a few years. You will make money from your fishermen friends so long as

196

Caesar fights his wars which, I still believe, could continue for years to come. You should begin thinking of planting orchards and vineyards next year."

"Oh, I have been, I have been," replied Guiamo, "particularly apple trees. You know how much I love fresh apples, though some are better than others. I shall need help finding the best saplings to plant."

"Choose wisely, for what you select will, like family, be with you the rest of your life," advised Gabinius. "I know several good sources, and there is always my own from which to draw."

Guiamo added, "I will plant an expansive orchard of these saplings, and my estate shall be known as '*Domus de Mali*,' " meaning 'the house of apple trees.'

As the men on Guiamo's estate made final preparations for the onset of winter, Guiamo invited Gabinius, Suadusegus and Susama to visit there with him. Suadusegus was feeling slightly feverish, so declined, but encouraged his wife to go. So, on a cool day with a welcome, warm touch from the sun, they mounted their horses and set off for the day. They traveled south to a bend in the river where the water was shallow, and easily crossed. They enjoyed the freedom of the trip, and Guiamo raced Honestia where the fields were smooth.

Three of the men were putting in the last of the stones to line the well, and Actus was supervising the storage of grain which Guiamo had purchased for them to last the winter. As Guiamo led Gabinius and Susama into the estate, Actus told one of the men to repair a torn sack of grain, and walked over to greet them.

Actus helped Gabinius dismount, and led his horse to a newly constructed stable. Guiamo helped Susama off her horse and led it and Honestia there as well. Gabinius and Susama waited patiently for the two to return. When the five at last were gathered together again, Guiamo introduced Actus to Susama. Politely, Actus offered to show everyone their progress.

As they walked across the fields, and through the cluster of small homes, Susama asked Actus about his life. He described his time of roaming with his men in the recent past, living off the land and the plunder of the unwary. He was surprised at the depth of her interest. When Gabinius and Guiamo turned another direction, she paused to face him.

"Did you tell him about these?" asked Susama as she pointed to a tattoo on his shoulder.

"He has seen them and knows they are curses," said Actus.

"Come now, you surely portrayed them as curses to you," she said, mildly rebuking him.

"They are curses to me. I have lived a life of desperation because of them," he retorted.

"Ah, now you are being evasive," she said. "These are curses, but not as you have led him to believe. I can read them. I know what they say. Shall I read them to him, or will you tell him? He needs to know."

"He must not know!" pleaded Actus. "Stolo will drive me away!"

"The damage is done, I fear. He needs to know. He shall know," said Susama.

"I do not have the strength within me to tell him. Will you tell him on my behalf? I shall stand there as you speak, but my tongue would betray me," said Actus, tormented with despair.

"I shall speak for you, and counsel him to make no rash decisions against you, but the decision will remain his to make," said Susama. "Come with me now. We must tell him today."

She quickly found Gabinius and Guiamo, and called them to meet concerning urgent matters. Actus let them use his home as a shelter from a growing wind. It was bare except for a long wooden bench before a firepit and in one corner his bedding lay.

Preferring to stand, Susama spoke gently to Guiamo. "I have been asked by Actus to speak on his behalf concerning things he has not revealed to you."

Gabinius became concerned and said, "Continue."

198

She said, "He has told you of the curses scribed into his body by evildoers in the land beyond the seas. What he concealed was the meaning of these curses."

Guiamo cautiously asked, "Are they not curses upon him?"

"No, Durmi, they are not curses upon him. They are curses laid in his skin to curse you." Susama said softly.

Gabinius groaned and covered his face. "What are the curses you have brought down on this boy?" he cried in anguish.

Actus hung his head and tears flowed from his eyes. "We were in such need! We heard your offer of amnesty and a hopeful future, and, as bees to a flower, we could not refuse! Forgive me, my lord Stolo, forgive me!"

Guiamo was shocked speechless and knew not what to do. Gabinius said again, "Speak the curse so we may know its face."

Susama said, "There are four curses upon his body. One on each shoulder and again on each thigh." Pointing to his left shoulder, she read, "He who prospers this thrall shall accursed be, that his wealth be wrenched from his hands and given to another." To his right shoulder she pointed and said, "He who shelters this thrall shall accursed be, that his way be lost, never to return."

Again pointing, but to his left thigh, she said, "He who protects this thrall shall accursed be, that sickness afflict him in his time of trial."

Finally, reading from his right thigh, she said, "He who befriends this thrall shall accursed be, that all friend and family be lost."

Gabinius mourned, "Each of these, Guiamo has done!"

Susama said, "I cannot stop the curse. It was written in the ancient tongue which has far greater power than the child language of Rome. Even the language of the Belgae is not powerful enough to defeat the words of old."

Gabinius said, "Is there anything that can be done?"

Susama replied, "I can only ask the gods of our fathers to protect him. Perhaps they will grant that each curse will happen only once or at different times, but happen they shall."

Gabinius turned to Guiamo. "You must live your life as if the curses have no affect on you. We cannot be certain that the curses were spoken correctly as intended. They must be spoken before they can be written."

Susama agreed. "The wicked one who set this curse may also have intended for you to change the course you would choose to live your life. This may actually be their intention. Malleolus is correct. Live your life as if this had not taken place."

Guiamo asked, "Why did the curse come to me?"

Susama said, "The evil ones surely know you are coming, and have so for many years. However strong their foresight, they know not who you are or where. They may also not know when you are coming. Divining that your destiny intertwines with theirs, they would have selected someone that they saw would also intertwine with your path. Actus, it would seem, is that one. In releasing him into the world, they have sent him as an arrow shot into the night, knowing only that it would pass near the target. They could not know if you would help Actus, but laid this trap before your feet in the hopes of ensnaring you. In this they have succeeded.

"You should always be cautions as you go through life. It may be that Actus is not the only one sent out into the world to poison your way.

"Now the power of curses goes in both directions. This I know; that it sometimes happens that a curse sent out may, in the end, return harm in equal measure to the one who sends it."

Gabinius said, "What must we do?"

"I shall take Actus and Durmius to a sacred grove atop a hill. There is a ritual of the *Druidae* to cleanse one from curses," replied Susama. "Is there a sacred hill nearby?"

Guiamo replied, "Yes! There is the sacred grove on the larger hill by Gobedbiacum where Salonius and I killed the great boar."

Susama was shocked, "You killed a pig in the holy grove? You may well have desecrated the sacred site! Its power could be destroyed!"

"No, Susama," said Guiamo. "The boar was only near it. I shot it on a trail leading into the oak grove."

Susama was visibly relieved. "Thank the gods!" she said. "The sanctification ritual to cleanse a sacred site requires the presence of twelve *Druidae* and the sacrifice of four white bulls."

"Four bulls could be purchased only at a tremendous cost," observed Gabinius, "and we have but one *Druides* priestess to call upon." He winked at Guiamo and said, "It is well that your shot killed the boar so quickly or its bloody squeals would have driven out every spirit in the grove."

Susama did not appreciate Gabinius' humor, glared at him, and then continued her thought. "A sacred grove blessed by priests of Rome has less power than *Druides*, for their charms are as the speech of babes, but I should hope it would be sufficient. We should destroy this curse tomorrow. I will make the preparations. Malleole, I need sulfur."

Clad in a white robe that touched her heels, and wearing a garland of mistletoe upon her hair, she led them into the clearing in the sacred grove only after Guiamo showed Susama the exact location the boar had died. Actus was nervous and entered with great hesitation.

Taking Guiamo aside so that Actus could not hear the secret details of the ritual of the *Druidae*, Susama explained the ceremony to her new pupil, "I will create a fire from the sulfur. When the clouds of smoke have risen thickly, you must pass through the smoke four times. The foul burning sulfur clings to the stench of the curse. As the sulfur smoke rises to disperse into the air, it takes the curse with it. When this ritual is complete, the potency of the curse should be diminished. We may learn only then to what degree the god will cleanse you of it.

"As for Actus, the ritual shall be painful. To remove the curses from Actus, he must receive a new tattoo depicting a serpent devouring each of the four demons of the curses. Only then will he be freed from his burden."

The cleansing ritual of burning sulfur was surprisingly quick. Susama gathered fallen twigs and sticks into a pile. When the stack was sufficiently large, she knelt down and said, *"Falamos!"* With a bright cluster of sparks and a puff of smoke, the wood began to burn brightly.

Guiamo was shocked at the use of magical words to spark the fire, and memorized the word Susama had spoken.

Satisfied, she began casting handfuls of sulfurous powder across it. As the sulfur burned, a most obnoxious odor of rotting eggs permeated the area and Guiamo nearly gagged on the stench. When the clouds of putrid smoke had lifted high and dense around the small bonfire, Susama told Guiamo, "It is time to pass through. Do this four times without speaking."

Guiamo walked through the smoke as instructed the four times. When this was completed, he looked at Susama and shrugged his shoulders as if to say, "Now what?"

Susama motioned for him to remain silent. She removed her gold serpent ring, and holding it to her lips, blew a puff of air through it. With a clear voice, she spoke loudly through the center of the ring, "What is the truth now of the power of the four curses?"

Susama held the ring to Guiamo's left ear, and he heard a faint whisper reply, "Once it shall be. Only one time shall each curse bear its wicked fruit."

As Susama had promised, Actus' four new tattoos were painful, and it took her the rest of the day to complete them. Throughout it all, though, Actus seemed relieved and eager for her to proceed. As each serpent tattoo was completed, he shouted with joy as if the pain of a firebrand had been quenched.

When the three walked the long trail back to Gobedbiacum, Actus told Susama and Guiamo the story of his life in the land beyond the sea. "I was newly married and content when they found me. They were brutish men who

202

served the evil ones. They came with sword and flame to my village. My brother was visiting, and they slew him as he tried to bolt the door. My wife fell upon the firepit as they dragged me away. The last thing I remember of my home was the stench of her burning flesh.

"I was taken away into the night, hooded and tied. When at last they stopped to rest, one of the evil creatures joined them to place the curses upon my body. I saw him not, but his voice was rough like a bear or wolf. His accent was strange, and he spoke our language with some difficulty. He was tall of stature and the creature stank. I was taken beside the fire, and he handled me roughly and struck me across my mouth. I cannot be certain, but I thought his hands had claws and not nails for his grip upon my shoulder left punctures which even today are roughly scarred. When he came near to my face, I nearly vomited from the sourness of his foul breath."

Guiamo interrupted him, "Are you saying that he was not a man?"

Susama answered cautiously, "It is possible. This world holds many mysteries that even the *Druidae* do not know. There are ancient stories told of monsters which live in a kingdom far across the western sea. They are said to be powerful and wicked creatures of the world of Ifurin, of chaos, destruction, and the ancient ever-swirling darkness. Some say they were cast out of the abyss of Domnu to punish the sins of men, but the *Druidae* think not. I have had little dealing with these legends of old, and most think them merely stories of simple folk told to frighten their children into obedience. It may be that these legends have some truth to them. I cannot say. Tell us of what then happened."

Actus said, "I was thrown roughly to the ground and held down by the men who stole me. The evil one chanted strange words as he carved my flesh in these four places, and when done with his work, he spat upon the wounds."

Susama took interest in this and said, "Did the spittle increase or lessen the pain of your tattooed skin?"

Actus replied, "To my surprise, it lessened the pain."

203

Susama seemed relieved. "The creature then had already poured out his strength into the cursing words. It would seem, then, that the curse has not the power to revive itself in later days. What happened next?"

Actus said, "After traveling many days still bound and hooded, we came to the coast and I was set upon a boat which bore me to the land of the Belgae. There I was released with not a word spoken.

"I sought help, but upon seeing the tattooed curses upon my body, was beaten and driven away. In desperation, I lived by my wits in the wild. After several years, I learned that the Belgae had named me the Lost Man of the Wood. I had been sighted from time to time and they had come to fear me.

"Eventually, I came to a village whose chieftain feared neither demon nor man. I came to ask for food and clothing, and was seized by some warriors as a trophy. They had at last captured the dangerous Lost Man of the Wood.

"The chieftain had been boasting to all of his strength and skill, and seeing me dragged before him, saw his chance to prove his might. He challenged me to fight for the food I wanted. I realized he would not free me, so agreed on the condition that if I won, I would receive not only his food, but also become the chieftain of this tribe. How they roared with laughter, for I was thin and haggard. A good jest, they thought.

"I said, 'Swear it, my lord! If I win, the leader of your tribe I shall be.'

"Turning to the clamoring crowd, he laughed and shouted, 'I so swear! By the gods, I swear that if this mouseling can kill me, your lord he shall be.' And they all laughed for they well knew his prowess in battle.

"With venom in his voice, he turned to me and said, 'And if I defeat you, while you yet live, I shall cut out those pretty marks upon your legs and shoulders and hang them on my walls to forever remember your insolence.'

"Little hope had I to survive this battle, but I had decided that I might best be able to run to the safety of the wood if a sword was in my hand. The crowd fell back to give us room to fight. I was given a sharp, but well-worn sword with which to fight. It was a *gladius* of Rome taken on the field of battle in years past.

"He came at me with a great sword and battle was joined. I fought not to win, but merely to survive. I saw a thin place in the encircling throng where I might break free, and maneuvered so that I should have a direct path to it.

"Then, to the surprise of all, a great black raven flew overhead. With a loud caw, it placed a dropping directly across both of his eyes. Blinded, he roared in frustration and wiped frantically at his face. I seized the moment, knocked his wavering sword aside and thrust my blade into his throat. The crowd gasped in surprise and fell silent as they watched him struggle and fall.

"As his blood poured out onto the ground, I shouted in triumph, 'Your lord, I shall be! With an oath to the gods, he swore it! Is there any among you who dares deny the gods their choice of lord?'

"Not one spoke aloud, though the murmurs of discontent were many. I called the elders to gather before me and reluctantly they came. I said, 'Take me to the house of your former lord. His house is now my house. His wife shall be mine. His children are my children. Take me there. We have much to discuss.'

"To my surprise, they did not resist. I was introduced to his wife and seven children." He looked at Guiamo and said, "As a woman, she had little to admire, and though she must have pleased him, I saw that she wept not at her husband's death.

"I met with the elders and spoke of their enemies, of their food supplies, and of what brought them prosperity. They saw that I would not bring tyranny, and so accepted my lordship. Still, they were frightened of the cursed marks upon my body.

"I ruled over them for nearly a year, and was content. Then another tribe attacked our village in the night. I had taken over half our warriors on a raid of our own, and so the villagers were unable to fight them off. When we returned from our raid, instead of a time of joy and the sharing of plunder with our families, we found rotting bodies and burned huts. None blamed me, but nothing remained to keep us there. Only the memory of our beloved remained to haunt us day by day. We left our ruined homeland and turned south to search out a new life in Gallia."

Susama said, "So that is how you came to meet with Durmius."

"Yes, priestess," Actus replied.

"Remember this day, Actus, when troubles arise and you wish to move on. To him you owe your life. You must stand loyally beside him always," she cautioned.

The weeks passed, and Guiamo worked as earnestly as ever with his lessons, but his heart was in the time spent with Susama, priestess of the *Druidae*. His work with Lúin became his joy in life, and her lessons in the ancient words quickly gave him a confidence in exploring the spear's capabilities. She had him practice the varying degrees of command which could be given.

"Take me through the increasing strength's of the words of Fire you have taught Lúin," instructed Susama.

Guiamo commanded *"Chothla!"* and the spear tip grew warm to her hand. He said, *"Votnerti!"* and Lúin's bronze point became too hot to touch. With a shout of *"Ebfulna!"* Guiamo told the spear to become molten red and it was so.

"Good, good!" said Susama, pleased with his skill and control. "Try this word now. Say *"banru."*

"Banru!" commanded Guiamo, and a flame of fire erupted out the top of the spear. It continued to burn as Guiamo quietly examined it.

"Now say, '*nef,*' " said Susama.

"Nef!" Guiamo said, and the flame went out.

"Nef is a word of Ceasing. It works with many things," she observed. "Now for something very interesting. Say, '*ignu-al.*' "

"Ignu-al!" said Guiamo, and Lúin's spear point began to glow brightly as the sun. *"Nef!"* he called out, intimidated by the power contained within this command.

206

"You already know *falamos*. Let us try another. I shall stand behind you when you say this one." She moved behind Guiamo and put her hands on his shoulders. "Think of a target and say '*thivinen.*'"

Guiamo held tightly to Lúin and commanded, "*Thivinen!*" An enormous bolt of lightning sprung out from the spear point, crossed the meadow and split an ancient tree in two, with the branches crashing to the ground.

As Guiamo gaped in awe, Susama quietly observed, "Great power Lugus has given you, Durmi, which you are now just beginning to learn."

Winter gave little difficulty to Actus and his men. The estate had been secured for winter, the fields prepared for plowing in the springtime, and food stored securely. Animals had been purchased, and the barns were full of lowing cows and bleating goats. Two of the men spent their spare time courting local girls, and the others looked on both in envy and humor as they saw their two friends behaving in foolish and embarrassing ways. Their lives were simple, but all were content.

Guiamo continued his regular routine of lessons upon lessons, and exercise and military drill. Gabinius gave him much latitude in his schedule, but Susama rigidly required his evenings for learning the ways of the *Druidae*. Guiamo, too, was content with his life and spent his free time enjoying the company of Actus and his men. And so the winter passed.

Chapter Five - 56 B.C.

"Do what is required, strike hard, and let the consequences be damned." Commodore Sir Horace Philip Stone, Battle of Jutland 1916.

Gabinius came to Guiamo's *cubiculum* one evening in the springtime, and sat down on his bed to talk. "Guiamo, I am an old man. I am now nearly seventy-five years old, and a time of change has come. Some weeks ago, I sent word to my two sons to come here. They should arrive over the next few days. The time has come that I should turn much of my industry over to them. In truth, it will be a relief, for my joy in work comes through my artistic masterpieces only. The drudgery of producing large quantities of simple weaponry wears on me. I enjoy creating the intricate details for which I am renown.

"My eldest son, Lucius, you know is a merchant of wine, grain and the oil of olives with eighteen good cargo ships sailing the *Mare Nostrum*. He is, I think, most interested and capable of continuing my work successfully.

"Quintus, my younger son, is highly skilled as a sculptor. He does stone portraits. There was once a time when he was considered to carve a bust of *Senator* Nasica, but Quinta's price was said to be too high. That is not altogether surprising, for from what little I have heard of the man, Nasica would not pay the fee to have his own mother carried in a *lectica* litter to see a physician when she was ill.

"Well, Quintus is very talented, and though I love him dearly, he is much too fond of his wine and a life of ease. He plays too much the rascal for me to give him my estate. He will receive instead a large sum of money for his inheritance when he arrives, and Lucius, the ownership of my lands and industry. I think both will be pleased.

"The day will come when I have died, and Lucius today has no knowledge of my suppliers and our agreements in business. I must secure for him a way to continue the industry uninterrupted.

"My merchants of late are becoming unreliable, and their shipments rarely arrive when they promise. I need to visit

208

with them soon and either secure their reliability or find new sources.

"I see that this will be my last trip to the coast. I am still able to travel, as you well know, but the enjoyment of travel is gone. Sleeping on the wet ground under the falling rain no longer appeals to me as it once did in the days of my youth.

"Many of my suppliers are located only a few days distance, and I will go with Lucius to visit them all. The most urgent trip is to the tin and copper merchants on the western coast. This is the trip for which I purchased Suadusegus. With the knowledge you have of many tongues, you are to be the ever-present ears for Lucius and me."

Guiamo said, "It should prove an interesting trip."

Gabinius replied, "Yes, it will. Particularly so, since the word I am receiving is that a tribe to the west, the Veneti, is clamoring to challenge Caesar's governance. We will have need to tread carefully between the Veneti and Rome."

Guiamo asked, "When do we begin our travels?"

Gabinius replied, "Some weeks from now. Once I have given Lucius the estate, and Quintus his inheritance, we will leave for the coast."

Guiamo replied, "The timing is good, for it will not be long before Actus has finished sowing our first crop of wheat. I should like to see his work completed before we set out. While we are gone, his men will be planting vineyards."

Lucius was dark of skin and nearly as tall as his father, but not as broad in the shoulders nor as muscular. Guiamo discovered that he had never chosen to serve with a *legio*, turning to the sea to make his living instead.

In a short two years, he had managed to earn enough to purchase his first merchant ship. It was a leaky fishing boat, single-masted, and only four *passuum* long. He hauled it ashore with a borrowed team of oxen, and scraped the hull clean of barnacles. Rotten sections of the wooden hull had to be replaced, and he inspected every plank from prow to stern. The sail was old and ragged, and he worked hard to stitch it back into usefulness. After two months of laborious efforts, he dragged his boat back into the sea.

From that moment on, he sailed, carried cargo on his back, bartered, transported goods, hired crewmen, and his fortunes began to grow. Now equipped with eighteen proper merchant ships with deep hulls, sail and oars, his fleet plowed the seas of the *Mare Nostrum*, taking goods between Rome, Greece and Egypt.

Lucius knew how to build wealth upon wealth. At forty-six years old, he had also developed a farming estate nearly as impressive as his father's. He had married the daughter of a minor noble, and she bore him seven children, of which five sons survived to pass through the coming of age ceremony of *Liberalia*.

He came unannounced one day, riding on a powerful brown steed which wore an elegant ermine fur-lined collar. Six years had passed since Lucius had seen his father, and their reunion was a time of joy and feasting.

Gabinius had quickly introduced Guiamo to his son and told Lucius his story, but as the days passed, Guiamo began to feel shunted aside. Suadusegus, seeing the boy's sagging spirits, kept him focused on his lessons, and Susama stepped in to help by playing the role of loving mother to him.

Gabinius and Lucius spent most of their time together and quite happily, and Gabinius taught his son every aspect of his business he could think of. Seven days passed and Quintus finally arrived driving a two-wheeled cart. Gabinius greeted him with as much pleasure as he had with Lucius, and the three spent the next two days reviewing Gabinius' estate and speaking of the future and the past.

Guiamo was pleased that there was no jealousy or strife between the two sons. He realized that Gabinius knew his sons well, and that his decision for each was best suited to them both. Gabinius formally transferred title of his estate to Lucius who graciously gave his heartfelt thanks. Quintus, too, was delighted with the vast fortune his father passed over to him, and blessed his father for the tremendous generosity he had shown to his younger son.

Quintus stayed for twenty days before returning to his home in Rome, and spent this time completing two carved portraits of his father in white marble. After painting them in vibrant, lifelike colors, one was presented as a gift to Lucius, and the other he kept for himself. Gabinius was delighted with the work, and humbled by the honor paid him by his son.

While Quintus labored on the sculptures alone in a private workshop, Gabinius and Lucius sat together speaking mostly of business, politics and war. Lucius came to learn how closely entwined his father's business had become with the aspirations of Governor Caesar. He also learned more about Guiamo's talents, the roles of Calidius and Gabinius, of oracles, and the boy's developing estate and fortune. Gabinius showed Lucius the documents of Guiamo's financial account, and made his son swear to keep the records true and honor the boy's ownership of the money. Lucius dutifully agreed to his role of stewardship and promised to faithfully turn the money over to Guiamo when the boy celebrated *Liberalia* the next year.

With many tears in parting, Quintus drove his wagon down the lane wondering if he would ever see his beloved father again. Once he passed out of sight of his father's home, his thoughts turned to his lovely wife and their three young children impatiently awaiting their father's return, and switched the horse to a faster pace.

As his youngest son departed, Gabinius turned to Lucius and said, "It is time now to go to the west to introduce you to the copper and tin merchants. Salonius and Guiamo will accompany us. Will you help organize our supplies? I am weary from seeing my dear boy departing."

"Yes, father," Lucius replied. "I have prepared the list of supplies we need. All should fit into the two wagons. With some help, we should be able to leave in the morning."

The first day of the journey was the eighteenth day of *Iunius*, and after the morning passed, they stopped to eat. Guiamo, who had been riding with Salonius in the following wagon, stepped forward and spoke to Gabinius' son, "Lucius, what are the best and worst things you have seen in the sea?"

Lucius said, "The best thing a sailor sees is his wife waiting for him on the pier after he has passed through a terrible storm."

Guiamo asked, "And the worst thing?"

Lucius replied solemnly, "There was a time when I went out to sea in my first small boat. It was equipped only with a single sail, and a storm came up which raged all night. It blew me into an area of the *Mare Nostrum* where pirates are known to live. As I sailed around trying to find my bearings, I came upon a terrible sight. I saw another small sailing ship sitting calmly in the middle of the sea. From a distance, I could hear the weak voice of a man crying out for help. As I drew closer to give him aid, I saw that his ship was stranded in a vast bed of kelp, unable to break free. My own ship started to slow from the drag of the kelp, and I was forced to turn away before becoming stranded as he.

"He cried out that I must help him, for he had no food and was starving. With tears, he shouted that he had been caught there for fifteen days, and would soon perish from hunger and thirst. The pirates had seen his plight, but, laughing, had refused him aid since he had no cargo of worth to them.

"My ship was similar to his with but a single sail and no oars. I could not help him, and had to sail away. Later, when I came to shore, I told all I found with ships of the man's dire condition. When I described the location of the kelp beds, they all said for fear of the pirates, they could not help him. And so he must have perished there all alone, trapped in the beds of kelp."

Hearing this sad tale, the four fell silent, and they turned awkwardly to their meal.

Gabinius broke the silence by changing subjects. With the three others quietly eating a simple meal of bread and salt pork, he spoke of the days to come.

"Guiamo," said Gabinius, "when we arrive in Aremorica, you will dress as a slave. In all your behavior, you must play this humble role. We must not allow the tin and copper traders to think you important. Most of all, you must always remember to speak to me as *Dominus* Malleolus. To name

212

me Gabinius would reveal my plan to them. Lucius shall be Malleolus to you. Can you do this? It will hurt your pride, I assure you."

"Yes, *Dominus* Malleole," said Guiamo with a smile as he tried out his new business role.

"Good!" replied Gabinius. "You must also never speak to the traders or look them in the eye. Behave as a slave. Spend your time near their servants, but pretend to not understand them. They will speak more freely than their masters. Listen carefully at all times.

"For my part, I will prolong the bargaining across two or more days. This will give you time to glean what you can before decisions must be made. Having Lucius with me as my heir will give good cause for a lengthy negotiation.

"Saloni, your role is as guardian. You will act as if Guiamo is an untrustworthy slave who might bolt to freedom if given the chance. Take deliberate action which they can witness to keep weapons out of his reach."

Salonius showed a mischievously wicked grin to Guiamo and said, "I am to be guardian to Durmius the slave! Oh, I shall enjoy this day! Kneel slave and grovel!"

Guiamo growled at him in feigned anger.

Gabinius corrected Salonius, "You also must take care to name him Guiamo and not Durmius, a name of Rome."

Turning back to Guiamo, he corrected himself, "Guiamo, It may be wise of you to speak the tongue of the Bellovaci openly. Perhaps some of their servants will understand it, and you could gather even yet more knowledge of their dealings. Commonality among people tends to make the tongue wag."

Salonius and Guiamo nodded as Gabinius continued, "We shall need to take your knife and gold *bulla praetexta* from you, for they are certainly not to be found on a slave."

Lucius was surprised at the audacity of his father's plan, and appreciated his insight in dealing with unscrupulous or unreliable men.

Early in their travels, they learned that Caesar had attempted to storm a Veneti *oppidum* situated on a narrow peninsula. To the dismay of the *milites gregarii* and Caesar alike, the low lying land between the mainland and the *oppidum* would flood twice daily as the tide came in.

A fat-faced Roman merchant with crooked feet and bandy legs they met on the road described how the first battle fared, "Caesar's man is *Legatus* Decimus Junius Brutus Albinus who does not seem to understand how to fight the Veneti. He planned to assault a fair sized *oppidum* with normal Roman tactics, and was soundly thrashed. He had his *milites gregarii* build a long, narrow mole of earthwork out into the tidal flats. When Albinus had exhausted his men with weeks of moving stone and earth, spent the treasury dry on food and supplies, and they were nearly ready to assault the *oppidum*, the Veneti outfoxed him. Do you know what they did?"

Gabinius shook his head and said, "No. Pray, tell me."

The merchant replied, "The Veneti brought in their fleet at high tide and evacuated everyone. To the astonishment of the Romans, they simply sailed away to another *oppidum* sited a short distance away on a similar peninsula. The Veneti bragged that the only thing of value left behind was the horse dung stained straw underfoot."

Gabinius observed, "The cost to Rome and the demoralization of its *legiones* must be tremendous."

"I agree," said the merchant. "I think Albinus has not yet recovered from his defeat, and still he does not know how to deal with the Veneti."

Gabinius thanked him for the information and the four moved on in their two wagons. As they headed northwest down the dusty road, Guiamo asked, "Gabini, why are the Veneti rebelling?"

Gabinius replied, "They rebel because they wish to be free of Rome. The cause, this time, is two-fold. They fear that Rome will usurp their trade with Albion, a great isle only a short distance beyond the northwestern coastline. The second cause of strife was caused when Rome pushed them too hard last year. Caesar had demanded hostages and they were only reluctantly given up. Then last *September* Caesar sent men to demand grain from the Veneti. Their harvest had

214

not been good, and they could not afford to spare any. After a brief council, the Veneti chieftains rebuked the Romans and took them hostage. They hoped to exchange them for their family members held by Rome. Caesar did not take this act kindly, and this spring, marched the Ninth, Tenth and Twelfth *Legiones* to put down the growing rebellion. The captive Romans were executed as soon as the first *legio* set foot in the land of the Veneti, and war began."

Salonius always kept a careful watch and regularly advised Gabinius to keep pace with other travelers for the safety to be found in numbers. Usually once each day, a Roman cavalry patrol passed by. The way was clear, the weather good, and they traveled quickly.

As they traveled, they gathered more information of Caesar's difficulties. Albinus had tried three times to seize an occupied Veneti stronghold. The results were always the same, with dozens of sailing ships fading from sight as they passed over the horizon, leaving only the stinging jeers of the Veneti to fill their ears.

They followed the westward flow of the river Liger, and as they approached the land of the Veneti after twenty-eight days of travel, Gabinius learned that Caesar had decided on a change in strategy. Caesar would fight on the sea to defeat the Veneti. Gabinius did not expect Caesar to be successful in such a risky battle. Gabinius had seen Veneti ships and knew they had two tremendous advantages over the Roman *biremes*.

The two-deck *bireme* rowing ships had lower sides than the Veneti ships, which made it extremely difficult for the Roman *classiarii* marines to scramble onto the Veneti ships for a coordinated assault.

The second obstacle facing Caesar was that his primary tactic of ramming the sides of the enemy ships would be unsuccessful, for the *bireme* underwater rams could not pierce the unusually strong hulls built by the Veneti.

Gabinius explained all this to Lucius, Guiamo and Salonius, and the four fearfully hoped Caesar would not drown entire *legiones* in a futile battle against experienced shipmen while Rome blundered along with unsuitable tactics.

At long last, on the twenty-second day of *Quintilis*, the four weary travelers came upon the Roman encampment on the southern banks of the Liger River near the coast. It soon became apparent that a battle was imminent.

Albinus had decided against building Roman *biremes*, for their construction would prove too costly and time consuming. Rather, he recruited a vast number of ships from among the friendly locals who saw a means to make a large profit. Many of their ships were built in a fashion akin to the strong Veneti sailing ships. They were flat bottomed ships with strong oaken sides, high bows and sterns, and with raw leather sails. Into these ships manned by experienced sailors of Gallia, Albinus planned to station many of the *milites gregarii* as *classiarii* clad in full battle armor to storm the enemy ships.

According to a *centurio* who was willing to speak to Gabinius, the battle would take place in two days. "*Legatus* Albinus intends to grapple with the Veneti ships and force a battle ship against ship."

Guiamo was listening by Gabinius' side and asked, "How will he catch them? With a brisk wind, I should think they could maneuver around freely."

"Yes, that day will be like trying to catch birds with a net," the *centurio* replied. "Now if they had no sails, it would be much easier." Looking down at the *druídes* tattoo on Guiamo's arm, he joked, "Do you have a magic spell to remove their sails?"

Guiamo thought a moment and replied, "Perhaps we could slash their sails so they could catch no wind."

"And how would we do such a thing?" taunted the *centurio* skeptically.

Guiamo mulled this over for a few seconds and then replied, "I do not think it would be so difficult. If we took a knife, or perhaps a scythe like they use for harvesting grain, and affixed it to an extremely long pole, our men could stab

216

into the leather sails as we passed by. As our ship passed theirs, it would slice cleanly down their sail."

Pausing to ponder the idea, he said, "I believe a scythe would work better than a knife, for its curved blade would grab into the sail and not pull out. It would cut cleanly downward. Bring your advance ships in with scythes and let the boarding *classiarii* follow. With sails in tatters, they cannot maneuver. You can board them as you please." With a smug look on his face, Guiamo said flatly, "*Roma victrix*, Hail Caesar."

The *centurio* blinked in surprise and his mouth fell open. Gabinius could see the idea sinking in. The *centurio* was so taken in by the brilliant simplicity of Guiamo's idea that he turned without speaking and dashed back into the camp to tell *Legatus* Albinus.

Albinus walked briskly out of the camp a short while later with an armed escort and several senior officers. The *centurio* directed him to Guiamo. After a quick introduction, Albinus said, "Durmi, would you care to watch the battle with Governor Caesar? I plan to meet the Veneti in battle in two days, and Caesar will be watching from atop a hill nearby. We have just enough time to gather the scythes you suggested and cut the long poles. You have given us the advantage we need."

"Yes, certainly I would like to witness the fight with Governor Caesar!" said Guiamo with great enthusiasm. "May Gabinius, Lucius and Salonius join me?"

"Without doubt, they can. Be here tomorrow evening before dusk and I will have a guard escort take you there," Albinus replied.

Gabinius led his three companions to meet the escort as instructed, and they were given horses to ride to their campsite. They found a tent with accommodations in the shadow of a hill, and were delighted with the fresh scent of the sea which wafted across the land. They settled in for the evening and soon fell asleep.

When Guiamo was presented to Caesar midmorning on the hilltop by the ocean, Caesar said, "It would seem, my fortune in battle is to be determined by the counsel of a mere youth!"

Gabinius replied, "A good idea from a youth is still a good idea. Thank the gods that this boy was born a Roman. If he had been Veneti born, it would be a day of disaster for Rome."

"Well said," replied Caesar, "but the battle is not yet fought and victory is not certain. I may yet be forced to put my tail between my legs and run like a beaten whelp."

Caesar glanced out to sea at the Veneti ships at rest in the bay and then off at the promontory point to the southeast. "Our ships have set out from the estuary of the Liger River. They are coming into the bay even now," he said. "Albinus will be in the center with a red banner."

Guiamo looked toward the southeast and saw three clusters of ships rapidly sailing toward the fleet of over two hundred Veneti ships at anchor in the bay below. He could clearly see the Veneti sailors scrambling to raise their sails and haul in the chains of the anchor stones. Several of the larger ships carried catapults, and the fires were being stoked in preparation to send volleys of flaming projectiles at the Roman fleet.

The wind favored Rome. The Veneti saw their disadvantage and turned west out to sea to better position themselves.

Caesar motioned to an aide who sprinted into the woods. He returned with six others bearing a table and chairs. When these were positioned to Caesar's satisfaction, they ran back to the rear again. The servants returned quickly loaded down with wine and food which was spread across the table.

With a gesture of his hand, he invited his staff to help themselves. He turned to Gabinius, Guiamo, Lucius and Salonius and asked them to eat as well.

Guiamo was hungry and enjoyed the feast of delicacies, but what surprised him most of the whole affair was the pervasive casualness with which Caesar approached the critical battle. He seemed more interested in a piece of chicken caught between his teeth than the moment by moment updates from messengers and signalmen.

Still, Caesar was fully aware of the developing sea battle. As Albinus' fleet moved to pursue, Caesar called Guiamo to him. "See how the Veneti have just turned to face our fleet. They can use the wind to advantage now, and they will close with Albinus' left fleet first. Do you see how Albinus has advanced his right fleet? Watch how he uses them."

Just as Caesar had observed, Guiamo could see the Veneti fleet began to pick up speed after they heeled about. Their sails began flapping at first, and then billowed out in full as they completed their turnabout.

"When our left becomes entangled with the Veneti, Albinus will signal his right to turn and maneuver to come across their bows. Watch for signals from Albinus' red ship."

Several minutes passed as the ships of both sides turned to gain advantage. As the Veneti closed upon Albinus' left, Guiamo saw four ships begin firing flaming projectiles, leaving smoking trails arcing across the sky. The first volley fell short.

The second volley managed one clear hit on the deck of a Roman ship, and the frame supporting the mast was destroyed. Without support, the mast started to lean and the sail began to drag in the water.

The bulk of the Veneti fleet bore down on the Roman left, but a dozen ships saw the threat from Albinus' right. They veered off to engage, but the winds were too contrary, and they could not turn adequately to meet them properly. Albinus' right mixed with the dozen Veneti ships, passing close enough in many cases to bump hulls.

To the surprise of the experienced Veneti sailors, the *milites gregarii* lifted long poles with cutting scythe blades attached. Before the Veneti could steer clear of this unexpected threat, the Romans impaled their enemy's leather sails, and with mighty pulls, tore the Veneti sails into strips.

Immobilized, the Veneti panicked. The leading Roman ships continued on to other targets, and the following ships filled with boarding parties chose their victims. With two or three ships attacking isolated Veneti ships at once, the *milites gregarii* stormed aboard from different directions and butchered the outmatched and unarmored Veneti sailors.

Once a ship's crew had been slaughtered, the Romans reboarded their own vessels and maneuvered methodically to their next victim.

The ships on the Roman right followed the same strategy, and Guiamo watched in awe as he saw his strategy obliterate the Veneti fleet.

Curiously, Caesar placed his helmet on the ground at Guiamo's feet. Gabinius and Guiamo were puzzled by Caesar's action, but the mystery was soon revealed. Messengers came to Caesar with battle statistics at regular intervals. Each time a report was given, Caesar reached into an armored box on the ground and pulled coins out.

After the first report, Caesar dropped fourteen newly minted gold *aurei* into the helmet. "One for each ship destroyed by young Durmius." Smiling, he patted Guiamo's back, and mussed his hair appreciatively.

The battle raged on and it became clear that Rome had won the day. Rather than flee, the Veneti stubbornly clung to the hope of victory. In the end, Albinus surrounded the Veneti with his center formation of ships, and every Veneti ship was taken. Most crews died to a man, but at the last when the winds died down, a cluster of barely mobile Veneti ships slowly approached to beg for mercy.

They received mercy, but it was the mercy of slavery. Guiamo watched as the Veneti ships were taken in tow and hauled back to the Roman port past the promontory to the southeast back to the Liger River estuary.

When the last ship was seized, Caesar said, "Count, Durmi. See what appreciation Caesar and Rome have for your genius."

Guiamo picked up Caesar's heavy helmet and, placing it on the table, began to count. When he finished, he had two hundred twenty-three gold *aurei*.

"The gold is yours, but the helmet, I need," said the smiling Caesar triumphantly. "Do you desire to own any

220

slaves? The Veneti have cost me dearly, and their debt will be paid in blood and flesh."

Guiamo replied, "Your gold is more than generous. I have need of no slaves. I am building an estate of my own and already have twenty-three men to work it."

Caesar was surprised. He asked, "At so young an age? How came you by so many workers?"

Guiamo said, "You may remember them for I purchased a pardon from you for them. They had been a company of brigands near Gobedbiacum."

Caesar was surprised and said, "That motley band that gave my cavalry fits for years?"

Guiamo replied, "Yes, it is they. They have turned out to be good men, and they work diligently."

Caesar nodded and said, "I am glad it worked out for you."

The officers and their four guests watched for a long time on the hill as the prizes of battle were secured and towed away. When they readied themselves to leave, Caesar said, "It is a rare day when the *Druidae* help Rome."

Gabinius replied, "Cannot a man be both holy and Roman?"

Intrigued, Caesar laughed in appreciation of his insight. "You are a most interesting pair. Farewell Malleolus! Farewell Durmius Sail-render."

As Guiamo, Gabinius, Salonius and Lucius were escorted back to their wagons at the Roman encampment, Caesar descended the hill to board Albinus' ship which had anchored near the shoreline.

With great cheers of celebration, Caesar was rowed in a small craft alongside Albinus' ship. A boom slung from the mast swung out over the smaller boat, and from it, a wooden crossbeam was lowered by rope. Caesar stepped up onto the swaying wooden bar, and grasping the ropes on either side, was lifted up onto Albinus' ship.

Albinus set sail north to the estuary of the Gwilen River, and Caesar was soon standing on its southern bank.

Awaiting him were the officers of the Ninth *Legio* which had marched deep into Veneti territory. "We await your orders," said the *Legatus Legionis*.

Caesar replied, "We march south to Darioritum. I shall have my vengeance upon the Veneti in full. Have all the men of the Tenth and Twelfth *Legiones* disembark from whence they sailed. We will march to meet them at the Veneti village.

"Sell the Veneti ships and the prisoners. Half the proceeds comes to me. One tenth goes to Albinus. One tenth shall go to the officers in proportion to their rank. Distribute the rest to the men of the *legiones*."

Caesar marched on to Darioritum and seized it without resistance. The governor was so infuriated with the warring tribe, and fearing a more widespread rebellion among the Galli, seized the Veneti chieftains and tribal ruling counsel. Without hesitation, he ordered them brought before him outside their great hall. As their wives and children watched, they were all beheaded in sight of the Veneti people.

As a warning to the surrounding tribes, he sold all the Veneti, from the aged to suckling babes, into slavery, and burned Darioritum to the ground.

Gabinius led the wagons north across the Liger River on a hired barge into the land of the Samnites. They then continued north through the land of the Veneti to the territory of the Osismii beyond where the merchants from Albion traded.

Gabinius and Lucius were appalled at the treatment of the new-made slaves, and Salonius occasionally told Guiamo to turn his eyes away from some particularly brutal scene.

After three days, they passed through the still-reeking and charcoaled ruins of Darioritum. The corpses of the ruling counsel members lay where they had been slain. Deeply disturbed by the horrific sight, Gabinius hastened the wagons past.

"Victory is an ugly witch, make no mistake about that," said the appalled Lucius.

"Indeed she is," replied Gabinius. "Indeed she is, but Defeat is a monster."

Guiamo was visibly relieved to leave the ruins of Darioritum behind as they continued north toward the territory of the Osismii. It took four more days of travel to reach their village of Vorganium and they arrived just before the sun set.

After they settled into their room at the inn, Gabinius had the owner bring four buckets of warm water. After washing away the grime of over a month's travel, the men felt refreshed as they had not for a long time.

When their baths were completed, Gabinius ordered soup and bread to be brought to the room, and for the rest of the evening, they ate and sat with their aching feet soaking in the cooling water. Lucius told stories of the sea as they relaxed the evening away.

"Tomorrow, we go to see our merchants," said Gabinius at last. "Scoundrels all, to be sure. Tomorrow will be an interesting day and I need a restful night's sleep." With that, he lay down on his bed. In no time, he fell asleep, Lucius quickly followed, and soon the four were soundly asleep.

The docks of Vorganium stank of rotting fish. The pungent odor wafted across their path as they drew near and was as palpable as a slap across the face. Salonius covered his nose with his sleeve and silently wished for the fresh scent of the wild woods.

Even Lucius was bothered by the rank odor and complained, "This is not the smell of the sea. Something died near here."

Guiamo pointed out toward the shoreline and they all saw the decaying carcasses of a dozen dead whales. The gulls dipped and circled eagerly above the twelve putrid lumps of moldering flesh.

Gabinius said, "The whale is a strange creature. It can break a ship's back by a slap of its tail, and is wary enough to stay beneath the waves for lengthy periods to avoid our hunters, yet they will cast themselves upon the sands for no reason. There they lie until the sun kills them."

Lucius said, "Perhaps the great god Neptunus casts them out of his realm for some offense."

"Perhaps," Gabinius replied doubtfully.

The four walked briskly away from the dead whales toward a market of fishmongers located on a cleaner stretch of beach, and were pleased to be overwhelmed with the honest odor of fresh fish.

Gabinius led them through the market where fishermen sorted their catch and sold the fish to eager merchants who had ready markets. Two dozen suntanned veterans of the sea sat quietly by the shore repairing the damage to their nets.

As they passed the fish market, Guiamo saw a cluster of buildings ahead and seven large wagons with pairs of hitched oxen. Four large merchant ships were anchored offshore. Outside the buildings were stacks of metal ingots.

As Gabinius led them closer, Guiamo distinguished the red tint of copper in one large stack. The rest looked like iron or tin.

Gabinius looked to his three fellows and said, "Actors, play your roles."

They drew close to the buildings, and Gabinius took them to the largest building furthest from the shoreline. He entered without knocking and motioned for Lucius only to follow.

"You are well met, Glévezen," said Gabinius to the burly, gray haired merchant seated behind a table.

"Malleole, my old friend, you are well met indeed!" said Glévezen as he stopped ciphering numbers on a wax writing tablet and set down his *stilus*.

He rose to embrace Gabinius, who received him with open arms.

Gabinius introduced his eldest son, Lucius, but said nothing of the transfer of the estate. As the two old friends reminisced, they spoke of the old days when Gabinius first met Glévezen near the harbor at Brivates north of the Liger River. Gabinius had been looking to find a source for a variety of metals, but discouraged, finally wandered back to the inn. In the mud beside a stable, flat on his back in the rain was Glévezen, who was fully consumed by drunkenness.

224

Gabinius stopped to help him into the stable where he found a comfortable hay pile to sleep off the power of the wine.

Gabinius came back in the morning to check on the man and found him snoring contentedly. After awakening him, Gabinius gave him a dry change of clothing and through the fog of an overpowering headache, their close friendship sprouted. Glévezen turned out to be an exporter of tin from Albion.

As the men spoke, Guiamo and Salonius sat patiently outside, waiting and observing. Guiamo watched metal buyers arrive to negotiate with other sellers. He noticed that they shouted angrily, and argued as they haggled. Guiamo guessed from their behavior that the price was unusually high, supplies were few, and the sellers were unusually content to hold fast to their prices.

Some purchased small quantities, and others stormed off empty-handed. The metal sellers seemed content with letting the latter go, confident in their high prices. Guiamo thought of Gabinius' advice of behaving like a slave, speaking the Bellovaci language and trying to outfox the merchant's servants through guile. He felt daunted by the complexity of Gabinius' plan, seeing that they might discover his accent to be inauthentic for his role. Rather than try out his role as Gabinius had planned, Guiamo decided to try a simpler approach.

Guiamo walked over to sit in the shade of a building so he could listen into the conversation. Salonius put his hand on his *gladius* and followed Guiamo as if guarding him.

When all the buyers left, the sellers gathered to pass the time. Guiamo remained seated in the shade listening to their conversation. Though Salonius could not understand their tongue, Guiamo did.

He listened as they talked quietly of home, women and rough seas. They talked of profits and troubles, and the defeat of the Veneti. And they spoke of warfare in Albion. Guiamo learned of the miners leaving their work underground to join the fight. Guiamo heard that the war was going badly.

Guiamo also learned that what little supplies of ores were available were being used in the war. Only the miners in the northeast of Albion were still producing. Guiamo realized the distribution of tin and copper from Albion into Gallia was in jeopardy, and that supplies were quickly drying up.

As he rested in the shade, he saw a girl about his age walking down a grassy trail from the village built higher up the hill. She carried a basket upon her head. As she drew near, Guiamo saw that she was very pretty with dark, beautiful eyes and glossy black hair tied into a series of ringlets around her brow. She was willowy thin, but showing the softening shapes of womanhood.

She moved with a rhythm in her step he had never before noticed in any other and, entranced, he followed her every step as she passed closely by. She was the most beautiful creature he had ever seen. As he stared, mesmerized, she took notice of him. She looked directly at him, and with hope in his pounding heart, he smiled up at her.

He was self-conscious, but steeled himself to say, "A good day to you! I am…"

She cut him off with a terse, "Stop staring at me, slave! Avert your eyes or I shall have them cut out!" Offended by his impertinence, she scurried away as fast as she could walk without losing control of the basket on her head. She entered the large building and slammed the door shut.

When she came out a few minutes later, she was followed by Glévezen and Gabinius. Angrily, she pointed at Guiamo. Glévezen picked up a long stick from the ground and headed for Guiamo.

Gabinius, seeing the trouble, called Glévezen back and said, "Friend, the boy is my slave, and I shall deal with him myself." Gabinius took the stick from Glévezen and told him, "Be at ease here. I shall beat him back into submission."

As Glévezen and his daughter watched, Gabinius stormed over to Guiamo. Seizing the boy roughly by the arm, he dragged the bewildered Guiamo to the side of the smaller building where Glévezen could not see.

He hushed Guiamo and said, "Cry out in pain at the right time. I will explain later." Then shouting angrily, he cried, "I shall teach you to show deference to the daughter of a freeman, you wretch!" He raised the stick and struck the side of the building again and again.

As instructed, Guiamo cried out, feigning pain being inflicted by repeated blows upon his back.

When Gabinius stopped striking the wall, he winked at Guiamo and patted him on the back supportively. "Vlatucia is a pretty thing, but you forgot to play the role of slave. Now follow me back to the shade and sit there like a beaten pup."

When she finally left her father to return home, Guiamo held his head down in respect until she passed him by. But he could not help himself from watching Vlatucia with longing eyes as she continued her way up the hill.

When evening came, the four returned to their inn to eat and rest. Gabinius was pleased with his reunion with his long-time friend Glévezen, but explained, "I have known Glévezen for over twenty years, and though he is my good friend, I know he is a bit of a scoundrel. The prices he is hinting at today seem high to me. I shall probably need to search elsewhere for better prices. Perhaps my suggesting this to him will encourage him to lower his prices to a more reasonable level."

Guiamo immediately spoke up, "Gabini, there is more that you should know. I listened to the merchants talking at length today as you desired, and there is much turmoil in Albion. War has broken out and it must be desperate, for the miners have joined the fight. Tin and copper will be in short supply for many months, if not years. The buyers are purchasing little or none at these prices in hopes that the prices will come down, but the sellers are content. They all see prices increasing further as supplies drop to nothing.

"My advice to you is to buy all they have here now. The price will continue to rise and you will have a goodly store of tin and copper either to work into weapons, or to resell to others."

Lucius said, "If what the boy heard is true, his advice is sound. We should buy everything here tomorrow and establish the prices however high on future shipments."

Gabinius was impressed, "The language lessons of Suadusegus have paid off. My little spy has done well. Tomorrow, Lucius and I will purchase everything here, make Glévezen happy, guarantee our supplies, and make a fortune."

The next morning, Gabinius and Lucius sat down with Glévezen to negotiate. Within two hours, Gabinius had purchased all the dwindling inventories from every tin and copper merchant from every mine in Albion which shipped to Vorganium, as well as all future shipments for the next year. Glévezen agreed to coordinate the transactions with the other merchants and provide transportation to Gobedbiacum. He also agreed that if anyone came looking to buy metal, they would be directed to see Gabinius.

With their business concluded, Gabinius greeted Glévezen goodbye and the four headed back home to Gobedbiacum. The journey was long, and the mystery of Glévezen's lovely daughter, Vlatucia, haunted Guiamo's thoughts throughout.

Susama seemed most anxious to resume teaching Guiamo, and he found that she had many words of power for him to learn.

He was anxious to be taught, but the first harvest required all his available time. The men labored hard to reap, winnow and place the grain in storage, but the work was a pleasure for the harvest was bountiful. They all felt satisfaction in the year's work, and the vineyards were showing progress.

When the harvest was completed, the cool winds of autumn came. Susama searched him out, and he eagerly resumed his lessons. She taught words whose meanings were related, but of differing intensities. They rehearsed the two words of Striking, *ibur* to pierce and *nétlis* to slash, and then explored words of Impacting which were employed using the butt of the spear.

228

He learned to say *dranda* and *nurdranda* to 'push' and to 'knock down.' 'Break down' was *fisóvet* and *vúimon* meant 'shatter.' Her favorite word of Impacting, though, was *hutsosh*. Trying out this new power, Guiamo placed Lúin against the ground and commanded "*Hutsosh!*" With a shuddering rumble, the earth began to shake endlessly in tremendous, rippling surges. Delighted, Guiamo finally commanded "*Nef!*" and the earthquake ceased.

Other lessons that autumn were words of Finding. First, she reviewed the word *betn'lina* which commanded Lúin to point east to the rising sun. With practice, he could have Lúin point to certain objects by saying *betn'dhorvo*. Eventually, he was able to search out things hidden without knowing where they were. By commanding "*betn'whúin atha,*" Lúin would find anything that Susama hid away.

One evening in mid-*September*, Guiamo led Susama down to the river. Placing his spear in his right hand, he said, "Watch, Priestess Susama. I have an idea to try."

He looked at Lúin and commanded, "*Ebfulna!*"

The spear tip began to glow red hot. Satisfied with Lúin's response, he extended his arm and placed the glowing spear point into the calmly flowing water. With a hissing sound, the water began agitating and bubbling from the heat. Several minnows floated to the surface and were pushed outward, away from the boiling waters. A great body of steam rose above the river. Guiamo held Lúin steady. The steaming action became so violent that clouds of mist began spreading to the opposite shore to envelope the trees growing on the bank.

Still Guiamo held Lúin firm. The water evaporated away so quickly, that despite the flow of the river, the water clearly was becoming ever shallower. Downstream, Susama could see just enough through the fog to know the river was drying up. Several fish were flopping in the shallows and their struggles were becoming more desperate.

When Guiamo was satisfied with his experiment, he cried, "*Nef!*" and the boiling cauldron went still. The river quickly refilled the low spots and after a short while was flowing normally again.

Guiamo led Susama up the hill where they could survey the valley. The mist went across the entire valley, obscuring his estate and beyond.

"Impressive!" said Susama in amazement. "I can see how this could be used in battle to confound your enemies. Just be certain you do not blind yourself."

Guiamo grinned back at her confidently, "With Lúin, I can command him to find my way out!"

"That you could, I see now," Susama replied. "What else would you like Lúin to do?"

Guiamo though about this for awhile before answering, "I would like Lúin to speak to me."

Susama was surprised by this request and she found a suitable answer difficult. She eventually replied, "A man may love his horse or hound, and they may understand his commands, even love him in return, but the gift of speech is beyond their ken. I suspect it is so with Lúin. Yet, if it were possible, the word to teach him is '*alfalel*.' It is a word of Speaking."

"*Alfalel*," said Guiamo, and he mouthed the word as if it was too precious to speak again. "If I should command him to speak, and he was not able, how do you suppose he would react?" he asked.

Susama again thought at length before replying. "It is difficult to say. It may be with frustration-driven anger, or with sadness. Perhaps you may find he must be taught each word and its meaning. Thus it may be with the speech of animals. Or, perchance he must teach you the words he knows already from the days of his youth," she said.

"How could he teach me words if he cannot speak them?" asked Guiamo.

" '*Melnothel*' is a word of Writing. Perhaps he can spell words to you by scratching in the dirt. I should be able to read the ancient words and teach you his thoughts. In time, you could converse with him without me," she replied.

Guiamo laughed, "A talking spear. I wonder what a spear has to speak of?" He thought a moment and then pretended at having a silly conversation.

"I say, 'Good morning, Lúin, I slept soundly last night. How about you? Are you well rested?'

"Then Lúin replies, 'I had a terrible night. I did not sleep a wink!'

" 'Why could you not sleep?' I ask.

"And Lúin says, 'You leaned me against the wall, and I was up all night!' "

With a groaning laugh, Susama put her hands over her face and said, "Oh, but your jesting is too painful to hear! Perhaps we should not teach him to speak after all."

Guiamo just grinned at her laughing rebuke.

Then, growing more serious, she said, "I recommend you work slowly first with "*melnothel*" before attempting "*alfalel.*"

Lucius left a week later to return to his family and his own shipping affairs. In agreement with Gabinius' advice, he left Petronius in charge of the craftsmen until his return in the spring so his father could work uninterrupted in his private smithy.

At supper that evening, Gabinius spoke with Guiamo about his future, "Guiamo, you are now fourteen years old. You have a fine estate and much wealth. This spring, it will be time for you to become your own man. I will prepare for you the celebration of *Liberalia* on the seventeenth day of *Martius* as is the custom of Rome.

"I have done all that was asked of me by Calidius. You and I have both been blessed by our time together. You have been faithful and true to me and a gracious student to Sertorius and Suadusegus. For this, I thank you.

"After *Liberalia*, you will live on your own estate, but will always be welcome in my home. You need to begin construction of your own home now. I have ordered materials brought here for the construction of your home, at your expense, of course. Not only materials will be shipped here, but also artisans to inlay mosaics into your floors and paint beautiful paintings upon the walls. You have the wealth of a *patricius* and you must live as one. They will build furniture befitting your station, and you must think of hiring servants to manage your home. I suggest that you ask Susama if any of her maidservants could be hired away. They all seem well disciplined and capable, and it seems they have not enough work to keep busy.

"I am thinking also of freeing Suadusegus after you celebrate *Liberalia*. You two have become quite close friends, and I no longer will need his service. I shall speak to him of this in the next few days, and it is my hope that he will choose to live on your estate as a guest teacher. A small payment for his lessons would retain him, I should think. Do not neglect to pay Susama as well, if she is willing, but I have heard the *Druidae* will not take payment for their instruction."

Guiamo grew sad, realizing that his life was about to change forever. He would no longer be a boy, but a man with responsibilities he had never before truly faced. His relationships with his friends would change and he knew that life would bring him challenges he was not sure he was ready to face.

Gabinius did not see his countenance fall and continued, "From word that has reached my ears, it looks that the supplies of tin and copper for which I bargained in Aremorica will still prove insufficient for my own needs. If you chance upon word of any other sources, let me know."

The supplies needed to begin construction of Guiamo's new home arrived over a period of three weeks. Gabinius organized the building process, and gave instructions to the crew bosses of what needed to be done. As an extra incentive to finish the work quickly and accurately, Guiamo promised bonuses to the best workers. The local men were eager for work, and they labored hard to outdo each other.

Guiamo and Ulleria enjoyed watching the artisans working on the floor mosaics, and spent hours observing their progress. Unglazed tiles of many colors purchased in Lugdunum were carefully broken into small cubes called *tesserae*, and Guiamo saw that the color was not just on the surface. Dies had been mixed throughout the clay prior to hardening. After each *tessera* was cut to shape, it was placed in groupings of like color and shading. Ulleria was amazed at the wide variety of shades made available to the artisans.

Gabinius helped Guiamo choose the themes and motifs for the flooring artwork, and the artisans began sketching their proposals on the hard flooring. Following the custom of many Roman homes, a portrait of a dog was selected to be placed at the entrance to the home to warn thieves away. Guiamo had Salonius bring Flaccus to the house so the artisans could work his image accurately into the mosaic.

Gabinius recommended that the largest mosaic, which was to be put into the floor of the *tablinum*, be a scene of Mars at war. At Guiamo's request, Lúin was used as the model for the spear in this scene. When Guiamo was not present, Gabinius instructed the artisans to create another person into their original proposed design. Standing boldly behind Mars and to his right, Gabinius had them draw a youth in the image of Guiamo also holding up a similar spear and ready for battle.

The wall paintings in the formal *exedra* entertaining room off the *peristylium* outdoor garden room were elegant pastoral scenes. The dominant painting depicted Selene, the Greek goddess of the moon, approaching the sleeping shepherd Endymion.

Opposite the *exedra* was the *triclinium* dining room. Carpenters fashioned the central serving table and three reclining *lecti* couches, and the artisans set to work carving elegant designs into them.

In the open-aired *atrium* toward the front of the home, a pool was built to retain rainwater as a source for the use of the household. Once it was completed, Ulleria brought pitchers of water from the river to bless the house with its first fill of water.

Ulleria took delight in preparing the soil in the center of the *peristylium*, and planted many beautiful ferns and flowering plants after the artisans had completed the flooring mosaics.

Gabinius instructed Ulleria to purchase all the tableware, cooking utensils and all the other household items appropriate to a proper Roman household. She purchased new bedding materials, oil lamps and cleaning materials. She enjoyed her work and delighted in the freedom given her to complete the house as she saw fit. Guiamo had little interest in these details and thanked her for graciously handling them all.

What bothered Guiamo most was that the construction of his house brought much attention from the neighboring families. Word quickly spread of the mysterious boy of fourteen whose wealth was reputed to exceed that of Gabinius himself. As the stories spread, his notoriety increased. Men brought their families to see Guiamo's estate, and some speculated that Guiamo was a son of Gabinius from another woman, and that he would inherit all of Gabinius' wealth.

The families became bolder in their attempts to get sight of Guiamo, and Actus found himself acting as guard of the estate, running off trespassers who wanted to tramp through the nearly completed home. One particularly brazen family snuck into the house and took some of the kitchen utensils as keepsakes.

Then, Guiamo found himself being invited to dine with nearby families who ranged from slightly known to complete strangers to Gabinius and himself. He politely refused, and after a dozen invitations came to him in one week, he told Gabinius.

His mentor explained, "I fear that my poor Guiamo has become the target of Cupid. You see, each of these fathers have daughters eligible for marriage. They might be anywhere from ten to fourteen years of age. You, my boy, are the wealthiest, most interesting potential husband in the region, and each of these fathers is set on marrying his daughter off to you."

"But I am a *Druides*!" exclaimed Guiamo. "I cannot marry for nineteen years! Besides, I have no interest in marriage. At least, not yet."

234

"Yes, you are *Druides*, and nineteen years of training await you, but these fathers do not know this," said Gabinius.

"What am I to do?" asked Guiamo. "I think it unwise to proclaim it to everyone. The *Druidae* are not welcome here."

Gabinius agreed. "I shall make it known that you have not yet celebrated *Liberalia*, and until then, I will not allow you to accept these invitations while you are under my roof. This will not cure all, but at least you shall be safe from the maidens until *Martius*."

He stood alone by the river. With the onset of winter, the sun was pleasingly warm and the chilling wind brisk. The occasional gust sent ripples across the flowing water. Lúin lay on the damp ground at his feet.

"*Melnothel!*" Guiamo commanded.

The spear tremored on the brown turf and Guiamo could hear the dried grasses quietly rustling.

"*Nef!*" he stated quickly, for he did not wish to torment Lúin, and the spear went still.

"That did not work so well," Guiamo said to himself. He picked Lúin up and held him with both hands. Though his stiff fingers were turning red from the cold, the boy could feel trust emanating from his spear. He decided to try again. "*Melnothel!*" he commanded.

Again the spear shuddered, but he felt it was different, as if Lúin wanted Guiamo to release him. Guiamo released his left hand, and with a lunge, the spear point rushed to the muddy bank. Guiamo held tightly to the end of the spear with his right hand, and in amazement watched as Lúin pulled and tugged against his grip while the spear point jabbed and slashed patterns into the mud.

Susama had been watching from a distance and hurried down the hill to see why Guiamo's arm and spear thrashed around so unnaturally. When she arrived, Lúin had ceased his wild motions and rested again in Guiamo's hands.

Guiamo was speechless. In the mud were clearly scribed letters which he did not recognize. Susama drew close and, seeing the writing, covered her mouth.

"Lúin wrote this, Priestess Susama," said Guiamo.

"Yes, I see. It is the language of the ancient world. Few but the *Druidae* now can read it," said Susama.

"What does it say?" asked Guiamo eagerly.

She replied, "It says 'I, Lúin, made by the will of Lugus, am.' "

Guiamo said, "Tell me how Lugus and Mars, gods of two different peoples, are both come to associate with the beginnings of Lúin."

Susama replied, "Lugus is a god of the ancient world. Mars is a child compared to him and weak. It is true that Mars crafted Lúin and Assal, but it was Lugus who taught Mars.

Guiamo looked at Lúin and back down to the writing in the mud. "What good is it that Lúin can write, but I cannot read his message?" he asked.

"Then I must teach you the letters of the ancient script." Susama replied. "Take hold of Lúin as before and say '*Haba.*' "

Guiamo held Lúin in one hand as before and commanded "*Melnothel haba!*"

Lúin pulled as before and scratched a round symbol into the mud.

Susama pointed to the script in the ground and said, "Guiamo, this is the letter *haba*. It is the letter representing the moon. See how my lips become round like the moon when I say the voice of the letter, and it sounds as the wolf who howls in the night. This is *haba*. Now let me teach you *samta*."

Susama patiently taught the ancient alphabet to Guiamo, and Lúin enjoyed writing the symbols into the muddy bank of the river. By suppertime, Guiamo had become fairly proficient with the thirty letter symbols.

Guiamo thought long throughout the restless night. When the light of morning shone through the open-aired *atrium*, he struggled out of his *cubiculum* to begin his lessons with Sertorius. He had slept through the time for his morning meal but did not mind for he had no appetite.

236

Sertorius saw Guiamo's reddish eyes and sluggish mannerism. "What troubles you, Durmi?" he asked.

"Sertori, I have a great mystery to solve and I cannot find its answer," Guiamo replied.

"What is this puzzle?" Sertorius asked as he set down a *volumen* for the day's reading.

"It is something only Susama can help me with," Guiamo said.

Sertorius saw how disturbed and burdened the boy was, so said, "Then go to her now. My lessons can wait another day."

Guiamo thanked Sertorius and went outdoors to see the priestess.

Susama was giving instructions to her maidservants when Guiamo arrived. She dismissed one girl to answer the door and Guiamo was shown into the house.

Susama motioned for Guiamo to sit, and after he settled into one of the carved chairs, asked him, "What brings you here so early this day?"

"It is a joy to command letters and words of Lúin, and I shall do my best to read his thoughts, but in my heart, there is something else I wish above all others," Guiamo said.

"Name your heart's desire, Durmi," Susama said.

"I wish to speak to the animals, but I am unsure how to attain this," said Guiamo.

"This is no small thing you are attempting, Durmi," said Susama in surprise. "Speaking to Lúin is one thing, for Mars has blessed you with him. Making speech with the animals is a different matter, and I know of no one who has done so. It is very likely that your desire will always be beyond your grasp."

Guiamo sat silently awaiting her sage advice. He waited longer than he expected he would have had to. She thought deeply and he could see her exploring different ideas, and ultimately rejecting them. Then her eyes brightened.

"Durmi, I think I have discovered a way for you to converse with the animals. Rather than commanding them to speak or understand you, I think it might be possible to put a word of power upon you; a command of Understanding,"

Susama said. "You would not be able to speak to them, but you would know their thoughts. This would at least be a beginning."

"I have thought of this, but how could it be done?" he asked. "A command of power spoken to me should have no effect, for I do not understand the ancient tongue."

"That is not entirely true," said Susama. "Words of power do have strength over nature and animals, and sometimes over men. Lúin understands the ancient tongue, and your commands are simple for him to comprehend. Animals and nature know the old words and the commanding power rules them. For men, it is similar, but a man may overpower the command if his will is strong enough."

"With you, a command of Understanding might work, but I suspect it will not. Lugus may have put a protection upon you that the words of power cannot be used upon you by the evil ones. Let us pray that this is so."

"Why do we not try the word of Understanding on me now and see?" asked Guiamo.

Susama sat back cautiously and warned, "To attempt to do so may cause untold damage to the one who utters the commanding words. I dare not."

"Then what can be done?" asked Guiamo.

"I shall have to think more on this," replied Susama.

Guiamo was not satisfied. He wanted an answer, and no longer had the patience to wait. "Perhaps I should just ask Lugus myself," he said impertinently.

Susama was surprised by his answer, but not displeased. She said, "You are a bold one! He is not summoned easily and we should certainly never do so for frivolous reasons. Still, you are favored by him. To do so, we would need to go to the sacred grove. Tomorrow morning, wear the white gown of the *Druidae* and wash in the river before you come here to my home. Bring enough gold to make a ring. It may be that Lugus finds you ready for a ring of your own. If all you have available are gold *aurei*, melt them down."

Guiamo brought Susama to the sacred grove atop the high hill near Gobedbiacum. Guiamo noticed that while the cold weather carried a wind, it was not strong enough to move the limbs of the trees which swayed dramatically along their way.

Susama noticed the activity of the trees, too, and observed, "Lugus eagerly awaits your arrival." They trudged along watching the branches moving energetically around them. Guiamo pointed out that the trees a short distance farther were nearly still.

Susama asked, "Durmi, did you bring the unformed gold?"

He reached into his *bulla praetexta* pouch and pulled out a lump of gold.

"Oh, Durmi, that is far too much," Susama said in a kindly tone.

Guiamo was not bothered. He replied, "I thought Lugus would take what he needed and leave me the rest. I just did not want to have an insufficient amount."

"No harm is done, Durmi. It will be so," said Susama.

"Do you really think Lugus will craft a ring for me today?" Guiamo asked. "I have studied for such a short time."

"From what I have seen of the oracles and *augures*, you may not have a full nineteen years before your life as a great warrior is to begin. Malleolus and I suspect it will begin when you are in your mid-twenties when your strength is at its greatest. That would give you about ten years to prepare and mature," Susama said.

Before long, they entered the sacred oak grove and the trees moved even more violently about. As before, Guiamo saw movement flickering just beyond his peripheral sight. Susama brought him into the center of the clearing and sat him on the ground. Guiamo saw her nervousness and realized she felt inadequate to her responsibility that day.

Susama gathered an armful of oak leaves and placed them in a wide circle one *passus* in front of Guiamo. Then, sitting beside him, she began to call in the ancient language, "Lugus *dithmero-mil!* Lugus *dithmero-mil!*"

As she completed the word of Summoning, from out of a clearing sky, a massive lightning bolt struck the ground in the center of the oak leaf circle. Rather than dissipate in an instant, it continued to blast the ground and, twisting, sent out tendrils of brilliant fire. Overwhelmed by the power of the sustained lightning bolt, Susama fell back in alarm, and Guiamo shielded his eyes with his arm.

As the lighting blazed in a dancing, arcing column to the sky, a voice deep and powerful as thunder said, "My son, today my powers are bestowed upon you."

Guiamo blinked his eyes at the words and was awestruck. The blaze of lightning continued to dance with power in the circle of oak leaves and Susama sat forward to kneel before the raging light. Around them the oak trees bent and swirled as from blasts of wind from a raging storm.

Lugus' roaring voice continued, "I have seen your heart's desire to speak to nature, to converse with the animals. Today, I shall give you the power to speak to my servants of war and to know the truth always. I cannot give you the ability to speak to all creatures, for only those who serve me in war do I command. Know this: the ancient tongue only shall they understand.

"Hound and hawk will understand your words. Caution is needed, for they shall obey only as they see fit. Their reply will be of limited understanding and they shall use but simple words.

"Horse, donkey and ox you shall speak to, and they will understand and blindly obey, but they have not the gift of speaking.

"Serpent is the healer of wounds but is a speaker of both truth and deceit. With him you will be able to converse as man to man, but you will be unable to command him. I shall give you the power of Discernment which shall bind his deceit and force the serpent's speech to the truth if he dares to speak.

"Bring forth the gold."

Guiamo removed the lump of gold from his *bulla praetexta* pouch and held it out with an open palm toward the light. With a blinding flash, a thin tendril of light streaked out and snatched the gold from his hand.

240

The lightning bolt intensified and then with a crash of thunder disappeared from sight. Susama gasped in surprise and looked around, realizing that the surrounding oaks had gone suddenly still, and he knew that the god had departed. Guiamo looked at the blackened ground within the circle of oak leaves which lay undisturbed. At its center lay a ring of cunning design. Guiamo stood and walked forward into the circle.

He reached down carefully and picked up the ring. It was a serpent ring, but different from the two he had seen before. Rather than being a single loop with the serpent swallowing his tail, this was designed as two parallel loops set half a finger's width apart. At the center apex was the serpent's head swallowing its tail.

The serpent ran diagonally across the top of the finger and then turned to wrap around the finger. As the loop came up the opposite side, it bent diagonally again to pass beneath the snake's head. It then wrapped again as a second loop around the finger. Rising on the other side, it then bent its tail to enter the serpent's opened mouth.

"Place it on your finger! Quickly!" whispered Susama. "Or it shall dissolve again."

Hearing her words of alarm, Guiamo slipped in onto the index finger of his right hand. It was a perfect fit. He turned to hold his hand up so Susama could see the double ring.

"I have never seen a ring of such design!" she exclaimed. "Its powers must be unique to you alone. Bless Lugus! He has given you tremendous power. You must wear it always, but never reveal its source." Overjoyed and with great enthusiasm, she said, "We must soon begin to discover its secrets."

Guiamo eagerly replied, "I wish to speak to Flaccus first!" and Susama agreed.

Susama and Guiamo searched out Salonius for much of the remainder of the morning, but it became evident that he was afield hunting. As they prepared to give up for the day, Flaccus came running up to Guiamo and nuzzled his hand. Salonius followed, dejected that his bowstring had broken just as he had drawn it back for a shot on a yearling buck.

Susama whispered a warning to Guiamo, "Not here."

Guiamo understood her concern that Salonius not listen in, and said, "Saloni, I would like to take Flaccus with me for a time."

"That would be fine," Salonius replied as he held up his broken bowstring. "I am finished hunting for today."

Guiamo took his aging dog with Susama down by the river where no one else could observe. He made Flaccus sit in the grass, and Susama watched in wonder.

Guiamo looked down at Flaccus and knelt in front of him, caressing his neck and ears. Upon hearing Susama urging him to proceed, he looked at Flaccus and commanded "*Alfalel.*" Flaccus blinked his eyes and looked directly at Guiamo. Without hesitation, the dog began to speak, and as he spoke, his words fairly tumbled out of his mouth. Flaccus chattered on and on excitedly, and so rapidly that Susama could hardly keep up with his enthusiastic thoughts.

Seeing the dog speaking without guidance, Guiamo tried to interrupt his dog's endless prattle by calling out "Flacce!" Three times he called out before the dog took notice and fell silent.

Guiamo turned to Susama and said, "Lugus said his words would be simple, yet Flaccus talks on and on!"

"Lugus spoke in generalities, not of each specific animal. Be thankful Flaccus can speak so freely," she replied.

Frustrated, Guiamo said, "But Susama, what is he saying? I do not understand any of his words!"

"Of course you do not," she replied. "He speaks the ancient tongue as Lugus promised. I can understand him with some difficulty for, though I know the words, it has been a long time since I have had reason to converse at length. Flaccus speaks in such haste that he speeds beyond my comprehension.

"I believe his conversation is thus: 'Hunt ducks. Quiet quiet still still still. Kill duck. Fetch duck fetch fetch. Rub my ears. Rub my ears. Rabbits fun. Rabbits quick quick quick but stupid. Rabbit tasty good. Fish tasty good good good. Bones bad. Bones stick stick hurt. Flaccus hungry hungry.'

242

"His thoughts are intensely focused, but he flits from one thing to another. We are finished with Flaccus for today. You will need to learn the ancient tongue so that you may converse with the animals. Come, we shall begin immediately."

Guiamo stroked Flaccus' neck and ears as he lay on the grass, and quietly commanded, "*Nef!*" Flaccus laid his head down on his paws, looked up with raised eyebrows, and wagged his tail.

Susama delved into her distant memory of lessons in her youth, trying to retrieve the words of the ancient language. The words came slowly but steadily.

Having already learned how to speak several languages from Suadusegus, Guiamo found learning the language of old to be rather easy and his mind quickly absorbed her lessons. He learned every word she could remember, and quickly became proficient not only with the meaning and pronunciation of the words, but also with constructing meaningful sentences.

Throughout, Susama was frustrated with herself for not having retained the language as well as she might have. But of what she did remember, she felt comfortable that the words were taught accurately to Guiamo. She began compiling a list of meanings whose words she could not remember, and told Guiamo, "When you return to Camulvellaunus, have him teach you these words." And the list grew long.

Gabinius saw that Guiamo's interest in the lessons and exercise of Sertorius and the daily working session with his craftsmen was waning. He did not mind, for he knew Guiamo had learned enough already, but in keeping with his original agreement, required his time and attention until *Liberalia*.

Winter came and Guiamo looked forward to *Martius* when he could move into his new home. His fortune was still impressive even after the costly construction of his home. The fields were ready for plowing and sowing the second crop. The vineyards were promising, though much work had yet to be finished. Actus and his men were well kept and content. Two men were planning on weddings, though the brides-to-be did not yet know it.

Guiamo exercised hard and his thin frame continued to grow ever more muscular. His fighting skills were more than adequate, and he had gained a healthy confidence in himself. He began to grow whiskers on his chin, and hair on his chest and back. He noticed one day he was taller than Sertorius, and his voice had taken a deeper tone. He carried himself with strength and bore the aura of command about him. Gabinius had commented on how the boy he met was now becoming a man among men. Nearly fifteen, he was ready to live his life on his own terms.

Chapter Six - 55 B.C.

"Some cannot achieve greatness at home." Dr. Alabaster Hawkins, lectures circa 1798

Liberalia was approaching quickly and the signs of spring were showing. Budding trees opened their leaves as the grassy fields turned green. Migratory birds flew across the sky to find suitable nesting sites and Guiamo was becoming restless.

The fresh, warm winds stirred his blood, and he became irritable when he had to be still for his lessons. Everyone knew the growing boy was bursting with energy, and they all found ways to cut their teaching time short.

Seizing upon the freed-up time, Sertorius lengthened his exercise and martial drills. He worked Guiamo mercilessly, and Guiamo loved him for it. He felt his strength growing and he pushed himself harder and harder each day. Gabinius allowed Sertorius to begin his exercise time early, consuming much of the workshop time, and even then, it was all Guiamo could bear to force patience into his time with the craftsmen.

Suadusegus spent little time teaching philosophy and changed his lessons' emphasis to practical exercises at being a king's counselor. Suadusegus practiced endlessly as king, and Guiamo as counselor, standing, posturing, speaking aloud, thinking spontaneously, and avoiding defeat in their verbal sparring. All his focus was on activity to burn up Guiamo's boundless energy.

The only time Guiamo could sit quietly at all was after the evening meal. He was so tired from his frantic pace that he could do little else than to sit and listen. Susama took advantage of his quiet attentiveness to teach him the language of the ancient world. He yearned to practice his words upon Flaccus, but Susama would not allow it, insisting all his time be spent with her.

She used the ancient words to give him advice on being a man among men, and as a man with women. She spent long evenings teaching him to be a man with a woman; a man with his woman, and Guiamo listened with rapt attention.

And she taught him to be patient, for he had over eighteen years to wait before he could take a bride.

Gabinius took Guiamo into Gobedbiacum on the sixteenth day of *Martius*. A priest had come to help the villagers, farmers all, to celebrate the annual Procession of the *Argei*. The simple folk had gathered together in the center of the cluster of simple huts and were talking excitedly about the day's festivities. Thirty human effigies made of rushes were lying on the ground at their feet.

The priest, Guiamo could see, was quite pleased with his role as chief of ceremonies, and he began giving instructions to the crowd. The people listened carefully as he explained that the god Saturnus required human sacrifices in the days of old. The original Greek victims were executed by being thrown into the river. He then said, "Since we have no Greeks to offer, we shall appease the powerful *Numina* gods with these *argei* figures. Praise the gods with song and sacrifice!"

With a voice lifted high in exultation, the priest directed the people to pick up the *argei* and follow him down the valley to the river.

Gabinius pushed Guiamo forward through the thin crowd and told him to pick up one of the *argei*. Guiamo felt very self-conscious, but did as Gabinius instructed. Following the example of the farmers, Guiamo held the rush figurine above his head and began to sing along with the priest. His voice was deep and strong, but he had trouble with the words, for he had never celebrated the Procession before.

Before long, the line of townsfolk reached the bank of the river which was muddy and swollen from recent rainstorms. The priest raised a prayer to the faceless *Numina* gods, calling for abundant rains. The villagers grew impatient with the longwinded priest, and murmured for him to finish. He pretended not to hear their complaints and prayed all the louder.

Guiamo looked over at Gabinius in exasperation, for his arms were growing tired. Most of the people no longer held the *argei* over their heads. Gabinius smiled at Guiamo and

246

motioned for him to drop his arms. Gabinius looked at the priest who droned on and on, and he rolled his eyes in comic exasperation.

At long last, the priest finished his prayer, and seeing the *argei* were no longer being held aloft, motioned for the people to raise them up again in respect. Once the people had complied, he called for them to cast the rush figures into the river for the guilt of disobedience to be taken away.

With a shout of cheer, the thirty bearers filed over to the riverbank and began to throw them into the flowing water. When his turn came, Guiamo dropped it casually and then turned quickly back to Gabinius.

Gabinius said, "So now you have witnessed the Procession of the *Argei*. What do you think of it?"

Guiamo said, "I felt silly. Surely Saturnus and the *Numina* are not so easily tricked as to believe we are offering real Greeks to them. The people are such simpletons."

Gabinius replied, "True. This is a ceremony for the simple farmers who live in the countryside. Though the priest tries to convey its importance to them, they do not understand. They are not interested in knowing. They are simply superstitious. That is the way of farmers. Recognize their ignorance, but do not mock them. The Procession gives them something to celebrate in their difficult, dreary lives."

Gabinius continued, "Now if you think this celebration is silly, you just wait until tomorrow when we celebrate your *Liberalia*."

Ulleria woke Guiamo in the morning. "Today is your *Liberalia*. I must shave your face before the celebration begins."

She led him to stand in front of a bronze mirror and pulled out a thin-bladed, iron *novacula* razor. The handle was ornately made in bronze and had two loops, each engraved with the image of a bird. She had water and a whetstone ready for the many resharpenings necessary for Guiamo's first shave; for she knew the iron blade would dull quickly.

She instructed him to stand still, and she stepped upon a footstool, for Guiamo had grown taller than she could comfortably reach. Holding a plate under his chin to catch the falling whiskers, she scraped the sharp blade against his face. Most whiskers were thin, for he was young, but the razor tugged and pulled at them. Guiamo winced several times when the blade nicked his face, and Ulleria had to constantly remind him to stand without moving.

The chin was the worst part, for the whiskers were thickest there and strong. After two or three scrapes, Ulleria had to resharpen the blade with the moistened whetstone. After each swipe, she carefully wiped the whiskers off the blade and placed them on the plate. His face felt raw. He bled from several places nicked, and she blotted the wounds too infrequently to suit him.

When she was finished, she handed him a bowl of water and a towel to wipe his face. She showed him the plate which held the whiskers which had been removed. The tiny pinch of facial hair seemed to him to be embarrassingly small.

Ulleria then asked Guiamo to take off his *bulla praetexta* pouch. When he complied, she removed the protective amulet and scraped the whisker shavings inside. She closed the *bulla* and handed it back to Guiamo, who put it around his neck again.

When Guiamo had finished his morning meal, Ulleria helped him dress. She gave him a new garment, the *toga virilis*. It was unadorned and off-white from the undyed wool, in keeping with the style worn by men.

When he stepped outside, he was greeted by a boisterous crowd of over one hundred craftsmen and workers. The craftsmen gathered around Guiamo and began to sing songs to him. When Guiamo heard the lyrics, he found they were so ribald and rude that he flushed red from embarrassment. His response led the men to compose even more crass words, and they laughed as they sang. They picked him up and tossed him onto their shoulders, spinning, twirling and dancing. They carried him down the path to Gobedbiacum where they were met by another festive crowd. The priest

248

who led the Procession of the *Argei* came forward to greet Guiamo, and the craftsmen set him down.

"Welcome to the day of Pater Liber, our great god of the vine and bounty," said the priest. One of the four elderly priestesses crowned with wreaths of ivy gave him an oil and honey *libia* cake. Seeing that Guiamo did not know what to do, the priest said to him, "Present the *libia* back to the priestesses, and they shall make a sacrifice of it to Liber on your behalf."

Guiamo self-consciously handed the *libia* right back to the same priestess who smiled and promised to present it before Liber.

The priest called everyone in the boisterous crowd to silence. "Today young... what is your name, young man?"

"Durmius," Guiamo replied.

The priest continued, "Today, our dear, young Durmius becomes a man!"

The crowd quickly became disinterested in the lengthy speech as the priest droned on and on. Guiamo became bored as well, and disliked having to stand like a prize in front of everyone. Guiamo's mind wandered.

He was startled back to the present when his name was called. He looked forward to see the priest standing in front of him. Guiamo stared at the priest and, with dismay, realized the priest was passing a strange object to him. With skeptical reservation, Guiamo took it into his hands. Then, with a look of profound dismay, he recognized what it was. He looked to Gabinius to rescue him from his predicament, but Gabinius just laughed back full of mirth.

Gabinius said, "Be the man today, Guiamo. Do your duty and carry the *phallus* through the fields for the blessing of a good harvest."

Guiamo was deeply bothered by his embarrassing assignment and wished he could set the figure down and melt into the crowd. With a face turned red, he steeled his resolve and followed the priest, holding the *phallus* high with as much dignity as he could muster. They walked up the pathway to Gabinius' house and then down to the valley and across the river to Guiamo's estate. As they passed through the fields, the following crowd sang songs as saucy as before.

When they finished blessing the fields and vineyards, the priest led the crowd to Guiamo's new home. Ulleria stepped alongside Guiamo outside the entrance and in her arms bore an ivy wreath. With a wave at the crowd, she lifted the wreath, and with great ceremony, placed it over the *phallus* symbol.

The crowd erupted into great shouts and cheers. Ulleria took the *phallus* symbol from Guiamo and set it aside. Then she reached around his neck and pulled up the necklace of his *bulla praetexta*. She removed it and led Guiamo into the house. She took him to the household altar where she placed the *bulla* pouch on the altar as an offering to the Lares household gods. Then, kissing Guiamo on the cheek, she led him back outside.

The priest held his hands high in the air and shouted, "Guiamo Durmius Stolo, a man of Rome!" The crowd cheered him as never before. The men picked Guiamo up and carried him all the way back to Gabinius' estate where a banquet had been prepared to feed hundreds.

When the day's celebration was completed and the sun began to set, Ulleria went back to Guiamo's home and quietly entered. She walked over to the household altar. She picked up Guiamo's *bulla praetexta*. Handling it reverently, she turned it over and over thoughtfully in her hands.

Quoting the words spoken by generations of Roman mothers, she said, "As a mother of Rome, I take this offering of noble manhood. As a mother of Rome, I vow to keep it safe. As a mother of Rome, I shall use this amulet to protect the name of Guiamo Durmius Stolo from the evil words of those envious of his successes. Bless the Lares. May the gods of this household protect and prosper Guiamo Durmius Stolo."

While Ulleria was at Guiamo's home, Gabinius sat him down for a final, parting talk. Guiamo was nervous, and Gabinius, somber and quiet. The air was turning brisk and gusty, and they moved out of the *peristylium* garden room into the *tablinum* where the air was still.

Once he had settled onto his favorite bench, Gabinius wrapped himself in a cloak for warmth. When he felt comfortable, Gabinius said, "Well, today is your day, Guiamo. I am pleased with your time with me these past years, and your uncompromising devotion to your daily assignments. A fine man you have become. Your lessons should prove invaluable to your success in life, but there are a few things more I wish to discuss with you before we part.

"I know your interest in girls in increasing. This is good. I will counsel you this; do not marry too soon," Gabinius said.

Guiamo objected, "Gabini, I am a *Druides*. I cannot marry for years to come."

Gabinius replied, "But not all *Druidae* finish their years of training. So it may be with you, so I shall advise you still. The girl you would be attracted to today will not be the same type of girl you would be interested in if choosing when you were a mature man of thirty. Wait for wisdom which comes with age before marrying, or you may doom yourself to an unhappy life.

"Beauty is a good thing, for you must look at her for the rest of your life, but always understand that beauty fades quickly. More importantly, the girl you choose to marry will be the mother to your children. Look for wisdom in the girl, and virtue, for the moral foundation of your family will be built upon the mother, not you. A rebellious, wild spirit in a woman will lead to riotous children and trouble in your marriage.

"Health in a wife is important. We cannot know what illnesses will come to us as we age, but be careful to marry a woman who has good health. Many years ago, my friend married a woman who had a coughing disease. He loved her with all his heart, and she, him, and so they wed. Their bliss lasted but a few months, and she fell deeper into her sickness. He stayed by her side, and her illness lasted for three years, and at last, she died. But he did not mourn her for long, for she had given him her disease and he followed her to his grave one year later.

"Money does not bring happiness, but the lack of it denies opportunity. In many ways, money is time. It allows you to do immediately what others must wait for. Now, too much money teaches someone to have no patience, and an impatient man is not a welcome guest. Work hard to make money, save much, and spend moderately. Time passes all too quickly, and the needs of your life change as you age. Forego frivolous things and extravagances.

"Be known as generous, but not to the point of impoverishing yourself. When a poor man wishes to give you something, do not force him to accept payment, for it is a vice to deny a man the opportunity to be generous. When a rich man wishes to give you a gift, do not regard it as a bribe unless it is clearly so, for a rich man may also wish to be generous. In both situations, rich man or poor, receive it with thanks, but allow no expectations of a response in like manner."

Gabinius stood and said, "Wait here, Guiamo." He walked out of the *tablinum* through the *peristylium* to his private *cubiculum*. After a few moments, he returned carrying a heavy iron chest. He placed it on a table and opened it with a key which he wore as a ring on his finger.

"I have kept track of your money all these years," Gabinius said. "You have amassed quite a fortune for a boy just celebrating *Liberalia*. Your first harvest was fairly good, considering the rough ground that had to be worked, and you will need to spend more money this year planting orchards and vineyards. Do not neglect to reward Actus and his men. They are diligent workers and you will want to retain them."

Gabinius showed Guiamo his ledger and the boy's eyes bulged at the sum he owned. Gabinius counted out the amount mostly in gold *aurei*, and they filled Guiamo's hand. "Keep it safe. Even a small amount left unguarded will prove a tremendous temptation. Here is my recommendation; have two strongboxes. In one, put a goodly amount which a thief might discover and steal. He will be content, for he will think he has all your treasure. Pay

252

your expenses out of this box and let it be the only one anyone ever sees. Put the majority of your money in the other box and hide it away within your home in a hole in the ground or wall. Repair the floor or wall so that it cannot be detected. In this way, your greatest wealth will be protected from theft. Trust only one person with the location of this strongbox, so that it might be recovered if you should die."

Seeing that he had grown longwinded, and the hour was late, Gabinius somberly said, "It is time to fetch your possessions before you go."

Guiamo went to his *cubiculum* and put his things into a large bag. Carrying the bag in his right hand and Lúin in his left, he walked back into the *atrium* where Gabinius stood patiently waiting.

With tears forming in both their eyes, Gabinius led him through the *atrium* and the *vestibulum* entrance hallway to the exterior door.

"Now embrace me as a son, for truly do I love you," said Gabinius. "As you have not forgotten Calidius, forget not Gabinius."

Guiamo leaned Lúin against the wall, and setting the bag down, hugged his dear old benefactor in parting. "I shall never forget your kindness," he said. "Thank you, with all my heart." Guiamo then stepped outside into the cold night air and strode down the valley to begin his life as a man.

He spent the night in his own home for the first time. The *peristylium* was beautifully arranged with ferns, flowers and herbs. The home was meticulously cleaned and elegantly furnished. His bed was comfortable and warm, and it was one of the loneliest nights he had ever experienced.

Suadusegus and Susama visited the next morning, having ridden in a wagon across the river. Actus welcomed them as they arrived, and removed the chair with wheels from the back of the wagon.

Guiamo was delighted to receive his first visitors and welcomed them inside. They brought a gift of fresh vegetables and loaves of bread.

His pleasure turned to joy when Suadusegus announced, "Durmi, today I am again a freeman. I now am a *liberti* and I wear the Phrygian cap to proclaim it. He pulled out a soft, red hat conical in shape and handed it to Guiamo. *Dominus* Malleolus has... Pardon me. I should learn to say simply 'Malleolus.' Malleolus has given me my freedom, for he no longer requires my services."

Guiamo was pleased to no end. "I wish to continue my lessons from both you and Susama. Would you consider allowing me to hire you?" asked Guiamo. "Your wages would be as Gabinius has recommended to me; twenty-three *denarii* each month for each of you."

"The distance from Malleolus' estate is prohibitive for daily lessons," said Suadusegus, "though your thoughts intrigue me."

Susama volunteered, "Our attachment with Gabinius is severed, and we are no longer bound to remain on his estate. Perhaps you would allow us to construct a home here on your lands. If so, your plan would work, but as before, I will take no wages for my instruction."

Guiamo liked this idea immensely, but countered with an alternative which suited him better. "Suadusegus, Susama, would you be so gracious as to live with me in this fine new home as my guests? I have need of companionship, for with all its loveliness and grandeur, it is most empty. Stay here with me and teach. I need servants to care for the household and I have seen that your maidservants lack for work."

Susama looked at Suadusegus for guidance. He thoughtfully replied, "A better fit is seldom found, Durmi. We have no desire to return to our homeland. We appreciatively agree."

As the maidservants delivered Susama's possessions, four of Actus' men helped move the heavier pieces into Guiamo's house. The women were appreciative of the help, and they could not help but noticing how overly polite the unmarried men were to them. The women flirted back at the men and everyone was in good spirits.

As the furnishings were being arranged, Guiamo stood aside with Suadusegus, allowing Susama to set up the house as she desired. Suadusegus yawned in boredom and Guiamo leaned against the wall at his side. Their talk turned to business and farming. Then Guiamo posed a moral question to Suadusegus.

Guiamo said, "Suadusegus, I am conflicted. I need to increase my profits and have an idea how to achieve this, but I believe that doing so would betray Gabinius."

Suadusegus asked, "What is this opportunity?"

Guiamo said, "I know where tin and copper mines are said to be still working. I failed to mention it to Gabinius last year, but it seemed of little importance then. He seemed to have purchased as much as he should want and more."

Suadusegus replied, "You have done your duty to Malleolus. You should have no fears that you are taking advantage of him by striking your own business arrangements. You owe him none of your profits and he would not expect you to forfeit your opportunities to his favor. You are your own man now. Seek out your future and prosperity. Go to these mines and see for yourself how well they produce."

Guiamo said, "Then go there, I shall. But first, I wish to see grandfather and Ursius again. Grandfather has not yet seen Lúin, and I have many things to learn from him.

Guiamo traveled light. He wished to return before harvest, so traveled as fast as he could without pushing Honestia beyond her limits. He left Suadusegus in charge of the estate and Actus was tasked with minding the farm. Gabinius was notified and asked to monitor the situation at a distance.

He set out to see his grandfather on the twenty-fifth day of *Martius*, and hoped to have time to visit with Ursius as well on the return trip. Confident in his martial skills, and feeling the need to travel without a nursemaid tending him, he decided that he would travel alone. Knowing that the road was more civilized than before and, with Lúin in a scabbard at arms reach, he decided he would be safe.

He had purchased Honestia from Gabinius and, still using his riding steps, rode confidently toward the land of the Bellovaci. He traveled with Roman cavalry patrols and merchant caravans whenever possible. He had no serious difficulties, and with an ample supply of *denarii*, was able to purchase whatever he needed. The trip was easy and exciting.

Camulvellaunus was delighted to see his grandson arrive on the twentieth day of *Aprilis*, and was pleased with the education Guiamo had received from Susama. Guiamo handed a parchment written by the priestess of the words of the ancient tongue needing to be identified for him.

Camulvellaunus' eyes were getting worse, and he had much difficulty seeing her script. He worked hard to read it and finally allowed Guiamo to read it to him. After several days, Guiamo finally knew the words Susama had forgotten.

Camulvellaunus asked him one day, "What do you intend to do with such a wealth of knowledge of the old words?"

Guiamo replied, "Grandfather, I have something which I must show you in secret. Where can we go that others may not see or listen?"

Camulvellaunus said, "To our sacred grove, we must go. There we shall be safe. Are you ready now?"

Guiamo said, "It is nearly dark now. Perhaps we should wait until the morrow."

Camulvellaunus replied, "My son, to my eyes, it makes no difference. Let us go now, for I sense what you are to say is of profound importance."

Guiamo agreed, and they walked through the dark of night to the sacred grove atop the hill. Camulvellaunus stumbled not once, for he knew the way.

When they arrived within the holy site of oaks, Camulvellaunus turned to face the young man he could no longer see. "Tell me your secrets, Guiamo."

With command, Guiamo said, "*Athibar!*"

Camulvellaunus visibly tensed, his countenance alert, as he recognized the word of power.

Lúin soared silently through the sky and nestled into Guiamo's outstretched hands. Guiamo took his grandfather's hand and placed Lúin into his grasp.

Camulvellaunus felt the weight of the spear and ran his hands along its length. When he reached the spearhead, he exclaimed, "The gods above! You have a spear of Lugus! The gods above! Is he Assal or Lúin?"

Guiamo replied, "He is Lúin, grandfather."

"The gods above! I hold the sacred spear which has been lost for over fifty generations. The gods be praised! Lúin has been found at last!"

"Let me show you what he can do," said Guiamo, and Lúin tremored in anticipation.

Villagers from all around watched in fear from a distance as strange glowing lights flickered from among the oaks of the sacred grove, and bolts of lightning blazed upward into the sky. Cloudy mists spread out of the oak grove and the townsfolk bolted their doors as they hid from the terrifying magic of the *Druidae*.

For over a month, Guiamo studied under the teaching of Camulvellaunus, and always in secret haunts in the wild. Usually they returned late in the evening, ate a quiet supper, and retired for the night.

Some thought it strange the way the young Roman, who always carried a spear, was kept from sight, and rumors spread that he wore a strange golden serpent ring upon a finger of his right hand.

On the rare occasion the two *Druidae* were seen, walking abroad through wood or meadow, the younger carried a dignity about him that few had ever achieved. His strength and command were palpable, such that the strong would grow silent in his presence, and the more timid would turn away.

When his time among the Bellovaci had drawn to a close, the young Roman *Druides* simply sheathed his spear, mounted his horse, and rode away to the southwest.

On the second day of *Quintilis*, Guiamo arrived at the fortification of the Seventh *Legio*. Leaving Honestia and Lúin outside, he walked into camp to find his friend. He found Ursius arguing over a meat allotment with the *praefectus castrorum*.

"If your hunters cannot find game, then your dogs can eat *puls* like the *milites gregarii*. I will not spend our scarce funds buying mutton for your hounds!" shouted the *praefectus*.

Ursius shot back angrily, "I would have had enough meat if your precious *centurionis* had not confiscated the deer we killed."

Guiamo interrupted their argument with a heartfelt laugh at his two red-faced friends.

They both turned to glare at the outspoken intruder, and it took a few moments for them to realize who he was.

"Stolo?" said the *praefectus* in surprise.

"Guiamo!" said Ursius, and they clasped arms in greeting. "Too long has it been, my young friend! But come now! I see from your *toga virilis* that you have finally celebrated your *Liberalia*! So, has old Malleolus finally rid himself of you?"

"Yes, Ursi," Guiamo replied, "I am a man of Rome at last! I am returning from visiting my grandfather, and since I was not in the area, I thought I would stop by to visit with you."

Ursius laughed politely at Guiamo's little joke and led Guiamo outside.

The *praefectus* called after him, "You know the rules. Be sure to abide by them."

Waving a hand in acknowledgment as he left, Guiamo asked Ursius, "What news have you?"

Ursius was surprised at Guiamo's tall, muscular build and commanding presence. He noticed the serpent tattoo and elaborate gold ring. Pointing to Guiamo's hand, he said, "The ring is beautifully done. A gift from a beautiful woman?"

"A gift it was," Guiamo replied.

Ursius laughed loudly and slapped him on the shoulder, "And I spend my time with hounds. Most of my days are spent much as when you left two years ago. It is all the same; dog training, handler training, feeding, grooming, and cleaning up their stinking piles. It is getting to be rather tedious.

"I have made use of your advice, you know. I have been learning cavalry fighting skills and tactics in my spare time. A *centurio* lets me borrow his horse to better myself at riding. In time, I intend to become a *decurio* in command of a troupe of ten mounted men. I will have to start out as a common *gregalis* fighting from horseback to gain some experience, of course, but my time here as *optio* should help me advance more quickly. My hope is to eventually become *praefectus alae*, but since I am not nearly experienced or old enough, that promotion would not take place for some years to come. Sometimes I am invited to practice with them. I am not as good as they, but I learn quickly and work hard at it. I hope to be transferred this year."

"Have you prepared a replacement yet?" asked Guiamo.

Ursius replied, "I am working with a young man named Asinius. He is capable, though not creative. I think he shall be able to maintain the force effectively, but expect nothing further. A few more months and he will be ready."

Guiamo asked, "So, tell me about Julius Caesar. Is he fighting anyone this year?"

Ursius replied, "He is off chasing the Suebi across the river Rhonus. No battles have been yet reported. They are a slippery bunch. I suspect Caesar will wear out his horse before he catches them, and he knows it. The favored plan for this autumn is abandon the chase and turn west to probe into Albion across Oceanus. There is much talk of turmoil there, and many suppliers here are in need of materials. Word has it that Caesar thinks wherever there is conflict, profits can be found. So, he plans an expedition soon, probably the Tenth *Legio* and our Seventh. He favors the Tenth, you know. The Seventh has been chosen, they say, because we were not involved against the Veneti last year. He wants to keep our skills honed.

"We have had time to heal and refill our ranks from our thrashing in the battle against the Nervii. We lost many good men that day. Too many good men."

Guiamo asked, "When does the Seventh *Legio* march?"

"Very soon, Guiamo," said Ursius. "It is said that we will leave in the middle of *Quintilis*. Why do you ask?"

He was thinking rapidly of the still-active mines to the northeast of Albion and the prospects of huge profits awaiting him. He ignored Ursius' question and asked, "Where will you board your ships?"

"Possibly in the land of the Belgae," Ursius replied. "The harbor of Portius Itius is good, and the sea is narrow there."

"Interesting," Guiamo said, seizing upon an idea to expand his business. "Is there any chance I could cross with the *legiones*? I desire to travel to Albion, and it would be safest to travel with an armed escort." Then, teasing Ursius, said, "The Seventh and Tenth *Legiones* should be powerful enough to protect a man of fifteen years, I should think."

Ursius rolled his eyes at Guiamo's jest and replied, "No, only the men of the *legiones* are going."

"What about you and the dogs?" Guiamo asked.

"Yes, we will be going as well," Ursius answered.

Guiamo mulled this information over awhile before exploring another idea. "Do you need any hired help?" he asked. "I could tend your dogs until we return from Albion."

Ursius saw where the conversation was going and replied, "Yes, in fact I do need helpers. I do not pay much. Just enough to feed you, really."

"That would be more than enough," replied Guiamo. "I just need a safe way to cross and some free time once I get there."

"That should not be a problem for Rome or my dogs," said Ursius.

"May I bring a weapon?" asked Guiamo.

"Yes, what do you have?" asked Ursius. "Your knife will not be sufficient for a campaign."

"I have an old spear," Guiamo replied, "and a horse."

"Can you use the spear well?" asked Ursius.

260

"Oh, better than you might think," Guiamo replied knowingly. "I have had much time to practice."

"Then bring it," Ursius replied. "When do you wish to begin your work as a hired man attached to the Seventh *Legio*?"

"What of my horse? May I bring her to Albion with me?" asked Guiamo.

"No," Ursius replied. "There is already concern there will not be enough ships. They will not let you bring your horse. We will march to the coast. Your horse must stay here until you return. Do not worry. The camp guard will tend to your horse with food, water and exercise if I order it."

"Will I be able to quit my employment with the *legio* when I so desire?" asked Guiamo.

"You will not be able to quit while on campaign unless I release you, but I certainly shall should you desire it," Ursius replied. "Since our departure could be very soon, and warfare is a possibility on those strange shores, the *legio* requires that you must write a will in the event you are killed or captured."

"Killed, I understand, but being captured requires a will?" asked Guiamo.

"According to the laws of Rome, a soldier captured in battle is legally dead," Ursius said solemnly.

"Such a comforting thought," Guiamo replied. "I will start work on a will tonight. Sign me up. I am ready for a trip to Albion."

"When your will is completed, turn it in to the *praefectus castrorum*. He stores all the wills during campaign," said Ursius.

When Guiamo turned his will over to the *praefectus castrorum* the next morning, he also hired a messenger to deliver a letter to Gabinius. Then Guiamo and Ursius signed a document accepting him for work as a dog handler with the *legio* for six months.

Compared to Gabinius' demanding daily regimen, Ursius' assignments for training and caring for the dogs was a vacation to Guiamo. He enjoyed grooming them and exercising along with them. His manner was calm and commanding. The dogs responded eagerly to his instructions and his praise.

The food given to the hired helpers was *puls* in the morning, bread and cheese at noon, and *puls* again in the evening. Guiamo reminded himself to not make comparison with Gabinius' elaborate meals. He really did not mind, for it reminded him of the simple, quiet years with Calidius.

Sixteen days later, on the nineteenth day of *Quintilis*, the Seventh *Legio* marched out of their encampment toward Portius Itius. Ursius' dogs walked along with the baggage train which stretched out beyond sight of the troops. The road was muddy and the dog handlers slipped frequently as the dogs pulled on their leashes. The walk was difficult, for the ruts were deep and filled with water. Guiamo longed for the ease of riding Honestia, but knew he had to endure this work to secure the profits awaiting him.

Lúin was stored along with their camp gear in the wagon assigned to Ursius.

Ursius traveled apart from the dog handlers, and Guiamo was surprised to see that his friend did not spend time walking with him. Ursius was quick to give orders to the handlers of any dog teams giving problems, and he treated Guiamo no differently. Ursius had his responsibilities and showed no favoritism.

The *legio* stopped rather early in the afternoon to build a temporary wooden fortification around their camp site. When the work was completed, and the wagons had been drawn inside, the men set up their tents for the night. The evening meal was *puls* as usual, dull but filling. Only when the men had finished their work did Ursius come to spend the remnants of the evening talking with his friend.

Each day of the trip was the same, varied only by occasional rain, and varying road conditions. They traveled north into the land of the Belgae and on the fifteenth day of *Sextilis* arrived on the outskirts of Portius Itius.

Portius Itius was a dreary town on the coast, but the harbor was excellent for ships bearing cargo from Albion.

They met up with the Tenth *Legio* and joined together to construct an even larger fortification.

Ursius was assigned a small area to house his dogs, and they seemed pleased to rest from the long journey. Several dogs had been given leather boots to wear on their feet, for they had been cut and bruised from the journey. Several were so injured that they had been carried on the wagon for days while they healed. Guiamo searched out the doctors of the *legio* to obtain a small quantity of Meridius' ointment, and with it, the dog's injuries healed more quickly.

Guiamo was not the only one frustrated with the scant amounts of reliable information of their campaign which was being passed down through the ranks. Not used to living as a soldier, Guiamo felt uncomfortably blind to the events going on around him. Rumors abounded, but none were reliable and frequently conflicted with each other.

Ursius said nothing during the day, but in the evening he privately told Guiamo what little news he had gleaned. No one was allowed outside the encampment without authorization, so facts were limited. While running errands for the *primus pilus*, Ursius had seen a dusty cavalry unit of five hundred pass by and head to another harbor to the south where the eighteen ships assigned to carry them would soon be arriving. Ursius also saw that while some of the soldier's time was spent cleaning equipment and sharpening blades in camp, most were tasked with carrying supplies aboard the eighty deep-hulled transport ships anchored in the harbor.

Guiamo saw that Caesar was planning to cross Oceanus to Albion with the full strength of the Seventh and Tenth *Legiones* and the men were eager. Guiamo also realized that the entire baggage train would be left behind. Once in Albion, everything would have to be carried on their backs. He worried that Caesar's invasion would not achieve much and he would not have the opportunity to venture northeast to the mines.

The messenger arrived late afternoon at Gabinius' estate on the nineteenth day of *Sextilis* to deliver Guiamo's letter. Sertorius received the letter on his behalf and delivered it immediately to Gabinius who was working in his private workshop.

Gabinius unrolled the parchment *volumen* and read the letter silently. Sertorius tried to appear patient as he anxiously waited for Gabinius to reveal Guiamo's message. After he had read it over twice, Gabinius looked at Sertorius and said, "Our young man has ventured into the wild to snare some profits."

Sertorius asked, "Where has Durmius gone?"

Gabinius replied, "He has gone to Albion."

"Alone?" Sertorius asked fearfully.

"No, he went as part of Caesar's army with Ursius and the dogs," Gabinius replied cautiously.

"Then he should be safe," replied Sertorius.

"The gods willing," Gabinius answered. He looked back at the letter, and remembering the oracle, replied, "I fear we shall not see Guiamo again."

Guiamo enjoyed working the dogs and a few days passed. He woke on the twenty-third day of *Sextilis* to the sound of trumpets. The blaring *cornicines* were calling for the troops to assemble, ready to board the ships. The well-rehearsed process of striking the tents and gathering their packs went smoothly. The men filed out in an orderly march formation through the gates and they passed the outskirts of town as they headed toward the harbor.

Guiamo marched out with Ursius' men, and with a heavy pack on his back and Lúin bound to it to keep his hands free, led five black dogs on leashes. The hounds were excited and pulled at his arms, yelping and jumping. The handlers all struggled to control the dogs, and Ursius shouted commands to keep them from tangling with others.

As they neared the harbor, Guiamo caught his first glimpse of the transport ships. He thought they looked much like the Veneti ships and rather mundane. What impressed him were the Roman *bireme* and *trireme* warships. With two or three rows of oars, they looked fast, sleek and deadly.

The harbor could dock twelve ships at a time. As a ship was loaded with over one hundred soldiers, it would then be pushed away from the dock to allow another in its place. The troops were hurried aboard and placed in the hold, cramped and miserable.

It took the entire day to put everyone on board, and Guiamo's turn came as the sun was setting. He led his dogs across a wooden plank which rose steeply from the dock to the deck of the merchant ship. When he reached the deck, Ursius told him to take the dogs into the hold and stay there. Guiamo descended the steps into the dark hold below deck and found a corner to sit with his dogs. The dogs sniffed eagerly at all the mysterious odors left over from previous journeys and urinated on the supplies in storage to mark their territory. The hull was filled with sacks of grain, barrels, *amphorae* jars and soldiers sitting and standing wherever they could find a place. The air was becoming stuffy and in the darkness, the men became gloomier by the moment.

Ursius brought three lamps into the hull and hung them from the ceiling. The flickering lamps cast just enough light to fend off confusion and fear. The ship was pushed away from the dock, and it gently rolled with the waves as it slowly turned to maneuver out into the bay. Many men were nervous at being at sea, and several became sick at the unfamiliar motion. With the nauseating odor filling the hull, many others became sick as well.

Guiamo was delighted when Ursius called him to stand with him on the deck. Guiamo handed his five leashes to another handler nearby and, carrying his pack, scrambled through the men and up the staircase.

The stars were bright, the wind steady, and drawing a full breath of clean air, Guiamo instantly felt better. Ursius showed him around the deck and introduced him to the ship's captain. They shared some bread and watched the ships maneuvering for space. Ursius allowed Guiamo to remain on deck the remainder of the trip and gave him a woolen blanket to keep warm.

In the middle of the night, just after the call for third watch, Caesar gave the command to set sail. The tide was favorable and the winds steady. Led by twenty warships, the ships began to move out into the open sea, and Ursius confidently said, "Now Caesar will take us to war."

Guiamo replied, "I just hope he takes us to victory."

Glossary

Latin Terms
Adytum - innermost chamber of a temple
Amphorae – two handled jars
Annales – epic poem by Ennius
Aprilis – month of April
Argei - effigies used in a religious ceremony
As – bronze coin valued at 16 per denarius
Asses – bronze coins
Atrium – reception hall
Augur - one who interprets behavior of birds
Augures – augurs
Aurei – gold coins worth 25 silver denarii
Aureus – gold coin worth 25 silver denarii
Auspiciis - to divine the omen from the flight of birds
Avunculus – maternal uncle
Bireme - warship with two rows of oars
Bulla Praetexta - locket worn by boys
Cella – storeroom
Centuria – formation of eighty soldiers
Centurio – centurion
Centurionis – centurions
Classiarii – marines
Cohors – cohort
Congius – measurement of volume
Cornicen - trumpeter
Cubiculum – bedroom
Culina – kitchen
December –month of December
Decurio – officer of ten men
Denarii – silver coins valued at 25 per gold aureus
Denarius – silver coin valued at 25 per gold aureus
Domine – master
Dominus – master
Druidae – Druids
Druides - Druid
Eques – knight of the Equestrian order

Equites – knights of the Equestrian order
Exedra – entertainment room
Fasces - bundle of rods carried before the high magistrate
Fauces – corridor
Februarius – month of February
Flamines Martialis – priests of Mars
Gallia – Gaul
Gladii – swords
Gladius Hispaniensis - sword used in the conquest of Spain
Gregalis – horseman
Ianuarius – month of January
Iunius – month of June
Lecti - reclining couches
Lectica – litter
Lectus – reclining couch
Legati – commanders of the legions
Legatus – officer
Legatus legionis – legion's commander
Legio – Legion
Legiones – Legions
Liberalia – celebration of manhood
Liberti- freeman
Libia – sacrificial cakes of honey and oil
Libra – unit of measure
Lictor – bodyguard who carries the lictoriae
Lictoriae – bundle of white birch rods carried to protect magistrates
Maius – month of May
Mare Nostrum – Mediterranean Sea
Martius – month of March
Milites gregarius – experienced soldier
Negotiator gladiarius – a manufacturer and dealer of military arms
Novacula – razor
November – month of November
Numina – faceless household gods
October – month of October
Oppidum – fortification
Optio - junior officer

Passus – pace, a double step measurement of distance equal to 5 feet

Passuum - paces

Patricii – wealthy Romans of the patrician class

Patricius – wealth patrician

Peristylium – garden room

Pes – measurement of height

Pila – javelins

Pilum – javelin

Pleb – commoner

Pontifices - high priest

Praefectus alae – cavalry commander

Praefectus castrorum – camp commandant

Praenomina - personal name

Primus pilus – centurion over the first century of the first cohort

Puls – porridge

Quartarii – measurement of volume - plural

Quartarius – measurement of volume

Quintilis – month of July

Roma victrix – Rome is the victor!

Senator - senator

Senatoris - senators

September – month of September

Sextilis – month of August

Stilus – writing stylus

Subligar – loincloth

Tablinum – office

Tertius pilus prior – centurion over the third century of the first cohort

Tesserae – colored clay cubes used for mosaics

Testudo – tortoise

Tirones   new recruits

Toga praetexta - garment worn by children over 16

Toga virilis – toga for men

Tribunus – tribune

Triclinium - dining room

Trioculis -three eyes

Trireme – warship with three rows of oars

Vestibulum – entrance, court
Via praetoria – central road in Roman fortification
Volumen – scroll
Voluminis – scrolls

Words of the ancient language
Ibur = pierce
Athibar = return
Chothla = warm
Votnerti = hot
Ebfulna = molten
Banru = fire
Falamos = ignite
Ignu-al = light
Thivinen = lightning
Nef = stop
Alfalel = speak
Melnothel = write
Dranda = push
Nurdranda = knock down
Fisóvet = break down
Vúimon = shatter
Hutsosh = earthquake
Betn'lina = find (point) east
Betn'dhorvo = find (point) to object
Betn'whúin atha = find (point) to hidden object
Nétlis = slash
Dithmero-mil = a summons
Haba = first letter of ancient alphabet.
Samta = second letter of ancient alphabet.

18541013R00144

Made in the USA
Charleston, SC
09 April 2013